Praise for The Art of Danger

"I can't tell you how much I enjoyed it. A treat. I'm a fan. A hugely entertaining story. A 'switch off the phone, park interruptions, sit back and enjoy the ride' type of novel. Characterisation is superb." *Crime novelist E V Seymour*

"Raymond Chandler's Philip Marlowe reinventing himself as a 21st Century English Art Investigator" *(Amazon UK reviewer)*

"Plot had some very cool twists" *(Goodreads reviewer)*

"I was entirely hooked by the plot line and read it pretty much at one sitting." *(Amazon UK reviewer)*

"Brilliant read. Strong characters" *(Goodreads Reviewer)*

THE ART

OF

DANGER

THE ART OF DANGER

Stuart Doughty

This action crime thriller is the first in a series about investigator John Kite whose speciality is recovering stolen artworks. To find out more about the books, the author and get an introductory, exclusive FREE story… join the Readers' Club at https://stuart-doughty.com/freedownload

To LIN

Chapter 1

They suggested I should have counselling.

I said no.

They said their *professional advice* was that I have counselling.

I said no again.

I wanted to stand on my own, not get sucked into a lifetime of therapy like – what's that weird American film director? – like Woody Allen.

I said no fifteen years ago and I haven't regretted my decision.

At least... Not until this story happened.

As they say, it all began just like any other normal day...

The woman from accounts was fussily checking the bundles of notes.

For a third time. Anyone would think it was her money.

I needed to get a move on.

I glanced out to where the sun was reflecting off the dome of St Paul's Cathedral and spun things round in my head. Had I forgotten anything for the handover? Criminals expecting a large cash hand-out are unpredictable. So I try to expect the unexpected. Logically impossible, I suppose, but you know what I mean.

'Seventy-five thousand?' the accounts clerk said with an annoying upward inflection. Like challenging us to dispute her figure.

'You tell us,' I said.

The woman gave a little toss of her head, reconfirmed the total in a clipped voice then said, 'Fifties would've taken less space.'

'Twenties was the deal,' I said.

No one except used car dealers and dumb tourists carries fifty pound notes.

I began to stow the seventy-five bundles in my Superdry sports bag.

'Is that safe?' the clerk said, looking at the bag disdainfully.

I was about to tell her where to get off but Fiona MacIver intervened:

'Kite knows what he's doing,' she said.

Thank you, I thought, for the vote of confidence and for shutting the other woman up. MacIver was my employer on this job and didn't suffer fools. But she was more diplomatic than me.

A sports bag is as safe a way as any to transport cash along a street. Stand in a queue for a bank cashier while shop staff pay in takings – you'll have plenty of time to watch. See how they carry cash in supermarket plastic bags. The only time a sports bag attracts attention is when it's left unattended in a public place.

The phone on MacIver's desk rang. She picked it up, listened, and looked at me.

'The car's ready.'

I zipped up the bag.

MacIver held out her hand and we shook.

'Good luck, Kite,' she said. Then after a questioning look, 'Haven't seen the suit before.'

'Final day,' I said with a smile. 'Thought I'd posh up.'

She didn't smile. She wasn't a smiley person. She just gave my suit another look, nodded approvingly and said, 'I expect there'll be others when this job's over.'

The accounts woman insisted on seeing me off the premises, as she put it. Insulting or what? I nearly asked for her defence strategy if we were attacked.

She also insisted on using the lift. Which delayed me further. MacIver's department is only on the eleventh floor and I always use the stairs. It beats going to a gym.

In the lift I looked at the accounts clerk. She could lose a few pounds. Too much sitting at a desk. Too many Snickers bars to ease the boredom.

The Art of Danger

Down in the street I got in the back of the car and put the bag next to me.

'Take care now,' the accounts woman said, like she was seeing a child off on holiday alone for the first time. Then she shut the door and gave me a little wave.

I didn't wave back but turned to the driver and saw a face I recognised.

We greeted each other and Jason set off at a lick.

'May I confirm the destination, sir?' said Jason with a knowing smile. 'TQ 332832?'

I laughed. He must have looked it up and memorised it. I was touched. Jason, whose grandfather was one of the few genuine *Windrush* immigrants, had only driven me a few times, but he was a bright spark.

'Grid reference right?' he said.

'Spot on.'

'That thing you do... It's real spooky.'

'No,' I said. 'We can't choose what we're born with.'

Like we can't choose our parents. If only we could.

'My girlfriend can't even find B & Q,' said Jason.

'Can she find H & M?'

'Oh yeah.'

'Then I don't think map reading's the problem.'

He laughed.

TQ 332832 is Hoxton, by the way. Still as cool and hip as it used to be? I didn't care: I was going to an office, not a bar.

It was where I was exchanging the seventy-five thousand for an early sixteenth century oil painting.

That's what I do: recover artworks. Stolen artworks. I'm an investigator, not a lost property man. I spent eleven years in the police, but I'm freelance now and work for owners or insurance companies. I scrutinise every aspect of an art theft, try to discover where the missing item has ended up, then bust a gut to get it back.

I was swapping my bag of cash for a picture by the not so famous German artist Christoph Amberger which had been stolen two years previously from a country house in Northamptonshire. A similar painting sold a few years ago for about £800,000. So £75,000 was a

3

good deal all round. For the bad guys. For the insurers. And for the owner.

BetterWork, the sign read in a self-confident sans-serif. And below it, *A new concept in office-space.*

Jason stopped outside and I told him not to wait. I would get a taxi later. Or maybe just hop, skip and jump back to MacIver's office with the picture.

BetterWork is one of those start-ups that go from being worth ten cents one day to a billion dollars the next. All they do is rent out office space. What a doddle. But these guys say their mission is to make work more enjoyable, more creative and more productive. Music to any employer's ears. But it sounds like mission impossible to me.

Even so, I have to admit the place I went into wasn't like anywhere I'd ever worked.

The building was a radically up-cycled nineteenth century warehouse. On the open-plan ground floor there was bold artwork in funky colours, vaguely in the style of Howard Hodgkin, with some vogueish, balloon-like structures imitating Jeff Koons.

I saw signs directing eager workers to a yoga studio, to a wellness room, to bike storage, to showers, to the games area, to the brainstorming room. Spa hotel meets students' union, I thought.

The location for the handover was the choice of the man I was meeting, Jamie Rind. He was a solicitor, the intermediary between me and the criminals. Jamie was far removed from the lawyers on TV shows like *Suits*. His suits – or rather his suit – always looked like it needed cleaning. His hair was shaggy and straggly and his shirts weren't Jermyn Street but George at Asda. Based in Streatham, south London, many of his clients were career criminals who'd put in long service.

We'd met previously in pubs, all of them within spitting distance of the Old Bailey or the Law Courts in The Strand where he frequently appeared. His favourite drink was what he called a Dry Legal Aid – in other words a spritzer. He said its curious nickname was an invention of his supervisor's when he was a law student, thirty years ago. It was an old fashioned kind of drink but it suited Jamie. His humour was dry and laconic and he certainly did lots of legal aid work. His chosen field was unglamorous and not a big earner. But he had a social conscience and believed however much previous an old lag might have they still deserved a fair hearing.

I'd had four meetings with him so far. He brought quality jpegs of the picture for me to check and in the end we agreed a price. But a pub was too public a location for the actual exchange of hard cash so Jamie Rind had booked a private space in this Hoxton office-fun-hub.

I went towards the receptionist who was standing motionless behind a narrow glass counter. She was a perfectly slim young woman with a perfectly slim Ultrabook in front of her. Her hair, make-up and skin were immaculate. Her short, black dress snugly fitted the contours of her body and her features suggested a grandparent from Japan. She was a real looker.

So naturally I gave her my best smile. 'Hi,' I said, 'John Kite. I've a meeting with Jamie Rind. I think it's on Level 2.'

Some women have told me my voice is sexy. All I know is it's deep and resonant. I'm muscular, but not excessively so. Tall, but not so I can't blend in with a crowd. My eyes are ultramarine and I have cheekbones sharp as razors. I was told once I looked like a young Brian Ferry – though the woman who said this was a bit drunk. Correction, she was so drunk her hangover lasted thirty six hours. I'm not trying to big myself up. Don't think I'm vain. I'm just pointing out I'm not pug ugly.

But the receptionist woman said nothing. She blinked once, so slowly I thought she was having a zizz, then registered my arrival with the thinnest twitch of her lips. She languidly lifted a finger, with its sublimely turquoise-painted nail, pressed a key and her eyes flicked to her screen. She was like those humanoid AI robots: both disturbingly sexy and strangely sexless.

Call me old fashioned, but I want people who stand behind counters in some sort of service capacity to be a teeny bit welcoming. And to give some bloody service.

'Level 2, Zone Delta, Room 6,' she said. It was dialogue from a sci-fi movie.

'Is there somewhere I can leave this?' I said, holding up my Superdry bag, which in this oasis of fashionistas seemed gross and ugly.

Her eyes scanned me up and down in a way that made me worry my flies were undone.

Then suddenly she was holding out a key which seemed to have appeared by prestidigitation. She nodded ever so slightly towards a bank of brightly-painted lockers.

You might think it dumb to leave £75,000 in a cupboard protected by a lock so feeble it could be picked by a four year old with plastic cutlery. But I had to see the artwork before producing the cash. And I calculated nobody would expect rich pickings in a place where people normally kept lunchtime bananas, bicycle pumps and a book to read on the tube home.

I stowed the bag. Then out of nowhere came:

'WAIT!'

I don't usually jump at loud noises. But I jumped now.

It was almost a scream.

Her voice no longer sounded computer-generated but drill-sergeant harsh and commanding.

She was staring at her screen, her face showed emotion for the first time.

'No...,' she said, looking pained and even trembling slightly. In her perfect world there was a glitch. A Houston-we-have-a-problem kind of glitch.

She eyeballed me, her eyes like lasers. 'Mr John Kite has already arrived. He checked in at the west door seven minutes ago.'

Her look was saying I was a con man, a danger to society, a potential assailant. I wouldn't want to face her alone on a dark night with her rape alarm and can of mace.

But I could read the situation better than she could.

If someone was pretending to be me it meant only one thing.

The meeting was compromised.

Which meant potential disaster.

I ran towards the stairs and raced up, my shoes clattering like machine gun fire on the bare oak treads. On the second floor, I followed the zombie's instructions and ran through an area where people with headphones were video-conferencing then raced down the corridor. The private office suites had doors painted in narrow vertical stripes of bright colours: red, blue, yellow, green arranged like bar codes. Presumably to dazzle workers into more creativity. Or give them headaches.

I halted by Suite 6 and put my ear to the door. There was no sound from inside. I stepped back and kicked the door hard. It was a strongly built thirty minute fire door but the frame was cheap whitewood and the ironmongery even cheaper. Timber splintered and metal alloy bent. The door crashed back against the plasterboard wall as I slipped back into cover beside the door-frame.

The only sound was the dry trickle of falling plaster where the door handle had punctured the wall. But the smell of detonation was unmistakeable.

I peered round the doorframe and saw the solicitor Jamie Rind in a swivel chair behind a desk.

He looked more unkempt and bedraggled than usual. He looked dead.

There was an unpleasant bullet wound to his head and some of his brains had made a mess on the wall behind him. Another man I didn't recognise was on the floor, also dead with bullet wounds. I assumed he was Rind's client, one of the gang who owned the picture.

I glanced around the little office. There were four swivel chairs with blue upholstery, three tables of beech-look laminate and a black plastic waste bin. The carpet still showed stripy marks from being vacuumed, the coffee in its stainless steel pot was scalding, three cups and saucers were nested together on a tray and mini-packs of homely custard creams and digestives were untouched in their cellophane.

Except for Rind's battered leather briefcase and the messy bodies, the space was as neat, clean and antiseptic as you could wish for in an office rented by the hour.

All it lacked was a fine piece of sixteenth century artwork.

Unique is an over-used word. People who know about grammar tell us it's an absolute; an adjective that can't be modified. Tough. I'm breaking the rules.

To steal a stolen painting which is about to be swapped for cash is an absolutely unique event. Extraordinarily, incredibly unique. An unheard of crime. Infinitesimally unlikely.

There's not even a word for it. "Re-stealing"? It doesn't compute.

Of all the unexpected things I could have expected – and planned for – this would never have figured among them.

I wasn't just gobsmacked. I was furious. I grabbed at the first thing within range – a pack of digestive biscuits – and hurled them across the room with all my strength.

Immediately, I controlled myself.

This was a crime scene. Forensics wouldn't appreciate biscuit crumbs on the bodies.

I crossed over and picked up the packet. The biscuits were pulverised but the cellophane was intact. The digestives went back on the tray.

But my mind was zonked.

Why would anyone want to steal a picture so brutally? It was a picture they could have paid for in the same way MacIver's insurance company was going to pay for it. Seventy-five thousand is not big bucks. Not to a professional gangster. Not if they were that keen on German Renaissance art.

I felt bad for Jamie Rind and his client. They shouldn't have been in danger. Had I been careless? Given something away? I didn't think so.

But I'd failed. It was a catastrophe. I felt abject.

I stumbled a few paces to the window and looked out. My brain was buzzing with theories, motives, consequences, explanations, repercussions, strategies, excuses.

My unfocussed gaze drifted down from the sky to the street outside and then suddenly became very focussed indeed.

A man in a shiny grey bomber jacket was walking briskly along the pavement carrying one of those A1 size carry cases that art students used to have in the days before digital.

The case had a distinct bulge in it. Like there was a framed picture inside.

I felt I was watching a reconstruction from a Crimewatch programme.

But this was real.

The man in the street was not behaving oddly. He wasn't looking around, not making any obvious check for observers. His pace was neither fast nor slow. He looked professional. But I detected an intensity about him, the air of someone on assignment. In a heartbeat, I knew he was the killer and the bulge in his carry case was the Amberger. As I watched, he flagged down a taxi.

I turned at once and raced out of the room, back the way I'd come, through the open area and down two flights of stairs. At the bottom I literally crashed into the torpid receptionist who was coming out of the Ladies. She reeled back in shock.

'Two dead upstairs.' I said. 'Get the police.' Her mouth gaped and she looked horror-struck. She thought I'd killed them.

'Call them,' I said and ran to the door, not bothering to look back to see if she'd fainted.

I came out on to the street in time to see the killer's taxi a hundred metres away driving north. There was a time, I think, in London when all so-called black cabs were actually black. But now many are brightly painted in advertising liveries and the escaping man had bizarrely chosen one of these. It was decked out in the red of Virgin Media. I looked around desperately for a taxi of my own but there were only delivery vans.

I cursed myself for letting Jason go.

Now there was only one option.

I started to run.

Chapter 2

In my first CID job I worked with a DS called Ryan who called me the Hulk. This wasn't because I was fat, my BMI has always been what it should be, but he reckoned I behaved like The Incredible Hulk. Ryan collected vintage comics and watched repeats of the Hulk TV show on obscure channels. He said I had the same overpowering urge to catch criminals and put things right as the Hulk did. He said I didn't have a red mist of anger but a green mist of vengeance and retribution. There was something in what Ryan said, though I never split my clothes or changed colour, thank God. So for a while at that nick, until everyone got bored with it, I was "the Hulk".

Well, a silly nickname is better than no nickname at all.

Right now the green mist had descended once again. There was a real pain inside me that two men had been killed, that the picture had slipped out of my grasp. I had a single-minded obsession to get the perpetrators at whatever cost.

The Virgin taxi was held at traffic lights and I sprinted along the pavement towards it. When I was fifty metres away the lights changed and the cab moved off, indicating to turn right. I ran on, gaining ground as it waited for a gap in the traffic. I vaulted over one of those metal barriers put in to stop you crossing the road at dangerous junctions, shot over to the other side of the road then turned right after the cab. I was running fast, but well within myself. I've finished a marathon in two hours fifty six and the average speed of central London traffic is not much quicker, ten miles an hour or so. Chasing on foot wasn't a hopeless tactic.

After half a mile the Virgin taxi was no further ahead. After three-quarters, I'd closed the gap to thirty metres.

Ahead of me, the pavement was blocked while a pallet of five litre cans of white emulsion was manoeuvred into a DIY store. I shouted a warning and did a steeple-chase jump over the whole pallet. There were jeers and catcalls from the yellow-jacketed delivery men, but who cares? I landed well, the paint was fine, I was fine. I carried on.

After a mile I was gaining further on the red taxi and beginning to relish the pursuit. I was expecting to catch it at the next traffic lights and began to plan how to tackle the gunman. Would he still have his weapon or had he ditched it? I was concentrating on this when I ran blindly across a side road. There was an angry shout from my right and the squeal of bicycle brakes. A courier in full Lycra crashed into me and we both fell to the ground.

I felt my jacket rip. But better that than a tendon.

'Fucking idiot!' the cyclist said, lying in the road.

I thought the same, really. About him. They're a bit of a silent menace, cycles. All very healthy and eco but they think they rule the roads.

I didn't have time to argue. I picked myself up and ran on. Apart from damaging my suit, the bike's front wheel had hit my right leg: it was painful and I knew it would slow me down. I hoped the cycle had been damaged as well.

I saw a taxi pull away from a hospital having dropped a fare. I waved frantically. It seemed reluctant to pick me up but the driver shrugged, did a U-turn and I jumped inside.

'See the red Virgin Media taxi?' I said. 'I want you to follow it.'

The driver eyed me suspiciously. He was at least sixty and I knew the type. He'd driven everyone: Sean Connery, Dick Van Dyke, the Beatles. Had loads of stories to tell. Boring old fart.

'You a journalist?'

'No...'

'Reality TV show?'

'No. I just want...'

'Just having a laugh?'

'For God's sake! Bloody follow that taxi!'

I pulled out my wallet and slapped three tens and a twenty down on the little plastic tray in the middle of the glass partition. 'Is that

serious enough for you? The man in the other cab's got stolen
property. Follow it.'

The driver glanced at the cash, shrugged and set off.

'I'm not exceeding the speed limit,' he said. 'Whatever he's
nicked.'

I exhaled loudly. 'Just don't lose him.' Though with Grandad
behind the wheel I wasn't fancying our chances and once again
wished I could be in Jason's car.

I perched on the edge of the seat, tense and staring forwards. If my
clothes weren't splitting like The Hulk's they bloody well ought to
have been for all the anxiety bottled up inside me.

Up ahead the red taxi was stationary as it waited to turn right. We
caught it up and joined the queue, six vehicles behind it, all waiting
for the filter light to go green. Then the red taxi driver took a chance
and slipped across in front of a Royal Mail van which was forced to
brake and blasted its horn.

'Can't you do something?' I said, frustrated my driver didn't have
the same spunky attitude as the guy in the Virgin taxi.

'I haven't got a flashing blue light, have I?' he said.

The red taxi had turned down a road that led to Kingsland Road
which is a main artery of north London and often congested.

'Don't follow it,' I said. 'Go straight on. Into De Beauvoir Road.'

'What?' said the driver.

'Kingsland Road's full of traffic lights. If we go straight on we can
get ahead of him.'

'Who's driving this cab? Me or you?'

'Who's paying?'

'And who's done the Knowledge?' said the driver, meaning the
taxi driver's qualification which involves years learning London's
streets.

'Yeah, yeah, but I know these streets, too. Go up De Beauvoir, turn
into Stamford Road and join Kingsland Road by Dalston Junction
station.'

The driver muttered and clicked his false teeth together.
Nevertheless he pulled away from the queue waiting to turn.

I'm not exaggerating if I say I know almost all streets. Almost
everywhere. I've always read maps for pleasure and can memorise

one in seconds. Grid references are second nature. I was born with a sixth sense for direction-finding which makes GPS and sat-navs redundant. Jason called it spooky and as a child I thought I was a bit of a freak. But my father told me not to fear the ability.

'It's a beautiful gift,' he'd said, 'like some people have perfect pitch, some can do square roots in their head, some can tell Chateau This from Chateau That.'

My driver was still muttering as he followed my route through the side streets. We approached the junction with Kingsland Road and I saw the red Virgin taxi drive across in front of us.

'See?' I said. 'Now, get in behind, close as you can.'

My driver slotted in one car behind the killer and gave me a look in the mirror which I took to be his version of admiration.

'How did you know he'd go north not south?'

If he'd been going south he'd have done so as soon as he left BetterWork. But I couldn't be bothered to explain. So I just said, 'Probability.'

Which seemed to impress the driver more than a logical answer.

'So what's the probability of my numbers coming up on the lottery this week?'

'As close to zero as makes no difference,' I said.

'What's he nicked, anyway?' the driver said.

'A painting.'

'Not one of them Turner Prize things? Load of rubbish they are.'

'No, it's sixteenth century. Worth a million or so.'

The driver was impressed and got the idea a piece of national heritage was in danger. His driving became more urgent. He suddenly seemed to be enjoying the chase.

I was convinced the red taxi would soon turn off into a residential street where I could tackle the gunman more easily. But it didn't. It kept going north and I got increasingly exasperated. We followed it through Stoke Newington, then into Stamford Hill. The miles were clocking up.

I had a miniature SLR camera in my pocket and I had to get a shot of the killer.

'Try to pull alongside the other cab,' I said.

13

But there were parked vehicles along much of the road which left space for only one lane of traffic. Further ahead I could see a wider section.

'Do it now,' I said.

'There better be no speed cameras,' he said.

'I'll pay the fine.'

'Yeah, but I get the points.'

He pulled out and pushed his foot down, overtaking the solitary car between us and the taxi. My camera was ready, pressed against the side window. As we drew alongside I could see the killer on the back seat, holding the big carry-case. I pressed the shutter several times.

'Keep going,' I said. 'I need a better shot.'

'There's a traffic island coming up,' said the driver.

'Overtake him. Force him to stop.'

'Jesus Christ. You want to kill us?'

'Get in front of him. Then just go slow.'

'You need a stunt driver not a taxi driver. Better still, you need the police. You should've called them.'

This had been on my mind for some time, but it was me who'd lost the picture and I wanted to get it back.

'We're on the scene,' I said. 'By the time they get here he'll have gone.'

Did I believe that? The man was armed: response time of SCO19 is bloody quick. But I had the green mist: it made me go on. I rubbed my hands over my face. How could something that had seemed so simple in MacIver's office go so spectacularly wrong?

Things were taken out of my hands by the piercing two-tone of an ambulance siren behind us. It was travelling fast.

'I got to let it through,' the driver said, slowing down and pulling in behind the Virgin cab.

The ambulance shot past.

There were more traffic lights and the Virgin cab went over on amber behind the ambulance. But we had to stop.

We were now in Tottenham.

On green, my driver got away fast and we quickly overtook three or four vehicles. Then we caught up with a huge car transporter which was between us and the Virgin cab.

Then the driver played another joker.

'I'll need diesel soon,' he said.

'For Christ's sake!' My opinion of the driver plummeted.

'I was just going to get some when you flagged me down.' I remembered the U-turn he'd had to make as I waved at him frantically.

But we had to press on. The road was wider now. Enough for two lanes in each direction.

'Overtake the transporter,' I said. 'Then overtake the taxi and make it stop.'

'It's forty grand's worth of cab I've got here.'

'If anything happens my employer will sort things out. They're an insurance company.'

The driver snorted. 'They're all so keen to get your business, then as soon as you make a claim they don't want to know.'

No time to argue. But he had a point I guess.

The red taxi was indicating to join the North Circular Road westbound, as was the car transporter. The red taxi accelerated down the ramp, joined the dual carriageway and we followed behind the transporter. But as we went down the ramp there were more sirens and we were overtaken by a police motorbike with lights flashing. The officer waved us to stop.

'Is it you they want?' said my driver as he halted, turning round and grinning like he'd said something funny.

The police bike stopped in the middle of the access ramp and traffic queued up behind us. I cursed again as I watched the red Virgin taxi disappear into the distance. I thought about getting out of the cab and talking to the officer, but I knew my sudden appearance on the roadway would unsettle him and I'd get no useful help. Then I noticed the road we were trying to join was suddenly empty of traffic. Then I twigged. And the driver twigged at the same time.

'It'll be royals or foreign high-ups,' he said.

The driver was an old git, but he was right and I had slowly warmed to him.

Just then a car from Diplomatic Protection and posse of police motorbikes flashed by escorting three black Daimlers. I saw CD plates on the cars and men in robes and Arabic head-dresses inside.

By the time we could proceed there was no chance of finding the red taxi so I asked to be taken back to the BetterWork complex. But first we had to stop for fuel. And I used the petrol station's ATM to top up on cash for the fare.

As I got back into the cab I saw a high-performance motorbike had stopped near us but wasn't filling up. The rider – a woman – seemed to be doing nothing except wiping her mirrors with that blue paper roll they have at filling stations. But there was something wrong. Her movements weren't urgent enough. It was like she was waiting for a cue.

I was immediately suspicious.

And angry. I'd just spent half the morning tailing someone. How dare anyone tail me. And if they were tailing me, why were they?

I asked the cab driver if he'd noticed the bike before.

'I've hardly looked in the mirror for the last half hour. Eyes glued on that bloody red taxi.'

I took some pictures but the driver's visor was down. It had a smoked finish and her face was invisible.

'Sure you're not a copper? One of those undercover guys?' the cab driver said as we set off back to central London. 'I've met them, you know. And the Secret Service,'

I was twisted round looking through the back window trying to see if the bike was following us. Then a supermarket home delivery van came in right behind us and comprehensively blocked my view.

'I was in the police,' I said, turning back to see the driver eyeing me curiously in the mirror. 'But not any longer.'

'What sort of stuff did you do?' Now the immediate pressure of the chase was off he assumed he could indulge himself in adding to his stock of stories.

'You'll have to wait till I write my memoirs,' I said.

I hate talking about the job. But everyone else loves to. People think they know what police work involves. But of course they don't. No more than I know what a stockbroker does all day. Or a corporate lawyer. Or a television producer.

But I'll break the habit of a lifetime and tell you a bit. Just enough so you don't think I'm a phoney. The thing is I never intended to become a police officer. For as long as I can remember I wanted to be an architect "when I grew up". I'd mapped out my future completely, dreaming of designing the kind of buildings that tourists photograph. But then things changed and I grew up all too quickly.

I had a good enough career, but I was never a yes-man or arse-licker and had the odd dust-up with senior officers. Mostly I kept my opinions to myself. I pretended to support Brexit, pretended to hate the Home Secretary, pretended to agree with the majority. I drank in the right pubs and joined the right clubs but I knew I'd get no further promotion. Not because I'd transgressed in any way, but because I just didn't have the right stuff to be a long-serving police officer.

I'd joined for the wrong reasons you see.

But that's all in the past.

Where I ended up was in the Met's Arts and Antiques Unit. It's a Cinderella squad, under-resourced and under-manned but I was happy there. I liked the fact that the unit's purpose was not solely to catch villains but to recover stolen artworks. It was this which got up the noses of the top brass. They thought that if Lord Claude had a few pictures nicked from his castle it was far less worthy of police resources than a kid getting knifed in Hackney or a woman raped in Kentish Town.

Well, yes. Up to a point.

Trouble is art crime isn't like it is in the movies. Art's not stolen to enhance the collections of Dr No types – mega-rich megalomaniacs. It's much more complex.

Today is a case in point. So complex I just don't get it. Not yet. But I will. Even if it kills me.

Why did they want this artist? Why this picture?

That's what I grappled to understand as we drove back, craning my head round every few minutes to look for the motorbike. But if it was there, it stayed well concealed.

The driver prattled on about police officers he'd known and then gave me his views on the football World Cup and which teams were dead certs for the semi-finals. Back in Hoxton I felt sorry for his next fare. He'd bore them rigid with a street by street account of our chase.

Back at BetterWork no one seemed to be working at all.

Except for police officers.

In the ground floor open area everyone was chatting excitedly, taking selfies, snapping the police and frantically updating their social media accounts. There was only one person who remained exactly the same as an hour earlier. The receptionist. She stood behind her counter scrutinising the jollity with a sherbet lemon kind of face. Like a referee about to blow up and wave the red card.

I went upstairs to the murder scene and made myself known. Detective Chief Inspector Bostock was in charge. I knew him by reputation but we'd never met. He was well-respected in the service and though he was near retirement age he was still full of energy with a frisky sense of humour.

He'd heard of me. Which was surprising.

'Ah, the art tart,' he said in greeting, but not unkindly. It wasn't a nickname I'd heard before in the Met, but it fitted the general sardonic impression of the Art and Antiques Unit as a bunch of limp-wristed fairies who sat about in smoking jackets sipping cocktails and reading *Connoisseur* magazine. Coincidentally I was also called an art tart at school, but so was everyone in the Arts Sixth. It was that sort of school. Members of the 1st XV were rugger buggers, the assembly hall was Big School and Big Side was a cricket pitch.

'Didn't know I knew you?' said Bostock with a grin. 'You'd be surprised what I know.' Then he stopped the side show and came clean. 'Miss Mikado downstairs gave us your name – after she'd frigging photocopied our warrant cards...' And he made a despairing, stone-me kind of face. '– so I looked you up.'

I told Bostock all I could and identified Jamie Rind. The other dead man was carrying no ID but would be traceable through Rind's office. Then I gave a full statement to one of Bostock's sergeants.

It was beginning to appear there were no witnesses and no descriptions of the killer apart from my own. No one had heard the shots either. Presumably a silencer had been used but many workers were wearing head-sets for phone conversations, Skyping, or just listening to music and were deaf to everything else. It seemed a good place to stage a murder for the same reason Jamie Rind thought it a good place for the handover of the painting. The office complex was so free and easy that extraordinary things went unnoticed.

I was hacked off I had nothing better to give the enquiry and I began to feel a bit of a spare part. I went downstairs and took the bag of money out of the locker.

Then I remembered what the Japanese receptionist had said. The bit about me already being checked in at the west door. I wondered whether Bostock's team had followed that up yet.

Perhaps I could get a jump ahead of them.

I trailed through the building and found the west door which was actually a goods and staff entrance not intended for the general public. Guarding it was a kid who looked about sixteen. He was wearing an England football shirt and listening intently to whatever was coming over his headphones. I started to introduce myself but he waved at me to shut up and pressed his earphones closer.

I tried to speak again but the boy, whose badge said he was Nathan, shook his head violently – not at me but at what he was listening to. Then he yanked off the headset despairingly.

'I don't believe it,' he said. 'Have you heard this?'

Obviously I hadn't. So all I did was shrug.

'It's the World Cup. There's some kind of storm coming in... in that place where it is.'

'Qatar?'

'Yeah. There's going to be a surge, a soon..., a soon...'

'Tsunami?'

'That's what they said.'

I just looked at him. I couldn't imagine what crazy stuff he'd been listening to. I tried to persuade him that weather for the imminent football would be perfectly fine and that I had something more urgent to deal with. He immediately assumed I was with the police and I didn't bother to put him right.

But his thoughts were still on football and Nathan could remember nothing about the killer he'd let in. My questions brought only furrowed brows and head shakes.

'Is there anything you can remember about him at all?'

The boy screwed up his face so much with the effort of concentration that he looked in pain.

'O.K., Nathan, thanks anyway,' I said. Then just as I turned to go:
'He did... he did talk funny.' Nathan suddenly spluttered into speech like an air-lock clearing from a water pipe.
'You mean an accent?'
'Yeah. He had an accent.'
'Russian? Polish? Arab?'
Nathan looked at me like I'd asked if he preferred Frank Lloyd Wright to Mies van der Rohe.
'It wasn't the accent that was funny.'
'What was then?'
'His voice was sort of squeaky.'
'High pitched?' I said.
'Kind of.'
'Sing-songy? Like Welsh, or Geordie?'
Nathan gave me the WTF look again. Then he gave a big sigh like he was frustrated I was so dense I wasn't getting what he meant.
'It was like when you've got a cold and there's snot stuck in your throat and... No... No. It was like...' Nathan stood up, elated he'd found the right comparison. 'It was like an app,' he said triumphantly.
'An app?'
'A voice changer app on a phone. My friend Fletch can sound like Brian in *Family Guy*. With this bloke it wasn't all the time. It was like his app was switching in and out.'
A foreigner with a voice that was intermittently squeaky, like it had gone through a graphic equaliser. Not much to go on. But perhaps more than Bostock had got.

Chapter 3

I returned the seventy-five thousand to the accounts department at Maskelyne Global then went to see Fiona MacIver. She was a long-serving executive who managed the loss adjusters and fraud investigators at the insurance group as well as special investigators like me. She was in her mid-fifties, twenty years or so older than me, but she'd kept her figure, invariably wore smart business dresses and always looked trim.

As did her office. Some people create an extension of their home with photos, nick-knacks, pot plants, posters. Her office was spare, tidy, unfussy. Not OCD, not a disciple of that de-cluttering prophet who does origami with clothes, just old fashioned neat.

Her style was a bit old school too, even school marm, but that's not necessarily a bad thing.

I'd already told her over the phone what had happened. And it hurt me to do so. I regard myself as a first team player and don't want to drop down to the reserves or sit things out on the bench.

I went into her office expecting a bollocking.

But what I got was worse. Much worse.

It was an unanswerable question.

'Ever heard of someone called Alex Broughton?' she said, hardly looking up from papers on her desk.

I couldn't have been more shocked if Fiona MacIver had stripped off and asked to suck my cock.

There was a swirling sensation in my stomach, a lightness in my head, a sudden sweat on my brow. It was a shock-induced nauseous vertigo that I never thought I'd experience again. It made me feel weak, unmanly. There's a book, which I've never read, called *The*

21

Unbearable Lightness of Being. I've no idea what it's about but I saw it on the shelves of a long ago girlfriend and I just fell in love with the title – though not with the girl. And it describes how I felt just then. Unbearably light-headed. Like I was floating away into some distant other world.

I looked at the floor, trying to give the impression of deep thinking, then took a few steps away from MacIver across the tarmac-coloured carpet – a similar shade to the one at BetterWork but without the bloodstains. I have never been a great liar so I grabbed the chance of a delaying tactic.

'Alex?' I said. 'A girl or a bloke?'

'A man. About your age apparently. In a similar line of work. Someone phoned up about him.'

I took a few more steps away from MacIver, tried to imitate the befuddled expression that the kid, Nathan, had put on, then turned back and shook my head in a way that I hoped looked conclusively negative.

'Name mean nothing to you at all?' She looked at me with her large tawny-brown eyes which always reminded me of a bird of prey. Not an owl, MacIver certainly wasn't owlish. Something more fleet, more dangerous. Maybe a peregrine.

'No.' I managed to say, realising my voice was a bit squeaky too.

MacIver shrugged. 'Oh, well… We've more important things to talk about. But you seem a wee bit… quiet this morning.' MacIver was Scottish but her accent was light.

'Well… bit of a cock-up wasn't it?'

'Let's call it a bolt from the blue.' MacIver was always fair: she didn't blame me. But I blamed myself. 'And it's a pity about the suit.'

The torn sleeve was the least of my problems. Though I was surprised Bostock hadn't made a crack about it.

'Do you think stealing this wee picture was the main objective or was it killing Mr Rind?'

'The picture's got to be fundamental,' I said, feeling easier now we were talking crime. My earlier shuffling movements round the office had developed into a definite pacing. 'Nothing else makes sense.'

MacIver looked at me with her unblinking eyes.

'Let's review the alternatives,' she said. 'One possibility is: someone wants to kill Jamie Rind. They do so. And also kill the other man...' She looked at me.

'Roland Sadler,' I said, having got the victim's name from Rind's efficient P.A.

'They kill Sadler to eliminate a witness. Then they see the picture and take a sudden fancy to it...'

'And they just happen to have with them a large carry-case to put it in,' I made a how-unlikely-is-that kind of face, pleased my heartbeat was back to normal.

MacIver nodded, conceding my point. 'Second possibility. Someone wanted to kill Roland Sadler. They do so, and also Rind because *he's* a witness. And then they take the picture.' Then with another nod towards me, 'Same objection as the first scenario. The third possibility is: someone wants to kill you...'

I took a breath to protest but MacIver went on. 'Let's imagine there are some dark and terrible deeds in your police career that a person or persons unknown wants to avenge.' She looked at me. Her falcon eyes were now twinkling and she had her trademark tight-lipped, half-smile,

I understood she was teasing, but even jokes along these lines send a shiver up my spine. Someone walking over your grave is what my grandmother used to say. I've never offered my past up for water-cooler chat.

'So the killer mistakes Mr Rind for you and does the deed...'

'He should've gone to Specsavers, then.' I tried to laugh. 'Rind is more your age than mine, he's shorter than me, plumper, different hair...'

'What about the other guy? Sadler.'

I thought back. Shit. Yes, he was my age. Similar size, too.

And there was that girl on the motorbike at the petrol station. Suddenly I felt sweaty again. I said nothing but, seeing me thoughtful, MacIver was pressing on.

'Let's try a fourth possibility. An obsessive fan of the works of – what's he called...?'

'Amberger.'

23

'...A fan of Herr Amberger who is too short of cash to buy his hero's work at auction kills two people in order to add a picture of an unknown German youth to his collection.' She paused and looked at me.

'Sorry, Fiona, all complete bollocks I think.'

Her carefully pencilled eyebrows slowly ascended.

'The fourth option could have a faint ring of truth.'

'In a movie, maybe. Except in a film it'd be a cyborg doing it, not the collector himself.'

'No motive for anyone wanting to murder Mr Rind?'

'None I know of, but I'm interviewing Rind's PA later.'

'What about you?'

I thought about the motorbike girl again. She wasn't sight-seeing. It was a powerful bike, she had good leathers and all the kit. Was someone after me? A friend of my father's? Why, after all this time? My pacing round the office speeded up.

'I'll take that as a no,' MacIver said and swivelled her desk chair round towards the window, kicked off her court shoes and put her feet up on the low radiator behind her. Her legs were exactly horizontal, her toes in their black tights were precisely pointed. It was early autumn and still warm so the heating was off, but it was her habitual pose when puzzling something over.

My pacing took me past one of MacIver's few personal items in the room: a map pinned to the wall in a discreet corner. It was of the Munros, the hills in Scotland over three thousand feet. On the map were several hundred plastic-headed pins, some green and some red. One of the few things I knew about MacIver was that she was a keen hill-walker. I guessed the green pins marked those she'd climbed, the red ones those she still had to tick off. She'd done over half of them, nearly two hundred. Impressive. Persistent. Dedicated.

'So tell me why someone's so keen to get their hands on this picture?' she said.

'If I knew I wouldn't be standing around in your office.'

This provoked a moment of irritation. 'You're not standing. You're pacing. You'll get nowhere fretting about what's gone. Sit down and relax a wee minute.'

I realised my restlessness had turned into a barefoot-bather-on-burning-hot-sand routine. I said nothing but slumped into a chair opposite her desk.

'There must be something special about this picture,' she said. 'The artist is awful obscure.'

MacIver was right. I can tell a Monet from a Manet, but Christoph Amberger is not a marquee name. I'd never heard of him before. I could appreciate the artist's skill but the picture didn't appeal, it felt remote and formal. It was called *Portrait of a Young Merchant* and was painted around 1520 in Augsburg where Amberger lived. He specialised in portraits of the rich and famous including the top European of his day, the Emperor Charles V.

Why did someone want this particular picture so badly?

I had to grasp at straws.

'There's the Shakespeare connection.'

'History isn't my subject but surely Shakespeare wasn't born when this chappie was painted.'

She was right again. 'Yes, but the frame is of later date than the picture and there's a legend the picture was given to Shakespeare by a supposed male lover.'

MacIver wasn't impressed and blew out dismissively. 'Like all those houses in Scotland where Bonnie Prince Charlie is supposed to have lodged.'

I nodded. 'Whether it's true doesn't matter. It adds value. And mystique.'

'So a fifth possibility is that a fanatical student of English Literature, who believes in fairy tales, killed two people just to get his hands on a wee wooden frame.'

MacIver sighed, put her elbows on her desk and rested her chin in her hands. My despondent mood had afflicted her. She picked up from her desk an A3 size print of the Amberger painting and gazed at it.

'What about the subject? The Young Merchant. Who is this boy?'

'He's probably a Fugger.'

The big eyes turned to me again. 'Is this rude? I saw a film about the Fockers once.'

'The Fuggers of Augsburg were the richest family in Europe at that time. They basically invented banking. But their descendants are not short of a Euro or two, so if they wanted a picture of great-great-great-great-great... whatever grandfather they'd just fork out the cash.'

MacIver nodded.

'Any other ideas?'

Since leaving BetterWork I'd had about twenty ideas. Trouble was I didn't like any of them much.

'Was the picture taken by mistake?'

'In mistake for what?'

MacIver was about to answer, then she realised there was no answer. 'O.K. Forget I said that.'

We sat silently a moment. MacIver's feet returned to their perch on top of the radiator.

I had one suggestion left but I'd purposely waited until we'd exhausted every alternative because I thought MacIver would think me crazy. It was one of those wild, high concept scenarios that you never come across in real life but are the stuff of movies. You know the kind of thing. There's often a scene which goes something like:

'Mr President, it's not just New York that's in danger. It's the country. The whole world.'

'In danger of what exactly?'

'Of total annihilation.'

Then the hero is sent out to stop the incurable virus, the rogue asteroid, or the extra-terrestrial invasion.

Yes, it sounds mad. But was the only kind of solution that even began to make sense. And it also indicated how serious the theft could be.

But how could I explain it to MacIver? Well, I just dived in.

'In my gut,' I said, 'I feel the painting's part of some bigger plan. Maybe not anything to do with art at all.'

MacIver swivelled back again. 'Like what?'

I had to ad lib. 'Extortion, blackmail, revenge, conspiracy...'

'Terrorism?'

'Possibly...' I was still groping. 'Something which would threaten the stability of...'

'Of the insurance business?'

26

'Could be…'

'Of *all* business? Of the nation?' MacIver's searchlight eyes targeted me again. 'If this is your view surely we should leave it to the police?'

'No.'

My voice was louder and my tone sharper than I intended but I was annoyed I'd prompted MacIver to suggest this. She was thinking of the corporate angle, company reputation, risk versus gain, profit and loss, health and safety. But I didn't want this case taken away. I was confident I could sort it. I do what I do because I have to. Because of my past.

MacIver saw my determination but didn't change her line.

'Why didn't you get the police involved when you were chasing the killer in the taxi?'

'I was so close to him. I nearly had him.'

'But you didn't. You lost him.'

'Only because of that bloody motorcade of Arabs.'

'You can't blame *them*. You might as well blame that irritating woman from accounts for delaying you this morning.'

I gritted my teeth and breathed in. Privately I'd already blamed the woman from accounts. If I'd got to BetterWork just a few minutes earlier I would have been there before the killer arrived. I could have…

But who knows what I could have done? I wasn't armed. I might have ended up as another of the killer's victims. It's no use trying to rewrite the past. I've learned that the hard way.

'Calling the police would have been sensible.'

I wasn't giving in. 'You hired me to get the picture back for the owner. That's what I'll do. Murders or no murders.'

My phone pinged and I looked at the screen.

It was a message from Bostock. I read the grim words and immediately felt more depressed. My instinct was to keep it from MacIver, but it was already too late.

'Bad news?'

I looked up, about to try and bluff it out.

'It's written all over your face,' MacIver said.

In the school lunch-break poker sessions I always lost. I'm not good at play-acting. I've got some kind of incredibly strong honesty gene that trumps everything. I had to bite the bullet.

'The driver of the taxi I was chasing. They've found him. Shot dead.'

'*Three* murders to steal one painting.'

I nodded.

'They didn't catch the killer?'

'No.'

There was a knock, the office door opened and Clark Munday hurried in. He was about my age and on MacIver's staff. He always wore an absorbed, serious expression as if he were wrestling with the world's toughest Sudoku. Perhaps he was.

He liked to claim his parents had named him after Clark Kent – Superman – because they were fans. Clark lacked flying ability but he was undoubtedly a superman when it came to digital stuff. An ace computer nerd and techno-freak with access to an illegally-wide range of databases. The only thing he had trouble accessing was a sense of humour.

'I was monitoring police messages.' he said. This was one of his private passions. 'Heard about the taxi-driver?'

'Yes. Where was he found?'

'New Southgate station.'

'A tube station?' said MacIver.

'No. That's called Southgate,' said Clark. '*New* Southgate's a mainline station. He could've been going anywhere.'

'Explain,' said MacIver.   She knew the Scottish Highlands intimately but not the outer suburbs of London.

'It's on the King's Cross line,' said Clark. 'Five or six trains an hour to Welwyn, change there and go onwards to Cambridge. Alternatively change at Hitchin for Peterborough and the eastern mainline: York, Newcastle, Edinburgh Waverly...'

'Too much information, Clark,' said MacIver, waving a hand at him.

Clark looked peeved. He was an anorak when it came to railways. I don't know whether he still stood on station platforms with a flask, sandwiches and an Ian Allan book of locomotive numbers but I'm sure he'd done so as a boy.

'He may not have caught a train,' I said. 'He may have been meeting someone. To hand over the picture.'

'How many people live within a mile, say, of that station?' said MacIver.

Clark was silent for a moment while he juggled numbers. 'Say thirty, forty thousand people.' Clark looked at me. 'Do you want me to correlate everybody living within a mile of New Southgate station against criminal records?'

'Not yet,' I said. 'What do you know about that party of Arab big-wigs?'

'Trade delegation from Qatar,' he said.

'What were they doing buggering about round the North Circular?'

'Plane was diverted to Stansted. Tyre-pressure warning indicator gave a false positive.' Clark was hot on all modes of transport.

'Is this a Buck House banquet job? Horses and carriages?'

'No. It's purely trade. Except for some reason a Culture Minister's come along, too.'

'What's he here for?' said MacIver.

'Going to scout round the British Museum earmarking items of cultural importance they want sent back,' I said.

Clark ignored me and just carried on.

'The department's actually called the Ministry of Culture and *Sports*.'

'If he's on the sports side why has he been allowed playtime? The World Cup starts any time soon. He ought to be checking the touch-lines are straight and the air-con goes all the way up to eleven.'

'Let's not get diverted,' said MacIver. 'Clark, I was trying to persuade Kite to leave it to the police. What do you think?'

This was the kind of question Clark couldn't handle. He looked uncomfortably between MacIver and me then after a lengthy pause said, 'Well, I think...' and then stopped.

So I jumped in.

'My view hasn't changed,' I said. 'I should still hunt for the picture. The police will deal with the murders.'

'But I don't want the murderer to deal with *you*,' said MacIver with heavy emphasis.

I said nothing but I thought of the biker. Was she part of the killer's team? If she'd wanted to kill me she'd have had every opportunity.

MacIver gave me one of her unblinking stares. The peregrine falcon looked about to strike. Then she exhaled. 'Very well. But I can't let this go on too long. You need to find the picture fast or I'll close the case down.'

How long did she meant by fast? A few days? A week?

'And your theory that there's something bigger going on... I see where you're coming from but it's an awful, wee scrawny thing to hang an investigation on. You need to put some flesh on the bone.'

Then she leaned forward, flicking at my torn sleeve with a finger.

'And you better get some new clothes... to put on the flesh.' MacIver surprised herself with her play on words and grinned.

I turned to go but something made me ask a question I'd been itching to know the answer to for the last half hour.

'This phone call about the Alex Broughton guy... Who was it who called to ask about him?'

'Nobody I know. And not the police...' She moved back to her desk to consult a note scribbled on a pad. 'A woman called... India Paine.'

There are some questions better left unasked.

It was another sledgehammer blow. I looked out over MacIver's head to the dome of St Paul's shimmering in a hazy sun and to control my churning stomach, thumping heart and woozy head I silently recited Wren's epitaph. *Si monumentum requiris, circumspice* over and over. Then the orders of architecture: Tuscan, Doric, Ionic, Corinthian. Repeatedly. And fast. Like a mantra for a man with his lover who wanted to stop himself coming too quickly.

I managed to say to MacIver that the name meant nothing to me, left her office and found the nearest Gents where I locked myself in a cubicle to recover.

I felt dizzy. There was a whirlpool in my stomach.

What a big girl's blouse.

I thought back to when they talked about counselling. After I'd said no twice, nobody mentioned it again. Fifteen years later I've begun to think those professionals could have been right.

But it's a bit too bloody late.

Chapter 4

Agreeing to leave the murder investigation to the police seemed to satisfy MacIver, but if I was to find the picture the first step was to chase down the murderer.

So I went to Clark's office to look at the shots I'd taken in the taxi.

Clark's room was as cluttered as MacIver's was neat. There was a bird's nest of cables on the floor powering an impressive array of equipment: screens, scanners and computers with high-powered software. He kept the blinds closed and the lights dim so it was difficult to tell if it was day or night. He also chose to remove time displays from his screens so thoughts of meal breaks or going home wouldn't interrupt his concentration. I couldn't work in such a timeless netherworld and after thirty minutes in Clark's office I always felt a need to see some sky.

As Clark uploaded my pictures I mentioned what Nathan at BetterWork had said about bad weather affecting the World Cup.

'Tidal waves in the Gulf?' he said, making a face like I'd said Atlantis had been discovered.

'Sources are quoting figures received from automated weather buoys. It's making...

a big splash online.'

I gave him an apologetic grin but Clark didn't register my naff pun.

'Some idiot's misread the data. They're confusing feet with metres. Millibars with inches of mercury.'

'The readings stack up. They've been checked.'

Clark shook his head dismissively again. 'It'll be human error... fat finger syndrome.'

'Or intentional misinformation,' I said.

That made Clark turn round from his screens to look at me. He said nothing, just nodded slowly, thoughtfully. The silence was broken by my phone.

It was DCI Bostock.

'You didn't tell me you funded the Barrington Prize,' he said.

'Well, Chief Inspector, you didn't ask,' I said with a casual sort of laugh. Somebody had been shooting their mouth off. I'd asked for anonymity when I made that gift.

'And an old mucker of mine says you're generous to the Benevolent Fund, too.'

'I guess... you know, every little helps.' I tried to sound embarrassed he'd uncovered my philanthropy. It wasn't hard. I was embarrassed.

'I heard it actually wasn't so little. And you're a fixer for pro-am golf as well?'

'Occasionally. But it's meant to be... discreet, confidential. I really don't like to shout about it.'

'Well, you ought to. It's not everyone would use an inheritance in that way,' said Bostock impervious to my hints. 'A rich granny, was it?'

I hesitated. 'Something like that.' Giving money to police charities or foundations sounds as bad as fixing the World Cup. But the money I donated was tainted. I couldn't keep it. I wanted to use it for good. And supporting police officers is surely doing good.

Do I get anything out of this do-gooding? Yes, of course. Like those stars who become ambassadors for the UN or for big charities. A famous face photographed in a war zone or drought area is good for the charity and does no harm to the star's image either.

So, I confess. I use the money to make contacts as well as do good. But the contacts I make help me do my job.

'So I thought I could – you know – do a *quid pro quo*,' Bostock was saying.

See what I mean?

'That's very kind.'

'Bollocks. We scratch each other's backs. That's what makes the world go round. Well, I'll cut the crap. The reason I called is there's CCTV of the murderer leaving the building in Hoxton. We can see he's carrying something picture-sized but we can't get an ID match. Either through software or with our recogniser specialists. He's not known to us. Clean skin. But I'll send it over.'

When the call ended, Clark had already loaded my shots and enhanced them as far as he could. Now he zoomed into the killer's face to show me what we had. He wrinkled his nose.

'It's hopeless. The face isn't lit and there's strong sunlight coming in the window behind him. *Contre jour*. Your auto aperture has exposed for the background light, not the face. It's the worst possible contrast.'

Clark didn't know about sugaring the pill, never minced his words. I gave him a look. But he didn't notice.

I peered at the face on screen. It was a man all right but his features were impossible to decipher.

'Anything else you can do to it?'

'I can't enhance what's not there.'

'O.K. Forget the man. Let's look at what he's carrying.'

Clark pulled back to look at the shot full frame then selected the artist's carrying case, where the picture-shaped bulge protruded through the PVC. He zoomed in. Perversely the exposure on the case was perfect. Part of the carrying case was black plastic but the central third of it was transparent. Through this section we could see the picture carefully wrapped. But there was something else as well.

'What's that white thing right at the bottom?' I said.

Clark enlarged the area further.

'Piece of paper,' he said, 'looks like a blank office letterhead. It'll be Conqueror brand. 120 gsm.'

I caught his eye. 'Sure it's not 100 gsm?'

Clark huffed. He didn't like his judgements being questioned.

It looked as if the sheet had been left in the carrying case earlier and had been squashed down to the bottom when the painting was inserted.

I thought of those government ministers who walk into Number 10 holding a secret memo, or a list of embarrassing notes in red felt-tip. They forget the waiting photographers will snap them, enlarge the image and publish for all the world to see. I hoped our murderer had been equally careless.

'Can you read the printing?' I said.

'What printing?' Clark was still annoyed by my quip.

'Right at the bottom there's something.'

'Oh, you mean the company information. Eight point. Very customer friendly.'

It was tiny but Clark magicked the image into something almost readable. I stared at the screen. There was part of a Company Registration number and part of a VAT number.

With further manipulation we had legible digits. But still only parts of each number sequence. Six out of nine of the VAT number and five out of seven of the Company Registration.

'Can you play with those and try to match them up?' I said.

'There's about five and half million companies registered in the UK and over two and a half million VAT registrations. Say fourteen million combinations.'

'That's a walk in the park for you.'

'Yeah, more like two hundred miles up the Pennine Way with a 30Kg pack.'

My phone pinged. It was the incoming CCTV from Bostock.

I transferred it to Clark's machine and we both stared at the screen. The image was similar to the glimpse I'd had from the BetterWork office window. The man was in his thirties or early forties, wearing jeans and a shiny bomber jacket over a plain white T-shirt. The bulge of the stolen picture was visible in his carry-case but not the piece of letterhead that showed in my shots. Most disappointing, as Bostock said, was that the man's face was half turned away from the camera. It would be difficult to get a positive ID.

Nevertheless, Clark zoomed into the footage, enhanced it as far as possible and I transferred the material to my phone. Then I left Clark to it – I'd had enough and he was happier that way. I was getting tired of the draught under my left armpit so I followed MacIver's instruction and went shopping.

My taste in clothes is kind of traditional but I like colourful things. And there's a practical reason. CID are mostly in suits while undercover cops dress down: black, grey, camouflage green, leather or denim. I don't want to be flamboyant or stand out in a crowd but I do want to give the impression of someone more interested in art and aesthetics than crime and punishment.

I bought an indigo coloured, wool jacket, a couple of shirts and some chinos, the ones with a bit of stretch to them, which means I can run, jump, kick, fight or whatever much better. If you're interested in footwear – I don't mean fetishly – I've an aversion to trainers. I find them sweaty, rubbery and too soft in a confrontation. I like something more robust: proper leather, solid sole, made in England even. They're supple enough to run fast in but can hurt if you're on the wrong end of them.

As I put my PIN into the shop's card machine I had a call from Clark. The marathon walk up the British Isles had become a five-minute stroll. True to form, he'd wrangled a company name from the incomplete numbers in double-quick time.

I left my torn jacket in the changing room and set off for the tube.

The company letterhead belonged to the Butt-Ansari Gallery in Golborne Road, W.10. Which, depending on your aspirations or whether you're an estate agent, is either Notting Hill, North Kensington or Kensal Rise. The company directors were Magda Butt-Ansari and Kadir Butt-Ansari.

The killer might have got the case from a charity shop so the sheet of letterhead might mean nothing at all. But the word Gallery excited me at once. Then Clark told me he'd checked the gallery's website and they didn't deal in pictures at all. Their business was middle-eastern antiquities.

But "middle-eastern antiquities" is a phrase that rings warning bells nowadays. Ancient art used to be an area of the antiques trade where little changed from year to year. Archaeology is a slow business. But now it's gold-rush time. Not the wild west but the wild east. The atrocities of ISIS, the Taliban and Al-Qaida are partly funded by the wholesale looting of museums and archaeological sites. The lawlessness in Syria makes it easy to transport the booty into the western antiques trade.

I left the tube at Ladbroke Grove and walked along Portobello Road to Golborne Road which is a confusing mixture of poverty and wealth. There are faded, cheap laundrettes and Hal-al butchers, but also designer upholsterers and a shop selling expensive, retro light fittings. I'd last been along there as an architecture student to study the notorious high-rise Trellick Tower built sixty years ago by Erno Goldfinger, the man whose name was famously pinched by Ian Fleming.

Typical of the hybrid nature of the area, the specialist Butt-Ansari Gallery was sandwiched between a downmarket Palestinian restaurant and an Afro-Caribbean greengrocer.

With steel shutters down and no lights on the building looked sad and unloved. A scrappy, handwritten notice stuck on the inside of the door said: If Closed, Please Ring Bell.

A bit contradictory but not unusual for this kind of shop. Maybe they dealt mostly with the trade and didn't want time-wasters. I gave them the benefit of the doubt and rang the bell. But nothing happened. I pressed it again and waited longer. Still nobody.

I moved away from the Gallery to the greengrocer's. Outside the shop was a rack of water melons. I picked up the biggest I could find and went into the shop. I paid for the melon and asked the cheerful guy behind the counter, who looked Somali, if he knew the couple in the antique shop next door. He did. They chatted from time to time. Used the same firm to board up their windows for the Carnival weekend.

I asked when the shop opened.

The man shrugged. 'When they want to,' he said. Perhaps it wasn't their main business I thought. But then he went on, 'Used to be every day. But recently… one day, two days a week only.'

'Why's that?'

He shrugged again. 'Brother, it's not Oxford Street.'

I nodded and smiled, waiting for more. Without prompting, the shopkeeper went on.

'The man, Kadir… I think he's ill or something. He's not been on the street for three weeks, four weeks… Longer.'

'What's wrong with him?'

The man laughed. 'I ain't no doctor.'

'Could be on holiday.'

'Without the lady? No way.'

The shopkeeper was remarkably open and didn't seem to mind answering questions. And this in an area of London where relations with the police are sometimes frazzled. I wondered if he was just spinning yarns or telling me what he thought I wanted to hear. But things changed when I asked him where the gallery owners lived.

'Don't know,' he said. 'But if I did know I wouldn't tell you.'

'It's all right, I'm not police.'

'I know that,' he said. 'Round here even the kids know who's filth and who's not.'

'I used to be in the police,' I said.

'Well, well... Obviously you've been out long enough to lose the...'

'The smell?'

He laughed loudly. 'Maybe. Or the way they walk. Or the way they talk. Or something.'

Then I gave him my card.

'That's what I do now.'

The man picked up the card and read it.'

'Specialist Investigator?'

'I'm an art specialist.'

He seemed to find this amusing too. 'Tell me, just how do you investigate art?'

'Stolen art.'

'Oh...' He immediately glanced at the shop next door and jumped to the wrong conclusion. 'They've had stuff stolen?'

'I want to talk to them about a stolen picture. They may not be involved at all but they're my only lead. When they open their shop what I'd like is for you to give me a call.'

I put fifty pounds on the counter. The Somali considered.

'What do they sell in their shop? I mean, where does the stuff come from?'

'All over. The antiques could be Roman, Greek, Egyptian...'

'African?'

'I expect so.'

'If you get inside the shop will you tell me if they have African things, Somali things?'

'If you want.'

'I do want. They shouldn't sell things from my country.'

Not a topic I wanted to debate, so I said nothing.

'O.K. I take your money. And I call you.'

'Thank you. And you can keep the water-melon, too.'

Now he looked mock indignant. 'Hey! Something wrong with my fruit?'

I smiled and we shook hands on the deal.

But I didn't expect to hear from him again.

Chapter 5

I had to hurry away from the Butt-Ansari Gallery because I had an appointment to talk to Jamie Rind's P.A., Kirsty. I'd asked to meet her as a formality but she became the source of some surprising information. And Kirsty, too, was a surprise.

Rind's firm, Rind and Buhler, was based in Streatham, SW2 and the office itself was like I'd imagined: chipped paint, well-trodden carpets, torn vinyl and old-fashioned grey steel filing cabinets. It fitted in with Jamie's crumpled clothes and unkempt hair.

Kirsty was different. She was in her late twenties and was tall, five-ten at least, with an athletic physique – a strong swimmer or sprinter I imagined. She was an eager and attractive woman with vivid eyes and dazzling blonde hair. Her clothes too were bright and fashionable, but chosen carefully enough to be in keeping with a downmarket legal firm. Jamie cultivated a shabby appearance as a kind of protective veneer, a cloak of invisibility to keep clients at arm's length, but Kirsty obviously preferred to mark out her individuality.

It wasn't just her appearance which made a statement. She had a sharp intelligence and expressed herself enthusiastically. Before I'd said more than my name, while we were still shaking hands, she was criticising what the police had told her.

'They think everything stemmed from someone wanting to kill Jamie. They're going through all his past clients, looking for a motive. They say the picture was just misdirection. To make us think it was important. They say it'll just end up in a skip. That's not true is it?' She gave me an intense look but, before I could answer, went on.

'Some of his clients were vicious, horrible men but Jamie always did his best for them. There were never any threats, no nasty emails that kind of thing. You get far worse on Twitter.'

She paused for breath. I liked her spirit. It was only hours since she'd had the news of her boss being murdered.

'The police aren't always right,' I said, fence-sitting.

'No. Otherwise there wouldn't be so much work for people like Jamie.'

'I meant, I used to be a police officer myself. So I know how things play out.'

She seized on this. 'Well, in that case can't you tell them they're mistaken? That they're looking at things from the wrong angle.'

I savoured what DCI Bostock's reaction would be if I told him how to run his enquiry. Then I explained to Kirsty why I wasn't surprised the police were mostly interested in the murders rather than the picture. But I also said I agreed with her. It was more complex than a grudge or a contract killing.

This pleased her.

'Thank you so much for saying that. But why did it happen? What do you think?' She leaned towards me, her eyes lighting up, keen for an answer.

I realised it was Kirsty asking all the questions and I looked at her wondering how to reply. Our eyes met. Hers were an unusual deep green with a hint of blue. The word viridian popped into my head.

Before I could give her an answer she bounced up out of her desk chair.

'I'm sorry. Can I get you a coffee? Tea?'

I said tea would be nice and with a 'Won't be long', she zoomed out of the office. I got up too and followed her to a little kitchenette off the hallway where she was filling a kettle.

'Bit grotty in here,' she said. 'Off limits to anyone but staff. Though I'll make an exception for you.' She flashed a smile at me.

The kitchenette had a Formica worktop with a burn mark on it and the tiled splashback was cracked. Even so it was no tattier than the rest of the building.

'Tell me why Jamie decided to stage the handover at that place in Hoxton?' I said as Kirsty dropped tea bags into a couple of mugs.

'There was a feature about it in *The Times* which read well. I think Scott Sage showed it to him.'

'Scott Sage? The PR guru? Jamie knew him?'

'They went to University together.'

'Really? Old friends, then?'

Kirsty wrinkled her nose. 'Not exactly *friends*. They spoke from time to time and Sage used to tap Jamie for free legal advice.'

That sounded right. Sage was a slime-ball who'd made a lot of money selling stories to the press. He represented celebrities and wannabe celebrities who needed publicity and had lurid tales to tell. Sage groomed his clients and rewrote their stories for maximum impact. I assumed much of the eye-catching and jaw-dropping material he pushed out was complete fabrication.

Kirsty handed me a mug of tea and we returned to her office which was adjacent to Jamie's empty room. I sat down where I'd been before, at the end of a row of three tired leatherette tub chairs with strips of gaffer tape covering rips. They must have supported thousands of crooks' backsides. Kirsty returned to the chair behind her desk and crossed her legs. Then she uncrossed them, got up and sat next but one to me in the row of three.

'Feels a bit unfriendly, me being the other side of the desk,' she said. 'It's not like you're charged with something.' And she gave me a big grin. Then she seemed to worry she'd been too friendly too quickly and said, blushing a little, 'These crappy old things are actually more comfortable, too.' And she slapped the seat between us to show it still had some bounce.

Then still trying to compensate for the thing with the chair she turned to me earnestly and in a serious tone said, 'So what can I tell you? Ask away.'

So I did. I asked first about the man with the squeaky voice and showed her the CCTV. Neither the image nor the strange voice meant anything to her. Nevertheless, her answers were concise and coherent. An uncommon skill among interviewees.

'Going back to Scott Sage,' I said, 'wasn't there a libel case recently?'

'Oh, yes. Mega. Sage asked Jamie to act for him, but he doesn't do, I mean didn't do, libel. Anyway Jamie suggested other solicitors for him.'

'Sage lost the case?'

'Yes. And then he appealed. And lost again. Jamie thought he was mad to take it to appeal.'

'How much would it have all cost?'

'Wow… Hundreds of thousands. He had a top QC. Maybe as much as a million. Or even more. Costs were given against him. Now apparently he's bankrupt.'

'So he says in interviews.'

Kirsty smiled. 'He says lots of things that are allegedly true but … impossible to verify. Even so I wouldn't be surprised if that were true.'

I liked her careful phrasing. She seemed too bright for this humdrum law office.

'Are you keeping notes? For the unauthorised autobiography?'

She laughed. 'Law's my thing, not writing. But I suppose I've got tales to tell if anyone wanted to listen.'

She gave me an inviting look and I knew I was being chatted up. I wasn't complaining.

'Does Sage collect art?'

Kirsty thought for a second, put two and two together and made about thirty six. Then she almost bounced off her comfy chair. 'Oh, wow! Has he just become a suspect?' Her green-blue eyes sparkled.

'Just a simple question,' I said, trying to calm her excitement, but smiling at her reaction nevertheless.

'I can't remember him ever talking about it. And obviously I've never been to his house.'

'Did he have any interest in the BetterWork office complex? An investment, I mean.'

Kirsty shrugged. 'I never heard him mention it before.'

'Why do you think he suggested it as a meeting place to Jamie?'

Kirsty was thinking hard. Then she got to her feet and took a few paces round the little office, galvanized by ideas racing through her head. Then she turned sharply to me.

'The most obvious reason is Jamie must have mentioned he was negotiating the handover of the picture. And Sage wanted to nick it.' There was a broad smile on her face as she snapped her fingers, 'You've got him! Bang to rights.'

'For someone who works in defence you're awfully keen to convict,' I said. But Kirsty was hard to dislike.

She gave me a repentant look and slapped one of her own wrists.

'A just rebuke,' she said. 'But he is a bit of a shit. Have you seen how he always fiddles with those fussy little nail-clippers when he's being interviewed?'

I hadn't.

'Plays with them like worry beads.'

'A way of putting off the interviewer,' I said.

'You are *so* right. And you know Scott Sage isn't even his real name?'

I didn't know that either.

'His real name's William Scott Savage. He chopped a few letters out because he thought Scott Sage was more cool and media friendly than Bill Savage. I mean, you can't really trust someone who changes their name just for effect, can you?'

'Well, people can have a valid reason for changing their name,' I said. 'And I wish it was so easy to nail a suspect. But Sage has a big public profile. All the media editors will know him. He's recognised in restaurants, is often on TV. You don't honestly see him as the man who organised a triple murder, do you? The man who'd have someone kill his old university friend?'

'No, I suppose not,' she said quietly and she sat down again. She drew her feet up on to the chair – she was wearing a long skirt – put her arms round her legs and rested her chin on her knees. Her mood was suddenly melancholic. 'Poor Jamie,' she said. 'I'll miss him.'

Then she began to weep.

It was only a few hours since he'd been killed but in any case Kirsty wore her heart on her sleeve. I wondered if she'd a relationship with Jamie. There was a disparity in their ages and Jamie wasn't David Gandy. Still…

Kirsty searched for a tissue in the daft place women often keep them, in the cuff of her top. But she didn't have one and she sniffed and wiped her eyes with her hand.

I always carry at least one handkerchief. It's an old-fashioned streak in me. Like preferring tea made in a pot to a tea-bag in a mug. I pulled out the clean handkerchief and gave it to Kirsty.

'Oh, thank you,' she said looking at the plain, white cotton. 'So beautiful.' As if I'd given her something of great value. Kirsty turned away from me as she wiped her eyes and blew her nose.

'Sorry. I apologise for that,' she said, the tears gone as quickly as they'd come.

We talked further about Sage and Jamie and the missing picture but Kirsty had no more revelations to make. I thought the information about Sage was remarkable but not game-changing. To me it felt more like an example of the six degrees of separation trope. An insignificant coincidence involving old university acquaintances.

As I was leaving, I casually asked Kirsty about her future. Was the chambers looking for someone to replace Jamie Rind? Her answer showed the ambition that was simmering under her lacey top. She found criminal work exciting but badly paid and was keen to move away from the small suburban law firm to get a job in central London. Jamie's death had concentrated her mind on her own future and she had no intention of staying in what she called the "social work" area of law.

'It seems an absolutely golden opportunity,' she said, 'I'd be mad not to go.' Then she put a hand over her mouth, aghast, and looked intensely at me. 'God! Do you think that sounds terribly heartless?'

'No,' I said. 'Just practical.'

She beamed.

'Thank you so much. That's what I hoped you'd say.'

Her sparkling viridian eyes made me want to find a reason to meet Kirsty again.

45

Chapter 6

I drove back home to Uxbridge. Unfashionable, anonymous, end of the line and ideal for my purposes.

If you live in a quiet suburban street as I do you get used to the cars that park there. Almost subconsciously you recognise that number fourteen has a Skoda, number sixteen a Hyundai, the young couple at eighteen a clapped out Golf and so on. You know which cars are kept clean and which are not. You know when they go and when they come back.

As I drove warily into my road I was looking for the motorbike I'd seen earlier. Or for any strange vehicles.

I parked. Then I walked up and down the street. There were no vans, which are ideal for covert surveillance, and none of the cars was occupied. There were no pedestrians lurking behind newspapers, no fake telephone line repair men. Everything looked normal.

I went indoors and cooked something from the freezer. Then I turned on the laptop, took care not to let my dinner drip on the keyboard, and delved into the backgrounds of the couple who owned the Gallery.

I'd persuaded Clark to give me access to some of his specialist databases and discovered that Magda Butt was a British citizen born in the UK to an Iraqi father and British mother. Kadir Ansari was born in Abu Dhabi, capital of the United Arab Emirates. He'd emigrated to the UK in the 1970s, had indefinite leave to remain, but didn't seem to have applied to become a British citizen. There was also no record of him ever marrying Magda, so presumably he remained a UAE citizen.

Magda Butt was something of an art tart herself. She had an M.A. in the History of Art and had taught at the Slade. She'd had a limited commercial success as an artist in the Nineties but had then abandoned painting for digital art. She had her own website full of highly technical data and seemed to be something of a leading exponent. Magda was trying to use new technology to produce art, rather like David Hockney exploited fax machines and iPads. Not my kind of thing, but good on her, I thought. Never too late to learn new techniques.

I turned my attention from the living to the dead. To Christoph Amberger himself.

I'd rubbished the hoary old "mad collector" theory to MacIver but I was desperately short of leads and this crime was so weirdly unusual I began to reconsider. This was an aberration for me. Like developing an interest in creationist theory or considering the sun might actually orbit the earth.

Amberger's works are mostly held by European galleries. It was too late to call any of them now but the Met in New York has an Amberger and they would still be open. I phoned and got through to one of the curators with a special interest in the art of the Northern Renaissance. I asked if she knew of any obsessive collectors, single-minded academics or neurotic megalomaniacs who would literally do anything, including killing people, to obtain an original. Perhaps I didn't introduce myself properly, perhaps I didn't give enough preamble, perhaps I was too graphic. All that happened was she just gave a nervous little laugh. As if I was the one whose lift didn't go all the way to the top.

I tried to explain again but she was still wary. Was I really not making sense? She was obviously intelligent but did she never watch cop shows on TV? Then, keen to get the crazy man off her phone, she muttered 'Sorry,' and abruptly ended the call.

I reckoned it was a case of two nations divided by a common language.

Then I called Gus, an old contact of mine from the Art and Antiques Unit days. He'd worked in the art trade all his life including time at Sotheby's and Christie's. He was in the middle of dinner. He wasn't an expert on that period but immediately saw what I was driving at and promised to think about it overnight. Before he went back to his food he suggested I call a lecturer at the University of Birmingham who he thought had a special interest in German painters. I checked the data again and found that the Barber Institute of Fine Arts, part of the University of Birmingham, did have an Amberger in its collection.

I called the Institute, expecting only to get through to security, but when the phone was picked up I heard laughter and the buzz of conversation in the background. There had been an evening lecture and private view to celebrate something and there was an after-party. The guy who answered the phone thought Gus's academic was actually in the building. He asked me to wait and I heard echoey footsteps, various off-mic mutterings, a long pause, then more footsteps, the clink of a glass being put down and finally Dr Gerry Hugill was on the line. He was obviously an enthusiast for Amberger and listened good-naturedly to my story. Then he took me by surprise.

'You're the second person recently who's called to ask something strange about Amberger,' he said and I heard him take a sip of his drink.

'Who was it? And when?' I eagerly swigged my own drink. I felt like joining in the party.

'About four, five weeks ago. A man phoned to ask if I knew anything about the stolen picture from Northamptonshire, the *Portrait of a Young Merchant*. Apparently he'd travelled to see the picture but only discovered when he got there it was missing. I told him I knew it had gone but obviously had no idea where it might be.'

'Did he say why he wanted to see the picture?'

'No. I assumed he was someone with a special interest in that period of German art. But he would certainly fit your criterion of obsessive. He sounded driven, almost desperate to find the picture. But at the same time he didn't seem crazy in any way, if you know what I mean. He was aware that what he was asking was a bit odd. Sorry, I'm not explaining this well.'

'No. You're doing fine.' Better than I did for the American curator. 'Did he give a name? A number?'

'Yes… er. Hang on.' There was the sound of the phone being put on to a table, the rustling of clothing, the clink of something hard against a glass, a muttered expletive. He was looking at his mobile. Then the phone was picked up again.

'Abid Bashir he was called.' And Dr Hugill read out a phone number.

'Any idea where he was from?'

'I couldn't tell. But he spoke English perfectly well.'

'What about his voice? Was it unusual in any way?'

'God, I can't remember. My wife always knows who's doing a voice-over on TV but they all sound a bit the same to me.'

'Did his voice sound...' After my experience with the American I hesitated a fraction. I didn't want this guy to think I was off my trolley. 'Did it sound... squeaky at all?' It was the oddest description, but all I had to go on.

'Squeaky? You mean like Pinky and Perky?'

Who? I'm not good on vintage pop culture. Clark would know who they were but I just said, 'Maybe... Or like he had a cold? Or a bad throat?'

'Not that I can remember.'

'Did you call him back?'

'No. To be frank, the more I thought about it I felt it may have been some kind of wind-up. Student prank. That kind of thing.'

Over the phone I heard applause and cheering: the evening was coming to a climax.

'If you'll excuse me, I ought to get back to the party, Mr Kite. I'm supposed to be doing a vote of thanks.'

I was disappointed Bashir wasn't the squeaky-voiced murderer Nathan described but his call to Hugill couldn't just be coincidence. Amberger was such an obscure artist to be interested in. I phoned the number Hugill had given me and wasn't surprised it was out of service. Presumably it was a burner. Which convinced me the man who gave his name as Bashir had to be involved somehow.

Thinking the unthinkable had got me half a lead. Maybe Copernicus wasn't a hundred per cent right after all.

Before I turned in I went outside to check my road again. As I stood in the porch I saw a car parked nearby with its interior light on. I opened the garden gate and took some steps towards it. As I did so the engine was hurriedly started and the car drove away.

If they were so easily scared off they couldn't be much of a threat.
Next morning there was an email from my auction house contact.

To: John Kite
From: Gus Lamport
Subject: Amberger obsessives
Can think of two candidates: The Margravine of Falkenstein-Neuburg, who (erroneously) claims direct descent from the Holy Roman Emperor Charles V, has a crush on Amberger because he actually met the Emperor and of course painted him. She's often out-to-lunch, but not yet certifiable. Second, an 80s rock star you won't have heard of who's made a packet in music production. Something of a clothes fetishist, hence fond of Amberger's treatment of silk, velvet etc. Currently trekking near Everest base camp. Kind regards, Gus.

I was impressed with Gus's knowledge. It was a top auctioneer's job to keep tabs on all potential buyers but he moved in rarefied circles. Both these characters were clearly rich and powerful, but they were also eccentric. Too eccentric to be involved in a triple murder.

But it was worth checking out Abid Bashir with him.

I emailed back and got a reply almost immediately.

Yes, I knew him. A dealer in top quality middle eastern carpets: Kilims, Kermans, Isfahans ... everything. Charming man but I'm afraid he's not a suspect. He had no interest in European painting and, more to the point, he died several years ago.

And I thought I was getting somewhere.

Chapter 7

The owner of the Amberger picture, Michael Cowper, lived at Nobottle Abbey, which sounds like a made-up place in a P.G. Wodehouse book, but isn't. It's at SP672634, which if you're not up to speed on grid refs is about ten miles north-west of Northampton, close to junction 15A of the motorway.

Northamptonshire is usually somewhere I drive through to get somewhere else. It's an undemonstrative county but is surprisingly unspoilt and green. In contrast, its attractive old villages are a jaunty orange colour because the local stone is full of iron.

Cowper's home, Nobottle Abbey, has medieval monastic origins but has been a family house since Henry VIII's dissolution. It's open to the public on Fridays and Saturdays in July and August but receives few visitors. Its near neighbour Althorp, the birthplace of Princess Diana, easily outdoes it in terms of fame and popularity.

In the Great Hall, the oldest part of Nobottle, there was a symbolic empty frame on the wall where the Amberger picture had once hung with a notice explaining the theft two years previously. Nobottle had never had a prize art collection and *Portrait of a Young Merchant* was their most valuable piece.

Michael Cowper, in his seventies, was wearing tomato coloured trousers and a lemon short-sleeved sweater over a bold red check shirt. He was a plummy-voiced raconteur and reminded me of the more eccentric radio cricket commentators I listened to as a boy. Those commentators did twenty minute spells so, just as their quirks were getting annoying, a fresh voice with altogether different quirks

51

took over. And after twenty minutes with Cowper I began to wish there was someone else to take over from him.

I apologised for not recapturing the Amberger picture and explained I wanted guidance as to who might be so desperate to own the picture they'd commit a triple murder.

Cowper began with a mini-lecture on the supposed Shakespeare connection.

'It's all to do with the frame, old boy,' he said. 'The frame is later than the walnut panel the picture's painted on.'

Then he rambled on about dendrochronology tests and strange marks on the bottom of the frame which were believed to be letters in some ancient, hard to read Gothic font. Then he was on about Shakespeare's sonnets and their dedication to a mysterious Mr W.H. Then he quoted an entire sonnet, though I wasn't sure why. Then he came back to the frame. The letters, if they were letters rather than just graffiti, wear and tear or woodworm, might – just might – include WH. They might, if you half closed your eyes or ate a magic mushroom or it was the summer solstice, they might also include the letters WS.

I got the point. This WH might have given WS the picture with a secret carved dedication on the frame. And since some of the sonnets were written to a man, not a woman, it might suggest some kind of relationship between WH and William Shakespeare.

Big deal, I thought. Enough of the folklore, let's have some facts.

'But the inscription, if it is an inscription, on the frame could be anything?' I said.

'Of course. Anything. Or nothing. But a few hundred years of legend is hard to eradicate. Gullible tourists still pay to go on Nessie-spotting trips on Loch Ness, I understand.'

'And before the picture was stolen it brought in gullible tourists for you?'

'In abundance. And, to be fair, plenty of sceptical ones too. But intelligent people have written long academic papers about it in serious journals.' He laughed loudly. 'Ridiculous, isn't it?'

'Have you come across anyone who's obsessed with the picture? A repeat visitor, maybe?'

He shook his head. 'I can't recall any loony groupies.'

'Did anyone know we were on the verge of recovering it?'

'As instructed, old man, I told no one apart from the family. But there was that plug the *Daily Mail* gave us.'

I don't read the *Mail*. But I gave an interested look.

'They did a feature on the picture and hyped up the possible Shakespeare connection. It was a couple of months ago but it was written like breaking news, not old tosh from four hundred years ago. Obviously a quiet day and they were looking for filler stuff. Annoying thing was it didn't mention the picture had gone. So we had carloads of visitors arriving to look at it. Some of them thought Shakespeare had lived here, or slept here or, pardon my French, fucked some pretty boy here.'

A neatly-dressed woman in her sixties walked into the Hall. At first I thought she was Michael Cowper's wife, but then I noticed she was wearing a badge: Volunteer Guide.

'Morning, Rosemary,' said Cowper.

'Morning, Michael. All well?'

'Never better. Rosemary, pop over a sec, would you. I think you might be able to help our visitor here.'

The woman came over, Cowper introduced me, then asked the woman if she'd experienced any visitors taking an unwholesome interest in the Amberger painting.

'You mean before it was stolen?' she said.

'No. More recently,' I said. 'After the article in the *Mail*?'

Rosemary thought for a moment, then said: 'There was a gentleman who was really upset to hear it had been stolen. He couldn't believe it at first and had the newspaper article with him. He even took a picture of the label.'

'The label on the wall?'

'Yes. He asked if it was correct. I said I had no reason to believe it wasn't.'

I walked over to the wall where the empty frame hung and read the label that remained there: *Christoph Amberger. Born c.1505 Swabia, Died 1562 Augsburg. Portrait of a Young Merchant. Oil on panel. 66cm x 45cm.*

'Some authorities give 1500 as his birth year but...hey ho.' Cowper said with a shrug.

I read the label twice then stared at it letter by letter, looking for a hidden message, an anagram, or a verbal trick. I could see nothing, not even a misprint. It seemed absolutely harmless. Then, like the visitor, I took a shot of the label. I wasn't sure why.

'What kind of person was he, the man who photographed the label?'

'He was in his fifties, I'd say. Asian. Well dressed. Actually, more than well dressed. I would call him dapper, even debonair. And he was on his own. That's unusual. Visitors tend to come in pairs or family groups.'

'Was he British or a tourist?'

'He spoke English well. But I don't think he was British.'

'Why not?'

'His English was almost too correct. Like someone who'd learned the language from a textbook. And many British Asians have recognisable regional accents, London, Glasgow, Birmingham etc., but he didn't. However, there was something interesting about his voice.'

I jumped in quickly.

'It wasn't squeaky, was it? A bit science-fictiony… like computer generated? Or as if he had a cold or catarrh?'

Rosemary gave me that condescending look that people who are experts give to people who ask them a question they know to be nonsense.

'In terms of voice production it was completely normal. What was interesting was that, while his native tongue had to be Bengali, his spoken English showed a definite Arabic accent. I assume he must have lived in the middle east for a while.'

Her tone grated but she spoke with such confidence that for a moment I was steamrollered. She saw my surprise and continued with a smile.

'Before I retired I was a voice teacher. At the Central School of Speech and Drama.'

'The one in north London?'

She nodded, 'Swiss Cottage.'

She was that rare bird, a witness with expert knowledge who knew exactly what she was talking about. Voice was obviously a life-long speciality. This curious Bengali visitor had to be the man who phoned Hugill and I really wanted him to be the killer.

'Sorry to press you on this, but could someone listen to the voice you heard and think it sounded squeaky, high-pitched...'

'...Or as if the man had catarrh?'

'Yes.'

'No. They couldn't. Unless they were being purposefully misleading or deceptive.' There was something of the martinet about Rosemary, a little bit of MacIver, too. But the voice teacher didn't have MacIver's wit and sparkle. I don't think I'd have enjoyed being in one of Rosemary's classes.

I showed Rosemary Bostock's CCTV of the man in the street, which Clark had enhanced to the hilt.

'Doesn't ring any bells at all. I'm sorry, I'm good on voices, bad on faces. I'd have been hopeless as a casting director. Sometimes at the RSC I actually shut my eyes for a while, ignore what's happening on stage and just listen to the beautiful words.'

'Forgetting the Asian man who came here, what, if anything, could make someone's voice like I described?'

'Squeaky? Like science fiction?'

'Yes.' She gave me the imperious look again so I ladled out some flattery. 'With your expertise and your long professional experience have you ever come across anything like that?'

She was polite enough to think for a moment before answering. Then I could see she was surprised by a memory and changed her answer. 'Well, many years ago, when I was a hospital speech therapist, there was a man who sounded like you describe. It was down to a congenital deformation of his larynx. He'd be dead now, of course.'

If you were mad enough to try to track him down, she seemed to infer.

This was becoming a job about voices. I now had not one but two men with unusual voices. Interesting, but intangible and ethereal. And no use for establishing an ID.

Back in the car I had a momentary fantasy of a purely vocal version of the traditional police line-up in which suspects were invisible to the witness but each had to say something. Inadmissible, Bostock would tell me. And probably Kirsty, too.

The article in the *Daily Mail* was at least something physical so, back in the car, I called the features department to get hold of the writer. He was called Benjamin Gold and I pretended to be a producer from BBC Radio, hinting I had some work to offer him and got his mobile number. Everyone is freelance these days and most journalists work from home. That's where I found Benjamin Gold.

I immediately came clean and explained who I was, but he was happy to talk, having just emailed his copy for the next day's paper. He'd been a journalist all his working life and now, nearing retirement he'd fulfilled most of his ambitions and was happy to write filler pieces or whatever he was asked. He told me the idea for the Nobottle piece came from a researcher who had discovered the story in an old edition of *Country Life* from the 1930s. Gold had spoken to Cowper and had learned about the robbery but he'd underplayed it and written what he called a frothy piece.

'I could've done the opposite,' Gold said. 'Gone for the "tragic loss of masterpiece from stately home, criminals are destroying our heritage" angle, but it was the Saturday before the May Day bank holiday and there was a lot of advertising linked to country weekends and all that stuff. In fact there was a sudden pressure on space and, unknown to me till afterwards, all mention of the picture being stolen was subbed out.'

'Did you get any feedback from the piece?' I said.

'It wasn't controversial or political so not the kind of thing that gets feedback from readers. Though annoyingly there was some comeback from the man who calls himself the King of PR.'

'Who's that?'

'Scott Sage.'

'Tell me what happened'

'Well, he's always talking to journalists, usually trying to sell a story. You know the kind of thing he peddles: Queen Victoria was a man, Putin to become American citizen, the night I shagged the Prime Minister. Anyway, we met at some press junket a month or so after the piece appeared. Apropos of nothing at all he told me the piece I'd done on Nobottle was bollocks. He said it wasn't true. Though he doesn't know what the word means. He said the picture I'd mentioned had been stolen. I told him I knew this and explained that several pars had been taken out by the stone sub at the last minute.'

'Why was Sage so keen to tell you this? Does he collect paintings? Have an interest in art?'

'I doubt it. But he's always having a go at me. I wrote a profile of him a couple of years ago which he didn't like. Kept belly-aching. Complained to my editor. He takes any opportunity to stick the needle in.'

This seemed thin-skinned for someone who worked in the media and I said as much to Gold.

'But he has a paradoxical relationship with journalists. He needs us to promote his clients but he also despises us for doing so. Despises us for apparently accepting his scams and made-up stories at face value. But we've got to fill the bloody space with something. He was just trying to get one up on me.'

Even so, a fuse of suspicion was starting to smoulder.

'And he's supposed to be broke.'

'Possibly, but he's got a secret new project.'

'Secret? How do you know about it?'

'Journalists do detective work too, you know. I've not always written puff pieces on stately homes. Google me and you'll find I started out on Granada's *World in Action* and I've done three investigative books on the troubles in Northern Ireland.'

I felt embarrassed. 'Sorry… I…'

'Don't apologise. Different generation that's all.'

'What can you tell me about this new business?'

'I don't have enough to stack up a story yet. It's hearsay, supposition and unattributable, but you're welcome to share it. He's set up what he calls a training centre, a PR Academy. He's got a load of kids there and he says he's training them all in new concepts of public relations. My arse. He wouldn't spend a cent on training anybody. Anyway it's at some god-forsaken industrial estate near Heathrow and Sage is refusing to answer any questions about it. Which for him is deviant behaviour. He's always blowing his own trumpet.'

'So what's he up to?'

'Could be anything. Low-cost drug trials. A rival to Facebook. Artificial Intelligence. Illegal immigrants growing cannabis under sun lamps. I've no idea but it's not registered as any kind of educational establishment. If you find out, tell me first.'

I ended the call with Benjamin Gold more confused than I'd started it and I sat in my car looking out at the tranquil Northamptonshire fields.

The road that runs past the end of the drive to Nobottle Abbey is straight and Roman and unfrequented. I heard a high-powered motor-bike approaching at speed. As it approached the end of the drive it slowed appreciably, the figure in the saddle glanced towards me and then accelerated away. I managed to clock the reg. It was the same bike I'd seen yesterday at the petrol station. But this time the driver was male, not female.

They were certainly keeping observation on me but their tactics were confusing. They seemed to have no fears about being seen. Either today, or yesterday. I had no idea who they were or what they might want.

I was hit with a wave of paranoia and felt suddenly vulnerable.

Was there a tracker on my car? I got out, checked the wheel arches and the boot, looked under the bonnet and then opened the petrol filler cap to look inside. I found nothing. Then I lay on my back on the drive, squirmed under the car and searched the underside. Still nothing.

I got up, brushed dirt, leaves and gravel from my clothes and saw an oily patch on the shoulder of my new jacket. I was angry with myself for being so anxious.

'Bloody big girl's blouse,' I said aloud.

But I was even angrier that somebody was diverting me from, interfering with, my hunt for the stolen picture.

Chapter 8

'Scott Sage Associates; how may I help you?' said a female voice that was neither quirky nor unusual but just breath-takingly sexy. Actually the sexiness was a bit OTT, like the speaker was trying too hard.

'My name's John Kite. Is Mr Sage available?'

'I'm afraid Scott's abroad. Can I help you? My name's Lorella.' She was almost purring now and I amused myself imagining what Lorella looked like. Was she as decorative as her voice suggested? Or was the voice just a come-on? In any case, Lorella's name sounded as unreal as Sage's stories.

'I'd like to talk to him. When will he be back?'

'Do you want representation? Do you have a story for him?'

'I could have a story for him…'

'Something personal? Have you been a victim? Are you in trouble?' She spoke persuasively. Both luring and alluring. She was probably a key member of Sage's team.

'The story's about murder and the theft of a valuable painting.'

Lorella gave a sharp inrush of breath.

'Don't get it wrong. I'm not the murderer. Nor the thief.'

She'd sounded shocked, but was just excited. 'Of course you're not. You've just got a great story for us. I'm *so* pleased for you.'

'I know who the murderer is. And I have video.'

Another gasp. 'Wow! That's so cool. And of course so terrible. Are you with the police?'

'Why do you ask?'

'We get all our really sexy crime stories from police officers. Though I shouldn't really tell you that. Did you *used* to be with the police?'

I didn't answer. Her voice went into boudoir mode.

'I think you were with the police but did something naughty and had to leave. Am I right, or am I right?'

I was enjoying her performance but it was time to end the theatrics.

'You're wrong. When will Mr Sage be back?'

Miss Temptress disappeared and Miss Efficiency was back. 'Give me your number, Mr…'

'Kite, John Kite.' I dictated my number.

'Scott will get back to you as soon as possible.' A beat, then it was Miss Temptress again. 'And I must tell you, Mr Kite, I could listen to your voice all day long.'

The call ended. What a pantomime. If even his P.A. lived in a lurid fantasy how seriously should I take Sage, himself? Benjamin Gold felt he was a threat to national security but perhaps Gold was over-reacting.

Trouble was, as I drove back to London, I realised the whole job had elements of a surreal charade.

The crime was as bizarrely unique as any crime can be. The location for the crime was a dreamlike, anti-office kind of office. The theft of the picture demanded incredible split-second timing which was, well… incredible. The murderer's escape was helped by the chance intervention of a party of foreign bureaucrats which seemed almost magical – Kirsty had called it a real *deus ex machina* moment, whatever that meant. The killer has a voice from a Sci-fi movie, there is a mysterious Bangladeshi who photographs labels, the missing painting has a hocus pocus connection to Shakespeare and Scott Sage, a player on the fringes of the action, is a man who lives by selling fake news stories.

If that wasn't enough, someone's following me and making odd phone calls to MacIver.

I began to wonder if I'd suffered an accident some days previously and was actually dreaming while lying unconscious in a hospital bed.

Then as I joined the M25 I saw the red Virgin Media taxi again happily driving along with no sign of damage. My heart began to thump and my stomach to churn. I felt sweaty and my vision started to blur. What was going on? The blood-smeared taxi had been low-loadered away by the police for forensic examination. I accelerated hard, caught it up and stared at it like it was a hypnotist's watch on a chain.

The taxi was real enough but it wasn't the one I'd chased. It had the identical red Virgin livery, same year and place of registration but the final three letters on the plate were different. Then I realised I was getting dangerously close to it. I hit the brakes, pulled the car into the inside lane and then on to the hard shoulder. I skidded to a stop in a cloud of dust.

For the third time in as many days I'd experienced the tortured feelings I'd not had for fifteen years. Since the time my parents were killed.

I was angry with myself. And worried. Was I losing it?

Then my phone rang and I was pleased to be brought back to the here and now. It was someone I never expected to hear from. The Somali greengrocer from Golborne Road. I was cheered to know there are still folk who do exactly what they say they will. He told me Magda Butt was opening up the shop.

Thirty minutes later I parked in Golborne Road and saw lights in the Butt-Ansari Gallery. Would the picture be inside? It seemed an even bet and I felt a tremor of excitement as I went to the door.

I rang the bell and the door was opened by a woman in her sixties, who didn't seem to be in the mood to sell antiques or anything and eyed me suspiciously.

'Magda Butt?' I said.

She agreed she was but didn't let me in. Her complexion echoed the mixed-race parentage I'd uncovered, but her English was accentless.

'Are you open?' I said.

'I usually only sell to the trade. To people I know. What do you want?' Like the BetterWork receptionist she'd win no prizes for customer relations.

'I collect the kind of thing you sell,' I said, 'and heard you have particularly good stock that's hard to source. May I look around?'

Even now she was reluctant but I could see her thinking that refusing me entry would look suspicious. Letting me in was a safer option.

So she did, then shut the door firmly behind me. I wandered around pretending to be interested in her stock while scanning everywhere for the picture. The shop had a good range of what I judged were Roman pieces but they were low value items of no great rarity. Nothing jumped out as being worth looting from a battlefield.

'Anything take your fancy?' the woman said.

'I don't want to be rude but many of these things are fairly common. Roman lamps and so on. These are for amateur collectors. What I want are rare items, things which are often hard to come by. S*pecial* things,' I said, looking directly at her.

Her brow furrowed.

'How special?' she said.

'Museum special. I'm interested in items from Mesopotamia. Have you anything from Palmyra? From Nineveh, from Mosul? I'm particularly interested in the Assyrian period.'

'Palmyra was destroyed by Isis. And Mosul too.'

I gave her a hard kind of look.

'I don't think *everything* was destroyed.'

There was a pause. She was staring back at me and I was calmly holding her gaze. I could almost hear her calculating the odds.

'You think I'm some kind of policeman looking for stolen treasures?'

The woman said nothing but kept looking at me.

'I'm interested in the artefacts, not how you acquire them. I'm interested in things that won't come up for sale on the open market.'

She looked me up and down, taking in my brighter-than-Scotland-Yard-normally-wears clothing. Her tone mellowed slightly.

'Who told you about my stock?' Magda said.

'It was a guy at the Berkeley Square antiques fair...' I said and feigned trying to think of a name and hoped that the Berkeley Square gig was too grand for the likes of Magda Butt to attend. 'He was... an Asian guy.' To my surprise this got a reaction from Magda.

'What kind of Asian guy? What was his name?'

There was no harm in throwing out the name Dr Hugill had given me, even though it seemed an alias.

'He was called Bashir. Abid Bashir. Do you know him?'

She shook her head. Convincingly. But it was plain she knew *some* Asian guy in the antiques trade. No surprise there, I suppose. But my persistence had worn her down. She shrugged in an offhand way and said,

'O.K. This way.' She walked to some stairs, at the top of which I registered the details of a state-of-the-art intruder alarm. Then I followed her down to a basement.

I'd already exhausted my scant knowledge of ancient art but the cellar was packed with stuff that looked, even to an amateur, extremely old and rare. There were stone reliefs and carvings which looked three, four or five thousand years old. There were Egyptian pieces and quality Roman or Greek work which I guessed was from Libya. Several of the bigger stone pieces had new-looking chips to a bottom corner or edge, other pieces had recent abrasions made by a wire brush. I reckoned these had been looted from museums and someone had crudely hacked or scraped at them to remove the accession numbers.

But I was there to search for a painting. And I was bitter that I couldn't see a single canvas or panel or ikon, not even a section of frame or a bit of stretcher. Let alone the missing Amberger.

'Is your partner around? Mr Ansari?'

She frowned. Then after a moment said. 'He's on a buying trip.'

'That must be interesting. Whereabouts?'

'Even if you're not a police officer you might be a dealer. You find your own sources, don't steal ours.' On top of her wariness, there was a fiery, belligerent tone to her voice.

'I'm not a dealer. Actually I'm looking for a painting.'

'We don't have any paintings here.'

'You're a painter yourself.'

'*Was* a painter. I don't paint anymore.'

'I'm sure you still have the equipment. Paints, palette, easel, canvasses, water-colour paper... Even one of those carrying cases maybe.'

'You said you were a collector. Now you sound even more like a police officer.'

'I'm not a police officer but I am an investigator. Looking for a stolen painting. It's an old master. *Portrait of a Young Merchant* by Christoph Amberger.'

I looked hard at her face but she seemed to be willing herself not to react. Her jaw was clenched. Her eyes were averted.

'Do you know the artist?'

'I've heard of him, that's all.'

'The man who stole it put it in a carry-case. In the case was a piece of your gallery's letterhead.'

She reacted, but covered it well. 'I don't believe you.'

'I have a photo. A photo of the thief holding the painting. In your carry case.'

She snorted. 'Photos! They're easily faked.'

Her response was curiously specific. Why had she mentioned faking? The Amberger picture wasn't something anyone would want to fake.

'It isn't a fake. The man in the photo murdered three men to get the painting I'm looking for.'

She gasped. There was an instant change in her demeanour.

'My God! Who were they?' It wasn't an idle question. She was palpably worried. She knew people who were involved.

'A solicitor called Jamie Rind, a taxi-driver and a criminal called Roland Sadler. Do you know them?'

She shook her head and the tension left her face as quickly as it had arrived.

'How terrible,' she said with emotion in her voice. She seemed disturbed by talk of murder and began to fidget, then pointedly looked at her watch. 'If you don't mind... I'm sorry I can't help about your stolen painting.'

I held up my phone with the CCTV shot of the killer 'Do you know this man?'

She peered at it for several seconds. 'It's not very good quality.'

'He wouldn't pose for me.'

If a person being interviewed is shown a photo of someone they know, but don't want to admit they know, a common subconscious reaction is to criticise the photo's quality. This has the effect of psychologically boosting them for the lie they are about to tell. After all, if the photo is poor how can they tell who it is?

Her eyes stayed on the little screen. 'You can't see his face. It could be anybody.'

'He has a distinctive voice. Kind of squeaky, high-pitched.'

Her eyes flickered. I could see her getting nervous.

'You know him, don't you?'

She looked again and shook her head. Her eyes looked down, away from mine.

'This man is dangerous. If you know where I can find him or any of his associates you should tell me.'

Her eyes stayed looking at the ground.

'When will your husband be back from the buying trip?'

'Soon.'

'How long has he been away?'

She gave me a suspicious look.

'He's not on a buying trip, is he? Is he ill?'

She looked up but said nothing.

'In hospital?'

She just looked at me.

'In prison?'

She started to say something but stopped herself.

'Having an affair?'

'No.'

'Where is he? Do you know?'

'Get out. Get out.' She started to cry and pulled the door open. I handed her my card.

'Call me when you want to tell me the truth.'

Chapter 9

I couldn't meet Scott Sage yet but at least I could look at his new-concept PR training school. Or whatever it was.

The journalist, Benjamin Gold, described the location as a god-forsaken industrial estate and he was right. Boston Manor was a curious location to kick start a start-up but maybe a good place to hide something you didn't want exposed. That part of west London has a raw, industrial feel and the air is flavoured with aviation fuel. Planes are constantly overhead, minutes from touch-down at Heathrow. The trading estate interspersed large shed-type structures with small office blocks and along with Sage's Academy the companies included a commercial laundry, a scrap metal dealer, a wholesale plumber's merchant and a self-storage depot. The usual low-rent, no-questions-asked, edge-of-town mix.

Sage's enterprise occupied a faded 1980s block with an unadorned exterior. Letters spelling out the previous occupant had been removed from the frontage, but the old company name was still legible in sooty shadows left on the concrete.

PR is about razzamatazz but there was only a dull and discreet sign by the entrance announcing this to be KEATS.PR. Named after the poet? Surely he had nothing to do with publicity.

I went through the front door. In contrast to the bleak exterior, the reception area was brightly lit and garishly, but cheaply, decorated in Day-Glo candy colours. A bank of monitors played BBC 24, CNN, Fox News and MTV to nobody except an attractive young woman behind a desk whose badge told me she was called Yasmine.

She looked Arabic and was as theatrically bright and in-your-face as a grand bazaar. She had bubbly brown hair, heavy make-up and a low-cut, faux-silk blouse tight across her chest, on which a Keats ID card on a lanyard bounced distractingly. Her smile was so big it would have made most daytime TV presenters feel inadequate.

'Hi!' she said. 'Welcome to Keats PR. How may I help you today?'

What was this woman doing here? Everything about her was at odds with the grim location, the grubby exterior, the relentless drone of aircraft. I would have liked to ask her why the place was named after a dead poet but I doubted I'd get a sensible answer. So I started by explaining that my eighteen year old nephew was keen on a career in PR and had asked me to pick up a prospectus for the training they offered.

'That's wonderful. So good to hear,' she said. 'Unfortunately there's been such demand for our documentation that we've had to print more. They'll be back from the printers in a day or two. If you give me your nephew's address I'll get one sent over to him straight away.'

'Don't you have anything online?' I'd looked for their website but there was only an "under construction" one pager.

'We're so new the site is still being developed,' Yasmine said. 'It'll be up and running in a day or so.'

'Is it possible to have a look round at your facilities?'

'Of course, that's our usual procedure but I'm afraid there's no one available right now. I'd love to show you round myself but I'm afraid I can't leave the front desk. So busy.' She flashed another big smile.

I nodded and smiled too, trying hard not to be sidetracked by the ID card bobbing around her cleavage.

'There's one more thing,' I said. 'I need someone to do a PR campaign for me. Do you run campaigns as well as training?'

'Of course we do. Tell me what you're planning.'

I explained that I represented Michael Cowper from Northamptonshire who owned a rare painting by man called Amberger which had been featured in the *Daily Mail*. We wanted to run a little campaign of our own to piggy-back on the press story to encourage visitors to the house where the picture was.

'That's fab, absolutely fab,' she said. 'Such a good idea. What sort of spend were you thinking of? Our minimum fee is £5,000 plus VAT with media costs on top of that of course.' Her reaction to my bare-bones cover story suggested she'd never heard of the picture. I felt whatever I'd said I would have got exactly the same scripted answer from her.

'Of course,' I said. 'Is there someone I can talk things through with?'

'As you know, we're hardly up and running yet so not all the creatives and designers are in place. Our Executive Producer is out at the moment interviewing as is the Head of Imaging.'

I nodded and smiled again as if this was all perfectly normal. Yasmine smiled back as if what we'd been discussing made any kind of logical sense.

Then my attention was grabbed by one of the TV screens. On CNN the scrolling news strapline read "Soccer World Cup: Ebola virus threat." I stared at the screen wanting to know more but the sound was muted on all the screens.

'Did you see that?' I said turning to Yasmine, concerned. She hadn't of course and just smiled her synthetic smile back to me. I was in danger of sounding like the gormless Nathan. I asked her to turn the sound on and she did so.

The story was that the several cases of Ebola had been reported from rural areas of Qatar and the World Health Organisation was worried about the impending arrival of hundreds of thousands of football fans for the World Cup.

I made some generic sort of comment as you do in response to awful news but Yasmine only replied that she wasn't very interested in football. The smile hardly left her face.

I kept watching the TV but realised Yasmine was watching me. So I turned towards her.

'Whereabouts are you from?' I said.

'London,' she said, looking surprised to be asked.

'And your parents were from the middle east?'

'Oh no,' she said. And didn't elaborate. Asking about people's ethnicity is a minefield and I didn't like to press her, though it seemed obvious that she had Arabic parentage.

The Ebola story sounded desperately worrying but Yasmine had muted the TV again and I felt like an unwanted guest. There were lots of best wishes and see-you-arounds as I left but I was conscious that Yasmine's eyes didn't leave me until the front door was closed. After that she would have followed my progress on the many CCTV cameras positioned around the building.

What was Sage up to? Taking untrained young people off the streets and throwing them into the hurly-burly of industry isn't a new idea. Celebrity chef Jamie Oliver did it in front of TV cameras with a start-up restaurant, the model industry regularly plucks unknowns from shopping centres and turns them into *Vogue* cover material and it's the same with some film directors who are excited by the "reality" of completely untrained actors.

But this Keats place didn't add up. It felt insubstantial. Unreal. Another incongruous component of a dreamscape.

I walked around the outside of the building not really caring if I was observed on CCTV. There was a staff entrance at the back, with swipe card access. The windows were all treated with a mirror finish so nothing inside was visible from the outside.

Then I came to where the rubbish and recycling bins were. They looked so sparkling bright and clean I wondered if they were real. I opened one of the recycling skips and there was stuff inside: energy drink cans, Diet Coke cans, milk bottles, plastic tubs that had contained hummus, yoghurt, olives. In another: hard copies of newspapers and magazines with stories or adverts razored out in the traditional way, copies of *Campaign* magazine, *Metro*, A4 printouts of TV overnights and other BARB ratings, rate-card information for radio stations, printouts of details of Google Ads and Facebook Advertising with various handwritten notes and comments.

Everything you might expect.

I continued my circuit and came to an area where I had to push through thigh-high nettles and rampant buddleia. An untended wilderness. Maybe it had been left as such to deter burglars or reporters. Or to keep the staff from wandering. Or it was off-set and never used therefore it didn't matter if it was a mess.

I walked back through the car park and headed towards a greasy-spoon café fifty metres down the road.

The café interior had been amateurishly painted in scarlet and white. Eye-catching, but crude. On the walls were some 1960s colour prints of holiday destinations – Rome, Paris, Amsterdam. Had they been there fifty years or were they meant to be ironic and retro? Hard to tell. It was the kind of place that specialised in all-day breakfasts for lorry drivers and sandwiches for workers from the trading estate. It opened early and now in mid-afternoon it was preparing to close. Nevertheless the owner was happy to serve me a cup of tea and an Eccles cake – bizarre choice, I know, but I've been fond of them ever since I first bought them from my school tuck shop. Yes, it was that kind of public school.

I asked the café owner if he knew anything about Keats PR.

'They don't come in here much,' he said.

Hardly a surprise. 'Those that do come in, what are they like?'

'They're just kids.'

'Have you met Scott Sage?'

'Who's he?'

'The guy who owns the company. The celebrity PR man. He's on the news a lot.'

'Well he's never come in here.'

He went back to mopping the vinyl floor and standing chairs on the metal-legged, laminate tables.

I took my tea and sat down by the window with a view across to the side of the PR Academy. It had nearly convinced me, but not quite. Had the site not been so hidden away, had Yasmine not been so obviously lying, I might have believed it was a genuine training set-up for would-be PR people of the future – a vanity project for Sage, let's say, an attempt to resurrect his career after the disaster of the lost libel case.

But it just smelled odd. Benjamin Gold thought so. And I agreed.

There's a school of painting called Super-Realism, in which the realism is so intense, in such sharp focus and high definition, that pictures start to look *unreal*. I'd got a similar feeling about Keats PR. The bins were too perfect. Yasmine was too perfect.

I used the café's Wi-Fi to chase up the Ebola story which was now being reported everywhere. The government of Qatar was issuing blanket denials that there were any cases of the lethal virus in the country. A cynical person might think 'they would say that, wouldn't they?' since they patently wanted to safeguard their football spectacular. But the story was more confusing. The World Health

70

Organisation had evidence that four people had travelled from an infected zone of the Democratic Republic of Congo to Qatar. They gave names and dates of travel. Qatar responded by saying there was no record of these people ever arriving into Qatar and the flight data given by WHO was simply incorrect.

I was puzzling over this news and trying to work through the Eccles cake, which was stale, when a vehicle went into the Keats PR car park.

Something about the driver looked familiar but his face was turned away and I couldn't immediately place him. But the woman with him was instantly recognisable. It was Magda Butt. The man had a worryingly firm grip on Magda's arm and steered her towards the office block where they both disappeared inside.

After less than a minute the man reappeared without Magda. I realised what looked familiar about him was his grey bomber jacket. The material had a shiny finish just like the one in the CCTV of the murderer and it caught the light. But there was no branding visible and one grey jacket is much like another. Then bomber jacket man opened his car boot, took out a leather briefcase and, as if he were auditioning specially for me, walked straight towards the cafe.

He came in, asked for a coffee to go and I was on alert at once. The café owner exchanged a few platitudes with him about the weather and the upcoming football and every word the killer said made my nerve-ends tingle. His voice confirmed Nathan's description. He spoke with an eastern European accent and on certain syllables his voice was high pitched and squeaky, almost a whistle.

With a heart-stopping thrill I knew he was the one in the CCTV footage. The man with the congenital defect in his larynx. The triple murderer.

He paid for his drink and made for the door as I scrabbled in a pocket for my camera. I ran off a few shots through the window as the man went back into the offices.

I hurried out of the café and got from my vehicle something I always travel with: a miniature tracking device. The battery only lasts a week and they're not cheap, but their great advantage is they're magnetic.

I looked at the killer's navy Nissan Qashqai. It was brand new and presumably hired. I took a shot of it then worried about being seen on the security cameras. Most of them were angled on the building perimeter but a couple covered the car park. Then I looked at the Indian Summer sun which was bright in a clear blue sky and low enough to leave long shadows. It was shining directly towards the wall-mounted cameras. Even better, the front half of the Qashqai was sunlit but the rear half was in shadow. I thought back to what Clark had said about my failed photography. *Contre jour.* The CCTV camera trained on the area where the Qashqai was could not expose correctly for both the shadow and the intense sunlight. If its aperture was correct for the sunny side, then the shadowy side would be dark and obscure. Useful.

I walked out of the car park towards the café. When I guessed I was out of range of any CCTV, I about-turned and headed back, approaching the Qashqai from the rear and keeping strictly in the shadows.

I reached the car and bent down on the side furthest from cameras and office windows. It was a clean, new car with no mud under the wheel arch which meant good adhesion for the tracker. In a few seconds it was installed.

Practical problems can be overcome but moral problems are more difficult. I now had a dilemma. Correct procedure would be to phone DCI Bostock and tell him the location of the murderer. Police would be on the scene in a few minutes. But arresting the killer wouldn't help me find the missing picture.

Occasionally you can arrest a suspect too soon. There are times when keeping a suspect on the streets may lead you to the whole gang. Or to the picture. I told myself that was true in this case.

My job is to hunt down pictures, not murderers. And I'd kind of promised MacIver – well, with crossed fingers – that I'd leave the murder case to the police. So I would do exactly that. And I wouldn't tell Bostock.

Aiding a criminal is an offence and I was arguably doing just that. So if anyone got to know I could be charged. My blue-eyed boy status with DCI Bostock would evaporate and MacIver would never hire me again. But at the moment I didn't care.

You think I was valuing an old painting more than human life? You could think that. The "whistling man" wasn't just any criminal, he was a multiple murderer.

So I had a pang of guilt.

Was I doing right or doing wrong? Once, when I was eighteen, I was convinced I was doing right. But then everything turned out wrong. Or maybe it was the other way around. Since my parents died I've learned the hard way that morality is a grey and murky area.

I decided to give myself a deadline. Twenty-four hours. I would keep tabs on the whistling man via the tracker and, whether I got any leads or not, I would contact Bostock in twenty-four hours.

Or maybe I wouldn't. Nobody would know about the deadline except me. It was a little mind-game. A way of giving a sop to my conscience.

I took another turn around the Keats building but found nothing new. As I turned towards my car, trying to work out what Magda was doing there, I heard a car door open and then click shut. What attracted my attention was its very quietness. People normally slam car doors without thinking. Somebody behind me was trying to be surreptitious.

I didn't look round, and couldn't hear any footsteps but I felt someone's presence.

Was one of the Keats people following me?

Chapter 10

I ignored my vehicle, walked right past the car park and out of the trading estate. At the main road I turned right and kept an eye on the traffic, waiting for a gap. I saw my chance and jogged across the road. The person behind me stayed on the other side of the road, walking in the same direction. After a few minutes they too crossed over and began walking behind me. I walked on until I came to a petrol station where I went across the forecourt and into the shop. I bought a Mars bar but my purpose was to get eyes on my follower. As I paid, the figure was standing in front of the petrol station apparently talking on their phone. They were wearing a bulky jacket that was too big for them, with baggy jeans, trainers and a large cap pulled well down. A rough and ready disguise. They didn't look like 1st XI opponents, but who were they working for?

It was likely I'd been spotted interfering with the murderer's car. Or was the tail something to do with the girl on the motorbike? Or the man in the car outside my house the previous night?

I came out of the shop and walked on. I passed a funeral director's shop and in the highly reflective black-painted window I saw my tail still behind me. I hesitated a moment while I checked the traffic. The person behind me slowed and did the phone dodge again.

Then I was off. Over to the centre of the road, then hesitating a moment while a car passed, then off again at top speed to the far side.

My pursuer tried to follow but he mistimed it. A car hooted and he had to pull back. That was a mistake. Drawing attention to themselves. I ran fast down a side street and ducked into an alleyway at the rear of some houses. It was overhung with trees and shady even with the strong sun. Peering out from concealment, I saw my tail finally make it across the road then walk down the side street towards my hiding place. They had an odd way of walking. Not a limp exactly, but there was something ungainly about them as if they had an injury, or even an artificial limb. An ex-soldier? As the figure came level with the alley I moved out from hiding and grabbed him by his lapels, pulling him round in a circle so his back slammed against the brick wall which ran along the alley.

'Why are you following me?' I said, realising as I spoke it wasn't a man I'd got hold of but a young woman.

The woman thrust a knee towards my groin but her angle was off and she hit me on the thigh, though still painfully. Then she punched her palm hard at my face aiming just under my nose. It was a good move but I'd seen the blow coming and jinked left, which meant I let go my hold on her jacket. The woman pulled away then made a kick-boxing attack which I parried with my arm, followed by another kick aimed at my knee. I made a grab for her foot and held on to it, twisting her leg round. My extra strength unbalanced her and she fell on to her front. I grabbed her arms and held them behind her back in a classic restraint hold. She was now face down on the dirt path. For good measure I rested a knee on the small of her back. She tried to kick backwards up at me, but she could never exert enough power from that angle to worry me.

'You've demonstrated a few nice moves, now tell me who you're working for,' I said.

The woman was silent.

Gripping her slender wrists together with just one of my hands I used the other to search her bag that was lying on the ground. There was no weapon inside, not even a can of pepper spray. Then I found her driving licence. Her name was Rochelle Smith and she had an address in Willesden.

'Clean licence. Very commendable, Rochelle,' I said. Then I flicked through various papers in the bag and pulled out a business card. 'Well, here's a surprise... Private Investigator. And what's this..?' I took out a laminated ID. 'A police Warrant Card? Obviously fake.'

'No, it's not!' These were the first words she'd spoken. She tried to raise her face from the ground. 'It's not a fake.'

'Moonlighting?'

'No. But the Warrant Card's genuine. At least… it's a copy of a genuine card. I *was* in the police. I resigned last year. And you needn't tell me impersonating a Police Officer is an offence. I've never actually used it. It was a mistake to copy it.'

Her story sounded unlikely enough to be true. Rochelle seemed a kooky type and I could understand why she'd resigned from the police. But why had she joined in the first place?

'Can I get up? There's some dog muck on the ground just in front of me.'

That was true. And real smelly stuff.

I pulled her up but kept a grip on her arm. I couldn't believe she was working for the whistling man. Or for Magda. But Sage was a possibility.

'Why are you following me?'

'You were nosing around the PR place.'

'I went to see if they could run a campaign for me. What's wrong with that?'

'You were searching the waste land at the back and photographing a car.'

'You work for the PR company or for Sage?'

'I've never met Mr Sage.'

'What do you know about the Butt-Ansari Gallery in North Kensington?'

'Never heard of it.'

'What about Nobottle Abbey?'

'I've heard of Northanger Abbey. And Downton Abbey. And Westminster.'

She fancied herself all right.

'How about Christoph Amberger?'

'What is this? *University Challenge?*'

Yeah, bloody intellectual type.

'I'll tell you why I was nosing around. I'm on the trail of a stolen picture and a triple murderer. Like you, he seems to work for the PR firm.'

'How do you know?'

'His car's in the parking place.'

'How do you know I work for the PR company?'

'Don't you?'

She ignored the question.

'Why haven't you arrested this murderer?'

'I'm not a copper. At least not any longer. I resigned like you say you did. After eleven years. I had a spell in SCO19 and finished as DI.'

She listened to this without reacting, but then she jerked my arm.

'You don't have to hold me, you know. I won't scarper.'

Even if she did run off I'd be able to catch her again. I released her arm and she grunted a curt word of thanks.

Then she brushed dead leaves and mud off her jacket and took off her cap. She carefully undid her hair and shook it out. A bit ostentatiously, I thought. Then she opened a little foil packet from her bag and took out some kind of wipe. She rubbed her face and hands with it and there was an astringent smell of lemon-scented cleanser.

'It's O.K.,' I said, 'you won't catch anything from me.'

She gave me a look through her eyelashes.

'I was thinking of the dogs,' she said.

Judging by another pervasive whiff, it wasn't just dogs who used the alley as a lavatory but late night boozers caught short on their way home.

As she wiped, I had a chance to look at her properly. Her hair was long, glossy and luxuriant. She was wearing no make-up but was an attractive woman of about thirty. I couldn't imagine how I'd mistaken her for a man. I looked her up and down.

'Walk a few paces for me,' I said.

'What?' Rochelle said, giving me a combative look.

'Just walk up and down.'

'Why?'

'Because I'm asking. Go on. Indulge me.'

Rochelle made a face like I was some kind of pervert, and then set off down the alleyway in a flouncy, look-at-me sort of way, like she was a 1950s Hollywood starlet playing Marie Antoinette.

It wasn't helpful.

'When you were following me you did something to the way you walk. I thought you were a man. A man with a bad leg maybe.'

Rochelle smiled like she'd got one over on me. Which I suppose she had.

'That's the effect I want. There's a difference in the way men and women move. So I try to disguise my walk, make it slouchier, more... clumpy. I wear a bloke's jacket that's too big for me, a loose jumper to hide my boobs and I don't wear a bra.'

I looked for her breasts. They were indeed well hidden.

'I try to look a bit of a saddo, the kind of person that no one notices.'

'Where did you learn that? Not at Hendon?'

'No. Look, having this chat is great fun but actually I'm dying for a wee. Can we go to a pub or something?'

I smiled.

'Always a problem on obbo jobs, isn't it?'

'It is for women. You can always piss behind a tree.'

'All right,' I said. 'But I'll hang on to your purse and phone so you don't run off.'

We found a pub not far away but I'd downed nearly half my pint before Rochelle emerged from the Ladies. But when she reappeared it was immediately evident how she'd spent her time. I'd thought she was good-looking before but now, having sorted her hair and applied lipstick and mascara, she looked head-turningly attractive. Her breasts were still concealed by her oversize, shapeless jersey but I wondered how they'd look under tighter clothes when she put her bra back on.

She picked up her glass of wine and took several large sips.

'Thank you,' she said, 'that's nice.' And for a moment she relaxed and actually gave me a smile.

I held my phone out towards her and showed her the picture I'd taken of the biker at the petrol station.

'That's you, isn't it? Yesterday.'

Then the smile faded and once more she was intense and stand-offish. She looked at the picture but said nothing.

'Powerful bike,' I said. 'What is it? 750cc?'

'847 according to the spec.'

'Not too heavy to handle?'

'You didn't see me fall off did you?'

'The same bike was in Northamptonshire today. Somebody else was riding it.'

'I didn't say it was *my* bike.'

She took a drink and turned squarely towards me. 'Tell me why you think Keats PR would employ a murderer.'

She seemed interested, concerned almost, but I couldn't work out her angle. Whose side was she on?

'Why are you following me?'

She ignored me again. 'Who is this murderer? Who did he kill?'

I saw no reason to tell her the details so I just showed her the pictures I'd taken of the man in the car park. And bounced a question back to her.

'Have you seen him around here before?'

'No. But I've not been here before. It's only my second day on this job.'

I had to smile. Her honesty was disarming. But it was plain she didn't think being a newbie weakened her position.

'What's his name?' she said.

'I don't have a name.'

Rochelle snorted. 'Brilliant.'

'But as well as myself I've got a witness who can ID him.'

'Still sounds flaky. Who's your witness? Little old lady with thick glasses? Defence brief will have you for breakfast.'

I was getting tired of being interrogated. I wanted to know whether Rochelle was a threat or a possible ally.

'Never mind my case. What the hell are you doing following me? Who are you working for?'

She just stared at me in silence. Appraising me like I was on a dating app.

'Why are you interested in me?' I said.

Her eyebrows flicked up and she flashed me a burlesque sort of smile. 'Hey... Don't get any ideas, honeybunch.'

I sighed in exasperation. She took another slug of sauvignon blanc and sat back in her chair. Then she said, 'Look, give me the phone back. I'm supposed to check in every few hours.'

I held out the phone. She took it and tapped out a text message.

'Who are you reporting to? What did you tell them?'

'I said I was interrogating a suspect but didn't think he was dangerous.'

It was my turn to laugh. 'I got the impression I was interrogating you and I can be as dangerous as you want.'

She laughed too. Then suddenly stopped. 'I hope that wasn't one of your clumsy pick-up lines.'

'Dates couldn't be further from my mind. Though maybe they're on yours. You were so long in the ladies primping yourself I started to think you'd jumped out through a window.'

She looked just a tad embarrassed by my accusation of vanity. Her cheeks coloured a little.

'Primping?' she said. 'What kind of word's that?'

It was my turn to give a silent stare. So with a toss of her head she went on,

'Undercover work's over. I get out of character, that's all.'

'And what exactly is your out-of-character character, ex- Detective Constable Smith?'

'There you go. Invading my privacy.'

Was she joking? Or repeating a mantra? 'If that's your attitude I'm guessing you didn't resign, you were kicked out of the Met. Did you start some sex-discrimination case? An accusation of inappropriate touching in the patrol car?'

Rochelle's eyes narrowed, her mood changed instantly and she let rip.

'You make me sick,' she said. 'Bloody swaggering, chauvinist tough guy from SCO19 who thinks he's got all the answers just because he can wrestle a woman who's forty pounds lighter on to the ground. Where did you end up? Counter Terrorism?'

Her sudden aggression puzzled me. I just continued gazing and said,

'Arts and Antiques Unit.'

She gave an incredulous laugh. 'You're joking.'

I told her I wasn't.

'Must be nice arresting Ming vases and Rembrandts instead of murderers and rapists.'

I sucked in breath, controlling my temper. If she wanted a fight I wasn't going to give her one.

'If you want to see what a Chinese guy did to me with dadao – that's a kind of machete by the way – when I was rescuing something he'd stolen from the Soane Museum I'll have to take my shirt off.'

'Not now, please. It'll put me off my dinner. You don't have to recite your hard-man credentials, I got a taste of them first hand.'

Neither of us spoke for a few moments but I was aware of her eyes on me. Then she leaned towards me and, with another mood U-turn, she made a big play of pinching my biceps and prodding my pecs, like a farmer might poke at livestock in a rural auction ring.

'Don't get many of those for the pound. You a gym bunny?'

'No. You just need to be fit in my game.'

'No good being fit if your brain's atrophied.'

I sighed. 'Can we stop all this pissing about and point-scoring? You might think it's fun, but it's actually a bit juvenile.'

I saw her take a breath to reply, but then think better of it. Perhaps she agreed with me. Perhaps she was stumped for a sharp enough come-back.

There was another pause while we both sipped our drinks, kept our powder dry and wondered how the conversation would proceed.

'You're obviously part of a team. How many?'

'Tell me why you're interested in this Keats business.'

Rochelle was back in professional mode again and competitive, the sniping all forgotten. It was my turn to say nothing.

'I saw you go into the office, then you came out, nosed around a bit, looked in the bins, went to the café – and then the so-called murderer drove up. And you put a tracker on his car.'

I smiled. 'Cards on the table time? If I tell the truth, will you do the same?'

She tossed her head from side to side as if weighing up a decision. 'It depends on what you've got for me,' she said sounding almost flirty. Her mood seemed to change minute by minute and I couldn't

81

tell whether her bolshie attitude was the real thing or just a put-on. Maybe a way of getting an edge. Maybe just a defence mechanism.

She didn't answer my question so I said, 'O.K. I'll go first.'

I outlined the work I did for MacIver and explained about the Amberger painting. I described what happened two days before in Hoxton. I was suspicious that Sage was involved in some way, but I didn't know how.

She listened without interrupting but gave no reaction to what I said.

'The thing is,' I said, 'the reason I've not brought the police in yet is I get the feeling this murderer is not the main man, not the star attraction, but a supporting artist.'

I looked at her but all she said was:

'I was a supporting artist once.'

I was fazed by her non-sequitur. Maybe that was her intention.

'I went to drama school before going into the police. That's where I got the different kind of walking from. You know those Shakespeare plays where a woman pretends to be a man and it leads to all kinds of confusion.'

'You were an actress?'

'That was the idea. But can I point something out? Most people say "actor" now for men and women. It's more egalitarian.'

I rolled my eyes but the drama school background explained at least part of her character. I wondered how much of Rochelle's persona was just an act.

'I did bits of extra work – they're technically called supporting artists – but I saw enough to realise it wasn't for me.' Rochelle paused, then said brightly. 'Well, any more to tell me?'

I had been taken aback by her digression.

'No, that's all. What do you think?'

'I'm not being paid to sort out your stolen picture case. That's down to you, tough guy. But I'd like one of those pictures you took of the man with the blue Qashqai.'

I looked at her and said cynically.

'You don't mind divulging your private number?'

She hadn't thought about it until I raised the issue. There was a second's pause while she worked out a suitable response.

'Don't think it's an invitation to anything.'

I smiled at her pretended ferocity while I sent a picture to her phone.

'What are you smirking at?' she said. This time the ferocity was more genuine. I got the feeling she was irked I'd begun to see through her, and was even beginning to send her up.

She checked the download on her phone.

'You name's... John Kite,' she said.

'Is that why you were following me? To get my name and phone number? You should have just asked.'

'Don't be ridiculous.'

'What do you want from me? What do you want to know?'

Rochelle Smith stood up to go. 'Thanks for the drink.'

'Tell me what you're after. I might be able to help.' I said.

She paused and looked at me.

'I'm freelance so I just follow instructions. Everything's on a need to know basis and I'm too far down the food chain to need to know.'

That might be true, but if it was, I thought Rochelle's self-esteem wouldn't let her admit it. She was just holding out on me.

'How long will you be tailing me for?'

'Until I'm told to stop. Or I get a better offer. See you.'

And Rochelle Smith walked out of the pub.

Chapter 11

I sat for a moment worrying as to why Rochelle Smith should be following me. PI's like her spend a lot of their time on matrimonial work, suspicious partners checking up on their other halves. But I don't have another half. And things are quiet on the sex front.

It had to be related to the call MacIver had from India Paine, asking about Alex Broughton. If India had hired Rochelle it suggested she was in London. But what was she trying to do? What did she want after so long?

I was moving to the bar for a refill when there was a tone on my phone from the tracker app. The murderer was on the move. I left the pub and was back at my own car in a few minutes. The whistling man was heading into central London.

I followed him first via the tracker but soon caught up with his car. He was driving carefully, well within the speed limit. I kept him in sight as we drove into Knightsbridge then went north up Park Lane. He turned right, following the one-way system to cross over the central island and come back down Park Lane the other way.

Reversing direction, like going twice round a roundabout, is a classic counter-surveillance tactic. Was he worried about a tail? Had he spotted me? No. Neither. Because he turned into Curzon Street and slowed right down. He was looking for a place to park. Difficult round there. The small amount of on-street parking is mostly reserved for residents. He turned into Chesterfield Gardens where I didn't follow since it's a cul-de-sac. He'd spotted a woman loading shopping bags into a BMW and obviously about to leave. He did the usual thing of putting his hazard lights on and waiting, double-parked. I continued down Curzon Street where miraculously there was a space. I snuck in quickly and phoned my card details through to the parking people. I hurried back to Chesterfield Gardens but the BMW woman was only now moving off. I had a long phone conversation with myself while the Qashqai took the BMW's space. The murderer got out of the car and walked past where I was standing. I let him get twenty metres ahead and followed.

To follow a suspect properly you need a big team. At least four or five agents at any one time with different modes of transport at their disposal. Even then the suspect can slip away or spot he's being tailed. On my own, on foot, it would be a big ask to follow him for any distance.

As he continued along Curzon Street he took out his phone, dialled a pre-set number and had the briefest of conversations. Presumably checking his contact was in place. He walked on and I realised with an inner smile that we were going past Leconfield House. The long ago headquarters of MI5. There was scarcely time for the name John le Carré to flash through my brain before I saw the whistling man disappear inside a hotel.

I increased my pace and went into the hotel eight or nine seconds after he had. It was a big hotel, smart and modern but only mid-range, not true Mayfair luxury. The kind of place where you can get a decent room for a two hundred quid or so.

A big hotel is a maze. Five or six floors, a hundred bedrooms or more. Bars, dining room, lounges, sauna, therapy room, whatever. Losing the whistling man would be frighteningly easy and as I stood in the busy foyer scanning around I couldn't see him anywhere. I moved further into the hotel and looked around again. I saw four guests standing together all grouped behind a single copy of the London *Evening Standard* with the headline "ANOTHER THREAT TO WORLD CUP – Qatar gives health pledge to FIFA." Then one of them folded the newspaper and they all moved away to the bar deep in conversation.

Revealed behind them, waiting calmly for a lift, was the whistling man.

I moved towards him, a lift descended, its doors opened, people got out, the whistling man and others got in and I followed. The murderer pressed the button for the fifth floor and I glanced sidelong at him. As when I'd seen him leave BetterWork, his manner was calm, untroubled, professional. On the walk down Curzon Street he hadn't looked around, hadn't made any obvious counter-surveillance moves.

I shifted forwards a little to check for the tell-tale bulge of a shoulder-holster. He looked clean but he could easily have a weapon concealed elsewhere.

At the fifth floor I let the murderer out first then stopped in front of one of those hotel signs that tell you which rooms are to the right and which to the left. My target turned left without hesitation. He had been here before.

I followed him at a suitable distance. He stopped and knocked on the door of 518 and the door was opened almost immediately. Thankfully. That saved me the extreme embarrassment of getting all the way to the end of the corridor then having to make some lame-brain excuse – like I'd got out at the wrong floor – while the whistling man stood in the corridor watching me.

With the door of 518 safely closed and only a low buzz of conversation from inside I retreated to a sofa in an alcove by the lifts. Ten minutes passed and the door of 518 opened. I jumped up from the sofa, slid through a door on to the emergency staircase, went down a few steps and waited. The hotel carpet was too thick to hear any footsteps but after a few seconds I heard the sound of the lift ascending. It stopped at five. Then went down. I cautiously opened the staircase door and peered out. No one there.

I went back down the corridor and knocked on the door of 518.

I heard a man starting to speak even as he was opening the door.

'Hey. What you forgotten...?' The occupant of the room stopped speaking abruptly as the door was open enough for him to see it wasn't who he'd expected.

'Sorry. I thought you were...'

'The man who just left? Yes, I know,' I said.

The man was disconcerted. He was an Arab, about my age and wearing evening dress with a burgundy coloured bow-tie. After a lengthy pause during which I enjoyed staring at him and listening to his brain working he finally said:

'What do you want?' He had a strong middle eastern accent but his English was good.

I smiled a cheery smile. 'Your friend. They guy with the unusual whistley voice. Did you know he was a murderer?'

Again the Arab was taken aback. He opened his mouth, then shut it. He looked up and down the hotel corridor as if looking for help. Or checking if I had back-up.

'What's your association with that man? How do you know him? Why was he visiting you?'

'I cannot answer police questions. I have diplomatic immunity.'

This was a surprise.

'Really? You couldn't get accommodation inside your embassy?'

'I cannot answer questions.'

'What is your nationality?'

'I cannot answer questions.'

'Tough. I'll just keep asking. By the way, I'm not a police officer. I work for an insurance company. And whether you have diplomatic immunity depends on your ranking in the embassy staff and the nature of the crime that may or may not have been committed.'

'Go away. I've nothing to say.' He gave the door a firm shove but my foot was quicker. Thick soles of decent shoes are effective door stops and he was shocked as the door sprang back towards him.

'Stop that. Or I'll call the police.'

'Be my guest. I'm trying to recover an oil painting that was stolen by the man you've just been entertaining in your room. And for the avoidance of doubt, since it may be illegal in your country, when I say "entertaining" I'm not implying any sexual congress between the two of you. O.K.?'

He didn't appreciate my humour.

'Go away.'

'You are involved with a multiple murderer and thief. You may avoid prosecution in this country but you will certainly be expelled.' Then I hardened my voice. 'I don't give a shit about your supposed immunity. I want to know where that picture is.'

He started to look just a little worried.

'I know nothing about a picture.'

'I think you do'

'I haven't killed anybody.'

'Didn't say you had. But your friend has.'

He pushed the door harder, trying to move my foot. I never did much physics at school so I don't know what Law applies but it's strange how one foot on the ground can resist a shit-load of pressure from a door that's so much bigger. My foot stayed where it was. So did the door.

'Take your foot away and leave me alone.'

'What was his name? The man you met?'

The Arab's eyes were swivelling round wondering how to get rid of me. He then did something really strange. He let go of the door, walked back inside his room, picked up the phone and pressed a number.

'Hello? Reception...?'

What more invitation did I need? I simply followed him into the room. It was a reasonable size, a junior suite it would be called. Nice décor. King-sized bed. Small sitting area.

I walked over to the man who was still waiting for Reception to pick up and yanked the phone cable from its socket.

He shouted some abuse in Arabic and advanced towards me, his eyes burning, intent on doing me some damage. He pulled back his arm and swung a punch at me. But I just dodged back and his fist whizzed past well in front of my face. The effort he'd put into the blow unsteadied him and I seized my chance. I grabbed the front of his dinner jacket and pulled his face close to mine.

'I don't necessarily want to hurt you. But I can. What I want is information. Who was the man you met? What's his name?'

The man spat at me.

As I turned my face away to avoid the spittle I saw something I recognised on a table.

To keep the man quiet, I punched him in the stomach, twice and he collapsed on to the floor.

'Stay down,' I said. 'Unless you want blood on your nice dress shirt.'

I kept my eyes on the Arab and took a step backwards. What I'd seen on the table was a swipe-card ID on a lanyard. It was identical to the one I'd seen bouncing against Yasmine's tits at the Keats office. I swept it up from the table and looked at the name.

'Nassir Hameed,' I said. 'That's you?'

The man said nothing.

On the same side table was a wallet and passport. I looked through them and confirmed that Hameed was the man lying on the floor and that he was a citizen of Qatar.

I looked up from the passport and saw he was rapidly pressing numbers on his mobile. I aimed a kick at his hand, the phone shot across the room, dented some quality Victorian skirting board and the phone's back panel flicked off.

I started to search the room. But even junior suites have few places where you could hide a painting. I pulled open the wardrobe, the drawers in a chest and those in a dressing table. The I checked the bathroom. The picture wasn't anywhere.

Hameed was still groaning on the floor, trying to recover his breath and nursing his bruised hand so I pocketed his swipe-card and went to the door.

'I hope you enjoy your function this evening,' I said as I left.

I checked the time: 19.12. twenty one hours thirteen minutes left of my self-imposed Bostock deadline.

Back in my car I thought about the Arab. I'd seen from a pass in Hameed's wallet that he had a post in Qatar's Ministry of Culture and Sports. Presumably he was part of the trade delegation that had got in my way on the North Circular. And, pound to a penny, he was the delegate who had no interest in trade.

But at least I'd discovered why he'd blagged his way into the UK.

I pulled out my phone to call my Foreign Office contact, but then remembered he had a thing about talking on mobiles. Since any radio communication can be intercepted he believed it was sensible to assume *all* radio communications were being intercepted. A stringent application of what they call Moscow Rules.

Less than an hour later, back home in Uxbridge, I dialled him on my landline.

'Somerscales…'

There was the buzz of conversation coming down the line. It sounded like a big party.

'Hello Leo. It's John Kite. Have you a moment?'

'Hi, John. I'm in Ankara. At a reception as you can probably hear. Can I call you back tomorrow?'

'Yes, of course.'

'Thank you for your latest donation to the Fund, by the way. Much appreciated. The General Secretary should have sent a note.'

'Yes, she did, thank you.'

And the call ended.

Next I phoned Clark. He often moaned about being over-worked but didn't seem to mind being called at home. I suspected he had no one else in his life and research and IT systems were his hobby as well as what paid the bills. I guess being called at home also made him feel needed.

He answered after a couple of rings and I heard what sounded like Buzz Lightyear's voice from his TV. Clark confirmed it was.

'I'm watching all the *Toy Story* movies tonight in sequence. I wanted to compare and contrast. You know how it is...'

I pretended I knew how it was and filled him in briefly on what had happened at the hotel. Then I asked him to find out anything he could on Nassir Hameed and also Abid Bashir. But I heard a note of panic in his voice and got the impression his *Toy Story* marathon had some end result, apart from personal pleasure. Under pressure he revealed he was writing a "major appreciation" on the films for what he called an "influential animation blog".

I said tomorrow morning would be soon enough.

And next morning as I was about to leave my house Clark did indeed call. Like clockwork, I thought. But he wasn't phoning with news on Nassir Hameed. Apart from confirming he was a member of the trade delegation he'd been unable to find out anything about the man, which in itself was unusual enough to ring alarm bells.

Likewise, he'd found nothing at all on anyone called Abid Bashir.

But while other people listen to music or news over their tea and toast, Clark had breakfast monitoring police radio messages. The real purpose of his call was to tell me a body had been pulled out of the Thames near Lambeth Bridge. What had made Clark interested was the dead person was classified as IC6 – an Arab or North African – and members of both SCO6 Diplomatic Protection and SCO15 Counter Terrorism Command had been called to the scene.

Clark was pernickety and pedantic – with a touch of Asperger's I thought – but he was first-rate back-up.

On the Embankment the site was easy to find. There was an ambulance, a patrol car and three unmarked police vehicles on the side of the road. I found a place to park near Tate Britain.

Looking over the embankment wall I saw a lifeboat from the Tower Bridge RNLI station standing by and a boat from the Marine Policing Unit tied up at Millbank Pier. Among the uniformed and plain clothes figures on the pier there was one I recognised. He was walking back along the pontoon towards his car.

'Kite. I don't believe it,' said Bostock as he stepped back on to the shore.

I felt a twinge of guilt as we met. I ought to be telling him about the murderer, his blue Qashqai and his link to Scott Sage. But all I said was:

'Morning Chief Inspector. An Arab body?'

'Yes. But he wasn't holding a painting.' Bostock gave me a cheesy grin, enjoying his witticism. I smiled back. I wanted to keep him on side.

'Have you told the Embassy, yet?'

'How did you know he was a diplomat?' Bostock was surprised.

I nodded towards one of the vehicles. 'Recognised the SCO6 car.'

Bostock made a disbelieving face.

'Murder?' I said,

'Have to wait for the PM. He's been in the water overnight and was at some kind of party last night.'

Now I was the one to be impressed. 'He was drinking? You've done a blood test already?'

Bostock snickered and teased. 'No. I just used my eyes. Like you do looking at pictures, I guess.'

'He was in fancy dress?'

Bostock grinned. 'Could say that. He's wearing a dinner jacket.'

Wow.

Nassir Hameed? My mind fizzed with possible scenarios. Had I been seen coming out of the hotel room? Had the whistling man targeted Hameed?

'Black tie?'

'Oh yeah. Full monty.'

'I mean was it a black bow tie.'

'What other colour bow tie d'you wear?'

'Burgundy,' I said. 'Or navy blue, dark green, Paisley.'

Bostock made a dismissive snort. 'Art tart stuff. Too poncey for me. And for this chap. He had a black tie that was black.'

I relaxed a bit. But how many other Arabs were at evening dress affairs in London the previous night? Ten? Twenty? Fifty? Maybe Hameed and the dead man had been at the same function.

'Got a name yet?'

Bostock gave an exaggerated weary sighed and pulled out his notebook. 'The name on his credit cards is Jamal Ahmed.' And he kindly spelled the name for me. 'Right. I think you've got your money's worth. You know as much as I do now.'

This wasn't true, but I took his point. I needed to give him something before he'd give me any more. I felt a wave of guilt again.

I felt Bostock's eyes on me and I looked up.

'Yes..?' he said with a half-smile. 'Go on.'

'What?' I said, playing dumb.

'I'm sorry. I thought you were going to tell me something...'

He seemed to be enjoying embarrassing me. Again I played dumb.

'...About events at a hotel in Mayfair? It was you, wasn't it? Your sudden interest in, shall we say, Arabian nights made me put two and two together.' He was in a jovial mood for some reason.

I had little choice but to confirm a minimum of details. Then to move things on I mentioned the name of Abid Bashir.

'At least *he's* not a Sheik of Araby,' said Bostock, noting the name. 'Your enquiry's getting very cosmopolitan.'

'He seems to have a link with the stolen picture and possibly with illegal imports of looted artefacts from the middle east.' It was pure supposition and I was talking it up but even so Bostock wasn't excited.

'More art tart stuff,' he said. 'Is he the murderer? That's the point.'

I said I didn't know. And I didn't. Even though the name was probably an alias I felt I'd done something. Something to ease my guilt, even if nothing to materially help Bostock.

Chapter 12

The previous evening, *News at Ten* had led on the puzzling threats to the World Cup for which nobody seemed to have a convincing explanation. They'd enterprisingly grabbed Scott Sage as he arrived at Heathrow for his opinion on how Qatar could repair the PR damage to their big jamboree. But Sage largely ignored the reporter's questions and, as Kirsty had mentioned, he used nail clippers as a prop, trimming, or pretending to trim, his nails in a way that was casually dismissive. To my surprise, he then publicly announced his new enterprise, Keats, which he claimed would transform the PR industry. It already had several millions worth of commissions, he said, and his young staff would rewrite the rules, they would be the stars of tomorrow and he was privileged to give opportunities to the wonderful kids he was in the middle of hiring. The visibly irritated reporter tried hard to drag Sage back to the point of the interview but he still got in one more plug for Keats.

I stood on the Embankment after Bostock had been called away and the body carried into an ambulance and phoned Lorella. I reminded her of our previous conversation and told her I would be at Sage's office at eleven. She protested that was not doable. I said I was sure she could persuade Scott to fit me in, particularly since she'd been so excited by my story. And because she liked my voice so much.

She still said today was not workable.

'Just say Nassir Hameed to him. He'll see me.'

'Say what?'

'Nassir Hameed.' I spelled the name out for her. 'He's from Qatar.'

There was a pause. Lorella was obviously thinking fast. But I got the impression the name meant nothing to her.

'I'll be there at eleven,' I said and ended the call.

Sage's office was in the centre of the West End, a location that in style, class and mood was the exact opposite of Keats's trading estate. Goodwin's Court is off St Martins Lane, just down from Leicester Square tube. It's a narrow lane with an attractive row of eighteenth century buildings which have somehow avoided development. It's a hidden gem, a secret spot right in the heart of theatreland. In the Court are two Literary Agents, four Theatrical Agents, a high class Italian restaurant, a film company, a creative consultancy and Scott Sage (Publicity) Holdings Ltd.

Lorella in the flesh was not quite as decorative as I had imagined on the phone. Her succulent voice promised more than her body delivered and she was older than I'd thought. Late forties, early fifties. She was also less eager, more restrained. She greeted me in a friendly, but not effusive, way and said she had twisted Scott's arm to make time to see me. I sat down on an enormous leather sofa to await his readiness.

Lorella's perfume suffused the reception area and apart from me she was the only person in the room. Three bare, unoccupied desks near hers seemed to prove that Sage's firm was in trouble. I guessed it was only recently that their occupants had been given an hour's notice and a brown box to pack their possessions in. The impressive switchboard in front of Lorella was forbiddingly silent.

I heard feet thudding down a staircase and Scott Sage appeared.

'Hi John. Welcome,' he said, grabbing my hand. 'Thank you so much for coming. You've a hot little murder story for us I think. Come on up and tell me all about it. I can spare just ten minutes. We're rushed off our feet as always.'

He disappeared upstairs. I glanced at the under-employed Lorella who avoided catching my eye and I followed him. On the floor above there were another two empty desks by his office door. I surmised Lorella had once been his P.A. but had been reassigned as receptionist and general factotum when the others had been let go.

The inside of Sage's office showed no signs of asset-stripping. There were two more oversized leather sofas, a huge Carrara marble coffee table whose weight must have put a strain on the eighteenth century joists, a couple of Damien Hirst spot pictures and lots of other swanky stuff.

Sage was not as large as I was expecting: probably wide-angle TV lenses exaggerated his size. He was in his fifties, wearing a dark suit with a patterned Paul Smith shirt but no tie. He had an open kind of face that wore an almost permanent smile. He looked remarkably trustworthy. He also looked like a salesman, which is what he was.

'So, John,' he said, rubbing his hands together, 'are you looking forward to being on the front pages?'

I smiled. 'I guarantee I won't be on any page. The murder story involves you, not me.'

Sage did a startled look which turned into another confident smile. The kind of thing that Donald Trump did so well.

'Hey! This some kind of teaser? Bring me up to speed.'

'You know Jamie Rind was killed this week?'

'Shocking and terrible. Most shocking. I've phoned his widow already.'

'Yes, I heard you were a friend of his.'

Sage shook his head. 'He was an admired business colleague and legal adviser.'

'And you were at University together.'

'So long ago. I've almost forgotten.' He laughed.

He took out his small nail clippers and fiddled with them, casually inspecting his finger-nails at the same time. It seemed a displacement activity or nervous tic, as well as a way of unsettling anyone asking him questions.

'Jamie Rind had been negotiating with me regarding payment to encourage one of his clients to return a valuable painting. I believe you advised him to stage the handover at the BetterWork complex in Hoxton.'

He stretched out his hands, peering at his nails. 'I didn't *advise* him to do that. We may have talked about it. We talked about lots of things.'

'Jamie Rind's P.A. said the venue was your suggestion.'

'I don't remember. Was something wrong with the venue? Besides the obvious, I mean. Apart from that Mrs Lincoln, how did you enjoy the play?'

He laughed at the old gag. I couldn't tell whether he was exaggerating his crassness for my benefit or whether he was just naturally insensitive.

'I guess you talk to journalists a lot?'

'All the time, every day. It's what I do. It's how I keep the cash rolling in.'

'You may remember talking to a journalist called Benjamin Gold a little while ago. He'd written a piece about the painting I was trying to recover. You complained to him his article wasn't true because the picture had been stolen.'

'So? That's right isn't it? Gold is a right tosser who gets up my nose. He's accused me of selling stories which don't stack up. I wanted to show him he'd cocked up. People in glass houses etc.'

'Have you ever seen the picture?'

'How could I if it's been stolen?'

'Before it was stolen.'

'Jesus! No. I've no interest in this bloody picture. I've no interest in art at all. Except as a bit of decoration.' He waved his hand towards the Hirst on the wall.

I took out my phone, selected the picture of the murderer I'd taken in the office car park and passed it over.

'Do you know this man?'

His reply was instant. 'No.' And he handed the phone back.

'Have another look.' I pushed the phone back towards him.

'I understand you're an ex-police officer, Mr Kite. You're behaving as if you still are one. I thought you had a story for me, but all you've done is ask me questions. Do you think I've done something wrong?'

'Your name has come up twice in my investigation about the stolen painting so it's my job to ask a few questions.' I pointed to my phone. 'He's the other reason I wanted to talk to you.'

Sage picked up my phone again.

'Who's this?'

'The man who killed Jamie Rind.'

'Why hasn't he been arrested?'

'He will be.' I paused a moment. 'You may recognise the building he's standing outside of. It's the Keats PR office.'

He grabbed the phone again. 'It looks like our office. Maybe he knows one of the students.' Then an abrupt tone change. 'Have you been inside? You ought to. It's really cool. All those kids. So keen to learn. So dedicated.'

'This man seems to work there.'

He spread his arms wide. 'I'm not involved in recruitment.'

'I thought you'd hand-picked everybody.'

'No time. No time.'

'Your TV interview last night made it sound that way.'

'That's just good PR. I'm promoting the enterprise, lending my expertise. You've seen *Dragons Den, The Apprentice*? It's that kind of thing. A start-up. The CEO is a lady called Poppy Brisco. They pick my brains but I don't lead. I advise, assist and guide.'

'I was out there yesterday. It's hidden away, isn't it? It felt secretive. Furtive.'

'Furtive? Don't be bloody stupid. I was talking about it on the national news last night.'

'It's not open to the public.'

'Course it's not. Not yet. The site's still being set up. More kids being recruited. It's like a play in the theatre. You don't let the audience in before the first night. Our first night's in six weeks' time. We'll be all over the press then. All over the internet. Mammoth.'

Yet the office below was so quiet. Where were the preparations for this big launch?

'And in what direction will you be advising, assisting and guiding the young people at Keats?'

Sage didn't like the way I'd picked up his own phrase. He gave me a knowing look.

'If you're interested, which I doubt, it's about a return to basics. There's so much fake news, false information out there now I want those wonderful kids to learn how to use the truth. That's information that's factual, real, honest and true. Facts are sacred. Facts have to be nurtured, guarded. People have to be weaned away from half-truths and lies and persuaded to listen to the truth. It's like a silver bullet. A cure-all. That's why I named the new enterprise after Keats. "Truth is Beauty", that's what Keats wrote. And we'll follow in his footsteps.'

So now I knew. How pretentious. He was getting carried away. Trying too hard. I couldn't stop myself reacting to the pompous reference to Keats and he saw my expression.

'You may snigger. You may think you're all squeaky clean, but journalists have to handle unsavoury information. Information that needs to be out there. I may present the facts in a dramatic way, a graphic way, sometimes a flattering way. But it's always the facts, always the truth. It's the bad guys that spread lies.'

There was no point in arguing so I paused and nodded my head a moment, as if mulling over his wise words. He relaxed a little and put away his annoying nail clippers. Still showing a thoughtful face, I leant forward and looked straight at him.

'How do you know Nassir Hameed?'

'Why do you ask?' he said immediately. His face showed no emotion, no unease.

'He has a security pass to Keats PR.'

'He came on a visit. Potential client.'

'Mr Hameed is a civil servant. From Qatar.'

'I know. I was with him at a dinner last night. Sponsored by the Anglo-Gulf Press Liaison Committee. The Middle East is hungry for news stories. We can provide training for their people.'

Sage had answers for everything.

He started to rise. 'Now, you've not brought me the story you promised so we need to wrap up. I've things to do.'

'Do you have any contacts in Qatar? Have you been there?'

'I've been to Doha. For the grand prix.'

'Are you going to the World Cup?'

'I may do. But what's that to do with anything?'

'Do you know Kadir Ansari and Magda Butt?'

'Who?' Once again he gave no indication he recognised the names.

'How about Abid Bashir?'

'Look, I'm getting sick of your interrogation. I want to ask you something. It's my turn now, otherwise I've been wasting my time.

You're currently on contract at Maskelyne Global. Yes? Working for Fiona MacIver?'

I agreed I was.

'Have you come across an investigator in the same line as yourself, a guy called Alex Broughton?'

I tensed.

'Why do you ask?

'I want to find him. Unlike you, I think he has a bloody good story for me.'

'How did you hear about him?'

'Through a client of mine, stupid. People bring stuff to me. They know I get results.'

'Who is this client?'

Sage laughed. 'Piss off.'

'Do you know Rochelle Smith? Have you got people following me?'

'Not more bloody questions. And what's with the paranoia?'

He paused a moment, recharging.

'Do you know Broughton?'

'No, I don't.'

'Shame. Well, look out for him. If you find him, let me know. I could make it worth your while.'

Sage stood up and opened the door.

'I'm sorry I can't help you with the theft of this painting. I would if I could, so help me. And Jamie's death was really sad. Absolutely tragic.' He squeezed my shoulder, then slapped it hard in a close mates kind of way. If it was meant to endear me to him, it didn't.

My experience of Sage bore out what Benjamin Gold had said about him and I couldn't take anything he said at face value. I thought back to an abduction case I'd worked on when I was still in uniform. A nine year old girl had gone missing from a tough estate in Mitcham. The father made tearful appeals aimed at whoever had taken her. He organised his friends on the estate into search parties. There was hysterical media coverage and just when everyone assumed the girl must be dead she was found in the father's house. It was a broken family and some stupid, devious, rancid scam to get back at the divorced mother.

Sage reminded me of that father. He was convincing in front of the cameras, too.

But if Sage was behind the search for Alex Broughton that worried me. I supposed his client would be India Paine.

I'd only gone a few hundred metres from Sage's office when my phone rang. It was Kirsty, Jamie Rind's P.A. Her voice was unmistakeable, sweetly-pitched but always to the point and purposeful.

'It sounds like you're out and about. Can you talk?' she said in her practical way.

'I'm on foot. On my own. Got something for me?'

'Well, Scott Sage just called me, asking personal questions about you. Were you married, where did you live, what jobs you'd done.'

He wasn't letting grass grow.

'What did you say to him?'

'I said I had no idea about your private life or where you lived. He said surely I had an address and I said Jamie had always contacted you by email, so I never had any reason to know it.'

I held the pause for a moment. 'Is that true?'

'I know you live in Uxbridge, Lancaster Road. But I wasn't telling him that. He wanted your email and phone as well. I said I'd have to ask your permission to pass them on. Then he asked something strange. He said did I know someone called Alex Broughton. I said I didn't and asked him to stop asking questions and leave me alone. Then he swore at me of course. Who is this Alex Broughton and why is he important?'

'Absolutely no idea. And I'm sorry Sage had a go at you.'

'Don't worry. It's not something I can't handle. Our clients aren't nicely brought up boys and girls who say please and thank you, or know how to hold a knife and fork. Well, some know how to hold a knife all right: that's why they're in court.'

I smiled at the phone. 'Even so, thank you for stone-walling.'

'I didn't want the little shit starting a press campaign against you. That's presumably why he wanted the information, do you think? So he could dig up some muck and discredit you?'

She was slap bang on the button. But I didn't want Kirsty to know she was right. Better to make a joke.

'Discredit me? Disembowel me probably. But don't worry. If things get physical I can usually take care of myself.'

'Ye-es...' she said, extending the syllable in a playful kind of way. 'That's the impression I got of you yesterday. Bit of an action man?' There was the amiable sound of approval in her voice. I find flattery from a woman hard to resist.

'Thought any more about moving jobs?'

'I've an interview in the City this evening.'

'Fast worker.' I was impressed with Kirsty. In every sense.

'It's maternity cover. They sounded a bit desperate.'

'I ought to thank you for defending me to Sage. After your interview do you want to meet up so I can buy you a drink?' This was certainly what Rochelle would have branded as a clumsy pick-up line. But there was no hesitation when Kirsty replied:

'Yes. Why not?'

'That'd be great. You choose a venue. Text me the place.'

'And I can give you back your handkerchief,' she said. 'It's washed and ironed.'

We both laughed and I praised Kirsty's efficient house-keeping. I ended the call feeling upbeat but the next call completely reversed my mood.

It was MacIver.

'Were you at a hotel in Curzon Street yesterday evening?'

There was no point wasting time, so I said I was.

'You met a civil servant from Qatar called Nassir Hameed?'

'Yes.'

'He's made a complaint to the Foreign Office. Infringement of diplomatic immunity. Rude and threatening interrogation. Physical violence. Damage to hotel property.'

'Yeah. That's me,' I said. 'I followed the murderer to Hameed's hotel. He's in it up to his neck...'

'Wait a wee minute. You followed the murderer? You mean, you've found him? Have the police arrested him? Has he got the picture?'

Bollocks. I'd been thinking of Kirsty and forgotten I'd not updated MacIver on the whistling man.

'He's not been arrested yet. But he will be. As for Hameed and the hotel, the only physical bit was my shoe against his door. And, well... maybe just a bit more.'

'Kite!' MacIver's voice had that "See me afterwards" tone I remember from school. She wanted me in her office within the hour.

Chapter 13

'I'm not happy that you're keeping secrets from the police,' MacIver said just over an hour later. Clark and I were in her office and the low sun was reflecting blindingly off the dome of St Paul's. 'I don't want to be answering questions before a Select Committee after this man's committed an atrocity,' she said.

'It's to prevent an atrocity that I'm hanging back.' I said.

'But you've got absolutely no evidence of what he may be planning. And if it was something dreadful, that's surely a compelling reason to let the police handle it all.'

'I'm not stopping them.'

'But you're not helping them.'

'All I want is for the murderer to lead us to the picture. When we recover it we can stop whatever they're planning to do with it.'

MacIver closed her eyes and wrinkled her forehead but stayed sitting squarely and bolt upright at her desk. It wasn't a feet on radiator meeting.

'I'm trying hard, Kite,' she said, as her normally gentle Hebridean accent became more acid in tone, 'to imagine how anyone could use an obscure and fragile, five hundred year old painting of a boy in fancy clothes as a tool for criminal extortion, political corruption, corporate chicanery, international espionage, human trafficking, or the mass manipulation of people's minds. Let alone global terrorism or military action.'

She opened her eyes and fixed them back on me.

'It'll definitely be one of those you mentioned,' I said. My flippancy was a mistake.

'Not the time for humour,' said MacIver in a dour tone which seemed to carry echoes of her homeland. I had a vision of those islands where she was brought up where laughter and games would be banned on the Sabbath, when even going for a walk was frowned on.

'You followed the murderer yesterday. He didn't lead you to the picture. He led you into trouble.'

'He led me to someone who's at the centre of the whole plot.'

'Nassir Hameed, the man from Qatar?' MacIver aimed her big, brown, unblinking eyes at me. The reflected sun was now in my eyes. 'Qatar is one of the richest countries in the world,' she said. 'If they wanted to start their own national gallery they'd just pay in cash.'

I couldn't disagree.

'And you definitely saw the murderer – the man with the quaint wee voice – you definitely saw him meet Hameed?'

I nodded. I'd already described in detail what had happened the previous evening.

'What about the complaint to the Foreign Office?'

I had to angle my chair away from the sun. Had MacIver arranged the seating on purpose to dazzle me?

'My contact's dealing with it. He knows the background.' I'd spoken to Leo Somerscales after MacIver had called me. He was also digging up anything he could find on Hameed.

'And where does Scott Sage fit into things?'

'He's a vainglorious shit,' said Clark who had remained so quiet I'd almost forgotten he was in the room. Both MacIver and I swivelled sharply to look at him. Clark seldom judged people, rarely slagged them off.

'*Vainglorious*?' MacIver quirked her eyebrows.

'And the rest. But I can't see him killing,' Clark said.

'I agree. He's involved in some way and his so-called training academy near Heathrow needs more investigation. But he's not the main man.'

'What about the Bengali or Bangladeshi man?'

'Abid Bashir.'

'No way,' said Clark. 'Abid Bashir is an alias. It could be anybody.' Why was he being so negative? Had his essay on *Toy Story* not gone well?

'There must be a connection through all this. Trust me.' I held MacIver's gaze. We glared at each other, then she looked away, annoyed by my stubbornness

'What about the car? The Nissan Qashqai?' she turned to Clark.

'It was a rental,' said Clark, 'from an Avis depot in Shepherd's Bush. In the name of Roderick Lestrange.'

MacIver raised her eyebrows in despair at the obvious false name.

'Bellatrix Lestrange is a character in Harry Potter,' said Clark. 'Played by Helena Bonham Carter in the movie.'

'Wasn't Lestrange a character in Sherlock Holmes too?' said MacIver.

'That's *Lestrade*,' Clark said. 'Inspector Lestrade. He was in *The Hound of the Baskervilles* and a dozen other...'

'O.K. We'll have the seminar tomorrow,' said MacIver, cutting Clark off sharply and visibly cross with herself for getting entangled in his net of trivia. She turned to me.

'Kite. I can't tell you how uneasy it makes me that you have a tracker on a triple murderer's vehicle but haven't told the police. He must be arrested.'

Well, I wasn't hunky dory about it myself.

'He will be,' I said firmly.

'Aye, but when?'

'Soon,' I said.

I'd hesitated only momentarily but she'd noticed. 'That's no kind of answer,' she snapped.

In other circumstances I'd have taken just the same line as MacIver. I understood the dichotomy only too well but the green mist was swirling around, driving me in a different direction. MacIver saw something in my face which worried her and wrinkled her brow.

'Are you all right?' she said.

'Of course.'

She didn't look wholly convinced but she couldn't possibly understand what drove me, what haunted me. No one knew. I sometimes wasn't sure myself. Was it guilt or was it rage? A long time ago I'd done something which I shouldn't have done, but I'd done it for the right motives. It had all gone disastrously wrong and I didn't achieve what I wanted at all.

'I don't like issuing threats,' said MacIver.

'Then don't.'

She drew in breath. 'But if you don't pass the information to the police by this time tomorrow I'll phone DCI Bostock myself.'

I said nothing. MacIver stood up, looked glumly out of the window where the sun had now disappeared behind grey clouds, then turned back to me.

'Well, you'd better get back.'

I got up and walked towards the door but stopped as I heard:

'By the way... I like the new jacket.'

In spite of everything, her altogether lighter tone brought a half-smile to my face as I left. Stick and carrot, I suppose.

What was going on at Keats? I couldn't get that question out of my mind. And there was one person I wanted to discuss it with. If they'd let me. If I could find them. But I knew where they *ought* to be – if they were doing their job properly..

As usual, I walked down all eleven floors to the ground, went through reception and stood outside the main door of Maskelyne Global. I looked across the road. There were two coffee shops that seemed suitable locations, one to the left and one to the right.

I crossed the road, went into the first and checked the tables nearest the windows. She wasn't there.

I went into the second. And saw her immediately at a table right by the window. Rochelle Smith.

I'd checked up on her police background and it was cast iron. Her service had been short but surprisingly impressive. She'd come across as prickly and reluctant to share anything but I hoped much of her animosity was not genuine, but simply role-play.

Today she was dressed completely differently. The oversized hobo disguise had been replaced with a short dress, now clearly with a bra beneath. The dress was in a stylish 1960s style geometric print in black and white. Together with full make up and lips which were as glossy as a coat of Dulux she had something of the look of a Mary Quant model.

106

Rochelle wasn't classically beautiful, but her demeanour, the tilt of her nose, her high cheekbones, her luxuriant hair, the angle and colour of her eyes all contributed to make her excitingly sexy. I'd have thought she had all the looks to be a great actor.

'Late lunch?' I said to her as I went into the coffee shop, though I could see there was nothing except a bottle of Pellegrino in front of her.

'Go away,' she said, crossing her legs, turning away and gazing out towards the Maskelyne Global building I'd just left.

I sat down at her table. 'If I go away you'll have to get up and follow me. So I've come to you. To save you the effort.'

'You're too kind.'

'What are you today? Some kind of honey trap?'

She looked at me with disdain.

'Are you being purposely offensive?'

I'd meant it as a bit of a joke, even a compliment. But Rochelle didn't seem to want to establish a rapport. Didn't want to connect. Maybe she just didn't like me. Well, too bad. We ought to be working together.

'Well, you're obviously not under-cover today: not the androgynous waif in charity shop clothes.'

'We have a rota,' she said painstakingly. 'There are two of us. Different day, different duty.'

'Ah. The man outside my house must have been the guy on the bike in Northamptonshire.'

'No comment.'

'You can play different characters on different days. That should suit your drama school training. Did you ever do... what's it called? Rep theatre, where they do a different play each fortnight?'

She spun round towards me.

'You think I'm play-acting? Is that what it is?'

Her disdainful style was both irritating and tantalising, repellent and attractive. I couldn't stop prodding. Like when you've got a sore tooth and you can't stop touching it with your tongue.

'Isn't doing this obbo duty a bit beneath you? Particularly as you said yourself I'm not dangerous.'

Her eyebrows shot up. It was hard Rochelle again.

'This a new tactic? You've got tired of insults so you're moving on to flattery.'

'Well... I looked you up.'

'You needn't have bothered.'

'Good career ...While it lasted. I thought you'd be more... ambitious.'

I saw her reflect a moment, then she said, 'Ambitious for what?'

I realised that Rochelle often paused momentarily before replying. Like she was trying not to say the first thing she thought of. Or like she was following a script she hadn't learned properly.

'I've not come to insult you. I've come to ask your opinion.'

She raised her eyebrows.

'What on? Films? Theatre? Politics? I know nothing about football, by the way, but everyone else in the world seems to know plenty.'

'I want to run a name past you. India Paine. Ever heard of her?'

She uncrossed her legs, turned away from me to look out once again into the middle distance, then crossed her legs again and pulled her dress down.

'No. Sorry.'

'Are you sure? She's about your age.'

'It's an unusual name. And a pretty one, too. India, I mean, not the surname. I think I'd remember it if I'd met her.'

Her volubility convinced me she was lying. But her body language confused me. What was all the leg crossing about? Was she trying to flash her legs at me or trying to cover up? Some women in short dresses are forever tugging the hem down. I'm never clear if it's modesty or attention seeking.

'Isn't she the woman you're working for? Or did Scott Sage contract you directly?'

'I told you I wasn't working for his Keats business.'

'No. That's a separate outfit. Yasmine seems to be in charge down there. Did you have a meeting in the Goodwin's Court office? With Sage and India?'

Rochelle said nothing but grabbed her Pellegrino and took a swig. Then she shuffled in her seat and there was more crossing and uncrossing of legs and pulling her dress down.

She looked steadfastly out at the traffic.

'Let's assume what I said is right. And move on from there. You may be surprised to know I'd like your input. Because you're wasting your time traipsing around after me.'

She turned to say something but I interrupted.

'Let me tell you where I'm at. Apart from the murderer I mentioned yesterday I have two other suspects. One is Nassir Hameed, a civil servant from Qatar. I followed the killer yesterday evening to Hameed's hotel room in Knightsbridge. You'd already clocked off. If they were paying you properly you would have followed me there. Anyway, Hameed was at a dinner with Sage last night and also has a pass to the Keats building.'

'There was an Arab pulled out of the Thames this morning.'

'Right. But it wasn't Hameed. Perhaps someone at the same dinner though. The other man of interest is Abid Bashir.'

'Indian?'

'Bengali, Bangladeshi.'

She nodded.

'We've checked the PNC and all the usual databases. But I think he's off the radar.'

She turned round quickly again and undid her legs. I could get to like it. She had great legs.

'You're not in the Job. How do you access the PNC?'

I gave her a that's-my-business kind of look.

'Smug bugger! And you were slagging me off for copying my old warrant card.' She looked at me and for a moment there was a spark of warmth and light in her eyes, her lips formed an endearing smile and her face was radiant. A vision of a different Rochelle.

'Let me ask you something, Rochelle. Give me a serious answer: don't just throw another question back to me. What do you think's going on at Keats? Is it genuine? A training centre for PR interns?'

'That's what he said on the news.'

'Yes, but that's not the vibe you get when you go there. It feels... covert, under cover, a tatty building skulking next to that self-storage place. Look at MI6 – great flash building on the Thames, or GCHQ with its snazzy doughnut office in Cheltenham.'

She looked at me for a beat, then said. 'I see where you're coming from, but you can't make crime-solving decisions based on *architecture.*'

'Maybe you can.'

'What do *you* think's going on there?' She paused, realising what she'd said. 'Sorry. That's another question.'

I felt I was making progress and acknowledged her concession with a smile. 'Ever seen *The Truman Show*?' I said. 'The film where everything in a guy's life is entirely scripted and pre-fabricated. His entire existence is within a TV show.'

'I saw it. So what?'

'Imagine Keats PR is like that. Imagine the whole thing is a set-up, a front. When I went inside there were no customers, no people, just Yasmine guarding the entrance. It could have been a film set.'

'You went through the bins. Weren't they real?'

'They looked real but they could be set-dressing. With Sage's knowledge and skill it would look the same, wouldn't it? A perfect illusion. That's what he does, creates illusions of truth.'

This idea caught her interest. I saw her eyes darting around and sensed her rapidly reassessing what she'd observed. She turned back to me.

'If it's a front, what's he really up to?'

Our eyes met. I felt Rochelle was keen to know the answer.

What I'd been thinking was that black propaganda or *kompromat* is all the rage. The Russians have huge teams of people sequestered in prison-like factories churning out lies and spreading them round the internet. Likewise, no doubt, the Chinese and North Koreans and, increasingly, political parties in the west. What was Sage really doing with all those kids he wasn't paying? Working covertly for the Russians?

But, still holding her gaze, I smiled and said: 'I hoped you could tell me. And I can tell *you* it'll be far more interesting and productive to sort out Keats than to troll round the streets after me. Whatever Sage or India may have said to you. And if you're also looking for Alex Broughton I can tell you where he is and save you the bother.'

Her eyes were intense and fixed on mine. Then in an instant her mood changed. She swivelled away from me again, crossed her legs and looked steadily out of the window. I'd seen similar from accused men who were on the verge of opening up, naming names and giving statements. Suddenly they'd have second thoughts or their brief would say something to them and they would clam up.

'If you have any thoughts, give me a call,' I said.

I walked out of the café. She came to the door and watched me all the way along the pavement. But she didn't follow. Maybe it was her side-kick's turn to take over.

In any case it was time to change focus because I'd been neglecting Magda Butt. She knew the murderer – thought their relationship didn't seem exactly friendly – and she was somehow involved with Keats PR. I wanted to see what else was in her gallery apart from looted archaeology. I would have to break in. But before I broke in I would do a little recce.

After leaving Rochelle I went to Golborne Road. The Gallery was closed as I expected, there were no lights anywhere and the building again looked deserted and unloved. Two shops along was a little side street. I walked down and found it was a T-shaped, dead-end road that ran behind the gallery and other shops and gave access to their back doors or yards. The arm of the T that ran behind the gallery ended abruptly in the tall brick wall of a primary school playground. At the other end of the T was another wall sheltering a four-storey block of flats. It was one of those quirky bits of streetscape that London is full of. A road that leads nowhere and has no obvious function. Probably a relic of some ancient stable yard or close where privies and a water pump may have stood.

A gate from the dead-end street led directly into a tiny yard at the back of the gallery, scarcely large enough to hold rubbish bins. The gate was padlocked but it would be simple to climb over the six feet of waney-lap fencing.

Looking through gaps in the fence I could see two locks on the gallery's back door. A Yale-type and what was probably a 5-lever mortise. The fence round the yard would shield me while I worked to open them. I could also see the green LED of the intruder alarm inside the gallery for which Clark had promised to supply me with the engineers' test code.

I needed darkness for this escapade. More than darkness. I needed the local nightspots to be closed as well. So there was time for some R and R.

Kirsty had picked Ye Old Mitre in Ely Court as our meeting place – one of the venues where Jamie Rind and I had negotiated the finder's fee for the Amberger. Her interview was at five in Chancery Lane so she'd suggested we meet at six thirty. I walked down Hatton Garden and she came through Ely Place and we both arrived outside the pub at exactly the same time.

Kirsty had a new look. She still wore the law office uniform of jacket, blouse and skirt but had moved away from Primark and Matalan towards Zara or Reiss. Executive level. Her clothes were sharper, sleeker, more fitted. She'd also sensibly ditched the Converse trainers she wore at Rind and Buhler for some heels. Her hair and make-up had been spruced up as well.

'Nice interview clothes,' I said. And I meant it.

She struck a little pose.

'You think I scrub up OK?' she said with a smile.

I certainly did.

'City lawyers are fussy,' she went on. 'Especially since I'm going corporate, not criminal.'

'Been rushing round the shops?'

'A bit. It seemed a waste to buy good stuff at Rind and Buhler. Jamie never made an effort.'

Perhaps I'd been wrong about an affair.

'Very smart. Very legal.'

Very leggy, too. Standing side by side at the bar in her heels, she was only a couple of inches shorter than me. We thought about ordering two Dry Legal Aids in memory of Jamie, but decided to forego the soda.

'It was a lunchtime drink,' I said passing Kirsty her viognier. 'So they wouldn't get too pissed for the afternoon.'

'Right. And now it's get-some-in-before-the-train-home,' she said nodding at the inrush of office workers.

'How was the interview?'

'Went well, I think.' She crossed her fingers.

'Wouldn't you like to be a lawyer yourself?' I said. I was surprised she was still going for PA jobs.

'Trouble is once you start as a P.A. you get stuck. My degree's in psychology so I'd have to spend several years qualifying. And the years go by so fast.'

I gave her a scrutinising look. 'You're not thirty yet?'

'Next year.'

'There's still time. If you want it, you should go for it. Don't hold back. Follow your dreams.'

What was I on about? I was the last person to give career advice especially if it was to follow a personal yen. I'd abandoned my first love – architecture – and chosen a career for reasons of guilt and retribution. The fact that I wasn't half bad as a copper was a lucky bonus.

'Thank you for saying that. That's what I was thinking.'

Kirsty's viridian eyes sparkled at me. "Viridian" went well with her new upmarket look and her new look had made me say what she wanted to hear. And I'd hardly tasted my drink yet.

'What's your degree in?' she said.

'I don't have one. I started an architecture course at Bath but gave it up.'

'And went into the police?'

I nodded.

'That's a quantum leap. What's the story?'

'You sound like Scott Sage.'

'Pur...lease.' She smiled. 'But why the change of direction?'

'Oh...' I hesitated in a way that made it clear I wasn't keen to tell.

'Sorry. I don't want to pry.'

But there was no reason not to repeat my standby line.

'Both my parents died.'

'How awful. Oh, God. I shouldn't have asked.'

'Don't worry it was a long time ago. A car crash.'

'I'm so sorry. So with no one to pay the bills, you thought you'd better get a job rather than hang around at university for three years?'

'And to qualify as an architect it's another four years. But it was all a long time ago.' And I'd said enough about it so I made an abrupt change of subject.

113

'No more questions from Sage?'

She shook her head. That was a relief.

'Thank you for what you did.'

'No problem.' She looked studiously at her glass of wine and said quietly, 'If there's anything else you want me to do... I mean, I'd love to help get the picture back if I could.'

I got the message loud and clear. An offer I couldn't refuse.

But it was risky getting an outsider involved in a job just because you fancied them. Morally dubious even. But this job was such a can of worms any offers of help were not to be sniffed at.

That's my justification, anyway.

'Well, there's one thing... If you didn't mind?'

'Yes?' She looked at me eagerly.

'I'd like to know if Jamie had any clients from Bangladesh or an Arab state.'

The light in her face slowly dimmed. I'd disappointed her.

'Sorry. Were you expecting a Wonder Woman mission?'

'Not exactly...'

'There's always next week.'

She laughed. 'I can scroll through files if you want. How far back shall I go?'

'Five years? There's one name I'm searching for. Abid Bashir.'

The chances of linking this name to Jamie were remote. Infinitesimal. But it was the only name I had and I couldn't let it go. I had to run with it till something better came up.

'No trouble at all.' She quickly noted the name down in her usual efficient way. Then she began to rummage in her bag. 'Now it's your turn.'

She pulled out three cards in their cellophane wrapping. 'I bought these today on the way to the interview. For my brother's birthday. Like you he's into art, which I'm not really. So, which should I send him?'

The cards were all blank-inside prints of artists' work. But not the usual Renoir, Monet, Hockney kind. None were by well-known artists. There was a 1930s group of jolly ramblers in the Peak District, a neat and clever abstract after Bridget Riley and a quirky, stylised still-life involving an owl and a clock in the middle of a field, kind of Dali meets Magritte.

I laughed. 'Is this some kind of psychometric test? Like the ink-blots?'

'The Rorschach Test. No... no.' She laughed, too.

'Have to be careful of people with psychology degrees.' I gave her a joshing look and our eyes met. I don't think she needed any kind of test: she knew a fair bit about me already.

'I can never decide what he'd like. It's the kind of thing I'd have asked Jamie and you've got a very ... *understanding* kind of voice. So I thought I could ask you.'

Kirsty was happy to lay all her cards on the table. And I was excited she wasn't pussyfooting around.

'O.K. Here's my verdict. Analyse this... The abstract's smart, but a bit cold for a birthday. The one with the owl looks symbolic but I don't know what the message is. I'd go for the hikers. I guess you bought it because he likes hiking.'

Kirsty chewed her lip. I'd obviously got it completely wrong.

'He doesn't like hiking but he works in the Peak District. He's into bird-watching and is fond of owls. The abstract one has exactly the same greeny-grey colour he painted his sitting room.' She smiled. 'But thanks...'

'Thanks, but no thanks,' I said. 'There's a lesson there somewhere.'

Then Kirsty clapped a hand to her mouth.

'No. I've forgotten your handkerchief. I meant to bring it.'

'Doesn't matter. I'm sure we'll meet again.' God. Whatever happened to cool and casual? This wasn't like me at all.

Kirsty looked at me, her eyes melting. 'That would be great.'

I thought I'd better slow the tempo before she got in my car and we drove home together. I looked at my watch in a way she couldn't miss.

'Just to warn you... I've got to work this evening. So I'll have to make tracks in half an hour or so.'

Kirsty was back to her practical self.

'Yes, of course. What are you doing?'

'Well...' I started and paused.

'Or is it a case of: if you tell me you'll have to kill me?' she said with a big grin.

I laughed. 'Actually I need to search somewhere.'

'So you've got your warrant sorted out...'

I shook my head. 'Only the police or HMRC can do that. What I'm doing is breaking and entering.'

I thought Kirsty would be shocked. But I was wrong.

'Wow...,' she said. 'That's really exciting.'

And I saw what looked like awe on her face.

Kirsty and I parted with chaste little kisses on both cheeks but our arms lingered around each other's waists. Holding her felt good. She felt hot as well.

She said, 'Take care tonight,' as we parted. And it sounded like she meant it.

Chapter 14

It was much later that evening – gone eleven o'clock – before I returned to Golborne Road. I'd changed into the jacket with multiple pockets that I keep for special occasions. I was going equipped and needed to conceal my tools. Secreted in the jacket were: a torch, a quarter-size crowbar, my wallet of lock picks, a couple of screwdrivers, pliers, glass-cutter, a mini battery drill and a few other odds and ends that have come in handy in the past.

As it was, I was still too early.

Golborne Road was still jumping. Most of the shops had closed long ago but the Caribbean-African fruit and veg store was only just pulling its shutters down and bars were still serving. The street was busy with young men and women strolling home, loitering, kissing, drinking, dealing.

I drove back towards the heart of Notting Hill and found a parking space in Chepstow Gardens. This is multi-millionaire residents territory and no one was out and about here. I waited an hour and a half and just before one o'clock drove back to Golborne Road. The T-shaped road was jammed full of cars and vans so I parked on Golborne itself.

I walked round to the rear of the gallery and was over the wooden fence in seconds. Then I got to work on the backdoor. I've never graduated to combination lock safes but I'm reasonably proficient on door locks. It's mainly a question of a delicate touch and a steady hand. This one took fifteen minutes. Bit slow, I thought. But my electronic pick made short work of the tumbler lock.

I opened the door and stepped inside. At once the LED on the intruder alarm changed from green to amber and began to beep. I moved briskly to the control panel and entered the test code. The beeping stopped, the amber light disappeared and the green light returned, though now it was flashing. I wondered how long the alarm would remain out of action. There would have to be a fail-safe mechanism that stopped an engineer leaving the system in test mode for any length of time. I'd allow myself twenty minutes max.

The ground floor looked different from my first visit. Many items had been packed away in bubble wrap inside plastic storage boxes. Was Magda moving out? Closing down? Making a run for it?

Perhaps I was only just in time.

I went up the stairs to the first floor landing. There were three doors, two of them were wide open but the third which led up to the second floor was secured with another Yale. This third door looked seldom used so I ignored it and went into the first room. It was a stock room with archaeological antiques similar to those downstairs but of lesser quality.

The second room was more interesting. It was an artist's studio filled with paintings, some hanging, some on the floor leaning against the walls. There were both watercolours and oils in different styles but all were derivative. There were local impressionist views of west London, some bold bright landscapes which reminded me of the Scottish Colourists and some quasi cubist still-lifes after Braque or Leger. This was obviously Magda's work. She was a skilful painter but very much a copyist. All the pictures were signed with her initials MB within a circle.

Judging by the dust the paintings were easily twenty years old but there were a number of radically different new works. They'd all been produced digitally and I remembered from her c.v. that she was a leading exponent in making art with new technology.

I checked the time. I'd been in the gallery just nine minutes.

I'd come across cases where a valuable picture has been hidden behind another in the same frame. So I started to examine every picture, the old ones and the new digital ones. I took them off the walls or picked them up from the floor. I looked at their backs, checked the frames, the mounts and the stretchers. I found nothing.

Then I opened a big cupboard which held the usual detritus of an artist's studio but no sign of the Amberger.

I'd now been there sixteen minutes.

I sat down on an old swivel chair in front of a 1930s office desk and opened the drawers. They were empty except for blank sheets of the same gallery letterhead I'd first seen in the shot of the killer in the taxi.

Under the desk was a plastic waste-paper basket, full to bursting. I searched through it. There were old receipts, empty printer cartridges, a palette knife with a snapped-off blade, cardboard packaging, a torn padded envelope. But at the bottom there was something interesting: an airline luggage tag. It was inbound to London Heathrow and dated two months previously. Where had Magda been visiting? I got out my phone and searched for the flight number printed on the tag.

It was an Emirates flight from Abu Dhabi.

Then the lights were switched on.

I swivelled round in the creaky old office chair and there was Magda standing on the landing in nightdress and dressing gown.

'What are you doing?' she said. Her voice was surprisingly calm.

'I told you I specialised in recovering stolen art. I'm looking for a sixteenth century...'

'Painting by Amberger, yes. You won't find it here.'

'You told me you'd stopped painting.' I waved my hand at the digital images.

She shrugged. 'It's not painting.'

'It's still making art, isn't it?'

She reacted to what I said and looked away. I'd worried her. Was she involved in forgery? But nobody would want to forge the Amberger picture.

'What's with all the packing cases downstairs? Are you selling up?'

She scoffed in an I-should-be-so-lucky way. 'Antiques fair at Kempton Park. I still have to try to sell stock.'

'Even though your partner has disappeared.'

'Yes.'

'If you want him back why don't you tell me about it.'

'I can't.'

'What's your relationship to Nassir Hameed?'

'What?'

119

'I saw him taking you into Keats PR yesterday.'

'I can't tell you.'

'What about the man whose picture I showed you... Does he have some sort of hold over you as well?'

She said nothing.

'What's his name? The man in the photo.'

She looked straight at me. 'I don't know.'

I stared back at her.

'That's the truth. I don't know his name. Nor anything much about him.'

'Where's your husband?'

She looked at me for a long moment before answering. 'I don't know that either.'

'He's being held somewhere? By the man in the photo?'

She turned away and refused to answer.

'What's he trying to do with the picture? Why is it worth killing people to get it?'

She just shook her head.

'If you tell me the truth I can help you,' I said. This was a sentence I'd used many times before. I'd said it to suspects being interviewed, to criminals being threatened by godfather figures and to victims of abuse. I always tried hard to sound convincing, but to my despair, the person I was talking to often thought I was bullshitting.

Magda felt the same.

'You'd better go,' she said.

Wa-wa-wa-wa-wa-wa-wa-wa...............

An ear-splitting din from the intruder alarm. The engineer's test-mode had run its maximum allotted time and the system had defaulted to emergency.

'Who's got in?' Magda looked terrified.

'Don't worry, it's only...'

But she darted into the room full of antique stock then came out grasping a vicious wooden club, the kind of thing Polynesians may have killed Captain Cook with, and disappeared downstairs.

I pocketed the airline tag and followed her.

She had already established there was no one in the basement or ground floor and was re-setting the intruder alarm.

'You did this?' she said.

I nodded.

'Get out!' She raised her club.

I could've disarmed her. Then tried to talk her round. But I'd searched the property and found nothing. There seemed little point in fighting a sixty year old woman who was determined to stay silent. It was two o'clock in the morning. Maybe she'd feel more talkative in the daytime.

I put one of my cards on top of an altar stone from a Roman temple.

'I can help you,' I said again. 'Call me.' I moved to the door, then turned. 'How long have you slept on the top floor?'

'Only since he went,' she said.

I went out of the backdoor and she locked it behind me. Then I climbed back over the wooden fence. As my feet touched the pavement a car's headlights were switched on full beam.

I was blinded.

I couldn't see who the driver was, how many people were in the car, or even what make of car it was.

It was stopped in the centre of the narrow dead-end road with parked vehicles either side of it. I was effectively blocked in between it and the brick wall of the school. Should I try to run past the car? Whoever was in it would certainly stop me. Behind me, the school wall was now perfectly illuminated by the headlights. It was maybe three metres high. If I could get over that I'd be safe. Unless the people in the car were fit and agile they wouldn't be able to follow. Unless the people in the car had guns. Or Polynesian throwing clubs.

I waited a moment. But it seemed pointless to start a conversation. Those in the vehicle must have bad intent. I could make out that both car doors were shut. Which meant those inside would lose a few seconds in getting out in the confined space.

Time to go time.

I turned and ran towards the wall at top speed, then jumped, launching myself as high as I could. My fingers got a grip on the brick coping course. The wall had recently been re-pointed and the brickies had used too much mortar. There was a definite ridge between each course of bricks and my toes found holds on the pointing. My fingers pulled me up and I got a good grip on the far side of the wall. In a couple of seconds my elbows were on top, levering up the rest of my body.

Then I heard footsteps on the road below. But it wasn't at all what I expected.

It was the click-clack of heels.

And a voice I recognised.

'Kite! Stop pissing about. Come down and get in the car.'

Rochelle Smith. Now in a red sweater, tight jeans and boots.

Chapter 15

I didn't move. Why had Rochelle followed me here? And offering help didn't fit at all with her spiky character. The ice had begun to melt earlier but, when I suggested we work together, the temperature had dropped again. She'd fooled me with her funny walk: was this all a performance?

'Are you alone?' I said.

Rochelle's response was immediate.

'Were you expecting someone else?'

'Where's your side-kick?'

'He's not my side-kick. He's... Oh, never mind him. Look, I'm impressed with the commando stuff. But you'll get a sore bum sitting up there all night.'

I was about to reply when I saw the flash of a detonation from the block of flats at the far end of the cul-de-sac. A split-second later I heard the sound of a rifle shot and the noise of the bullet smashing into the wall a foot from my thigh. Half a brick disintegrated along with a chunk of new pointing. The shot was wide and low.

Then Rochelle screamed. It wasn't an actor's scream.

That decided me.

I leapt off the wall as another shot went to where my body had been half a second earlier.

I hit the ground and saw Rochelle moving quickly to the side of the road, out of range of her own car's headlights. I followed her.

We crouched in the gutter behind a Land Rover Defender, hoping its high profile and tougher bodywork meant it could live up to its name.

'What the fuck's going on?' she said. She was tense, alert and serious. There was no pretence, no affectation, no posing.

'That's what I wanted to ask you. Why are you here?'

'Rescuing you by the look of it.'

'The gunman's not with you, then? Not the person you're working for?'

Her head whipped round and she glared. 'Shut up with the stupid remarks or I won't get you out of this.'

'Get me out of this? You helped to get me into it. Lighting me up like I was the star turn on stage.'

'I wanted to attract your attention, that's all.'

'Why not just hoot or something?'

'I didn't want to wake the neighbours.'

'Jesus.'

I wondered if Rochelle was always annoying. Even in life and death situations.

Then after a moment I felt a touch on my arm. The pressure was light, almost nervous, but new behaviour for Rochelle. I turned to her and her expression was one I hadn't seen before. She looked contrite.

'I thought about what you said. About the Keats place being so secretive. Like a front or film set. I'm sure you're right.'

She smiled at me.

'You're agreeing with me?' I said. 'You're on my side? Not chasing me on behalf of Sage, or India Paine?'

Her smile vanished. 'Yeah, well don't go on about it or I might change my mind.'

There had been no shots for a couple of minutes. We both peered cautiously round the Land-Rover in the direction of the gunman.

'Do you think he's got a night-vision scope?' Rochelle whispered.

'Certainly.'

'Then putting my headlights on would've screwed it up. That's why his shot went wide. So I think I could have saved you. So you could say thanks.'

I was so surprised I said nothing. Rochelle kept surprising me.

'If we can get to my car, I can get us out.'

I looked at her.

'What's your plan?'

'I'll drive.'

'What else?'

'I'll drive fast.'

'That all?'

'Do you want to sit in this gutter all night? We crawl up behind these parked cars until we've got beyond my car and out of the light. Then we make a dash. My door's open, yours isn't. My key's in the ignition.'

It seemed kind of crazily simple. But I looked at Rochelle and there was a confidence in her face that convinced me. For the first time I understood how she could be an effective and resourceful police officer and PI. Though probably always a kooky one.

'Ready then?' she said.

I nodded and we began to crawl slowly along the narrow pavement, keeping very low and in the shadows. I was suddenly aware of the silence in this usually noisy part of London. So early in the morning there were no buses, no tubes and little traffic to cover the faint sound of our movement. There was a faint clink from one of the tools in my jacket, an almost imperceptible rasping from Rochelle's denim jeans as she moved and the sound of our own steady breathing. In our tense state everything seemed unusually loud – like dead giveaways – even though they were not. Then there was a plasticky rattle from an empty food container blown along by the breeze and a shrill shrieking from a cat or maybe a rat. I saw Rochelle flinch, pause, then breathe out as she realised it was only an animal.

Then we were level with the rear of her car. We squeezed through a gap between an old Honda Civic and a Dacia Duster and crouched in the road.

'Ridiculous name,' Rochelle said in a whisper, nodding at the car.

Her own was almost within touching distance. It was a Porsche 718.

Then she grabbed my arm. More firmly than before. A brave new Rochelle.

'Go when I squeeze your arm.'

I heard her breathing deeply then she gave my arm a sharp squeeze and I was off. I scuttled round the back of the car, opened the door and I was into the seat within three seconds.

There was a shot and I saw the windscreen of a Mini disintegrate.

With a shorter distance to travel, Rochelle was already in the car. The lights were off and the engine was running. The car leaped backwards at what seemed forty miles an hour and I was thrown forwards into the dash. Rochelle then slammed the brakes on, spun the wheel and accelerated fast forwards. Back I went against the seat.

As we stormed out of the tiny dead-end road I saw a figure emerge at speed from the block of flats. I only had a split-second glimpse but it was enough to see the shiny surface of a grey bomber jacket illuminated briefly by Rochelle's headlights and to see the rifle the man was holding. It was the vocally challenged killer of Jamie Rind.

Rochelle was doing fifty miles an hour as we screeched into Golborne Road and was still accelerating. We bumped over a hump-back railway bridge and she took a sudden right, the rear end sliding away but she controlled it perfectly and we lost no speed. At a T-junction she went left in another controlled slide, then filtered left again into Harrow Road. We were doing sixty-five in a thirty zone.

'Watch the cameras,' I said.

'I know where they are.'

A buzzing was coming from somewhere.

'What's that noise?'

'Put you seat belt on.'

I fastened my belt and the buzzing stopped.

'Any one chasing?' I said.

'Don't think so.'

'Better zig-zag to make sure.'

Rochelle looked unsure for the first time that evening. 'Really?'

'Frightened of getting lost?'

I said it as a joke but her reaction told me she actually *was*. After bossing the escape so competently she'd gone all blonde and girly.

'I'll tell you where to go.'

She gave me a look.

'Next left.'

To my surprise, she immediately followed my instructions, sliding the car neatly round into a side street and accelerating to sixty again.

'Second right.'

The squealing tyres woke residents as she took the right-angle turn with ease.

'There's a T-junction at the end. Go right, then immediately sharp left.'

She did so. Her left hand moving perfectly from gear stick to wheel and back again. Her feet perfectly in rhythm, sometimes stabbing, sometimes caressing the pedals.

'Where are we going?' she said as she floored the throttle through Maida Vale.

'You'll see. Under the railway bridge then second left.'

Her headlights surprised an urban fox scoffing the remains of a take-away.

'Then next right... Then third right... Then slow down.'

'Why?'

'This is your street. Number fifty three, isn't it?'

She came to a halt outside a house in Willesden.

'It's thirty five actually. Big head.'

She checked the mirror for a final time.

'No one's followed us,' she said.

'Good work,' I said, turning and giving her a grateful look. I was genuinely impressed. 'Thank you for getting me out a hole.'

'No probs,' she said, acting as if this was the way she usually spent her evenings. 'Shall I get you a taxi?' It was like we'd just been down to the shops. I thought a cup of coffee at least might be in order.

'There's one problem. My house keys are in my car. Outside the gallery. I didn't want to weigh myself down with extra stuff when I was breaking and entering.'

This information seemed to disconcert her. I heard her swallow.

'I suppose you want me to ask you to sleep here?'

I looked at her but she was staring straight ahead through the windscreen. I saw the same emotional disconnect I'd seen in the café.

'Define "sleep here".'

'There's a sofa in the sitting room or you can have Emily's room. She's at her boyfriend's. But she may not have changed the sheets for a few weeks.'

'Either would be delightful.'

Rochelle seemed relieved I was happy with that arrangement. We went into her flat and she showed me the bathroom and Emily's room, which did pong a bit, and then made some coffee. I flopped on to the sofa in the sitting room and Rochelle produced a bottle of Lagavulin single malt.

'It's a smoky one,' she said.

'I like smoky.'

She poured a couple of doubles.

'I didn't think you'd ever worked in Traffic,' she said. 'I mean, all this turn left turn right stuff. Or were you a taxi driver?'

'I just have a sixth sense. A personal satnav hard-wired into my hippocampus.'

'Sounds painful... Though I guess it could be useful.'

'And where did you learn to drive like that? Police driving course?'

'Nah. It was Drama School really. Sort of.'

I look puzzled.

'Go on.'

Rochelle groaned. 'You don't want a full c.v. do you?'

'Tell me a bit. I'm interested.'

This seemed to surprise her.

'Are you?' she said.

'Well, yes.'

That seemed to please her.

'I've always liked cars,' she said. 'I breezed through the driving test after three lessons from Dad, then did an Advanced Test. I did skid-pan courses and training days at race circuits. Then, when I was at Drama School, I needed to earn some money so I talked myself on to a film as a trainee stunt driver. The hairy-arsed stunt co-ordinator seem to like what I did...'

I raised my eyebrows in a teasing sort of way.

'Not like that.' She grinned. 'But soon I was spending as much time stunting as studying. There was one shoot where I fractured a wrist and Dad said I'd end up like Evel Knievel if I wasn't careful.'

'The guy who used to jump his motorbike over rows of buses?'

'Yeah. He broke so many bones he was held together by bolts'.

'Like Frankenstein.'

Rochelle smiled. As she did so she looked incredibly attractive and not at all how I imagined a stunt woman to look. Though the more I think about it I don't have any kind of mental image of a female stunt person. But Rochelle excelled at not conforming to type. Always coming on as something of a rebel. This was part of her attraction and part of her irritation quotient. Yet deep down I think she was more conventional than she pretended.

Then her smile faded and she looked incredibly serious. She asked me who I thought was trying to kill me and I told her who I'd seen emerging from the flats.

'All that climbing and jumping. You've not made much progress.'

'I thought being shot at was a good sign. Proves I'm on the right track.'

Rochelle made a tutting sound and gave me a don't-be-so-stupid look.

'Don't swagger,' she said. 'Apart from anything else, it's dangerous.'

It might have been MacIver talking to me. But she was right. Rochelle's mind was as sharp as her tongue. And I was annoyed with myself. I hadn't earned any bragging rights on this job yet. Unconsciously I was doing what she'd accused me of doing when we first met – trying to chat her up. Truth was I was pleased – and relieved – that Rochelle was on my side. The relief had gone to my head. Or maybe it was the Lagavulin.

'Anyway, tell me why you came to the Gallery. And how you knew I was there.'

'What you said about Keats PR was ... intriguing. So I went back there this afternoon. Spoke to the café guy. He was useless. Then I went into reception and chatted to Yasmine. Talked about PR. Talked about clothes. Talked about shopping. Something she said made me think she's from the Emirates.'

'Why?'

'She said something odd about not liking Harrods.'

I couldn't see the connection.

'Harrods is owned by the Qatar Investment Authority. They bought it off Al-Fayed. If she was from the UAE she'd have a natural dislike of going there. And did you see the taser behind reception?'

Shit. I hadn't.

'That decided me. Then I just tracked your phone. I've got all the kit.'

'I'm glad you did.'

She waved away my thanks. She didn't seem to want compliments or personal remarks. The ice was rapidly thawing but spring hadn't arrived yet.

'I followed you because you think I'm some ditzy klutz...'

I tried to protest.

'You do. So... I wanted to show you I wasn't.'

'I reckon you achieved your aim,' I said, starting to feel that I was the klutz. How did I miss seeing the taser?

'Anyway, I want to talk about you rather than me,' she said abruptly. And then looked surprised at what she'd said. I couldn't tell if it was a challenge or a threat. 'You pay money to criminals, don't you, so they'll give back stolen pictures?'

'It's a negotiated settlement.'

'You buy back loot from the people who've stolen it.'

'It's not always from the robbers themselves. Art's become a commodity among criminals. Pictures get swapped for jewels, drugs, weapons.'

'Surely doling out cash encourages more art thefts.'

'Any money insurers offer is only about ten percent of the market value. Criminals settle because they know they can't sell pictures openly.'

'You're still rewarding them.'

I'd heard this argument many times before and it was difficult to rebut convincingly.

'Because artworks are a currency, if we get just one picture back it helps diminish the pot that criminals have to play with. It's important to save what art we can. Sometimes criminals get frustrated because they can't sell a picture and just burn it. Rescuing it is like rescuing a kidnap victim.'

'That's sweet,' said Rochelle. I gave her a look. I don't think she meant to be insulting.

'There's also a more philosophical argument...'

'Bit late for philosophy. But go on.'

I hesitated a moment. I find it hard to express complex emotions in words and I'm not a deep thinker. But I had to try to explain to Rochelle the feelings that underlie what I do.

'Well... if I said that every piece of artwork is unique and each work contributes in its own small way to our total cultural experience, to a huge catalogue of expressions of human feeling, to the record of our very existence and that catalogue, that record, needs to be preserved for future generations – if I said that you might think I'm a pretentious wanker, but it's true. And it's what I believe.'

There was a silence while she looked at me. Then she turned away and nodded, as if to herself. Had I got my message across?

'Your motives are certainly principled. And moral. And not pretentious. Nor wanky.'

'Thank you.' I seemed to have passed some kind of test.

'You better have another.' Rochelle poured another double into my glass and then sat down right next to me on the sofa.

That was a big surprise.

Then she said, 'Now I've cleared up the art side, tell me why you changed your name?'

That was an even bigger surprise.

'That's an interesting question,' I said, as if it was all a puzzle.

'Don't pretend you don't know what I'm talking about. Acting's not your strong point.' She was right about that, too. 'As you thought, I was hired by India Paine to track down someone called Alex Broughton. India is a journalist and went to Sage with a story to sell. He was interested but wanted more. Told her to hire a PI to dig around. She got my name off Google. I've never met Sage and don't know anything about what he does.'

'What's India Paine's angle?'

'No idea.' She paused and turned to face me. 'But I'm sure you're Alex Broughton.'

I didn't react.

'Before you joined the police there's no record whatsoever of anyone your age called John Kite. You fit the Broughton profile exactly. So the only conclusion is you've changed your name.' She looked at me with a QED kind of look.

I'd been fearing this moment for the last fifteen years. At first I was continually nervous about my identity being uncovered. Then as years went by my anxiety receded. Until I'd almost forgotten I was ever Alex Broughton. Astonishing that Rochelle had been relentless enough, or interested enough to suss the truth.

I nodded towards Rochelle and made a games-up kind of gesture.

'Why did you change your name?'

'The name annoyed me. With its silent "g". No one ever knew how to pronounce it, let alone spell it. I got Brawton, Bruffton, Browton...'

Rochelle gazed at me doubtfully.

'It's all very well for you to be disbelieving. Your name's Smith. No one's going to have trouble with that.'

'What did your parents think about it?'

'Nothing at all. They'd both died.'

Rochelle was taken aback. 'I'm sorry. Was it cancer?'

I shook my head. 'They were both killed on the M1. Police thought my Dad had probably fallen asleep at the wheel. They had a brand new Jaguar XJ, almost certainly going too fast. They hit a bridge support near Newport Pagnell and some poor ambulance crew had to scrape them off the tarmac.'

'How old were you?'

'Eighteen. Just left school.'

'Brothers? Sisters?'

I shook my head. 'No aunts or uncles either.'

'Poor orphan Kite. All alone in the world so he joined the police to find a family.'

Her tone was partly mocking but also partly sympathetic.

'No. It wasn't like that. Not at all.' It just came out. I couldn't help it.

My instant reaction piqued her interest and she turned round again to face me directly.

'Skeletons in the cupboard? I thought this name-nobody-could-pronounce stuff was hokum.'

She moved closer to me and looked hard into my eyes. Then in a voice that was soft and sensuous said, 'What were you trying to do? Ditch a criminal record?'

She was joshing of course but there was what seemed a seductive smile on her glistening lips. I looked at her sparkling wide eyes, smelled the peaty tang of the malt whisky on her breath and also the floral notes from her perfume. I looked down at her breasts, jutting through the tight sweater, her slim thighs in the denim. I didn't want to talk about my past. What I really wanted to do was take her in my arms, kiss her deeply, then rip her clothes off.

I put a hand on her leg and moved my mouth towards hers while my other hand laid gently on her back. She immediately sprang up.

'Kite! Stop that. That wasn't the deal. That wasn't the deal at all.'

Once again Rochelle had surprised me.

I sat back in the sofa and wondered how I had misread the signals. Or was it that Rochelle had done another U-turn? She was a real shape-shifter. I don't know why she hadn't succeeded as an actor.

Chapter 16

At seven-thirty next morning I was wrapping a towel around myself to go to the bathroom when there was a knock on the door of Emily's room and Rochelle came in wearing a nightdress and carrying a black bin liner.

'Brought you some clothes,' she said, dumping the bag on the end of the bed. 'An old boyfriend left them. He was the same kind of size as you. Take what you want and give the rest to a charity shop. They're all clean.'

I was seeing sides of Rochelle's character which I'd not imagined before. 'Thank you,' I said. 'And congratulations.'

'What?' She looked surprised.

I walked over to Emily's dressing table which was so extraordinarily messy it was like it had been designed that way. Like Tracey Emin's Bed. There was tangled jewellery, half-used cotton wool, hair sprays, an extensive collection of eaux de parfum and enough make-up to stock a small branch of Superdrug.

From among the mess I pulled out the invitation I'd found the previous night.

An invitation for Rochelle's wedding.

'He's a lucky man, your fiancé,' I said, holding up the traditional printed stiff card sent from Rochelle's parents to house-mate Emily.

'Emily never puts anything away,' she sniffed.

'Is he a copper, your bloke?'

'Not bloody likely.'

'Are these his?' I pointed to the clothes.

Rochelle shook her head. 'A long time ago man.'

'Getting rid of the evidence before he moves in?'

She didn't react to this but stood in front of me, pensive, and seemed to be staring at my bare upper body. Or maybe she was still half-asleep. In any case she was unembarrassed about giving me a good view of her breasts through the thin cotton of her nightdress.

'I'm sorry if I was... brusque last night.'

'It was my fault,' I said. 'I shouldn't have... If I'd known...' I pointed to the wedding invitation.

'Well, maybe I shouldn't have...' There was a pause.

Shouldn't have asked me to stay? Shouldn't have encouraged me?

'Maybe I shouldn't have... probed so much,' she said. Then she gave an embarrassed sort of smile and turned to leave the room.

'What are you doing today? Reporting back on me?' I said.

She nodded. 'I guess. I've done what they asked. Found you. So I'll put my invoice in.'

'So I won't have you on my tail any longer? Case closed?'

'Unless she wants more.' Rochelle gave me a long look. 'You never told me who she is.'

'I never said I knew her.'

Rochelle smiled. 'Come off it. She knows you. There's either some planet-sized scandal in your past she wants to expose, or else...'

'Or else?'

'She's your wife and she wants to get even. Or get your money.'

I'd got used to hearing India's name over the past days and no longer reacted.

'You may think that. I couldn't possibly comment.'

Rochelle made a caustic face. 'Piss off with your tired old quotations. If you won't tell me, I've got some matrimonial cases I need to get cracking on. See you around.'

And she was out of the room before I could say anything else.

I went through the bag of clothes and saw at once that Rochelle's ex, presumably like her fiancé, wasn't short of money. The underwear was almost new Calvin Klein, there was a John Smedley jumper and the shirts had an assortment of good labels including Ede and Ravenscroft who are legal and academic specialists. That convinced me the ex must be a lawyer. Probably specialising in some arcane but profitable area: intellectual property, patents or copyright. The polar opposite of Jamie Rind.

I've no problem with hand-me-downs. The Calvin Kleins fitted perfectly and so did one of the shirts – a jolly red, blue and white stripe, no doubt the lawyer's weekend wear.

I let Rochelle use the bathroom first and by the time I'd showered and dressed she'd disappeared, leaving only a spicy, tangy scent of make-up and perfume in the air.

I got a taxi back from Rochelle's to pick up my car, drove into the City, left it once more in the forty pounds a day multi-storey and started up the stairs at Maskelyne Global.

I came out of the staircase on to the eleventh floor just as MacIver was getting out of the lift. We said good morning and began to move away then MacIver turned back.

'Did you walk all the way up?' she said.

'Yes, and I'm surprised you don't,' I said. 'Be good training for the Munros. That is your hobby, isn't it?'

She nodded and seemed to be thinking about what I'd said. 'I'd have to bring a change of shoes, though,' she said, looking down at her usual smart heels, and walked off.

I watched her go.

One of the most telling things I'd been told about MacIver came from a guy who did similar things to her. He's called Charlie Duchamp and I've done a couple of art recovery jobs for him. He's based in Geneva and I'd better explain he was a geologist before going into insurance. He told me MacIver came from the Isle of Lewis and that part of the Hebrides has a kind of granite called Lewisian Gneiss – another silent "g" in case you didn't do geology – and he said the name described MacIver perfectly. Hard as rock, but nice as well. I liked that. And he was right.

In my office I called Leo Somerscales, now back in London. He did his usual thing of calling me back on a secure landline.

The Qatari complaint about my treatment of Nassir Hameed had been smoothed away with some diplomatic flim-flam. Hameed was previously unknown to intelligence agencies but after I'd alerted everyone to his meeting with a killer Leo told me that 'a file has been opened.'

'Is that all?'

'Of course not. I speak metaphorically.'

'What have you got on him?'

'Not much. He's unmarried. No known addictions, perversions, bad habits. Career civil servant. On the face of it as clean as a whistle but after your little contretemps we traced his bank account: suspiciously large balance for someone so junior. Pretty sure it's not drugs but no idea where the cash is coming from. So his file's just got a bit bigger.'

'Anyone tailing him?'

'After he met you he moved out of the hotel...'

'Into the Embassy?'

'Yes. So he's pretty much untouchable there. We've gone back over exactly how he came to be in the UK as part of this trade delegation and frankly it's muddled. We had a request he be included in the party but no one can trace where the request came from. He's in the Ministry of Culture and Sports and has no trade interests whatsoever. But HMG weren't too fussed, friendly nation, good export market etc., etc. Nobody vetted him too closely and someone green-lit his inclusion.'

'What's his job in the Ministry?'

'Something to do with the Doha Theatre Festival.'

'Not part of the World Cup organisation?'

'They set up a separate outfit for that. With a grandiloquent name. It's called the Supreme Committee for Delivery and Legacy. But Hameed's not involved.'

'What about the guy in the Thames?'

'In a way even more interesting. Jamal Ahmed is a freelance security agent. A mercenary. We've not encountered him in London before and we're not entirely sure what he was doing here. But some years ago he was involved in tracking one of those Princesses who absconded from Dubai.'

I remembered the story. An independent-minded daughter of the ruler of Dubai got tired of her life of glamorous isolation and tried to leave the country against her father's wishes. She made secret preparations, hired a yacht and a skipper but was tracked and brought back. Presumably to life imprisonment inside a magnificent palace.

'So are you thinking... he's searching for someone in London, but his target was tipped off and eliminated Ahmed before he could strike.'

'That's credible. But we have no clues as to any target. But I have to ask, John... What the hell's all this got to do with art?'

'My boss was asking me something similar,' I said.

And with a wave of guilt I checked the time. When was I supposed to tell Bostock about the killer? I realised I'd forgotten. Stuff it. It didn't matter.

'The last name on the list, Leo. Anything on Abid Bashir?'

I could sense Somerscales looking at his watch, wondering when he could get back to his day job. Donating to charitable funds was all very well, but Somerscales personally wasn't on the payroll. I relied on his goodwill. A delicate balance I didn't want to upset.

'Apologies if I'm pushing too hard, Leo.'

'I don't mind, but I'm due at Number Ten fairly soon. So briefly: Bashir is an alias. He's better known to us as Fawaz Menon though that may not be his real name either. He first came to notice twenty or so years ago. We have video of him addressing a rally in Dubai.'

A rally? Criminals don't usually address political meetings.

'Bashir – or Menon – was a construction worker. He was trying to organise other labourers into some sort of trade union. Hopeless task of course in the Gulf. All the heavy lifting – literally – is done by immigrant labour and they're mostly treated like shit. He was on our radar as an activist for some years then disappeared. We assumed he was in prison. Or had met with some accident.'

'Like falling off a tall building?'

'Exactly. If he's still alive and you come across him you'll see he's missing the top half of one of the fingers on his right hand.'

'That's brilliant, Leo. Great. I'll let you go, now.'

The call ended.

Gus's deceased carpet dealer Bashir was presumably someone quite different from this would-be trades unionist. But was the man who phoned Dr Hugill the political activist or another person entirely? If it was the same man what connected a Dubai construction worker to a blood-thirsty art theft?

All I knew was I was even more convinced now that the *Portrait of a Young Merchant* was at the centre of some international plot.

Then my phone bleeped: it was the tracking app. A pleasant surprise. I'd thought the battery had died or the device had been found and disposed of. The whistling man's Qashqai hadn't moved the previous night yet he had me in his sights in Golborne Road. He obviously had help and transport. Maybe the Qashqai was kept for special jobs. If he was driving it now perhaps something serious was going down. I hurried to pick up my car from the multi-storey and set off in pursuit.

The Qashqai was moving south west from the business park. He was only about twelve miles ahead of me but I had to travel right across London. The worst kind of journey. An hour's driving time for most people but I had to do it much more quickly.

I relished the challenge and used every short cut, every rat run, every taxi-driver's secret snicket. I avoided traffic lights, notorious bottle-necks, routes I knew to be congested. My zig-zag, roundabout route was clocking up the miles but it was clock time I was concerned about. The whistling man had taken a big sweep around Heathrow and on westwards through Twickenham. Here he seemed to get lost and double-backed on himself. By the time he was heading towards Kingston I was already south of the Thames near Richmond and catching him fast.

He went beyond Kingston but he, or his satnav, made some bad choices around Hampton Court and I could see he was stuck in heavy traffic. I thought he was heading for the M3 but he wasn't.

He came to a stop at Kempton Park racecourse.

Where Magda was trying to sell her looted antiques.

I arrived at Kempton Park only twenty minutes after he did. The racecourse has a regular antiques fair with hundreds of dealers operating from stalls inside the stands and outside on a huge tarmacked area. The place was crowded with cars, trucks, people and of course antiques, vintage stuff and old junk.

I parked and went to look for the Qashqai.

I found the car easily, but the whistling man was not inside.

139

Stuart Doughty

I scanned the crowds. There were professional dealers, serious collectors, people having a day out. I really needed Rochelle and five others to search the crowds. Even then he could evade us.

Assuming he'd come to contact Magda I started by looking for her. At least dealers were stationary by the stalls, not milling around. Problem was there were so many dealers. I moved as fast as I could but I got frustrated fighting through the bargain hunters and browsers. Then I found myself where many of the dealer's vehicles were parked: a sea of Transits, Lutons, Combos and Berlingos.

Then I saw him.

My target was walking among the vehicles, checking registration plates. Once again his manner was untroubled and he wasn't looking around or making any checks for observers. His pace was neither fast nor slow, but he had an intensity about him. He was on assignment again.

His interest was taken by an elderly, white Transit. He checked the plate against details on his phone and seemed satisfied. He tried all the doors and found them locked. Then he bobbed down to the ground and I lost sight of him for a few seconds. But was out of vision for too short a time to have tampered with the vehicle.

He came away from the Transit and walked more briskly now to the area of public parking. He walked past his own car, past my car and came to the edge of the huge parking lot where he made for a top of the range Lexus. As he got near the car its door opened and the driver stepped out holding a green and gold Harrods bag. The whistling man took it and nodded but no words were exchanged.

I got some shots of the Lexus and its driver then followed the killer again. I assumed he would go back to the Transit, but he didn't. He returned to his own car, putting the Harrods bag on the front passenger seat.

What was going on?

I sent registration details to Clark and he got me the owner's details within seconds. The Transit was indeed owned by the Butt-Ansari Gallery and the upmarket Lexus by a company called the Gulf Financial Settlement Ltd.

I made some rapid assumptions.

First: Magda was in danger. Second: the Harrods bag wasn't the killer's picnic lunch. Third: the chauffeur would be working for Hameed, or if not him then Fawaz Menon.

I asked Clark to chase down the company ownership.

Clark huffed and puffed. MacIver had lots of fraud investigations ongoing. He didn't think he had time. It could take all afternoon. Longer. He was going out in the evening.

Clark always wanted you to know how in demand he was, how privileged you were to have him researching for you. This wasn't due to pride or arrogance, but the reverse. He was full of self-doubt. He was a brilliant researcher but introverted and reserved. He needed constant reassurance.

I told him he was so skilful he would sort it out quickly, with just a few mouse clicks. Then he said:

'You know flattery, like tipping, is a way of oppressing the servant classes.'

Was he joking? Was he serious? Was he quoting Marx? I didn't know and didn't ask. I simply asked him to squeeze my request in when he was able.

The whistling man was sitting in his car and I took out binoculars to see what he was doing. He was bending over the passenger seat fiddling with what I assumed was the contents of the Harrods bag.

I walked round the car park without taking my eyes off the Qashqai. I completed a circuit but the man was still inside the car.

I made another long-range circuit of the car park. Buyers and browsers were starting to leave the fair, parking spaces near the Qashqai were emptying and the whistling man's car was becoming isolated.

I raised my binoculars again to search out Magda's Transit. It was still parked and Magda was nowhere to be seen. Did she have something in her van that he'd come to collect? Was her payment in the Harrods bag?

Then I recalled MacIver's use of the word "atrocity". Was he planning to kidnap Magda? Kill her? I couldn't think what motive he'd have but I knew what a vicious and dangerous man he was.

There was no point in delaying any longer. I had to make a move now.

141

He would be armed. But I had to stop him.

I was sixty or seventy metres away and started to walk directly towards the Qashqai, my shoes crunching softly on the gravelly tarmac.

Fifty metres from the car a pair of geese flew over from the nearby Thames, honking plaintively. I paused momentarily to watch them then, as I turned back, I noticed the Lexus and its driver were still hanging around, parked over a hundred metres away.

I continued towards the Qashqai and could see the man through the rear window. Now he seemed to be sitting doing nothing.

I readied myself to pull open the driver's door and drag him to the ground.

I moved forward steadily. Forty metres, thirty metres, twenty-five... I decided to sprint the last twenty metres to take him by surprise and limit the chance of him being able to aim his weapon properly. I was on the point of breaking into my final run when –

A ball of flame erupted from the vehicle accompanied by a deafening explosion.

I was hurled to the ground by the blast.

Pieces of metal, plastic, glass and human flesh flew into me. I covered my head with my arms and pressed my body to the asphalt. The roar of flames was in my ears and I felt the intense heat of the fire on my back but I lay there not moving. Then fragments started to fall from the sky. Heavier fragments first, painfully landing on my body or bouncing on the tarmac, then lighter bits fluttering down.

When the rain of debris finally eased I turned over, sat up and looked back at the devastated and burning hulk. I was covered with slivers, splinters and shards. Stuck to my clothes were scraps and lumps of melted things I couldn't identify – and others I had no wish to identify.

I knew what had happened.

The murderer was assembling an explosive device in his car which he was going to fit under Magda's Transit. But his assembly, his arming of it, or his adjustment of the timer was so ham-fisted that he'd only succeeded in blowing himself up.

I heard screams and cries from the crowd at the fair. People ran towards me. Other people ran away. Some jumped in their cars and drove away. There was panic. Mayhem.

'Are you all right?' shouted twenty people as they converged on the scene. Daft bloody question. But what else could they say?

The crowd swept up to the burning car, then just as quickly retreated, beaten back by the heat and small secondary explosions.

Two male members of the racecourse staff arrived with fire extinguishers while a middle-aged woman in office clothes ran behind them holding one of those little first aid kits in a green plastic box.

'I think he's beyond any treatment you've got in your box,' I said.

She turned away from the inferno and saw me on the ground.

'I'm a trained first-aider,' she said.

'He needs a trained undertaker.'

'Poor devil,' she said and moved away from the car over to me.

'How do you feel?' she said, looking earnestly at my face and opening her first aid kit. Another daft question.

I assured her I was fine but she picked up my hand to take my pulse and insisted on applying an antiseptic wipe to my head followed by a small dressing.

When she finished. I stood up and brushed some of the bits that had fallen from the sky off my clothes.

I looked at the mess spread around me and recognised a piece of the tracker I'd placed under the car. Then I saw a briefcase on the ground. It was the same one I'd seen him take from the car at the Keats offices. It had been blown out of the boot. The leather covering was badly scarred but the case was intact. I picked it up, tried the catches and they opened.

Inside were printouts of Googled pages on Nobottle Abbey and Boston Manor with maps and directions. There were other documents printed in a Cyrillic script. I read a little Russian but it didn't look like Russian. Then I came across a driving licence issued in Kosovo. It named the driver as Valon Morina and the photo confirmed he was the man I'd been following. So the Cyrillic script would be Serbian, one of the several languages of Kosovo. I assumed that Morina, like most of the population of Kosovo, was Islamic but had no clue if this was relevant.

Beneath the papers in the briefcase were two house keys on a ring. I slipped them into my pocket with the driving licence.

I walked as close to the still-blazing wreck as I could. The extinguishers had been emptied but had made little impact on the blaze. I could see no remains of the whistling man. He had been blown to mincemeat and incinerated.

But my thoughts were not for the triple murderer blown apart. My thoughts were for the Amberger painting. Had it been in the vehicle when it exploded?

I had no way of knowing.

I'm not normally squeamish around dead bodies but I didn't feel like hanging around. I was annoyed the murderer could not have been taken alive because he was my only substantive lead. I'd finally learned his name but it was too late. I was back to square one again.

Then something made me look at my watch. It was 15:20. And I remembered. It was five minutes before my deadline. At least I hadn't broken the promise I made to myself.

'Did you pick up any bargains today?' said the first-aider, waving goodbye as she saw me move towards my car.

'Just some metalwork,' I said, jingling the keys in my pocket and marvelling at her tunnel-vision enthusiasm. 'And I hope the hole in the car park isn't too expensive to fix.'

I drove out and headed towards central London. It was only a few minutes before I heard a cacophony of sirens approaching. Flashing past on the other side of the road I saw Armed Response Vehicles. Following at various intervals and in no special order were unmarked cars with detectives from Counter Terrorism Command, cars with SOCOs and local area patrol cars. Mingled with the police vehicles were three fire engines, a fire service incident commander's vehicle, two paramedic cars and three ambulances.

The investigators' obvious inference would be that the whistling man had been killed by a third party. Eventually forensic and explosives officers would work out he'd blown himself up but the least I could do was to phone Bostock now and save the investigators hours of wasted time.

I found a place to park and called the Chief Inspector. I told him about the explosion, how I thought it had been caused and that his murder enquiry was effectively over.

'Jammy, fluky sod,' said Bostock after he'd contacted the officers responding at Kempton Park. 'How did you find the bastard?'

'Old fashioned gumshoe stuff really,' I said as I picked at a piece of melted plastic welded to my trousers. 'Being in the right place at the right time.' But nearly the wrong place at the wrong time.

'Give me the name again,' said Bostock. I heard him tapping Valon Morina into a search box. There was a pause, a few more taps on his keyboard, then:

'He's a clean skin as far as the UK's concerned but there's a European Arrest Warrant out for him, issued in Germany. Must've got into the UK on a fake passport. But if he was arming a bomb or setting the timer what was he doing with it? And by the way, we're not getting anywhere with that Abid Bashir. Are you sure he exists?'

I nearly said something, but then I remembered that I had after all kept to my deadline. So I echoed what Rochelle Smith had said to me.

'I'm not doing any more of your work for you. I've got a picture to find.'

Chapter 17

The bomb had been in the Harrods bag given to Morina by the Lexus driver. Why was Morina so ham-fisted as to blow himself up?

Time to think: what if?

What if Morina had been duped? Suppose he'd been given instructions for some fictitious mission. He'd been handed an explosive device and told to set the timer then place it. But suppose there was no timer.

The Lexus driver had operated the explosive by remote control.

The intended victim was Morina.

Either his handler wanted rid of him before the police caught him and he talked. Or, once he'd obtained the picture he was simply expendable. Or, taking the fantastically unlikely view that his boss had some kind of morality, maybe the boss had been disturbed by the unnecessary loss of life and thought it was time to remove him from the scene.

But why the charade? If they wanted rid, why didn't they just shoot him? Cosh him on the head? Push him under a train?

I reckoned they wanted to set Morina up. He was an Islamic Kosovan and they wanted him to look like a failed terrorist. This would divert the police down a blind alley and away from whatever it was they were planning.

If I was right, it meant the three murders were simply collateral damage. The sole purpose of what happened at BetterWork was to steal the Amberger picture.

I'd always believed this but now the theft felt even more significant and troubling.

I found myself doodling an ornate picture frame on my office A4 pad. Then I put a big question mark in the space where a picture would go.

I stood up and paced around the office. Well, in a manner of speaking. The room wasn't big enough for pacing so I mooched across to the window and gazed out. I had no view of St Paul's from there but I could see the church of St Lawrence, Jewry. One of the great survivors: destroyed in the Fire of London, rebuilt by Wren, bombed in the Blitz, then repaired and restored. I wasn't after spiritual guidance. It was just the most beautiful object I could see from my window. 'Truth is beauty', Sage had told me self-importantly, as if he were announcing the discovery of a new vaccine. As if he were Einstein chalking up his General Theory in front of the Royal Society. Well, I'd looked up Keats's poem. The line actually starts, "Beauty is Truth". It comes from his Grecian Urn ode. And what I'm afraid came immediately into my head was the silly and ancient schoolkid joke, 'What's a Grecian Urn?' To which the answer was, 'Twenty Euros an hour.' Was Sage just a bad joke or something worse?

I turned from the window, put my hands in my pockets and the feel of Morina's keys brought me back to the here and now. I pulled them out, weighed them in my palm, tossed them on to my desk.

People keep keys in a pocket or bag. Leaving them in a briefcase in a car's boot meant Morina didn't need them often. Also, people tend to clutter up key rings. They have a fancy fob, maybe some kind of ID tag, supermarket discount cards, and a car key as well as house keys. Morina's keys weren't personal. They were keys to a place he didn't own and visited only occasionally. An office. A rented flat. A storeroom.

One of the keys was new-looking and made in a silver-coloured alloy. It was longer than the other and had the manufacturer's trade mark stamped on it. It's the kind that fits modern UPVC doors which can be double-locked by turning the key a complete revolution.

The other key was much older. It was dull, brassy and well worn. Moulded on its bow was *Lightheart Locksmiths* and a phone number. The area code was Thanet which covers East Kent. A search located a small chain of Lightheart shops across the south of England, one of which was in East Kent at Margate. But one of the frustrating oddities of the Internet is that information never goes away, even if it's out-of-date. Phone calls and further searches proved all the Lightheart shops had actually closed years ago and the company was dissolved.

If the keys belonged to a flat, the silver key would be for a modern, secure, street door, a common entrance to the property. The old, brassy one would be for the unmodernised front door of a flat somewhere inside the building. Given the age of the brass key, the property would be a big old house converted into flats. And Margate had many properties like that. It had been a prosperous holiday town in the mid twentieth century but was now depressed with many dilapidated houses.

I wanted to believe the Amberger painting was hidden in this unknown property in Margate. But if so, why did Morina go to New Southgate immediately after the crime?

The door opened and MacIver came in.

'I had a call from Scott Sage...'

'An offer you couldn't refuse? Full page profile in the *FT*? Feature on Maskelyne Global in *The Times*?'

'He was complaining. About you. Vehemently. My ear is still throbbing.'

I thought Sage had given me as good as he got. But I couldn't explain that to MacIver so I said, 'I think that's par for the course. Him complaining, I mean, not your ear...'

If MacIver had possessed less self-control she'd have stamped her foot. As it was, her feelings were only given away by her voice being tenser and sharper than usual. 'Is he involved? Yes or no?'

'There's a lot of circumstantial but pinning him down is like...'

'Trying to catch the wind?' she said.

What a perfect description, I thought. Then her metaphor rang a bell. 'Is that Bob Dylan?'

Suddenly calmer, she smiled and shook her head. 'Donovan. 1965 or thereabouts.'

I nodded as if I knew who Donovan was. I'd have to look him up.

'I see your clothes took the brunt. Pity about the jacket. And the trousers.'

I hadn't changed since the explosion and made an easy-come easy-go kind of expression.

'What about the face?'

I smiled. 'Think I'm stuck with the one I was born with. No, it'll be fine in a day or so. Thanks for asking.'

Now she let her feelings out and her eyes blazed: it was the peregrine about to strike. 'It's not a joking matter, Kite. A bomb. Fifty yards away from you. Why did I have to hear about it from Clark?'

Like me, she hated lying, hated double standards, hated deceit of all kinds.

'I didn't want to...'

'Didn't want to worry me? It's my job to worry about you.' She took a quick breath. 'Right. That decides me. We're not going any further with this. It's beyond our capabilities. We have four murders, a bomb, a foreign government involved and a volatile and unpleasant PR consultant. From a straight-forward business point of view it's cheaper to let the owner keep the insurance pay-out and forget the picture. I'm taking you off the case, Kite.'

'No,' I said, looking her straight in the eye and matching her tone.

'Aye, I am,' said MacIver. 'I've thought hard about it. I have a duty of care – both to the company and also to you. It's become too risky.'

'I'm happy to take that risk.'

'I'm not. It began as a stolen picture case...'

'And it still is. I've worked everything through and I still believe the picture is at the centre of it all. All that's happened is because someone *needs* this picture. I don't know what for but we must stop them, because they won't have good intentions. If we don't get the picture back there will be... ramifications, consequences ...'

'You just don't know, Kite. So don't pretend. Rhetoric, half-truths, innuendo – that's what Sage does to perfection. But you don't. So don't try.'

She was right. But I was determined.

'I refuse to give up the case.'

'Refuse?'

'Give me 24 hours,' I said.

I'd said something similar to a DCI when I was a young Detective Constable. He'd simply laughed and told me to follow orders.

Now it was MacIver's turn to laugh. 'Things must be desperate,' she said.

'I'm sure they'll *become* desperate,' I said. 'If we stop now and something terrible happens, you wouldn't want that on your conscience, would you?'

It was an unfair argument and MacIver knew it.

'Don't try that angle,' she said.

Then I held up the two keys.

'I know where the picture is. These were in Morina's briefcase.'

MacIver's face lit up. Then immediately looked worried again. 'Well, why haven't you got it?'

'I know the area it's in. Not the specific property.'

MacIver gave me her hard look again, assessing what I'd said.

'Are you absolutely sure the picture's there?'

'Ninety per cent.'

Her eyes narrowed. The peregrine eyeing its prey.

'Only ninety per cent?'

'I'm being honest. Not bluffing. No rhetoric.'

'Ninety per cent's not enough. I'm closing down the case.'

I respected MacIver. But whatever she'd said to me, however she'd threatened me, I would have ignored her. I felt the green mist suffusing my body. I was in its thrall. I had to find this picture.

'Well, I'm continuing with it.'

'What?'

Her raptor's gaze pierced into me once more.

'I'm carrying on. Whether you pay me or not.'

'Don't be ridiculous.'

'It's what I do. What I have to do.'

'Not on my watch. Whatever you do from now on, legal or illegal, I have not authorised it and will deny all knowledge. Understood?'

'Understood,' I said. 'Absolutely.' I picked up my things and walked out of the office. I went to the stairs and in my usual way walked down all eleven floors, my pace getting faster and faster as I descended.

I came out of the Maskelyne Global building feeling pumped up. Arguments energise me. Morina's keys were in my pocket and I planned to go to Margate straight away.

As I walked to the car, I thought more calmly and changed my mind. If Sage had been on to MacIver as well as Kirsty I must have rattled him. I thought about Rochelle's conversation with Yasmine about Harrods. And the bag given to Morina. And the taser behind reception. I needed to penetrate further inside the Keats building. I still had the pass card that I'd taken from Hameed's hotel room. I would go there next.

In Boston Manor I parked in the space that Valon Morina had used when I bugged his car.

Going through the front door seemed a needless risk. Yasmine on reception might look like a glamour queen air-head but I now marked her down as an important member of Sage's team.

When I'd walked around the building before, I'd seen a swipe-card point by a staff entrance. I went back through the patch of nettles and buddleia and found the door.

I swiped the card on the lanyard and the screen told me I was Nassir Hameed and my card was valid until 31st December 2030.

Such optimism.

A light flashed green. I tried the door handle. It turned. I went inside. If anyone was monitoring entrances and exits they would quickly be aware someone purporting to be Hameed was in the building. And they would come looking. My time was limited.

Through the glass panel of a door to my left I could see reception which was deserted as usual – apart from the solitary figure of Yasmine minding the shop. Ahead of me were toilets and store-rooms and to the right was a boiler room and air-con plant. Nothing of interest there so I went to the stairs which were unadorned concrete with a plain metal rail.

On the first floor landing I looked through a glass panel in the nearest door and saw a room with desks and rows of screens. Behind each screen was a boy or girl working hard at their keyboard. The oldest was maybe twenty-one, the youngest in their mid-teens. Occasionally one of the kids would consult another, but there was no tuition taking place, no one was supervising them. It wasn't a college but a workplace. Everyone seemed to know their task and was getting on with it. I moved along the landing to another door and looked through. There was a similar scene. Twenty sets of young fingers flying over keyboards. The fingers were assured, positive, experienced. They were gamers' fingers, hackers' fingers, coders' fingers.

Not students but professionals and they weren't playing games. But what code, what data were they writing? What were they hacking?

I desperately tried to read the screens but those with script or images were too far away. Then a boy in his teens, wearing an Alan Turing T-shirt, came into the room from the far end and walked towards me. I ducked down below the frame of the glass panel. I realised I was next to a door. Would the boy come straight through the office and out of the door next to me? I crawled along the floor and squatted on the hinge side of the opening, ready to defend myself.

The door stayed closed. So, after some seconds, I raised myself up and looked through the glass again.

The kid was sitting only a metre away with his back to me. His monitor had previously shown a screensaver but now he was back at work it had been replaced by a logo. I took a shot of his screen just before he tapped away and the logo disappeared.

I wanted to watch what he typed but I had to move on. Yasmine may already have sent a search party to find me.

Leading off the landing was a locked double door guarded by another swipe-card slot. I inserted my card and once again the LED turned green. I opened the door and went inside.

The room was spacious – maybe ten metres by five – and flooded with light. North light. The kind that artists crave. There was also a distinctive smell. I got white spirit and oil paint but there was something else, too. The dusty smell of hot electronic equipment.

I went past an easel, a table with tubes of paint, brushes, and a palette. Nearby was an Apple computer linked to a router and a top quality printer with a stack of photographic paper. There was also a machine I hadn't seen in the flesh before. A 3D printer. It was a small model, the kind able to produce objects only a few centimetres in size. That was the source of the unusual smell. What the hell were they doing with it?

I went briskly across the room to where there was a sofa bed with a pillow and duvet. Against a wall was a sink and some simple cooking apparatus. A door gave access to a small bathroom.

The space was geared for work but there was also something of the prison about it. A penitentiary version of BetterWork. And it looked as if the work had been finished. The paint on the palette was drying and a dirty coffee mug sat in the sink next to an empty plastic bottle of milk.

Magda. It seemed obvious this was or had been her cell. Driven here by Morina and neglecting her gallery. I went back to the table and picked up the palette. On the underside in black marker were the initials MB inside a circle.

There was nothing else to see. It was time to get out. But just as I was moving to the door it opened and in walked Yasmine. She didn't look so welcoming now. She looked very much in charge.

'He's in here,' she called to someone in the corridor.

A young well-muscled man in jeans and a T-shirt walked in. I'd seen him before. He was the Lexus driver at Kempton Park. The man who'd blown up Morina.

I was thankful he wasn't holding a remote control now, or a gun. He was just making do with the taser Rochelle had seen earlier. But it's not a smart idea to get on the wrong end of 20,000 volts and as he pointed the machine at me and I didn't doubt he would be only too happy to shoot. Getting fried wouldn't help my quest.

'We'd like you to leave, please,' said Yasmine. 'Now.' In spite of her glitzy, low-cut top, her stance was balanced, poised and confident. She looked trained. Ex-military perhaps.

I backed away towards the centre of the room. Very much aware that the bad guys were between me and the exit.

'You heard what Yasmine said.' It was the man with the taser. 'You've broken in. You're trespassing.' He moved further into the room.

'I don't want to have to call the police,' said Yasmine.

'Calling the police would be good,' I said. 'You can explain what Scott Sage has been doing. I believe he kept a person up here under duress.'

I reached the table with the painting apparatus and stood with my back to it. Yasmine and the taser guy came towards me and I casually picked up one of those big paint brushes which have wooden handles about a half a metre long, ending in a point. I waved it towards the two employees.

'In an artist's hands these create beautiful pictures. In my hands they're lethal weapons,' I said. 'Through an eyeball. Through an eardrum. Not nice.'

'He's a tosser,' said Yasmine. 'Bluffing.'

'I'm looking for the old picture. I guess Magda was working with it up here. Where is it?'

The taser man walked towards me aiming his weapon. I let him get nearer, fifteen feet, ten feet... Just before he could fire I snatched up Magda's palette from behind my back and spun it hard like a Frisbee towards him. The thin hardwood palette flew through the air better than any discus and hit him right in the throat. He cried out and dropped the taser, coughing and spluttering. Seeing her colleague in trouble, Yasmine launched a martial arts attack on me. It wasn't a discipline I recognised but she'd had combat training and was agile and more powerful than she looked sitting behind a desk.

I side-stepped to avoid a lunge from her booted leg directed at my balls, then bobbed away from a straight-arm thrust heading for my face, I jigged around to avoid a chopping blow aimed at my throat but which still hit my arm painfully. I parried another jab from Yasmine but didn't see an incoming side-swipe from her leg. My feet went from under me and I tumbled to the floor. I rolled away from her and was back up again in seconds but she'd had time to grab the taser her colleague had dropped.

She advanced towards me, looking for the best shot. I moved back towards the table. She still came onwards. I turned quickly to grab a couple of the long paint brushes I had brandished earlier and, thinking I was distracted, she fired. But I was completely aware and my reaction was instant. I used the wooden paintbrush to fend off the snake's tongue tip of the taser, rapidly wound the brush handle round the wire and yanked the device out of her hand.

She advanced towards me again, looking for an angle, working out a decisive, final line of attack. I backed away. She came forward. I saw her tense for her attack and as she lunged I grabbed the artists' easel and side-swiped her. My blow was mostly taken by her shoulder but part of the easel struck the side of her head. She went down. Semi-conscious.

Then I was grabbed around the neck. It was taser man, now recovered. He was untrained, his style amateur and intuitive. But he was strong. And his stranglehold was efficient. I swung hard at his balls with my arm but couldn't make contact. Then I stamped hard on his toes with the leather heel of my shoe. He was wearing trainers and it hurt him.

A bit sneaky, you think? Bit girly? Not heroic or Queensberry Rules? Bollocks to that. It was effective and that's all that matters.

He staggered and his hold loosened. I jabbed an elbow into his ribs and he let go of my neck. I hit him three times and he went down.

I didn't hang around. I just ran out of the room, down the stairs and through the deserted reception where the multiple screens were still playing unwatched.

On the way back to Uxbridge I constantly checked the mirror for the taser man, for Yasmine, even for Rochelle or her colleague on the motorbike, but I wasn't being followed.

Then as I went into my road I saw a car I didn't know. It was a Saab, six years old, in excellent condition, clean and well-polished. There was nothing explicitly odd about it but the Swedish car just didn't belong. Wasn't a local. I parked in my usual spot, walked over to the Saab and looked inside. The interior was as well-valeted as the outside. No child seat, no sweet wrappers, no old newspapers, no scattered CDs, no petrol receipts, no out-of-date road map, no abandoned clothing. No old crap of any kind.

A visitor. But who were they visiting?

I walked back to my own house and assessed the situation. The rusty gate which guards the three metre by four metre front garden was in the same position as it had been that morning. I walked down a side road and along a path that gave access to my back garden. The weeds by my back gate looked healthy and undisturbed. The back door of the house had not been bust open. I went back round to the front where the door looked normal with no new scratches on the Yale. I opened the letterbox and looked through. Nothing unusual.

So I opened the door and went in. I checked the house from top to bottom but there was no sign of any intrusion. But still I was nervous.

I unlocked the back door and left it wide open. An escape route in case of trouble at the front. It's what burglars do.

Then I opened some wine. Thirty minutes later while I was wondering about dinner there was a knock on the door. I never have unexpected visitors. Not even neighbours. It's not Coronation Street.

I went to the window of the front room and peered out towards the porch. I was so taken aback that I stayed rooted to the spot in plain sight. The person on the step casually turned in my direction and saw me peering out.

'Don't just stand there,' MacIver said. 'Open the bloody door.'

The Saab made sense now. It was hers. Neat, trim, efficient.

She apologised for door-stepping me but said she had been upset by our disagreement and believed you should never let the sun go down on an argument without making up. I thought that only applied to couples, but I let it pass.

'I want to know if you're all right,' she said. 'You're sometimes intense, I might say obsessed. Is there any wee thing mithering you?'

I told her there wasn't.

She was unsure how to proceed and we stumbled for conversation for a while. Then I offered her a drink and, although she was driving, she enthusiastically accepted a glass of the Chenin Blanc I'd opened earlier. Then she walked around the ground floor, not overtly looking for evidence as to my mental state, but I felt that was what she was doing.

'Lot of architecture,' she said, looking at the pictures on the walls, many of which were of buildings.

'My first love,' I said. 'Structure. Form. Function. Stability.'

MacIver's big tawny eyes swivelled towards me. 'Sometimes buildings fall down,' she said. 'How are your foundations?'

I had to laugh. Or rather smirk a bit. 'Enough of the metaphors and analysis. Or you'll read that picture of the Chrysler Building as a phallic symbol.'

She smiled and looked at the New York photo. 'Have you been there? Seen it in the flesh?'

'Of course.'

'Art Deco isn't it?'

'Absolutely.'

'Do you know the work of Charles Rennie Macintosh?'

'Of course. Brilliant. Innovative. Bit of a rebel. Put people's backs up.'

'Aye. A great man. But Scotland didn't really get him. Apart from a few.' She nodded as if she'd known Macintosh personally, though he'd died in the 1920s.

Then she cut to the chase.

'I spoke to Charlie Duchamp after you stormed out. I wanted his take on things.'

Charlie Duchamp was MacIver's equivalent in the Swiss insurance firm, Geneva-Toto. We'd had some long, boozy dinners together putting the world to rights and I wondered if I'd told him too much about myself.

'Charlie said you had a thing about your parents.'

I shrugged casually. 'They both died a long time ago.'

'I know. I wasn't meaning grief. I got a hint from Charlie there was something more akin to... well, hatred.'

Charlie had obviously dug deeper than I remembered. Or deduced more.

'Did they hurt you in some way?'

'I don't really want to talk about them,' I said.

'I think you should. Whatever happened you shouldn't bottle it up. Have you ever had therapy?'

'No.'

Yes, maybe I should have done but I wasn't going to admit that to MacIver.

'Did they abuse you?' Her voice was gentle and coaxing, a world away from the office. I'd never reckoned MacIver as a social worker. Maybe she had a calling.

It might have been easier to let MacIver think abuse was the problem. But I couldn't.

'No. It wasn't that.'

'I had a difficult relationship with my parents,' she went on. 'So if you tell me, I will understand.' Had she been in therapy? She looked at me, hoping I'd continue.

157

But I didn't. So she had to.

'They were pure against me leaving the island and going to England. Lewis is one of the most Scottish parts of Scotland. There's a tradition of Presbyterianism and narrow-minded creeds. The "Wee Free" and all that. I'm a Gael. I can still speak Gaelic if I try hard but for my parents it was their first language. For my grandparents it was their only language. I wanted a wider culture, a more cosmopolitan lifestyle so I rejected everything my grandparents' generation believed in. I left and moved to England. They saw it as betraying Scotland.'

'Your parents saw themselves as Scottish, not British?'

'Of course. Sure, the English made mistakes, screwed the Scots sometimes, but there were many benefits in the union. And it was all such a long time ago. I mean, do the English hate the French because of the Battle of Hastings? Anyway, I turned my back on my home.'

She paused and looked hard at me.

'You've rejected your home, too, haven't you?'

I couldn't deny this. 'I've rejected what my parents stood for,' I said.

MacIver nodded, but I could see her trying to work out exactly what I meant. 'Do you know that poem by Philip Larkin about parents?'

I didn't.

'"They fuck you up your Mum and Dad." That's what he wrote.'

I laughed out loud. That was about it. But a weird thing for a poet to write.

'I don't want to know details, Kite. I respect what you do, I respect you. I don't like seeing you... disturbed. I've no family, as you may know, but if you want help any time...' Her voice trailed away. I could see her looking uneasy, worried she'd said too much. Then after a beat she came back stronger.

'But before you think I'm getting maternal in my old age, looking on you as the son I never had... That's not the case.'

She gave me a particularly warm smile and the wild thought came to me that she fancied me. I looked at her for a moment in a way I hadn't before. She had a good figure and wasn't unattractive. In her smart business dress, black tights and heels and with no hint of grey in her expensively tended hair, she was slim and sleek. She would fit the cougar bill.

Bloody hell.

I didn't know what to say or do. There was a pause. It felt like a minute but was probably only five seconds.

'If you won't tell me, very well, but I'd prefer we work together on this. And I'm prepared to go out on a limb. I'll keep you on the payroll. I'll even lie to the Board about what's going on. But go easy. That's all I ask.'

Her big tawny eyes were unblinking again and didn't veer from my face.

'Do you agree?'

I nodded. 'Yes, of course. Thank you.'

We stood up and she held out her hand. We shook and then she pulled me gently towards her and gave me a hug. Thankfully there was nothing sexual about the contact. On either side. It was a friendly, comradely, us-against-the-world kind of hug.

I opened the front door and we chatted a moment there before she strode away to her Saab. I watched her go, then turned back to the sitting room to pour myself another glass of wine.

I went into the room and stopped dead.

Rochelle was sitting in a chair examining the label on the wine bottle.

Chapter 18

'Who's the old lady,' she said. 'Aunt? Mother?'

I felt a momentary pang on MacIver's behalf at hearing her called old. I must be getting soft. 'She's my boss. How the hell did you get in?'

'You left the back door open.'

I smiled.

'How long have you been inside?'

'Not long. Just since she talked about parents fucking people up. But don't you want to know why I'm here?' She beamed a huge smile and actually fluttered her eyelashes at me. Very theatrical. No woman had ever done that to me. Had Rochelle changed her mind? Did she want sex after all?

I didn't want to say the wrong thing. I didn't want to misinterpret signals. So once again I said nothing.

'Dumbfounded?' she said, still looking pleased with herself, like she was about to make me an offer I couldn't refuse.

I shrugged casually.

'I got into the Keats offices,' she said. 'Don't you think that's fabulous? Got right inside. You'll never guess what I found.'

My erotic fantasy evaporated. Feeling like a little boy deprived of a promised treat, my tone verged on the catty.

'Lots of kids bashing away on keyboards, artist's studio-cum-holding cell, 3D printer. Magda was held there.'

Rochelle's face fell. I'd upstaged her, stolen her punchline.

'How did you get in?'

'I nicked a swipe card.'

'That's cheating. And you should have let me know you had a free pass. Could have saved me a lot of bother.'

'I nearly asked if you wanted to come along this morning, but you said you were busy with matrimonial cases.'

She shrugged.

'How did *you* get in?'

Rochelle gave me a cocky smile; 'Just because I went to drama school doesn't mean I can't do electronics.'

I didn't want to antagonise her. I held my tongue.

'I made a kind of ... reverse credit card skimmer and saved the code to a blank card with a magnetic stripe. Straightforward, really.' She examined the pass I'd stolen from Hameed. She asked where I'd got it and I briefly told her how. Then I mentioned how I thought Magda Butt had been kept prisoner to paint.

'Reminds me of double art on a Friday afternoon at school,' said Rochelle. 'What was she painting?'

'A copy. A forgery.'

'A copy of the stolen painting? Why?'

I'd been puzzling over that question myself.

I told Rochelle the notorious old story surrounding the theft of the *Mona Lisa* from the Louvre in Paris in 1911. It was said the theft was part of a forger's master plan. He'd made a number of excellent copies of da Vinci's masterpiece but was aware that if the original still hung in the Louvre he'd have no takers. But if the original was stolen, gullible buyers could be persuaded they were being sold not a copy but the original. It's a good story, but no one has ever proved it true.

Rochelle looked doubtful. 'But this picture of a young merchant by Mr Amberger isn't the *Mona Lisa*,' said Rochelle.

I agreed. 'Maybe she wasn't painting anything.' I said and mentioned the digital work I'd seen at Magda's gallery and talked about the computer gear at Keats PR.

'The Apple was an iMac pro,' said Rochelle. 'Top notch.'

'What were they doing with the 3D printer?'

Rochelle thought for a moment.

'Dunno,' she said. 'But get me a glass. This Chenin looks almost drinkable.'

I did so and we sat down in a matey way like a couple of old friends catching up with each other. The difficult moment of last night when I'd tried to kiss her had been sent to the recycle bin.

'Not bad at all,' she said drinking. 'Didn't have you down as a white wine man.'

I thought it was time for brass tacks. 'So… why are you here? I thought you were ending your contract with India.'

'I have done.'

'She didn't persuade you to stay on?'

Rochelle looked uneasy. Which was a rare sight.

'I told her everything about last night. She wanted me to stick around you.'

'So that's why you're here.'

'No. I told her I wouldn't. Honestly.'

Rochelle was vehement. But did I believe her?

'Then why are you here?'

Now she looked embarrassed. Like in the pub when I'd accused her of primping. Surely she wasn't here because she liked me. Or had changed her mind about sex.

She shrugged, did a bit of leg crossing and uncrossing, then said, 'Your case is interesting. Weird. Weirder than anything I've come across before. And… I'd like to work with you on it.'

Wow. I was suddenly Mr Popular. Kirsty, MacIver and now Rochelle all offering help. Was it something to do with the deodorant I used? It was only the £2.99 stuff from Morrison's.

But I knew Rochelle's problem. Boredom. Your average PI spends a lot of time working mind-numbing, going nowhere cases for jealous partners. She might as well be a Department of Work and Pensions investigator catching people wrongly claiming disability benefits.

'Why did you leave the police?' My sudden question startled her.

'Well, I thought the job would be exciting…'

'You watched too many cop shows.'

'Probably.'

'But you found it boring?'

She nodded. 'It wasn't just the routine and the paperwork and the rigidity that got to me. It was that not many of them seemed terribly bright. Plod by name, plod by nature. I thought it would be exciting *intellectually*. But it was schoolkid stuff. Your missing painting is a real PhD kind of problem.'

'Was it boredom made you give up acting as well? You've got the looks. You're good at … pretending.'

She wrinkled her nose, made a face.

'Thanks,' she said. 'But unless you're Hamlet, it is pretty tedious. Worse than tedious. Lots of waiting. Sitting about. Trying to resist the food from the butty wagon. Then you say your one line. It gets cut in the edit or the camera's on the star.'

Rochelle took a generous sip from her wine. And then another. She nodded approvingly.

'And I really can't believe you have a criminal record.'

Shit. I shouldn't have asked about her past. I should have talked about what was happening tomorrow.

'I don't. I told you.'

'Your parents then. There must have been something funny going on. Tell me.'

'I thought you'd done with investigating me?'

'I have. On a professional level. I'm doing this in my own time. Pro bono.'

Her eyes were fixed on me, glittering. She was half teasing, half serious. But she seemed genuinely interested. On a personal level. Or did I just want her to be? Was she flattering me to get information?

I'd never told anyone the whole story before. There was one person I should have told but I gave her only half-truths, ambiguity and equivocation. There was something about Rochelle which reminded me of that person. Their characters were worlds apart but there was a similarity in the way they spoke.

Maybe it was that which made me want to tell Rochelle. Maybe it was that Rochelle had damned near saved my life the previous day. Maybe Rochelle was a better copper than I knew and was extracting a confession from me. Maybe I wanted to keep her onside. Maybe it was because I fancied her.

Maybe I'd been ground down by MacIver. Maybe I no longer thought it mattered if someone else knew.

'If I tell you, you won't Facebook it, or Tweet it round the world?'

'I've closed my Facebook page. A protest against all the crap. I don't tweet. Too many nutters.'

I was impressed. I'd half thought Rochelle might be one of those nutters herself. That decided me.

'O.K.,' I said and, just like that, I started to talk.

I told Rochelle how as a child I hadn't ever thought much about Dad's job. He had a small building firm but never seemed to spend much time with it. It wasn't until I was 17 or 18 that the mismatch between apparent income and our lifestyle began to worry me. I tried to analyse the contradictions and conundrums in our everyday life but there was too much I didn't know. Even worse, I didn't know how much I didn't know.

I tried to question my parents, but they brushed me off and changed the subject.

I began my architecture course at Bath University. So I was getting to grips with lots of technical stuff about building structures but I couldn't forget that, well... my own family house seemed built on sand.

I took a sip of wine and went on.

'I decided to bring things to a head so I went home one weekend in my second term and searched the house when they were out. I felt guilty sneaking around opening drawers like I was a burglar and didn't know what I was looking for. But I sure as hell found a lot more than I was expecting.'

'Apart from regular bank statements, there were some from an offshore account and another from a bank in Islamabad. There were big balances in both accounts. Then in the loft I found a little metal box with £45,000 cash in it and, tucked under the notes, a replica Smith and Wesson.'

'Bloody hell,' said Rochelle. 'But a corny hiding place.'

'When my parents got back I confronted them. They tried to pretend nothing much was wrong, that it was no big deal. But if something's wrong no amount of special pleading will make it right.'

'I bet they thought you were a right pious little sod.'

'I was stoked up. Like a hellfire preacher, I suppose ...'

'Spare us...'

'...or a crown prosecutor. I wouldn't listen to excuses. I was condemning. I knew I was in the right and they were in the wrong. I threatened them with the police, with never speaking to them again unless they changed their ways. Then I stormed out.'

'And...?'

'And I never did see them again. At least, not alive.'

'That must have been dreadful for you.'

'You know, when someone dies, you start sorting out their things. That's when I discovered all sorts of other stuff which shocked me rigid. First, there was no mortgage on our house in London. Its market value even then was over a million, so that was weird. Nor was there a loan on their holiday house in Florida. My parents had bought them both for cash. With stolen money.'

'What did they do?'

'Traditional stuff: jewellery shops, safe deposit vaults, cash in transit, banks.'

'Your mother was involved as well?'

'She must've known about it. She'd at least be an accessory. Possibly she even organised things.'

'Were they ever caught?'

'My father was interviewed once or twice but only charged once. The evidence was flawed, the crown barrister didn't do a good job and he was found not guilty. I was never told about it at the time.'

'Would you have preferred him to go to prison?'

'Yes,' I said. If he had he would still be alive.

I went on. 'When they died, I was waiting for the proverbial knock on the door, or a demand from the Revenue, or something. But there was nothing. No one investigated and I got probate in the normal way. I'd inherited money that was supposedly legit, but actually bent and I felt incredibly guilty. I dropped out of my architecture course and came back to London. I changed my name, then I applied to join the police.'

'You mean to payback for what your parents had done? That's very noble.'

I shook my head.

I didn't feel noble at the time. I remember feeling scared, rather lost. I thought joining the police would settle me down. Give me

165

something to concentrate on. I suppose it was an attempt at doing good instead of doing bad.

'I sold both houses and bought this much smaller one for myself. Much of the cash left over I gave away to charities, always anonymously. I also used some to make contacts among the police and in various government departments. I don't mean bribery – I made donations to benevolent funds, funded sports events, a prize at Hendon Police College. It's low key, under the radar stuff, but it gets me close to the right people. Contacts I can tap if I need information I can't get elsewhere.'

'What was the prize you founded at Hendon?'

'The Barrington Prize for the best female cadet of the year. Barrington was my father's middle name.'

'Shit.' Rochelle looked gobsmacked. 'I won that.'

'I know,' I said. 'Guilty of receiving stolen goods, I'm afraid. Better it goes to you than it sits in my bank.'

'How much did you give away?'

I shrugged.

'Hundreds of thousands?'

'Probably.'

It was actually a lot more. I'd kept careful records. But I wasn't going to tell Rochelle. And I wasn't going to tell her the rest either. The worst bit. What still gives me nightmares. What I still feel guilty about.

Rochelle said she found my story exciting. She said it made her own life seem tame. She *envied* me my experiences.

I wrinkled my face.

'Really?' I said.

'No. That's crass... unkind. But my upbringing was calm, organised, fit for purpose. I'd have liked a bit of dysfunctionality. Something to react against. I only joined the police to rebel. Because my parents told me not to.'

I had to smile.

'And you found they were right?'

Rochelle nodded and gave a cynically knowing look.

Then after a moment she said, 'You know, Kite, I think you're unbelievably honest. In your situation I might've swanned off abroad and sat in the sun for the rest of my life.'

I was flattered by her praise but she was wrong. I had not been at all honest where it mattered the most.

I just said, 'I don't think you would.'

We sat silently for a while, sipping our wine. Her eyes were unfocussed, gazing at the opposite wall, thinking whatever she was thinking. My eyes kept being drawn to her body then, feeling voyeuristic, flicking away again.

The she sprang out of her reverie, ready for action, turning enthusiastically towards me.

'What do you want me to do, then?

'Sure you want to work with me?'

'I think you'll be a pain in the arse, but it's the best offer in town.' She smiled.

'Well as long as only one of us is a pain in the arse.'

She jokily made as if to slap me across the face. I grinned back at her.

'OK,' I said, wondering how best to use Rochelle. 'I told you about Nassir Hameed?'

Rochelle nodded.

'It would be useful to track him around London. See if he'll lead us to Fawaz Menon, if that's his real name.'

'You think Menon is the Mr Big?'

'Pretty sure. Trouble is Hameed's based in the Qatari Embassy. It's the pits for surveillance: few shops, no cafes, hardly any cover at all.'

'Don't worry. I'll cope.'

'It's Mayfair. You can't use your saddo person in the fat man's clothes…'

'Don't worry…'

'And you ned to be more careful than when you were following me…'

'Don't worry…'

'Hameed'll be on alert after I bust into his room.'

'*I'll cope.* Trust me.'

Stuart Doughty

She was right. Having offered her a role it was too late to have qualms now. And if she'd left the police because it wasn't intellectually challenging enough she'd be able to sort things out for herself.

Rochelle didn't stay the night as I knew she wouldn't. But a man can dream.

We talked about operational practicalities for half an hour, then she left. With a handshake. Which I hadn't expected. Then as she walked away from my front door she blew me a kiss. Which I hadn't expected either.

Was she a joker? Or a tease? I even wondered briefly if she had some kind of split personality. Like the Hulk.

Then I remembered something I'd forgotten. She was getting married in six weeks' time.

Chapter 19

Next morning the dead man's keys were still in my pocket, still calling me to Margate. And that's where I decided to go. After my confessional to Rochelle I fancied some bracing North Sea air.

As I was standing in the hall, about to leave, Kirsty called. She'd spend some hours going through the firm's records and found no trace of any interesting Arab clients except a few with minor drugs or shoplifting charges. I thanked her for looking.

'Do anything nice last night?' she said. 'Did you find any clues? Did you...er, catch anyone?' She laughed at herself. 'Sorry. I don't really know what guys like you do.'

'Not sure I do half the time,' I said. 'Things just kind of happen and then I react.'

'Hey... Don't do yourself down. Have you found out *why* it was stolen?'

'Not yet, but I will.'

'And when's my Wonder Woman assignment coming up?'

I laughed. 'Well, has Wonder Woman chosen which birthday card to send?'

Now she laughed. 'I bought a different one. It just said Happy Birthday in nice graphics. No picture.' She laughed. There was something refreshingly uncomplicated about Kirsty.

At that moment there was a rattle from my letter box as the local free glossy magazine fluttered down. You know the thing: a few articles on local businesses, plus lots of ads for women's fashion, restaurants, and estate agents. Mine normally goes straight to recycling but as I glanced down at it on the hall floor something

169

grabbed my attention. The magazine had fallen open at an advert for a new development. I picked it up.

'Hello...? Are you still there...?' Kirsty was saying.

'Sorry. You know I was saying things just happen? Well, something's just happened.'

'Is it a good something?'

'It's something I must follow up.'

'Oooh. That sounds so intriguing.'

'It may be nothing, but...'

'But it could be the breakthrough. You'd better chase it up.'

And the call ended with Kirsty in high excitement and wishing me lots of luck.

What I was looking at in the magazine was an advert for a development of *six new, high class, executive dwellings in a most prestigious area of north London.* The address of the development was New South Gate Mews, Finchley. New South Gate. Three words. Not New Southgate, two words.

New South Gate Mews. A street I didn't know. I imagined some chichi new houses, coyly named a Mews, built by the South Gate of a big house, long since demolished. All at once I understood why Valon Morina had taken the taxi where he did. He'd misheard the address over the phone and gone by mistake to New Southgate. Several miles away.

I knew someone who lived in a road called One Oak Drive. Every time he ordered something people thought he lived at Number 1, Oak Drive.

But who lived in New South Gate Mews that would have an interest in the picture?

I called Kirsty back and established that none of the firm's clients had an address there and nor did Scott Sage.

I was suddenly excited. Margate was off and Finchley was on. My speed nudged seventy as I drove round the North Circular.

New South Gate Mews was not at all like a real mews and not as I'd imagined. There was a group of three large detached houses built in the 1920s or 1930s and in a greenfield site beyond was the new development for six more properties where construction was still at the groundworks stage. By the main road, tucked away behind hedges and mature trees was a small lodge building– the South Gate – which, as I'd expected, was all that remained of the Victorian estate.

Of the three period properties, two looked as if they were lived in by families, happy or otherwise, while the third had a To Let sign outside. There was no car in the drive and the house, while not unkempt, could do with a tidy and displayed that lack of personality which hangs around rented property.

It was a large house with five or six bedrooms, set in a big garden and was the obvious one to search

I rang the bell and also hammered on the door with the heavy, lion's head knocker. I waited, then rang and knocked again. The place was deserted.

There was a prominent burglar alarm on the front gable. Looking through the ground floor windows I could see movement detectors installed and there were alarms on the ground floor windows.

I moved round to the back of the house. The garden had begun to look neglected. Climbing roses hadn't been tied in, there were perennials to dead-head and the lawn needed cutting.

I surveyed possible entry points. On the ground floor there were big and attractive timber sash windows. Original. Unmodernised. I don't like smashing up nicely designed things unless there's no alternative. So I looked higher up. At second floor level was an upper bedroom with a miniature balcony – an expensive architect's whim that was probably never used. But I could see replacement UPVC double-glazed windows behind. That looked ideal.

I moved a sturdy wooden patio table up close to the house. I jumped on top of it and scrambled from there on to the roof of an extension. I walked up the tiles and reached the back wall of the house at first floor level where a wisteria climbed all the way up to the guttering. I'm wary of using trees and shrubs as climbing aids. It's too comic capers, too Romeo and Juliet. But this wisteria looked strong, at least as old as the house and I began to scramble up it. There was a hairy moment as I reached the base of the second floor balcony but I transferred half my weight to a cast-iron, rain-water hopper. From there it was easy to grapple up on to the balcony.

The room behind the balcony looked unused except as storage for redundant furniture. I couldn't see any movement detectors: well, you wouldn't bother putting them this high, would you? I took out a knife and applied it to the window. Double-glazed windows are often only held in place by the rubber seal around the frame. The seal peeled back easily enough, there were no extra clamps – well you wouldn't bother this high up – and soon I had lifted the entire pane out of its frame.

I went inside.

There was nothing of interest in the bedroom or on the rest of the top floor so I went downstairs keeping an eye for movement detectors. There was one on the first floor landing and from there I could also see the control box of the intruder alarm. So I went for it. I ran down the stairs and the alarm started to beep its pre-alarm warning. Then I simply attacked the control box with all my force. It came away from the plaster and I wrenched it further away from the wall. With my wire-cutters I severed every cable I could see. The LEDs faded: the alarm system died.

The house was mine to search. For as long as it took.

I ignored the first floor bedrooms and carried on down an imposing *Sunset Boulevard*-style staircase to the ground floor.

The house was presumably let furnished and the style of décor was what I call post-modern rococo – a mixture of simplicity and extravagance. The dining table was a single piece of toughened glass on a central pillar with chairs to match, but one wall was papered with a complex eighteenth century design of lusty nymphs and shepherds cavorting. The main living room had huge settees with baroque curlicues upholstered in a rich purple velvet contrasted with severe modernist lithographs on the walls. Everything looked neat and clean. There was no clutter, nothing left lying around. These rooms had no spaces to conceal things and I didn't waste time searching them.

Disappointed, I went back upstairs and started on the bedrooms. The first two were unoccupied, the beds not made up. If anybody was living here they must be on their own and as tidy as MacIver in their habits.

The next room was very much in use. A trace of an expensive after-shave still hung in the air. There were clothes hanging in a wardrobe and an open suitcase lay on the floor. The clothes were good quality, stylish and expensive.

Then I saw it.

Propped against the wall not wrapped, not guarded, not protected in any way was the sixteenth century wooden frame of the *Portrait of a Young Merchant*.

It was undamaged and the mysterious lettering or markings looked just as they did in the photos that Michael Cowper showed me.

I remembered MacIver and I joking about a Shakespeare obsessive stealing the Amberger. Surely Hameed wasn't a Shakespeare fan. But the reason Morina took a risky taxi ride to New Southgate was to deliver the picture to whoever was lodging in that room.

As I picked up the five hundred year old timber and fantasised briefly that Shakespeare might have also held this object I heard the front door slam. Someone had come into the house.

I heard footsteps on the bare floorboards of the hall then a slight creaking from the staircase. I sensed rather than heard the person stop half way up as they noticed the damaged intruder alarm. Then I heard hurrying feet.

And the door opened.

A man of Asian origin stood there. He was on alert but not in attack mode. He stood still, naturally startled to see a stranger in his room. But he wasn't frightened. It was as if this was an event he'd considered, almost something he'd planned for.

He was in his late fifties or early sixties, weather-beaten, thin and wiry with grey hair. There was a small scar on his cheek and I took his slightly bent posture to be evidence of previous hard physical labour. But his clothes were elegant and expensive: a striped jacket like you see in pictures of the Henley Regatta, a crisp shirt from the sort of shops favoured by Rochelle's ex, tailored trousers and well-polished leather shoes.

'You broke in,' he said. A calm opening gambit.

I had to smile.

'You stole it,' I said, still holding the frame in my hands. 'Where's the picture? What have you done with it?'

He didn't react. He just said, 'Be careful with the frame. It's very old.'

Was this the Shakespeare obsessive we'd talked about?

'You don't believe all that Shakespeare crap, do you?'

The man laughed gently.

'Doesn't matter what I think,' he said. 'It's what the market thinks. A piece of oak caressed by Shakespeare… and his lover.' He held his hand up as if he were an auctioneer. 'Do I hear fifty thousand? A hundred thousand?' He smiled. 'I think it's worth about that.'

As he raised his hand I noticed the top half of one of his fingers was missing.

'You're Abid Bashir. Or should I say, Fawaz Menon?'

He smiled again. 'Neither is my real name. But I believe you are Mr John Kite.'

It was my turn to be surprised.

'You are a little younger than I imagined,' he said. 'And, though I'm not the best person to judge, better looking than the average investigator. And I guess you think yourself smarter, too. Smarter than the average bear, Booboo.'

I didn't get the reference and gave him a questioning look.

'Did you never watch Yogi Bear cartoons as a child? No..? Too young, I suppose. And they were screened earlier in the UK than in Bangladesh.'

It rankled that he knew me. And I had a sudden nightmare vision that Rochelle had been working for this man or there had been a host of investigators tailing me for the past few days. Which was why they had an easy shot at me behind Magda's gallery.

'How do you know me?'

'Your Art and Antiques Unit is well known. In certain circles. Their work is followed closely. And I have many contacts around the world. Apart from Magda Butt. I think you know Gus Lamport? I see him occasionally at art fairs.'

If that was true, Gus must know him as Menon or even under another name.

'Someone shot at me the night I went to the gallery. Did you book the assassin?'

He paused briefly, seemed to be reflecting on some bitter memory, then said. 'I can't discuss that.' I got the impression another killing hadn't been part of his plans.

'Where's the picture?'

'You won't see it again. Ever.'

'Why? What's happened?'

'It's been destroyed.'

This threw me. I knew of cases where stolen art had been destroyed by criminals but this was usually in frustration at their inability to profit from it and also a way to remove the evidence against them. But given the extreme lengths he'd gone to in obtaining the Amberger it was illogical behaviour. Also too depressing to take seriously. Besides, Menon was educated and intelligent. I said, 'If you're the connoisseur you're making out you wouldn't destroy such a picture.'

He nodded slowly, weighing my words. Then he took a breath and began slowly, 'We're both connoisseurs, I think. But you will appreciate that ends justify means. I have studied the Bard and I remember lines where Lady Macbeth talks about dashing out the brains of her child if it helped her cause.'

Dreadful stuff. I haven't read the play and I certainly can't quote lines. But...

'Isn't Lady Macbeth the incarnation of evil. Is that what you are?'

'No. But I have a mission.'

'What is it?'

He just smiled enigmatically.

I still held the frame in my hands and in spite of its age and value I was positioning myself to hurl it at Menon, as I'd hurled the palette at the taser man. I tried to distract him.

'What happened to your hand?'

'A long time ago,' he said. 'Another life.'

Then his tone hardened as he looked at me. 'I can see you're thinking of using the frame as a weapon. But you're a man of intellect and aesthetic sensibility. You won't want to harm something that old, will you?'

He'd read my mind.

I was bloody furious.

Then keeping his eyes firmly on me he took out what looked like a small phone. But it wasn't, it was an old fashioned pager. He pressed three buttons on it.

As he put the pager back in a pocket he glanced away for a split second and I took advantage. I hurled the frame at him. But it was too big and weighty to aim precisely. And it wasn't aerodynamic. A corner of the frame glanced against the edge of the door and the contact spun the frame into the wall where it removed a large divot of plaster.

Menon laughed. Then he turned, ran out of the room and down the stairs. I raced after him, surprised to see how quick and agile he was for a man nearly twice my age. He reached the front door as I was half way down the wide staircase. As Menon went out another man slipped inside and aimed a gun at me.

He shot twice.

But I was already rolling down the thickly carpeted stairs, trying to make as small a target as possible. The man shot twice more, hitting the wall above my head. I tumbled down to where the staircase turned through ninety degrees and flattened myself against the return wall.

If the gunman moved further into the hallway I was a sitting target.

But he stayed on the threshold and let off a couple more shots in my general direction, emptying the chamber. It seems he was discouraging pursuit rather than trying to inflict damage.

Then there was silence.

A car door slammed and a vehicle started up.

I edged out of cover. I couldn't be sure Menon wasn't bluffing and the gunman was waiting to ambush me.

But he'd gone. I was out of the front door in time to see Menon's car career onto the road as fast as Rochelle would have gone but with less control. I saw Menon in the back, the gunman in front and sitting stiffly in the driver's seat was the taser man, with a bandage round his neck.

It was the same vehicle I'd seen at Kempton Park.

I hurried to my car and jumped in.

But as soon as I tried to drive off I realised something was wrong. I got out and saw a parking violation clamp had been padlocked to one of my wheels.

Because he dealt with car insurance scams Clark knew loads of useful people.

It was less than an hour later that a two hundred and thirty pound man-mountain arrived driving a ten-wheeled heavy vehicle recovery unit. He jumped out of the cab, holding an angle-grinder and in a few seconds my car was free.

After calling Clark I'd phoned Gus Lamport who had told me he'd never heard of Fawaz Menon. I described the man in detail and the missing half finger was the clincher.

'He told me his name was Sabbir Rahman. I had no reason to doubt him. No reason to think it was an alias.'

'How long ago was this?'

'Few weeks.'

'And you talked about me?'

'Only because he told me he wanted to hire a specialist art detective. I sang your praises.'

So Menon had been checking out the opposition from an early stage. I was kind of flattered. But also bloody annoyed. I wondered how much I'd been followed. How much information had been fed to Menon. I'd been working with a ball and chain round my ankle for the past few weeks.

After I finished talking to Gus I loaded the Amberger frame into my car boot where it nestled cosily on Rochelle's ex's discarded clothes which were en route to a charity shop.

I'd also used the time to check how Rochelle herself was doing.

All I got at first was a selfie. But what a photo. She was dressed in a pale yellow short skirt which looked like leather, with a long-sleeved, floaty top in the same colour through which her bra showed. She had black ankle boots and sunglasses. The photo she sent showed her in an Instagram kind of shot standing outside a high-end china and tableware company near the embassy. She'd cleverly framed the selfie so that next to her head appeared the words "By Appointment...", which were emblazoned on the shop window and were obviously part of the company's royal warrant.

Rochelle was doing a wild, look-at-me act – the opposite of going under cover.

But I could see where she was coming from. Given the lack of concealment in the street by the embassy she was effectively hiding in plain sight. The assumption being that no one so noticeable could possibly be conducting surveillance.

Forty minutes later another selfie arrived. The caption was, "This is better. Blagged a place in stationery cupboard." The shot showed her still in the same clothes, sitting on the window sill of a small storeroom stroking a cat. The view through the window was unmistakeably that of the Embassy of Qatar.

God knows who she blagged or what she said but I was impressed and I hoped she was safe.

When my car was fixed I didn't drive home. I headed straight for the M25 which would take me via the M2 towards the coast. I was heading for Margate. I had to find the house or flat which the keys fitted.

If the picture wasn't at Menon's rented house or Keats PR then it had to be in Margate.

Chapter 20

Once my parents acquired the holiday place in Miami they didn't do English seaside any more.

But they had taken me to Margate once as a child. My vague memories of it were a sandy beach and a big funfair. The sandy beach was still there and to my surprise so was the funfair – called Dreamland. Over many years it had closed, reopened, gone bust again, closed and, hey presto! reopened again.

Soon after 6pm I parked in the Old Town. A few buildings still remain there from the time before the town became a major resort, when it lived off fishing. It's now an area of vintage shops, artists and potters. Across the road are the remains of the harbour where Turner would have landed after his trip down the Thames to see his girlfriend. Next to the harbour is the hulking box that is the new Turner Gallery. Galleries hold beautiful things inside them and their outsides should at least try to be beautiful, too. But this one has as much grace and beauty as the Vehicle Assembly Building at the Kennedy Space Center.

I walked past the Gallery and came to the Lifeboat station. It was situated behind the sea wall and across an area of tarmac from the beach. My mental image of a lifeboat station is at the end of a pier or jetty so the boat can slide down a ramp into the sea. This one was strangely land-locked and I wondered how this lifeboat actually got into the water.

But that was enough sightseeing.

I made my way to the site of Lightwater's, the firm that had cut the brass key way back when. It was now a pizza joint. My plan was to walk all the roads within a radius of the old locksmith's, looking for a property where the keys might fit.

I had all night. All the next day. I had as long as it took.

At right angles to the sea-shore are several streets of tall Victorian terraced houses. They're big: six storeys plus a basement. Seventy years ago many of them would have been guest houses and doing quite nicely thank you. Now the whole area looked desolate and decayed. Most of the buildings were still occupied and some were being slowly restored but many only provided third-rate rental accommodation for those who couldn't afford better.

This seemed a good area to start. The streets, bizarrely, were named after early Saxon kings of England: Athelstan, Edgar, Harold, Ethelbert, Godwin. Long ago some council planning chief and history buff had had what he thought was a bright idea.

After half an hour I had strode through a few hundred years of English history and was approaching the Norman conquest. But none of the properties I'd passed seemed right. They were either too lived in, or too empty. If Menon or Rahman was hiding the picture down here he would want to protect it. He wouldn't leave it in a house that was unoccupied. He couldn't let it get damp.

I'd tried the silver key in several new-looking UPVC front doors which seemed likely candidates. But it fitted none of them.

I moved my search further from the sea. It was dark now and, passing a fish and chip shop, I realised it might be a long night so I took advantage of food while I could. Fish and chips is supposed to be some kind of national treasure but it's often a national disgrace. These were certainly no prize-winners.

I seem to be giving Margate a thrashing. The Turner Gallery's architecture, the lifeboat station and now fish and chips. I get bad-tempered when I'm on edge. And I feel on edge when I sense the endgame is near. The house was here somewhere. It had to be. Keep going I told myself. Just one more street.

It was gone ten o'clock. A cold northerly wind was blowing hard from the sea bringing with it the pungent, salty pong of seaweed. Not as bad as farmyard slurry but not a fragrance to relish. I pressed on, working through the town area by area, concentrating on multiple-occupancy houses. Next day was collection day for rubbish and recycling and as I passed front doors I saw people bring out plastic bags of rubbish and boxes of recycling and dump them on the pavement. Then I saw lights switched off as the occupants went to bed.

Midnight chimed from a clock somewhere. I wondered if I was running out of the right kind of properties. Or what I thought were the right kind of properties. I had tried the silver front door key in five more houses but with no success. I found myself in a street not far from Dreamland, the amusement park. The big Ferris wheel was eerily lit by the moon and there were metallic creaks and clangs from it as the near gale whipped around the closed park.

On yet another street I saw the wind worrying at a box of cardboard and paper put out for recycling. An Amazon book wrapper on top of the box flapped and then flew off down the street. As I passed the box I casually looked down at it.

And I stood still.

With the Amazon cardboard gone, what was revealed on top of the heap was an Arabic newspaper. I don't read Arabic but the masthead was familiar. It was *Al Ahram*. The front page photo was of one of the new football stadiums in Qatar.

There must be several Arabic families in Margate but this old newspaper seemed significant.

The Amazon cardboard wrapper was in danger of being blown into the sea and lost forever so I chased after it and caught it at the street corner. The addressee was Mr Sabbir Rahman. The name Gus had been given by Bashir/Menon. This had to be the place.

The address on the wrapper was Number 19, Flat 3.

The main door of number 19 was UPVC and newish. I took out the silver key once more, realising how cold my hands were from the wind. I tried it in the lock. It turned easily and the door opened. My spirits jumped. My heart beat faster. Even my hands felt warmer.

I crept inside and quietly closed the door behind me.

The hallway was dark, with only the faint glow of moonlight coming through a skylight at the top of the staircase three floors above me. I took out my torch.

There was only Flat 1 on the ground floor so I moved to the stairs. The original Victorian mahogany handrail was still in place, dented and covered in chipped white gloss. The ugly brown carpet was the colour chosen by cheap rental owners because they think it won't show the dirt. The ploy is always unsuccessful. This one looked filthy.

Flat 2 was on the first floor so I went up the stairs again and found Flat 3.

I listened at the door but heard nothing. For the first time that night I took out the old brass key and slid it into the lock. It fitted perfectly and turned easily. Yes!

I opened the door and took two slow steps forward, testing the floorboards to check if they would creak before putting my weight on them. Then I silently shut the flat's front door.

Further down the hall I came to an open door. In the torchlight I saw a small, grubby, old fashioned kitchen. Next to it another open door showed an untidy living room. There were three other doors, all closed. One, judging by its door lock, was a bathroom and from another I heard the steady breathing of someone fast asleep.

I moved gingerly to the third closed door where my torch showed a shiny, new padlock. Significant. The door was too big for a cupboard. It had to lead into a room that must contain something valuable. The padlock might deter an opportunist burglar but not me. The hasp had been screwed, not bolted, to the door timber. I had a screwdriver in my pocket so I began to take out the screws.

I removed three screws, but the fourth was tough. It had been fitted carelessly by someone using an electric drill. The screw slot was badly burred and my screwdriver kept slipping. Each time it did there was the sound of metal scraping on metal. In the quiet of the dark hallway this faint noise seemed deafening. I held my breath listening for a change in the sounds made by the sleeper in the adjacent room. Eventually, with careful persuasion, the last screw was free, but it

182

slipped from its socket before I could grab it and fell to the vinyl floor. Once again, the noise it made seemed unfeasibly loud. But the heavy breathing continued unchanged.

I put my hand on the door knob. Would the Amberger picture be on the other side? Surely it had to be.

I turned the knob slowly and opened the door. The hinges squeaked. I winced at the sound then I shone my torch into the pitch black room.

There was a smell of old socks and unwashed bed linen. It reminded me of Rochelle's flat-mate's room.

Then I started.

A pair of brown eyes shone back at me.

A man was sitting on a bed, in T-shirt and underpants, wide awake.

Chapter 21

It took a second or two for my brain to compute the information.

'Mr Ansari?' I said quietly, creeping into the room. 'Kadir Ansari?'

'Who are you?' he said. 'What are you doing here?'

I motioned him to talk quietly, indicating the room across the corridor and pushed the door closed.

'You're being held against your will?' I said.

He nodded. 'I was kidnapped. I'm a prisoner.'

'Let's get you out. Put some clothes on.'

'I want to know who you are.'

'I'm a friend of Magda's. I'll tell you everything when we're out of here. Get dressed.'

He seemed strangely reluctant to move and appeared to resent my intrusion. Finally he consented to pick up some trousers. At that moment there was a surprised cry of pain from the corridor. Someone had trodden on the screw I'd dropped on the floor.

The bedroom door crashed open. An Arabic man stood there in pyjama bottoms, massaging a bare foot and holding a metre length of sawn timber.

'Stay where you are,' the Arab said, advancing towards me.

No one had switched on the light so I shone my torch directly into the jailer's eyes, but he hardly seemed to notice. The timber he wielded was hefty stuff, the kind that stud partitions are made of. Four by two it would have been called when my father had his building firm. I kept the torch on his eyes and my eyes on his spar of timber. In my peripheral vision I saw Kadir sleepily, far too slowly, pulling on clothes in a corner of the room. The Arab was jabbing the lump of timber towards me, forcing me back. The single bed took up almost half the space and there was little room to manoeuvre.

I took another step back and came up against a wall. The jailer smiled. I saw him tense his muscles ready for what he thought would be a killer blow. He pulled the timber back and thrust hard towards my throat. At the last moment I jinked left and the timber crashed into the wall beside me. It was Victorian lath and plaster and the force of the blow sent the timber straight through the plaster and into the void beyond. My assailant had been targeting me so the extra distance the timber travelled unbalanced him. He toppled forwards and I kicked him hard in the balls. I wrested the chunk of pine from him and as he doubled over in agony I swiped him hard with his own weapon and sent him crashing to the floor.

Kadir was still faffing about as if we had all the time in the world. I grabbed his arm and dragged him out of his prison. He complained he had nothing on his feet but there was no time. Even as I pulled open the front door of the flat I heard the jailer struggling to his feet and shouting curses at us. We ran down the two flights of stairs and out of the main door. The wind was blowing stronger now.

Almost as soon as we got into the street Kadir managed to tread on something sharp.

'My foot!' he wailed, stopping and lifting his foot to examine it.

But over the sound of the gale I could hear the jailer thumping down the stairs, screams of pain intermingled with shouted curses.

'There's no time,' I said and dragged Kadir onwards. My car was a quarter of a mile away. First aid could come later.

We'd not gone more than fifty metres when the jailer emerged from the house. He half ran, half hobbled, towards us with one hand trying to comfort his throbbing testicles.

As I looked back I saw he was holding a gun.

He raised the weapon and fired. The bullet went through one of the recycling boxes in the street, sending up a shower of broken glass. I pulled Kadir into a side street, thankful the jailer hadn't brought out the gun inside the house. Maybe it had been secreted somewhere and the timber was the first thing that came to hand.

Kadir and I ran down the street, then I pulled him left and then right, zig-zagging across town trying to lose our pursuer. We came out near the sea-front just above the Turner Gallery, which looked no prettier in moonlight than in sunlight. The quickest way back to the car was straight down the sea-front towards the harbour, then left at a crossroads. I listened for the sounds of our hunter but could hear nothing except the *woo-woo-woo-woo* of an alarm or siren somewhere. I decided to chance the direct route. We ran on, the sea wall was immediately on our right and the sound of breakers now mingled with the siren, which was getting louder as we approached the gallery. Then I realised the siren was coming from the lifeboat station. There was a call-out.

As we rounded a bend there was a blaze of light ahead of us. The lifeboat was emerging from its boat house on a trailer being pushed by a powerful tractor. So that was how it was launched.

At that moment I heard another shot and concrete fragments burst up from the sea wall. We needed cover. The tractor and trailer with the lifeboat were only moving at a fast walking pace so I urged Kadir on and in a few seconds we were level with the lifeboat, the crew already on board in their yellow survival gear. I pulled Kadir towards the bow of the lifeboat, putting as much solid stuff as possible between us and the gunman. We jogged in front as the boat made its way to a ramp which led to the beach.

One of the crew up above saw us running in front of them and yelled:

'Watch out down there! We try to save people not kill them.'

I waved in acknowledgement as another shot came in our direction. There was a metallic sound as the bullet hit part of the lifeboat's trailer. The boat crew heard it and there were urgent questions from the coxswain as to what the noise was. No one on board knew and I certainly wasn't letting on. The boat continued forwards. It reached the ramp to the beach and trundled down with me and Kadir still in front of it. Under my feet I felt the soft sand that had made Margate famous and the tractor speeded up, heading for the sea twenty metres ahead.

On the beach we felt the full force of the gale blowing off the sea. I looked back and saw the gunman walk past the blazing lights of the lifeboat house and on down the street. He hadn't seen us. On the beach we were safe in the darkness.

Sea water washed over my feet and Kadir gasped as the cold salt hurt his cut foot. Breaking waves crashed on to the sand and the wind whipped spray into our faces. When the water was up to our knees we backed away as the lifeboat was pushed past us into deeper water. A wave broke against its bow and the spray came splashing down on our heads. Then the clamps holding the lifeboat to the trailer were released, the coxswain put the lifeboat's engine into gear and it roared out to sea on its rescue mission.

We were both soaked from the waist down. Kadir was shivering and complaining his foot hurt and his legs were going numb. I looked back to the sea wall and could see no sign of the man who'd been shooting. Kadir and I waded out of the sea and made our way back across the sand, ignoring the odd looks and questions from the lifeboat tractor driver. We reached the road and the tractor went back to the boathouse while we turned the other way. Kadir was hobbling badly now so I pulled one of his arms round my shoulder and put one of mine round his waist. I half carried, half dragged, him back to the car.

The car was a welcome relief from the wind. I let the engine run for a while with the heater on full power to warm our limbs and begin to dry our clothes. Then I set off for London. It was a quarter to four in the morning.

As we drove, I filled Kadir in on how I knew Magda and what I was investigating. Then I heard his story. Magda had been visited some months ago by a man who had asked her to paint a picture for him. Magda hadn't said what the picture was or who wanted it. Kadir assumed she'd been offered a good amount of money, but she'd refused the commission. A few weeks later she'd been visited again. The first man brought a second man with him and they again tried to persuade her, but again she refused to do what they wanted.

'Who were these men?' I said. 'Can you describe them?'

'The man who came twice was very smartly dressed. And older than me. Not Arabic, but he spoke English almost like an Arab would.'

'And he had part of one of his fingers missing.'

'Eh...?' Kadir was puzzled. Then he remembered. 'Oh yes...'

'His name is Sabbir Rahman or Fawaz Menon or Abid Bashir or maybe something else. He's Bangladeshi and he trades in looted ancient art.'

'Looted?'

'Yes. Like you do.'

'He didn't tell us that. He knew some of the people we buy from and threatened to expose us to the police if Magda didn't do what he wanted. He seemed... respectable.'

'A lot of criminals are. They can afford to be. Who was the second man?''

'He never gave a name.'

'How did he speak?'

'He spoke English. Very well, but with an accent.'

'Not which language. *How* did he speak? How did his voice sound?'

'Oh. It was strange, actually.'

I turned to look at Kadir again.

'Kind of squeaky? Whistling?'

'How did you know?'

'His name's Valon Morina. He's from Kosovo and he's dead.'

'Good. He was very unpleasant. Threatening. Vicious. He was the man who kidnapped me.'

'How did that happen?'

'They just grabbed me one day in London. Tied me up. Put me in a van and drove down to the coast. I've been held in that house for eight, nine weeks. I was very worried I was going to miss all the football on TV.'

'They captured you to make Magda do what they wanted?' I said.

'I suppose.'

'You've no idea what they wanted her to do?'

'No.'

'She went to Abu Dhabi while you were held in Margate.'

Kadir was amazed. 'What for?'

'I thought you might know.'

'All I know is it's some plot by people from Qatar. The man who held me in the house was from Qatar. They've always hated us in the

UAE and that's why they captured me. It's something they're planning against my country. Is it because of the antiques we sell?'

He gave me a worried look. But I explained that his business, criminal though it was, wasn't top of my agenda.

Then I explained about the missing Amberger picture. He said he'd never heard of it and I believed him.

'That's what took me to Margate,' I said. 'I was looking for the picture, not you at all.' I smiled at the irony. But Kadir didn't find what I said amusing.

'You want me to get out of the car? Since I'm not so valuable?'

'Don't be stupid. I didn't mean that.'

'You think I'm stupid?'

'No… I meant… You know what I meant.' The longer I spent with Kadir the more the prospect of him getting out of the car appealed to me.

Around dawn we reached the Golborne Road. Too early for the market traders to have their stalls set up but the street was full of residents' cars and I had to park some distance from Kadir's shop.

I'd already explained to Kadir that Magda had started living in the flat above the Gallery because she was frightened. Kadir still had his keys so he opened up and went in eagerly, calling out Magda's name. He raced up the stairs and I followed at a respectful distance. I'd only got to the first floor when I met Kadir charging down again.

'She's gone,' he said with rising panic. 'She's gone. They've kidnapped her.'

Chapter 22

I ran up to look around the little flat. The kitchen table was bare, the sink area clear. In the sitting room there was a pile of weighty, large format art books, neatly stacked, with Post-its marking pages of interest.

I looked in the bedroom. The bed was made, clothes were folded on a chair and towels hung on a rail.

I pointed out to Kadir that everything seemed tidy and ordered and there were no signs of a struggle. He'd jumped to the wrong conclusion and it was more likely she was at Keats or somewhere else working on whatever it was she did for Menon.

He sat down in the kitchen, flustered and shaken. I made him some tea. He drank it without comment while I tried to explain what I'd seen at the Keats offices and roughly sketched what Magda might have been coerced into doing.

Then the house phone rang. Who else but Magda? Kadir was overjoyed to hear from her and I retreated downstairs while they spoke. I wasn't being tactful. The phone call's timing was suspicious and I wanted to check who was watching us.

Parked outside the Somali greengrocer's I saw a motorbike. Not Rochelle's. The rider, a large man in full leather and helmet, was pretending to inspect or adjust the bike's drive-chain.

After ten minutes, Kadir came down to find me. He was much relieved after speaking to Magda, though he was still complaining about his injured foot. He asked me to drive him to his house in Ruislip. This seemed the last place he ought to go because Menon's gang would certainly know his address. I didn't have an immediate alternative so I initially agreed while I planned something else.

I then threw Kadir completely by telling him we must leave by the back door. He thought I was being ridiculous. I didn't want to worry him, made out that my background made me extra cautious and finally persuaded him to do what I said.

We exited from the shop, went through the gate I had climbed over on a previous night and into the T-shaped back road where the mini with the shot-up windscreen had been removed. In the daylight the street looked dull and normal and my recent near-death experience seemed even more like an unreal nightmare.

We got to my car without the watching biker seeing us and I drove off quickly towards Ruislip.

A mile away from the house I pulled into the kerb.

'Lie down in the back of the car. On the floor,' I told him.

He couldn't understand why so I explained he could be in danger and I wanted to check the area round his house before letting him go home. He looked dubious at first, then, as I persuaded him of the likely dangers, he became concerned and twitchy. And complained again that his cut foot was throbbing.

'The salt water will have done it good. Killed any germs. That's what wounded soldiers at Dunkirk found,' I said.

He looked blankly at me, but there were bigger things to worry about than his foot.

'Just get in the back,' I said. Being awake for twenty four hours was making me short-tempered.

Kadir looked doleful but complied.

In a few minutes I drove into his road and was forced to stop as a learner having a before-college lesson made a pig's ear of parking and stalled the engine. I didn't mind. It gave me more time to scan the road ahead.

What I saw was a Nissan Qashqai with this year's registration. It was the absolute twin of the one blown up and no doubt from the same hire company. Perhaps booked in the name of Mr H. Potter or Mr B. Baggins.

The learner got the engine going again and drove on. The instructor gave me a generous wave of thanks and I followed at a distance.

In the Qashqai was a bored-looking man doing nothing in particular. I didn't recognise him and he wasn't Arabic. Presumably hired-in muscle like Morina.

I drove past the watcher and out of Magda and Kadir's road. I stopped a mile further on and explained to Kadir why he couldn't go back to his own house. He looked glum and asked me where he could go.

On the drive to Ruislip I had come up with what I hoped was an answer.

I called Kirsty. My impression of her was she was a bit of a thrill-seeker. An extrovert who was looking for new experiences, new adventures. She also seemed to like me. So what did I have to lose?

She was at home on a few days' leave pending a new lawyer being hired or her getting a new job.

'What sort of place do you live in, Kirsty? I said.

'What..?' She gave a little surprised laugh but had no compunction about telling me. 'Well, …an ordinary sort of place, I suppose. A flat. Third floor.'

'How many bedrooms?'

'Just one. It's a studio really…'

'Purpose-built or a conversion?'

'Purpose-built. Why do you…?'

'There's dual access? Both a lift and staircase?'

'Ye-es.' Her tone had gone from surprised to intrigued.

'Do you live alone?'

She laughed. 'This is up-front for this time in the morning. Yeah, I'm single. Just at the moment.' I liked her attitude.

'Kirsty. Think before you answer the next question…'

'I always do.'

'Good. If I asked you to do something that was… inconvenient, difficult, possibly even risky but would protect a man who's in danger, what would you say?'

'Wow… That sounds better than looking through files.'

'But not Wonder Woman stuff.'

'Who's in danger? You?'

'No.'

'Oh.' There was the faintest hint of disappointment that it wasn't me who needed protecting. 'Who then?'

'He's not a suspect. Let's say he's tangential to the picture theft.'

'Hey, I'm under-employed at the moment, so I need something to occupy me. What would I have to do?'

I told her my plan was to use her flat as a safe house for Kadir. He could stay there on his own while Kirsty moved out to a hotel. As I spoke I could sense her working through the logistics of what I was suggesting and becoming involved.

She didn't spend any time thinking and replied immediately that she had no objection to Kadir using her flat for a while but wasn't keen on living in a hotel. I asked her why.

'Well, you'll have a budget. It won't be the Ritz or the Savoy, will it? I don't want to be stuck in some B & B on the North Circular.'

'What about staying with a friend?'

'My friends who are single have small places like mine, or else share; so it would be on the floor or on the sofa. My friends who are couples have either just had babies or are about to have babies. I'm not sharing with screaming kids. Also I'd be in their way.'

'I understand,' I said. I was irked that she happily went along with the big ask, but was putting her foot down on what seemed minor issues. So I wondered whether to chance my arm even further.

'What about staying at my place?' I said as casually as I could. I quickly pointed out it was a house not a flat, it had two bedrooms, a lounge and dining room as well as a small study, kitchen and bathroom.

There was a moment's silence from Kirsty.

'Do *you* live alone?' she said.

'I do.'

I felt a twinge of guilt. It was a morally grey area.

'We can offer you some rent for your place,' I said, staying with the dull practicalities.

'Don't worry about that,' she said. 'Well, I can think of more exciting places than Uxbridge, but what the hell?'

It was all done and dusted in a matter of minutes and Kadir and I were on our way to Kirsty's studio flat in Crystal Palace. When we arrived Kirsty was dressed for another job interview in more smart new clothes, a crisp white top, jacket and pencil skirt with heels. But in the short time since our call she'd packed a suitcase for herself, changed her bed ready for Kadir, vacuumed the flat and ordered some groceries online for delivery later that day. Well-organized or what?

She gave Kadir a curious look as he limped in.

'No luggage?' she said. 'Oh... and no shoes, either.' She looked from Kadir to me and grinned like we were new arrivals at a fancy dress party. 'You're both all wet. And you smell of... seaweed?'

'I'm pleased it's only the sea,' I said. 'We've both been up all night.' And I promised to explain everything later.

I had stopped on the way to buy a burner phone to communicate with Kadir and I gave it to him now along with two hundred and fifty pounds I'd drawn from an ATM. I told him to buy some cheap clothes, shoes, toothbrush, razor and so on.

'There's a good charity shop on the main road,' said Kirsty with enthusiasm. Though I didn't get the impression she shopped there much herself.

'You probably want to go to sleep before going shopping,' I said to Kadir.

'No. I need to bandage my foot first,' he said.

'If you must.'

I had examined the cut and it was very minor. I've never liked moaners.

'There's plasters, antiseptic spray and ointment in the bathroom cupboard,' said Kirsty.

'Thank you very much indeed, miss,' said Kadir. 'You save my life.' He held out his hand and shook Kirsty's vigorously.

I caught Kirsty's eye and quirked my eyebrows. She smiled.

While Kadir was in the bathroom and Kirsty was doing some last-minute tidying for him I glanced around her flat. It was neat and efficient – "a machine for living in," as Le Corbusier had once defined a house. The furniture was practical, the décor minimal. It had the appearance of a stopover, a place to spend a year or so until she could afford better. There were no pictures on the walls, but a number of photographs. I picked up one which showed a bikini'd Kirsty diving perfectly into an outdoor pool and another of her in a women's cricket team. I'd been correct in my first assessment of her: a good athlete.

Kadir came out of the bathroom having washed and with a large plaster on his foot. Then he undressed and got under the duvet on Kirsty's bed. He was asleep before we left.

It was now gone ten o'clock so I drove Kirsty into town for her interview and explained the best way to get to my place later on. Then I drove home, put Kirsty's suitcase in the spare room with a couple of my best towels, pulled off all my clothes, showered and went to bed.

When I woke up I thought of Rochelle. She hadn't made contact since sending the selfies and I wondered what progress she'd made.

I phoned her mobile. It was switched off.

Should I be worried or was it just Rochelle being Rochelle? Independent, free-spirited, doing nothing by the book, full of surprises. I guessed she'd had a change of heart, come across something or someone more interesting – or even become embroiled in one of her matrimonial cases and forgotten all about me and art thefts.

I dressed, tidied the house and soon Kirsty arrived. I showed her round and things seemed to meet with her approval.

'I'll go up and change,' she said.

'You look nice as you are.'

She acknowledged the compliment with a smile. 'These are clothes for work. So I'll feel better when I'm out of them.' She took her time upstairs, unpacking, arranging her things, using the bathroom.

When she came down she'd changed into silvery, skin-tight trousers with a satin look a simple buttoned cotton top and high-heeled sandals. Not so legal but still very leggy. She'd loosened her hair and re-done her make-up. From the kitchen I watched her disappear into the living room.

'I'm just exploring,' she said. 'Don't mind me.' In a few minutes she was back and looking round the kitchen.

195

Stuart Doughty

'No photos?' she said. 'Where's your family?'

'No family.'

'Everyone's got a family.'

I shrugged. 'It'll take a while to explain.'

She gave me a knowing sort of look and tapped the side of her nose. 'I see... Man of mystery,' she said. Then she walked slowly towards me until she was so close I could smell the lipstick on her glistening mouth. Her voice was low, almost a purr. 'So what excitement have you got planned for this evening? A stake-out? A fight? A chase?'

'In my line of work excitement is usually unplanned.'

'Mmm... That's often the most thrilling kind.'

I laughed. Kirsty was flirting shamelessly.

'I thought we'd go out to dinner and we can... take it from there,' I said.

'Fine by me,' she said.

We agreed on a pub first, then an Italian. She was good, animated company and kept up a stream of conversation which ranged widely. We didn't touch on the murders or the stolen picture but she was engrossed by the crime stories I had to tell, the characters I'd met and difficult corners I'd been in. I'd seldom had such an enthusiastic audience and didn't even have to exaggerate the dangers.

As we walked the short distance back to my place conversation turned to sport. I asked her about the cricket team photo in her flat.

She'd played cricket for many years and was genuinely talented. She'd once had a trial for the Middlesex county team.

'Bowler or batter?' I said as I opened the front door.

'Fast bowler.'

I nodded. She had the height, the long legs.

'What's your best figures?'

'Six for forty-one.'

I expressed admiration as we wandered into the kitchen and I put the kettle on for coffee.

She relaxed back against the kitchen units. As we chatted my eyes drifted down from her lively blue-green eyes to her long legs in the skin-tight satin trousers. Then I noticed one of her hands was playing with the top button of her blouse.

196

'Trouble is, I'm hopeless at batting. My top score this season is six and I get hit a lot.'

'Hit?'

'Yeah. When I go in to bat I can never work out what the bowler's doing with the ball. I play and miss and get a lot of bruises. Look.' She lifted up the bottom hem of her top. There was a small dark bruise just above her hip.

I made sympathetic sounds and saw her fingers return to the button just above her cleavage.

'Don't psychologists think those kinds of gestures tell us something?'

She grinned. 'What?'

'Fiddling with your buttons.'

She smiled knowingly. 'Maybe they do,' she said with a coy emphasis. Our eyes met and we stayed looking at each. Kirsty smiled.

'I could help you out if you like,' I said.

'Oh..?'

'I could undo it for you.'

Her eyes widened.

'I'd like that.'

I took a step towards her. My fingers went to her top button and I undid it. The fabric parted a little and I glimpsed the top of her breasts.

Her breathing deepened. She put a hand around my waist. 'Go on,' she said. 'And you can show me the scar from the da.. what was it?'

'Dadao.'

Her hands went to my shirt. She undid a button.

I undid another of hers. She undid another of mine.

I undid another. She was wearing a diminutive triangle-style bra in the thinnest of fabrics.

'Is that what they wear in the High Court?' I said with a smile. 'Or did you change everything when you got back?' I imagined something equally flimsy down below.

She smiled. 'Might just mean I'm behind with the laundry.'

'I don't think that's in character. You're too efficient.'

She giggled. And undid the rest of my shirt. I put a hand round her waist and drew her towards me. Our lips came together, her hands began to explore my body.

'I should kiss your bruise better,' I said, leaning down, lifting the hem of her top and touching my lips to the bruise on her side.

'Last Saturday. I got a fast off-cutter. I inside-edged it straight on to my body.'

'Another bruise?'

She nodded.

'Whereabouts?

'Just here.'

She put a hand to a spot at the top of her thigh, just to the left of her groin.

'I'll have to kiss that one better as well,' I said.

She smiled again. 'I thought you'd never ask.'

Our lips came together again and there was no more conversation.

Chapter 23

I woke just after six next morning, one of Kirsty's long, athletic legs still entwined in mine. I felt a strong urge to drift my fingers over Kirsty's silky body, rouse her with a kiss and continue the action.

But I'd slept badly, my dreams full of middle eastern plots, stolen paintings and crooked antique dealers. I was painfully aware of how little I knew of Qatar, Abu Dhabi or Dubai and could conceive of no reason why any of them would want an old German portrait.

I would let Kirsty sleep while I did some research.

I slid out of bed without disturbing her, pulled on just some old jeans, because the late September morning was already warm, and padded downstairs barefoot.

Menon had somehow moved from being a poorly paid immigrant construction worker to a wealthy dealer in antiques who mixed easily among sophisticated Europeans. The key to his wealth was surely stolen artefacts and I assumed his Moslem background gave him an in with the Islamic extremists who had been selling off the cultural wealth of Libya, Iraq and Syria. But how had he educated himself? He was suave, cosmopolitan, urbane. A big transformation.

I Googled every possible combination of his names but found nothing new.

What about the Gulf states? I knew Qatar and the United Arab Emirates were among the richest countries in the world. But what else did I know? Not a lot.

I did the Google and Wikipedia thing and soon had much more.

Both states have been at loggerheads for many years. There are claims and counter claims about who is supporting Islamist terrorists, about who is hacking into whose infrastructure systems, about whose news service is telling the truth. Qataris have been expelled from the UAE and Qatari flights banned from UAE airspace. Even the World Cup in Qatar is a bone of contention between them with the UAE taking a similar line to European nations – a denigrating "who do they think they are?" While the UAE attracts huge foreign investment Qatar seems keener to invest some of its wealth in foreign countries. Both states have mammoth construction projects: Dubai has its pattern of artificial islands, there's a gaggle of the world's tallest skyscrapers, the World Cup stadia in Qatar, hotels with gold-plated fittings and shopping malls to exhaust the richest shopaholic. And spending continues apace: the UAE acquired the most expensive painting in the world, Leonardo da Vinci's *Salvator Mundi* for a mind-boggling £450 million to add to their treasure house of the world's rarest objects – the Abu-Dhabi Louvre.

Some of the squabbling between the states sounds a bit like my dad's bigger than your dad. Two spoiled, rich kids fighting over who gets to sit where at a banquet. It's easy to dismiss their antics as immature, self-centred and irresponsible but their squabbles affect the balance of power in an unstable part of the world. The wealth of Qatar and the UAE is so great that Russia, the US, Iran and European nations all want a seat at this gold-plated feast.

Absorbed in my laptop I was surprised by a noise from behind me. It triggered an instant reaction. I whirled round, slid off my chair and grabbed it as a potential weapon.

Kirsty was there in a bath-robe. I'd completely forgotten she was in the house.

There was a bemused smile on her face. 'Very good,' she said as she looked me up and down.

'Sorry,' I said, replacing the chair. 'I got involved.'

'Don't apologise.' She walked over to me and looked at my A4 pad, covered in notes and questions.

'Time for a break?' she said.

I looked at the tantalising way the edge of her bath-robe skimmed round her breasts, leaving most of them exposed. I moved towards her and circled my arms round her waist.

She rubbed a hand over my bare chest then slid it down to my jeans, where in my quick exit from the bedroom I'd not bothered to fasten the top metal stud. She tugged the zip down a little.

'No knickers,' she said. 'How perfect.'

I undid her bathrobe and we indulged ourselves longer than we should.

Kirsty was on leave but I hate to be late. I was in and out of the shower in a minute, shaved without drawing blood in thirty seconds, dragged clean clothes on to my partly dried body, while Kirsty watched with amusement. I barrelled out of the house breakfastless and with hair still wet.

I'd been in my office at Maskelyne Global only a matter of minutes before MacIver came in. I was rebuttoning my shirt, having missed one in my speed dressing attempt.

I looked down and saw she was wearing a brand new pair of trainers. She followed my gaze and said,

'Bugger. I forgot to change. But a good idea of yours.' Then she launched into what she'd come to say. 'I'm not here to check up on anything. I don't even want an update from you. I've come to give *you* an update from *me*.'

She sat down in front of me. Had she resigned? Been promoted? Been fired? Got an O.B.E.?

'Had a routine session with the MD yesterday evening,' she said. 'Naturally he wanted to know the latest on the missing picture. Well, I exaggerated a few things, embellished some others and spun a few yarns.'

'You told some lies?'

'I'm afraid I did.'

'About me?'

'Aye. Who else?' There was an edge to her voice that made me feel like the class trouble-maker.

'I told the MD you are currently under-cover in a critical and dangerous situation but on the verge of a break-through. You have knowledge about the location of the Amberger picture and also of the identity of most of the criminals involved in its theft. But you are not able to recover the picture immediately for fear of alerting the gang who will flee abroad. Your plan is to bide your time until, with the help of a cohort of police officers assigned to work with you, you can arrest everybody involved and recover the picture safely.'

There was a moment's silence before I said,

'Are you writing a novel in your spare time?'

MacIver gave me one of her looks.

'The MD accepted what I said. Absolutely. So I suggest you stay away from the office, get back on the road and try to follow my scenario. I don't want to hear that the picture wasn't at Margate, that you've attacked Scott Sage, that another Embassy has made a complaint about you, or that you've caused a war to break out in the middle east...'

MacIver was still in attack-dog mode but I was knocked out by her support for me at high level. Shit, there was almost a lump in my throat. I had to say something nice to her. Something comforting.

'By the way, the embassy complaint... That's all sorted. Or will be soon.'

'One of your magic contacts, I suppose. I wish I had people like that to get me out of trouble.'

'And some late news. I've got the frame of the picture.'

'The frame? Just the frame? Don't tell me the picture's destroyed.'

'No. I'm sure.'

'Sure it's not destroyed?'

'Yes.'

'Ninety per cent sure?'

'More than that.'

Jesus! What was I saying? Menon had told me categorically the picture was destroyed and I'd never see it again.

Menon was astute, cunning, scheming. But I had to believe he was also a lying bastard. I just had to.

'Where is it? The frame.'

'In... my car.' Somehow I'd never got round to taking it indoors.

She said nothing: her look said it all. Again I felt an urge to reassure her.

'It's as safe there as anywhere. I'll return it to Nobottle as soon as I can.'

'You mean when you've got the picture to go inside it.'

'Of course.'

'Now before you think I'm doing this because I've got a soft spot for you, or because I've lost my mind, think again. I'm doing it for my own sake. Better to work with the devil you know. I decided not to fire you. But... And it's a big but. I'm trusting you to deliver. O.K.?'

'Yes. Thank you.'

'But remember I'm an insurance executive not the bloody Foreign Secretary. And you're a private investigator not an MI6 agent. And I don't want the MD to find out I've been telling stories.'

I nodded. 'Absolutely.'

She paused a moment, then said quietly.

'Finding a new job in your middle fifties isn't easy.'

This shocked me. Self-pity from MacIver was as rare as a Higgs boson. I realised she must be seriously rattled: her behaviour was atypical and emotional. Perhaps she was menopausal. I wanted to comfort her. Touch her hand. Pat her shoulder. But that was the post-coital glow from Kirsty talking. MacIver would call the men in white coats if I did anything physical.

I just said, 'I'm sure that won't be necessary.' In as concerned a tone as I could muster.

'We'll see...' she said.

Her voice was quiet, with none of its usual strength and certainty. I looked at MacIver's eyes. The usual intense gaze had become unfocussed and watery.

There was an urgent knock on the door and Clark burst straight in. He was about to say something but, unusually for him, he sensed a private moment between MacIver and me. He hesitated.

'Am I...?' said Clark and paused. This was new territory. He didn't know how to proceed.

'If you're going to ask if you're interrupting. The answer's yes,' MacIver said, her voice strong and assertive again. 'But go ahead, what's happened?'

'There's a newsflash about Sage. He's missing.'

I turned on the TV and we stood around the screen.

There were shots of the Keats PR building with its empty car park and of Sage's house in Beaconsfield from where the reporter was talking to camera. He told us Sage had mysteriously disappeared, his

203

businesses appeared to be closed, but there were no records of him leaving the country. It was suggested he might be severely depressed after losing the libel case. The programme cut to an interview with Lorella standing outside the office in Goodwin's Court. She gave a good impression of shock and grief. It may have been genuine, or she may have had a ticket to Panama in her bag. Finally the reporter reminded everyone of the death of newspaper magnate Robert Maxwell who, when his debts became catastrophic, had mysteriously disappeared from his yacht in 1991. Had something similar happened to Sage? And if so, did he jump or was he pushed?

I faded the sound as the programme moved to a different story.

'Thank you Clark. That's useful,' said MacIver. Clark didn't always pick up hints, but today his social antennae were finely attuned and he realised MacIver was dismissing him. It was plain he was eager to stay, but he turned and left.

'Suicide, Kite?' said MacIver in a dismissive tone. 'Is that likely?'

A few minutes ago MacIver herself seemed on the edge of depression.

'No. He's a conjuror, a manipulator, a showman. He sets things up which appear to be true but aren't. He's disappeared in a puff of smoke and it's all an act.'

'So where is he?'

'Counting his money somewhere.'

'I thought he'd gone bust.'

'He'll have salted something away. Or done a secret deal. He'll have prepared an exit strategy. He's not stupid.'

'Who would he do a deal with?'

'The man who dreamed up the plot. Fawaz Menon.'

I'd not mentioned Menon to her before, but I tossed the name out easily, as if I expected her to recognise it.

She gave me one of her long looks, her tawny eyes unblinking.

'Who... is... Menon?' She spoke slowly, as if asking a class of six year olds.

I feigned surprise she didn't know and pretended I'd already told her. But she wasn't buying that.

I felt a bit mean, particularly after she'd stuck her neck out to protect and defend me. So I told her everything I knew. Everything Leo Somerscales knew. Probably everything anyone knew.

She listened in her usual careful way. And then asked a few supplementaries.

'How is Magda Butt involved?'

'Menon's using her for something vital. I think forging.'

'Forging what?'

'I don't know yet.'

'How is Menon, or Bashir, linked to Sage? Who's in charge?'

'Menon's in charge. If the PR place really is a training centre for young people then Menon has leased it and is using it for his own purposes.'

'Which are?'

'Some online strategy he has to do with the stolen painting. If Sage has really disappeared it'll be because his part in the show has finished. Maybe it's just waiting for someone to flick a switch. So I think Sage has bailed out.'

'That sounds convincing,' MacIver said. Then with a tart smile added, 'But so did what I told the MD.'

She got up and headed for the door.

'Any other instructions?' I said.

'If you're in dire straits, you know my number.'

I watched her go then turned to the window, lent my elbows on the sill and gazed out. But St Lawrence Jewry gave me no inspiration or enlightenment.

My phone rang. The caller's number was withheld.

'John Kite,' I said, 'who's calling?'

'Hello Alex,' said a woman's measured voice. 'You were probably expecting to hear from me.'

I had been. But I had no idea what to say.

'Aren't you going to say something,' she said.

'I could say… sorry.'

'You could. Though I'm not sure that's appropriate.'

'Really? Why do you say that?'

'If you listen to what I can tell you… well, it may change your view of things. *Should* change your view of things.'

205

Stuart Doughty

'What are you going to tell me?'

'Not over the phone. Can we meet up.'

'I suppose we'd better. You know where I live?'

'Yes. Rochelle Smith told me. She's good, isn't she? Though a bit off-the-wall sometimes.'

'I suppose I must have seemed off-the-wall last time we saw each other.'

'More than that. You were a gibbering wreck.'

That was an exaggeration. And unkind. But I just said, 'Thanks.'

'Sorry. But you were strung out, manic, nervous.'

'I'm sorry.'

'Don't apologise. I understand now...'

'What do you understand?'

'Everything.'

Jesus, I thought.

'How about your place in two hours?'

I agreed and the call finished.

I picked up my things and was about to leave the office when I remembered the TV was still on but with muted sound. I grabbed the remote and pointed it at the screen. But I didn't get around to switching it off. What I saw made me turn up the sound.

On the TV was the same logo I had seen on the kid's screen in the Keats workroom. It was the logo of the main ticket distributor for the Qatar World Cup.

The newsreader was talking about rumours of a serious crash of the ticketing systems and an irretrievable loss of data. The fear was that hundreds of thousands of World Cup tickets paid for online by fans around the world would simply cease to exist. Billions of dollars would have been spent in vain. The effect would be catastrophic. Fans were due to arrive soon and the chaos at the stadiums would be unimaginable.

The Qatari organisers were vehemently denying any such event had occurred. They admitted the main ticket website had suffered a denial of service attack but it was now up and running again. They were adamant that no data had been lost, all paid-for tickets were valid and fans had no reason to worry. They claimed their website had been hacked by unknown criminal elements and fake stories were being spread around the internet deliberately.

I checked quickly and their ticket website appeared to be working normally.

Was Sage and his Keats outfit targeting the World Cup? And if so, why? Or were they fighting against the hackers? Hameed was a Qatari. Had I got him wrong? Was he actually a good guy? Had he discovered the plot against his nation's sporting bonanza and was using Keats to stop it? Was he working undercover to bring down Sage?

I didn't know. I didn't know anything and I felt unsure. Unsure of everything and of everybody. Including unsure of myself.

And now I had to head home for what would be a difficult – potentially excruciating – meeting with the woman who'd called me. A woman I hadn't met for fifteen years.

Fifteen years ago was the last time I felt as insecure as I did now. The last time I didn't know which way was up.

India Paine was my girlfriend at University fifteen years ago. My first love. She was studying English while I was doing architecture. I taught her about buildings and she tried to teach me about poetry and novels. When I discovered about my parents, I decided I had to leave university and split up with India. I wanted to make a break from my past life and start completely afresh. New name, new life, new person. India was heartbroken I was leaving her behind. 'You're running away from something,' she emailed later. 'I don't know what, but I don't think it's me. I just hope one day you can stop running and find peace.' She was a better psychologist than she knew.

Why had she spent so much time and energy – and presumably money – to search me out now? It was almost half a lifetime ago that we'd parted. No, not parted. That I'd walked out.

Chapter 24

I watched her park her car outside my house. A Toyota Prius. It was the kind of car which suited my memory of her. Efficient. Innovative. Wholesome.

I opened the door. We didn't kiss or hug. Just clasped each other's hands in an unsure way. She was still beautifully attractive. Her hair was shorter and different. She'd gained a few pounds but was still slim. She was wearing a brightly patterned shirt that looked like silk, but probably wasn't, with a black leather jacket over it and black trousers. Were these work clothes? Deputy Head Teacher? HR Manager? Something in local government?

I saw her giving me a once-over, too.

'You haven't lost any hair,' she said.

An odd opening after so long. But she had no reason to be nice to me.

'Bloody hope not,' I said.

'Some of my friends are thinning.'

We sat down.

'I'm sorry to spring all this on you,' she said.

I nodded. 'Is it what you'd call a *Deus ex machina* moment?' I said.

She suddenly laughed. Warmly, not unkindly. 'Not really... That's more – well, never mind. But it's not a phrase I'd associate with you.'

'Someone I'm working with... A lawyer's PA. She used it.'

'Is that... Kirsty?'

Bloody hell. What was this? The Day of Judgement?

'What's going on, India?'

'I'll start at the beginning.'

'Please do. Why? After all this time...?'

'O.K. I'm a journalist. Freelance. You may not read the papers I work for or see the TV shows I work on but I'm doing OK. More than OK, I suppose. I was researching a crime story from fifteen years ago – a cold case – and one of the names I came across was your father's. I'd always had a weird feeling that either your father was a spy who...'

'A spy for the Russians?'

'Yes. Kim Philby type.'

'God.' Would I have preferred Dad to be a *traitor*? Maybe. But I smiled at India. I suppose it was an amusing idea.

'Either a spy who'd been unmasked and had to leave the country, or else some kind of criminal. In the end I sort of settled on some financial crime. I had this image of insider trading or using investors' money to gamble with ...'

My eyebrows raised. It was like the fanciful story MacIver had told the MD. Extraordinary how people concoct imaginary lives for others. India caught my expression.

'I had nothing much to go on,' she said apologetically.

'Maybe I'd have preferred that kind of bank robbery to doing it with a gun.'

That brought us down to earth again.

'Anyway, the years passed. I didn't think about your father again until I was working on this new research. Once I uncovered some of your Dad's story I abandoned the cold case and concentrated on him. I found some new information which was startling and I saw there was a good story about the son of a criminal who was so shocked by his parents' criminality that he'd walked out on his girlfriend and his education and joined the police. I suppose to make some kind of retribution.' She gave me a questioning look.

'So you wanted to find me just for the story? And you got on to Scott Sage.'

'Yes, I contacted Sage. Whatever you think of him he's effective and practical. The trouble was I couldn't trace you. I knew you'd joined the police but didn't know you'd changed your name. Sage suggested I hire an investigator then go back to him when I had more. So I got Rochelle.'

'Why did you think I'd want my life publicised?'

'I wouldn't have done anything without asking you first. That's why I had to find you.'

I thought about telling India my thoughts on Sage and his Keats outfit. But that could wait. First I had to tell India what I hadn't told Rochelle.

'There's one bit of the story you don't know – no one knows – which means you'll never get this published anywhere.'

'I'm pretty sure I know it all.'

'You don't.'

'What don't I know?'

I hesitated. How could I say it?

'If it's important, you've got to tell me.' India had acquired a harder veneer over the years. I could see she'd be a successful journalist. She'd get stories from the most reluctant interviewee.

'I can't.'

'Can't?' she echoed. 'Or won't?'

'Can't.'

'Alex, don't be a wimp.'

'It's John, by the way.'

She sighed. After fifteen years of putting India on a pedestal as a wronged and angelic figure I was beginning to think she'd grown into a bit of a pain.

'What's the bit of the story I don't know?' she said finally.

'How they died.'

'I know exactly how they died. I've read loads of stuff. That's the new information I've found.'

'You can't know this. It won't have been recorded anywhere.'

'Are you sure?'

'Positive.'

India sat forward on her chair. I saw her discreetly take out a notebook. She was hooked all right.

'Go on, Alex. I mean... John. Tell me.'

Could I say it? I was on the brink, but I hesitated.

'Go on.'

I had to. I couldn't leave her in the lurch twice. I cleared my throat, shifted in my chair. Then I said it.

'I... I killed them.'

India's reaction was not what I was expecting. She was surprised by what I said, but also looked puzzled.

'No you didn't,' she said emphatically. 'They were in a car crash.'

'But I got my father drunk.'

'What?' She still didn't believe me.

'After I'd found out the truth about them I spent ages working out what to do. I thought about sending anonymous tip offs to Scotland Yard or the *Crime Watch* programme. But it felt too much like poison-pen letters in an old fashioned detective story. And also too cold-blooded. And I imagined cops coming round to the house with a print-out of my email... Anyway, what happened was there was a drinks party in our road. An old guy's seventieth birthday. We couldn't not go. My parents were driving up north for some reason so they made a thing about going easy on the drink. But my father liked the booze and I had an idea. I thought if I got him over the limit he might get stopped by the police and then his car might be searched, they might find something, put two and two together...'

'Creative thinking,' said India.

I shook my head. 'La la land. I was clutching at straws. My father drank vodka. Not proper Russian or the flavoured stuff, just basic Smirnoff. Not a lot of taste under the tonic. I bought a half bottle and made sure his glass was topped up. He didn't seem to notice. But I got him pissed enough to drive into a bridge.'

'You've been blaming yourself ever since?'

I nodded.

'God.' India dropped her head, put a hand over her mouth. She looked as sad as the day I'd said goodbye to her in Bath, fifteen years ago. 'That's so sad,' she said looking at me. 'Poor you.'

Then tears dripped down her cheeks.

'Why are you crying?' I said. This wasn't what I expected at all.

I handed her a handkerchief. She wiped the tears away.

'The new information I discovered is to do with their death. There's no way you're to blame. You were never to blame.' She wiped her eyes again.

I looked at her. I'd thought of her as my guardian angel when we were at university. Was she now lining up to be some kind of saviour, too?

'What do you mean?'

'This new information – it's why I thought there was a story here in the first place. I discovered that in his last year your father had become a bit like Kim Philby. I mean he was a double-agent. A police informer. He'd been arrested for a robbery and had obviously done a deal with somebody. To spy on other criminals and pass information.'

'Who did he do the deal with?'

'I don't have a name.'

'Someone in CID?'

'Presumably. But records are missing, some have been redacted, you know how it is.'

I couldn't believe it.

'He was getting evidence against other criminals?'

'In his last months, yes. There was a gang being investigated who were running a VAT scam involving buying and selling precious metals. He'd infiltrated it. Been accepted into the gang and was passing information to the police. But the gang got suspicious. He was ordered up to Manchester one night and while he was on the M6 they forced him off the road.'

'Forced him off the road? How? That's difficult to do.'

'I know. But it's true.'

'Were they caught? Why wasn't it mentioned at the inquest? Why did the police tell me something different?' I looked at her intently. Then it dawned on me.

'A bent copper? Several bent coppers? There were police involved in the VAT scam?'

'It looks that way. There may be files hidden away that I can't access but I've spoken to serving and retired officers and to some of the criminals involved. Everyone who's still alive thinks that's what happened.'

I sat silently for a moment.

'A waste of vodka, then.'

'A waste of a lot of things.'

Chapter 25

India stayed for an hour or so. Both of us were drained by the meeting. Neither of us wanted to talk about old times but we caught up with each other's lives. India was married and had two children. She seemed content with her home life and happy enough with work. I was pleased for her.

We swapped numbers and addresses and talked about meeting up sometime. But both of us knew we wouldn't.

As she was leaving I thanked her for what she'd done. She'd started out a bit selfishly, trying to get good copy out of the problems of my life, but had ended up doing me a service.

'I feel like I've had a nagging tooth for fifteen years and you're the dentist who's come along and extracted it,' I said.

'Without anaesthetic' she said.

We laughed.

'More or less.'

I kissed her on the cheek and she gave me a hug.

She got into her Prius and drove away. As I closed the door I realised I'd never told her my suspicions of Sage and the World Cup rumours.

My phone beeped. An email.

I'm not a phone junkie. I was still thinking about India and could easily ignore it.

Another beep.

It only would be advertising. I ignored it.

Then came the clicky tone for a text. Then another. And another. And more emails. And more texts.

I picked up the phone. What was going on?

There were ten texts and eight emails.

The first was from Hudson Cassoni, an art investigator friend based in Los Angeles. It was around dawn there but he was certainly wide awake and excited:

We should get a piece of this action. I'll ask $1500 a day each. Call me soonest.

There was something similar from Marcus, an old colleague in the Arts and Antiques Unit.

I'm scuba diving in Red Sea but cancelling everything and assembling a team to offer assistance. Similar deal as with the Munch in Norway. Are you available?

Before you ask, we don't insure them! That was from Charlie Duchamp my former boss at Geneva-Toto.

Then another from an old mate based in Rome:

I'm teaming up with Marcus. Are you in?

Then there was one from DCI Bostock.:

Did you fix this? Part of your pension plan?

And from MacIver:

Don't let it get you sidetracked.

And so on.

I turned the TV on.

It was unbelievable.

The world's most valuable painting, Leonardo da Vinci's *Salvator Mundi*, for which the UAE had paid $450 million, had been stolen from the brand new Louvre Museum in Abu Dhabi. To call it the theft of the century was an understatement. It was an event of Goldfinger proportions. And I don't mean the architect.

I opened my laptop and found a blizzard on social media, a hurricane-strength blast of online posts, tweets, and comments.

The word was that the crime had been carried out by an unknown terrorist group but no one was claiming responsibility.

The UAE government stayed quiet. All it would say was that the Abu Dhabi Louvre Gallery would remain closed today.

The Qatar government – their press officers already at action stations and keen to get their denials in first this time – categorically rejected any connection to the theft, even though no one had accused them of involvement. They stressed the picture was of little interest to an Islamic nation. Da Vinci was a European artist and the picture was a Christian image.

Online, people were claiming that a Christian picture had been targeted specifically to strike a blow at the western tradition. An Al-Qaeda tactic.

But among all the online verbiage there were no hard facts. The BBC, ITN, CNN, Reuters and other news sources were struggling to report any hard facts at all.

I clicked away from the noise and looked at the Abu Dhabi Louvre itself which is a mixture of the National Gallery, the Tate and the British Museum. There are priceless paintings by many European masters. But some of the rarest items are more ancient artefacts. There's a marble sixth century Buddha from China, a superbly chunky gold bracelet from Iran that's nearly three thousand years old and a magnificent Egyptian sarcophagus of a similar age.

I gazed at these sumptuous images, zooming in to admire details in close-up then moving on to another masterpiece. At last I came to Leonardo da Vinci's *Salvator Mundi*. I'd seen it in the flesh at the National Gallery's da Vinci blockbuster show in 2011. And what a crush that was. I was squinting at pictures over people's shoulders, under their armpits. Even so I came away gob-smacked.

But looking for the da Vinci wasn't on my to-do list today. I had another picture to find.

I answered some of the emails and texts, explaining my lack of availability for an adventure in the middle east and got into online conversation with a few colleagues. We all agreed it was as puzzling as the World Cup stories. What could anyone do with the most expensive picture in the world except give it back?

My phone rang. Number withheld again. Not India again?

It was Rochelle, on a poor connection which made her voice sound tinny and attenuated. India and I had drunk nothing but tea; even so I felt in a light-headed, intoxicated mood.

'How's things?' I said breezily, realising I was pleased to hear from her. A chat with Rochelle would be a welcome relief. 'Lovely pics, by the way.' I paused for a second, remembering how stunning she'd looked in the selfies. 'And what deal did you have to do to get into that office?'

'Never mind that. Why haven't you come to rescue me, you pillock?'

I was surprised into silence for a moment. 'What are you on about?'

'I've been stuck here for days. I thought you'd at least come and look for me. Weren't you worried about me?'

Well, no, I hadn't been. But I couldn't be that honest. 'I tried to call you a couple of times, but... I didn't think you'd want a bloke fussing round after you.' I thought Rochelle would like that angle. But she didn't.

There was a big, grumpy sigh from her. 'Thanks.'

But she sounded worried as well as glum. And now I was too. India was forgotten. The intermission was over.

'Tell me what's happened.'

'I'm a hostage, aren't I?'

'A hostage for what?'

'Not a hostage. Maybe just to keep me out of circulation.'

'Because we're on to them?'

'They must think we are, at least.'

Perhaps my encounter with Menon had frightened him. Perhaps Rochelle's presence had frightened him more. It felt like their plan – whatever it was – was coming to fruition.

'Tell me what happened.'

'I sat in the little stationery store for hours, sitting on boxes of A4 and glued to the window. They were getting fed up with me drinking their coffee and using their loo and about to chuck me out when I saw him come out of the embassy. He's better looking than on the shot your gave me. Really quite hot. Anyway I tailed him – did you know the old MI5 office was just round the corner? I felt all sort of goose-bumpy and like I was in *Tinker Tailor*.'

'And how quickly were you spotted?' I felt a bit cruel. And Rochelle growled down the phone.

'Not quickly at all.' She paused. Then lowered her voice. 'Well, it didn't seem quick.' She sounded defeated.

'Go on.'

'He walked towards Park Lane. Casual, confident. He crossed Park Lane by the subway, which I always try to avoid, and went into Hyde Park. He walked past a fountain of a boy with a dolphin...'

'...The one on the way to the Rose Garden...'

'Er... I think so. Then he sat on a bench near another statue...'

'Diana the Huntress.'

'I didn't know it was called that. Anyway he sat there a while. Oh... I forget to say he was carrying one of those green Harrods bags. I kept my distance, circling round and finding a seat about a hundred metres away. The park was busy enough to give me cover. At least I thought so.'

'After about twenty minutes Hameed stood up, still casually, picked up his bag and set off. I saw a man in a suit walking towards him on the same path. And the second man was also carrying a Harrods bag.'

'I get the picture. They were going to...'

She interrupted crossly. 'Who's telling this? Me or you?'

'Go on then.'

'Well, you know what happened. They walked up to each other like two complete strangers. They probably were I suppose. There was a tiny flurry of movement as they swapped the bags but it was done professionally. Quick. Subtle. No one would have noticed except me. And you of course, if you'd been there.'

'A brush pass.'

'Yeah. Classic. Never seen it done for real before. I almost took a photo.'

I snorted a laugh.

'What do you think Hameed passed to the other guy?'

'No idea. The bag looked pretty empty. Notes, paperwork maybe.'

As Rochelle said, a classic piece of tradecraft. A prearranged way for two people, unknown to each other, to pass information from one to the other without any conversation, without any electronics and hopefully without anyone noticing. Strangely crude, but its very simplicity makes it effective.

'I decided to leave Hameed and follow the other man.'

'Sensible.'

'I thought so. He walked out of the park to Knightsbridge, crossed over the road, then tracked back along Knightsbridge the other way. Just past Owen's, the posh car dealers, he ducked into a little alleyway…'

'Old Barrack Yard it's called.'

'Whatever... This led into a mews which looks like a dead end but there's a footpath…'

'It leads down to Wilton Row by The Grenadier pub.'

'Yes. My target went along there, then into Grosvenor Crescent. See? I do know some street names. He seemed to be doubling back and I got worried. Then I looked at the building I was passing and I thought … Yeah! Bang to rights. It was another Embassy. Embassy of the United Arab Emirates. You always said the Arabs were behind it all.'

'He went inside?'

'No. He made a quick phone call, then he continued back towards Grosvenor Place and Hyde Park Corner. We were still doubling back but I put this down to a counter-surveillance tactic. Then I saw him dodge into another funny little alleyway. It looked private but it wasn't. It skirted round the big hotel there.'

'It's the Lanesborough Hotel and the alleyway is Lanesborough Place.'

'How do you know all these bloody back roads?'

'No idea. It's like having a head for heights, or good eye-hand co-ordination, or being a horse whisperer.'

'Well, don't whisper in *my* ears after you've been with a horse.'

I paused a moment. Rochelle had certainly changed. Wanting me to look for her and now talking like this.

I carried on. 'Is that where they got you? Lanesborough Place actually goes under the hotel. Good spot for an ambush.'

'Bit late to warn me. Yeah… There were two men. Big, bigger than you. Verging on Sumo size. I did my best, but…'

'So, where are you now?'

'I don't bloody know, do I?'

'You must have some idea.'

'I haven't. I was blind-folded when they brought me here. I'm in a sort of shed. Like a Nissen hut. An old storeroom, maybe. But before you ask there aren't any handy tool-kits or sledge hammers or axes lying around. I've looked already.'

I bet she had. I couldn't imagine Rochelle sitting on her hands for long. 'Why didn't you call before?'

'Because it's taken me two days to make this phone work. I'm using an old 1960s handset on a landline. I've been cutting cable with my teeth, turning screws with my finger nails.'

I was impressed.

'I was amazed the GPO box was live.'

'GPO box?'

'General Post Office. They used to run the telephone system before BT was invented. Trouble is I don't know how long my terminal connections will last. I need some solder really.'

'Who's holding you? Are they Arabs?'

'Yes.'

'Did they interrogate you?'

'They wanted to know about you of course. I told them a load of bollocks.'

'They believe you?'

'I've not had burning cigarettes stubbed out on my tits yet.'

I winced.

'What about your mobile? Didn't they find my number on your phone?'

'They didn't search me at first. Bit dumb really. So when we got here I ditched the phone. Literally. In a ditch.'

I smiled. Rochelle deserved better than the PI's daily grind of matrimonial enquiries.

'And there's another woman being held here. In a different part of the shed. Haven't seen her but I heard crying and shouting. Could be your painter woman'

'Magda? Yes, it could be.' I paused a moment. 'O.K. Let's try to work out where you are. How long did the journey from London take?'

'Couple of hours.'

'Is there a window where you are?'

'Yes. But before you ask, even if I smash the glass there are big iron bars over it. My nails are strong but they're no good on painted-over Gauge 10 Pozidrivs.'

'What can you see through the window?'

'Fields, a wire fence, some houses, a road...'

'Big road? Small road?'

'Small-ish. Occasional traffic.'

'Can you see a street name?'

'No.'

'Any other names or signs? Shops, factories, offices?'

'It's all a bit bleak.' There was a pause. Then a delighted cry. 'Yes. If I press right against the window. It's a café ... looks like Berlin.'

'Berlin Cafe?'

'No! No! It's Merlin Café. Merlin, like the wizard. Like in King Arthur. At Tintagel. Do you think I'm in Cornwall?'

'Does the scenery look Cornish?'

'I've never been to Cornwall.'

I breathed out hard. Rochelle was a difficult person to help. 'Rocky cliffs by the sea, small fields with deep, narrow lanes through them, granite walls, moorland, warmer and wetter than London.'

'I don't want a weather forecast, Kite.'

'Does it look like I said?'

'No. It's fairly flat. No sea visible. No moorland. But I can see a seagull.'

'You get those everywhere. Describe the houses you can see.'

'Small. Pretty dull. Not the kind of house I'd ever want.'

'What are they *built* of? Brick? Stone? Concrete slab? Half-timbered? Is there weather-boarding? Are the roofs tiled? Made of slates? Or thatch? Are they modern or old?'

'Hang on, Kite, hang on... You do the architecture. I do cars and electronics. Well, one of the houses has got – I don't know what it's called – walls made of... like shiny stones.'

'Shiny stones?'

'They're glinting in the sun.'

'Flint. Are they flint?' Surely she'd seen a flint-walled house before. 'The flint nodules are split open and the flat, shiny surface is used to face the building. Is that what you can see?'

'I guess so.'

'What else can you see?'

I could hear movement as Rochelle climbed on something to get a better look.

'There's another sign. Orange. Not the company, I mean it's painted orange. A long way away. It's just initials. I think it's RVP. That's Rendezvous Point, isn't it?'

'Exactly. So you're near an airport.'

'I've not heard any planes.'

I thought for a moment, running many options through my mind. Then I got it.

'No. You wouldn't have.'

'What?'

'I know exactly where you are.' Though I was puzzled as to why Rochelle had been taken there. What were they trying to do?

'Where? For God's sake.'

'TR 347661'

'Give over with the clever dick stuff. What's that in …'

The line went dead.

'Rochelle…?'

There was no tone, no static. Just silence.

Either her jury connections had failed or someone had pulled the plug on her. If a third party had cut the link it meant someone had been listening in. Which meant someone had intended for Rochelle to make contact with me. She herself had found it odd that a fifty year old terminal box was still operational. Maybe it was made operational just so Rochelle could get in touch with me.

Then my mobile rang again. It was Kadir Ansari calling from the burner phone I'd given him. He'd had another call from Magda who said she had been held a virtual prisoner by unknown gangsters but had now been released and asked him to meet her at the Gallery in Golborne Road.

'Don't go,' I said.

Kadir protested vehemently.

'It's some kind of trap,' I said. 'Magda won't be there. They want to grab you again. Believe me.'

He didn't.

'No. You have something against me. You tell me what to do all the time. Like you didn't think my foot was hurt bad.'

I sighed loudly. 'How is your foot now?'

'Much better thank you. I put on the lady's Savlon cream twice a day and also spray with Dettol. Her medicines have cured me.'

'Excellent,' I said with more than a little sarcasm. 'Look, if I had anything against you do you think I'd have rescued you from that squat in Margate? And if you weren't involved in selling stolen antiques you and Magda wouldn't be in this mess at all.'

'We try to make a living, that's all.'

'There are plenty of other ways of making a living. What you do gives support to the terrorists.' I felt pompous and self-righteous but Kadir had a way of getting under my skin.

'Has she told the police anything about this?'

'No.'

'Why?'

'I don't know.'

'I'll tell you why. Because she's still being held and they forced her to make the call to you. It's the very people who recruited her to work for them. The same people as held you in Margate. And they're planning a terrible crime.'

'What kind of crime?'

'You've heard about the stolen da Vinci?'

'What?'

'The stolen picture in Abu Dhabi?'

'Yes. I saw it on lunchtime news. But I was more interested in what they said about the football.'

'O.K. But let me ask you something. If your fellow countrymen were attacked by Qatar, their long term rivals, what would you think?'

'They're not my fellow countrymen.'

'You're Emirati.'

'No I live in the UK. I'm British.'

'You've never applied for citizenship nor are you and Magda married. You have leave to remain in the UK but that's all.'

I heard a long sigh. 'I know. I meant to…'

'You could make up for all that now.'

'How?'

'Come and help me. Show you're on our side by stopping them doing something idiotic.'

'I'm not a soldier. Or a policeman.'

'I know. But I could use another body.' Even such a pain in the arse as Kadir.

'I don't like fighting.'

'Nor do I much.'

'I don't want to get hurt.'

'I'm not a masochist either.'

'Come and help me. It'll mean you see Magda more quickly.'

'What do you want me to do?'

'Stay at Kirsty's flat till I pick you up. Then we'll drive to Kent.' He groaned. 'Not the seaside again?'

'Not Margate and not the seaside. I'll see you in an hour.'

From my shed in the back garden I selected an axe, a large crowbar, a 7lb sledge hammer and bolt-cutters. I loaded them into the car boot where I always keep a range of smaller equipment in a tool box bolted to the bodywork. The Amberger frame had already been moved inside my house and Rochelle's ex's clothes were in my hall on the way to a charity shop.

I got to Kirsty's flat in Crystal Palace and, surprisingly, Kadir was ready for me. Even more surprisingly he had a foil-wrapped package in his hands.

'The lady made me sandwiches for the journey,' he said.

'Lady?' I said.

Then I heard a cheery 'Hi there!' from inside the flat. Kirsty.

In the bedroom, Kirsty was bustling about, looking through her wardrobe.

'I think you might be able to move back soon,' I said.

'Have you worked it all out?'

'Not everything. But it looks like the beginning of the end. Or at least the end of the beginning.'

'Well done,' she said, looking bright and sparkly.

'What are you doing back here?'

'I got the job.' She raised her arms up in a victory wave. 'Isn't that great?'

'Well done to you.' I moved over to give her a kiss. But she moved at the same time and it turned into a peck on the cheek. I quickly realised Kirsty was completely absorbed in her new future.

'My new boss is taking me out to dinner tonight. Result or what! He's very dishy.' She paused and put her arms round my waist. 'Not that you aren't of course. And sexy.' She kissed me quickly on the lips.

Dishy but not so rich, I thought.

'I thought that kind of thing, private work dinner for two, was a bit... you know, iffy these days. Specially in a law firm.'

'No, no, it's fine. It's just a briefing. A getting-to-know-you kind of thing. And apparently he can get World Cup tickets.'

'I thought cricket was your sport.'

She flashed her eyebrows up. 'A first time for everything.'

No doubt he could get her into the pavilion at Lord's and the Royal Box at Wimbledon, too.

'So you've come back for your best frock?'

'Well, yeah. We're not going to MacDonald's.' She laughed. 'And I must find some decent underwear.' She began rummaging in a drawer.

I'd thought the underwear she'd worn the previous night was pretty special. I tried to imagine what her five-star stuff was like. I didn't blame Kirsty for flinging herself at this new man. He could no doubt advance her career ambitions as well as give her a good time. But I'd sure as hell miss her body.

I moved to the door where Kadir was patiently waiting.

'Bye then,' I said. 'And thank you for putting up Kadir. And everything.'

'Thank you, John, very much. For pushing me in the right direction.'

Chapter 26

The first thing Kadir asked when he got into the car – a bit like a child, but a natural enough question – was where we were going to.

'Manston Airport,' I told him.

'If we're catching a plane I haven't got my passport.'

'It's a disused airport. When the French have a strike at Calais they use it for parking lorries. They call it Operation Stack.'

The most helpful clue Rochelle had given me was the name Merlin Cafe. This had nothing to do with King Arthur's friend but everything to do with engines. The World War II Spitfire and Hurricane fighters were both powered by Rolls-Royce Merlin engines. Manston was a World War II fighter station and today there is a Spitfire Memorial Museum on the airfield perimeter, near which is the Merlin Cafe. The North and South Downs which run through Kent are chalk hills containing billions of flint nodules which have been used as resilient building facings for centuries. The RVP sign that Rochelle saw clinched it. Few disused airports still have RVP signs but Manston only ceased operations recently and there are ongoing attempts to revive it.

The fact that Magda had called Kadir around the same time as Rochelle had called me convinced me we were being manipulated. Menon wanted us at the same place as Rochelle and Magda.

Presumably so they could kill us and continue with their plan uninterrupted.

Kadir and I were heading into danger but going directly to their nerve centre seemed the best way to stop their plans. Not that I could mention any of that to Kadir.

While I drove I thought back to when I'd taken Kadir to the flat above the shop after rescuing him. I remembered how tidy the little flat had been and the neatly stacked pile of art books I'd nearly tripped over. It hadn't seemed relevant at the time but it struck me now that all the books had been about Leonardo da Vinci.

I couldn't get da Vinci or his half billion pound picture out of my mind. I'd researched the picture extensively online and something was nagging me about its technical aspects. But I couldn't work out what it was.

Kadir, slumped in the seat beside me, was telling a rambling story about problems he'd had buying a roller blind for a small window in the gallery. He was complaining about being unable to find anything the right size and I was trying to blank out his voice as I concentrated on my own thoughts about *Salvator Mundi*. But he droned on.

'It's only forty-five centimetres wide and a sixty-six centimetre drop, but they had nothing that was so narrow,' he said. 'I had to go all the way to Oxford Street and get one made specially.'

He unwrapped a sweet and put it in his mouth.

There was silence in the car for a moment. I was gazing at the car ahead of me. I registered subconsciously that its registration started BJ66. Nothing unusual in that.

But something jogged my mind. 'You were talking about blinds…'

'They weren't in stock.'

'You mentioned some measurements. What were they?'

He gave me a suspicious look.

'Why are you interested? Do you make blinds.'

'Of course I don't. Just tell me what you said earlier.'

He shrugged and raised his eyebrows. 'I said I needed a blind for a small window…'

'The measurements. What were the measurements?'

'I don't know…'

'You told me five minutes ago.'

'Oh. Yes. Sixty-six centimetres by forty-five.'

We were passing the slip road to Medway Services on the M2. I yanked the wheel hard to the left, cut up a driver on the inside lane, and slammed on the brakes as we shot up the exit ramp too fast.

'Hey! You trying to kill us?'

I controlled the speed and found a slot in the car park.

'Why we stopped? You hungry? You should've had one of the lady's sandwiches. They were good.'

'Hang on.'

I got my phone and flicked through recent photos. Then I found it: the picture I'd taken of the label on the wall in Nobottle Abbey. I enlarged the shot and read:

Christoph Amberger. Born c.1505 Swabia, Died 1562 Augsburg. Portrait of a Young Merchant. Oil on panel. 66cm x 45cm.

'Sixty six by forty five centimetres,' I said aloud.

'Yeah. That was the size of the window,' said Kadir who thought I'd cracked.

'I'm going into the café,' I said, getting out of the car.

'So you are hungry?'

'I need the wi-fi.' My phone battery was low.

'O.K. I can go to toilet then.'

I bought a cup of tea because it feels mean to use their technology without buying anything. I thought about an Eccles cake, but they didn't have any. Fine. I felt too tense to eat anyway.

Then I frantically used my laptop to Google the dimensions of da Vinci's *Salvator Mundi*. It came up immediately. 66cm by 45cm.

That was the reason Menon took a picture of the label.

I called Nobottle Abbey and Michael Cowper himself answered.

'It's John Kite. I haven't got your picture yet, but I'm close. I'll go so far as to say I think I know where it is. But there's just one question.'

'Fire away, old bean,' said Cowper. 'I'm all ears.'

'What kind of wood panel is the Amberger picture painted on?'

'Walnut,' he said without hesitation. In that single word I could hear his pride in the quality and rarity of the work, even though he no longer had it. 'Have you heard the dreadful news about the Leonardo in Abu Dhabi...?'

'Yes, yes. I have. That's it, Michael. Thank you.'

I ended the conversation abruptly.

Oak was a more common timber to use for panels but da Vinci had used walnut for the *Salvator Mundi* as well.

I was beginning to see why obtaining the Amberger picture had been so vital for the plotters. They wanted a picture which exactly matched the da Vinci in age, size and material. But what were they going to do with it? Had Menon orchestrated the theft of the *Salvator Mundi* from the Abu Dhabi Louvre? It seemed likely.

I thought of Magda. If her role in Menon's gang was to be a forger, what was she forging? She had been playing around with digital imagery but the 3D printer at the Keats offices was far too small to reproduce anything the size of a painting.

I heard a voice behind me. Then realised it was Kadir.

'What?' I said.

'I said, can we go now?'

I thought we probably could.

'You haven't drunk your tea,' he said. I hadn't and it was cold now anyway.

Manston airport is positioned on a dreary, strangely unpopulated plateau of north Kent, near the sea but with no sight of it. Its proximity to France made it an obvious location for a fighter base in World War II but its distance from London and the fact that it's bypassed by the motorways make it less obvious as a modern transport hub. Which is why it's now deserted. Except it's not quite deserted. There's the Spitfire museum, a helicopter company and a few other small scale flying operations.

First, I drove all round the airport perimeter keeping to public roads. A sign by what had once been the main passenger entrance proclaimed this was Kent International Airport but weeds and grass grew tall in car parks and on taxiways. There was some minor activity around the helicopter company where a Bell Jetranger had just landed but little else. On the far side of the airfield, away from all commercial activity and next to a sign advertising workshop space to rent I identified a building which must be where Rochelle was incarcerated.

It was indeed a Nissen Hut, with roof and walls made of corrugated iron, curved into a semi-circle. Next to it was a group of other sheds and some more substantial brick buildings.

There was no physical barrier to stop me driving through the main airport entrance, on to the tarmac and up and down the runway:

nothing except a sign saying No Unauthorised Access. But driving up the runway would attract attention.

So I drove around the perimeter again towards the buildings I'd seen and parked the car on the verge, behind some convenient tall shrubs and hedging which would shield it from spying eyes. I woke up Kadir who had dozed off and explained what I was about to do. He was to wait in the car and I checked he still had the burner phone. He said he was cold and wanted to keep the heater switched on. So I gave him the car keys.

I cut an entrance through the metal fence, bent back the wire strands and scrambled through. I took my tools and ran with them to the Nissen Hut. There was only one window. It was barred on the outside and Rochelle had said it was barred on the inside too. I looked through and saw Rochelle pacing up and down. I tapped on the glass and she whirled round, shocked at first then relieved to see my face.

I moved round to the front of the Nissen hut and saw two Mercedes S Class Pullmans driving across the runway. They drove to a brick building a couple of hundred metres away and parked outside alongside other vehicles. Both cars had CD plates affixed.

I was in the right place.

I lay low while the five people got out of the limos and went into the brick building. I recognised Nassir Hameed, Yasmine and the taser man.

Rochelle's Nissen Hut prison had a modern galvanised steel door with a quality lock and also a new padlock for good measure. I didn't want to waste time opening locks or bashing solid steel so I looked for the weakest point. The door frame was old and wooden, with areas of wet rot. I attacked the frame with a hammer and chisel and the timber broke up encouragingly. Soon the screws holding the door hinges were exposed and I set to with my crowbar. The hinges gave way and the door would have fallen flat if its opposite side had not been held by the padlock. I yanked it open and went in.

Rochelle was there with her hands on her hips.

'Finally,' she said.

Which I didn't think was much of a greeting.

Each time I saw Rochelle she was dressed differently. The sexy clothes from the selfies had disappeared and now she was wearing a faded vintage boiler suit in RAF blue, which was far too big, with an equally ancient battledress top over it. But on her feet were the smart heels, now scuffed and dirty, she'd worn during the surveillance of Hameed. She had no make-up and her hair was frizzy as if it had been washed then left to dry.

But like movie stars who always manage to look hot even if they're stranded in space and facing certain death, Rochelle had that same remarkable quality too.

I tried to ignore this aura that hung about her and instead quirked my eyebrows at her clothes. 'Ready for action?' I said. 'Or are they prison fatigues?'

She snorted. 'There's a crappy shower here and an antique loo but I obviously didn't pack a suitcase. So I needed clean clothes. I found these in a locker. They're three sizes too big and the material's dead itchy. And I've got no knickers or anything underneath.'

She saw me looking at the faded old uniform and gave me a sharp look in return. 'I hope that doesn't get you excited or anything.'

I was glad imprisonment hadn't softened Rochelle in any way.

'Maybe if you were wearing silk or satin. But not serge.'

She rolled her eyes.

'Let's get going,' she said.

But I ignored her and looked at a steel shelving unit filled with thirty or forty 1960s black plastic telephones. On the floor nearby, with a cable snaking to the Bakelite telephone connection box that Rochelle had described, was a bright red telephone of similar vintage.

'You chose the only red one,' I said.

She shrugged. 'Thought it could be the Wing Commander's or the Control Tower's. You know, better quality.'

'You did bloody well to fix it all up.'

'Thanks.' My compliment seemed to please her. 'But what about you working out where I was? That was bloody clever, too.'

Mutual admiration? I almost blushed. We'd have to stop this before it got out of hand.

'But everything went dead,' said Rochelle. 'That worried me.'

Our eyes met.

'Think it was some kind of set-up?' she went on. 'The red phone was bugged and they turned the power on just long enough for you to guess where I was? To bring you into the net?'

I'd considered this before. But Menon could have finished me earlier if he'd wanted to, at Sage's house. A trick with the phone seemed too byzantine, like trying too hard.

'I think it was just a fluke,' I said.

'I'm glad you think so. I was worried I'd led you into a trap.'

I shook my head. 'I had to come. I think the painting's here.'

'Really?' She was open-mouthed. 'Why here of all places?'

I told her who I'd seen arriving. I think this is a meeting point for all those involved before they set off east.'

'East?'

'I came face to face with Menon – at the house he's rented.'

I outlined what had happened there. First she frowned trying to take in the implications of what he'd told me. Then she winced as I talked about the shots fired. Her hand stretched out as if to touch me, then she thought better of it and her arm dropped down again.

Then I filled her in on the da Vinci theft from Abu Dhabi. I told her I thought I'd worked out what was going on and was about to explain when Rochelle said,

'No. Don't tell me. I'll work it out for myself.'

'What?'

'I don't want you to spoil the surprise.'

I had to laugh. This was daft.

'You're nuts.'

She thought for a moment and smiled. 'Better than being a klutz, I suppose.'

We walked cautiously out of Rochelle's prison shed and I glanced towards my car. I could just see Kadir in the passenger seat, presumably still dozing.

I picked up the tools I'd left outside and led Rochelle across a few metres of long, rough grass to the next building which was of similar construction: sheets of corrugated iron curved into semi-circles. There was a rusty Danger No Smoking sign nailed to the door but the door was unlocked. Inside there were puddles on the concrete floor from where the roof had leaked and ranged along one wall were large iron tanks, flakes of rust hanging from the surface. The building had been a World War II fuel store. There was still a distinct smell of aviation fuel in spite of the passing years and the leaky roof.

This next building was more substantial and in better order. I crowbarred the door open and we went inside. The building had been modernised. It was weather-proof, centrally-heated and with a fine new hardwood floor. Some rugs, yucca plants and a quantity of new conference room furniture were tastefully arranged to show prospective tenants how the space could be used for meetings. It was empty of people – and paintings.

We moved on to the next building – a similar brick structure which had been likewise renovated. The double width doors were secured with a high quality modern padlock. But once again my crowbar removed the defences.

Inside, it was immediately apparent this building was different. It hadn't just been renovated recently but there was the hum of air conditioning. We moved from a little vestibule through an air-tight door into a clean room with filtered air and humidity controls. Dominating the area was a huge machine about three metres long by two metres wide. It looked like something out of a power station or a piece of kit from the villain's lair on the set of a futuristic action movie.

Rochelle and I walked around the machine as if it had just been teleported from another planet. We mounted steps which led up to a little gantry where a technician could oversee operations and found a large glass panel in the top of the machine with a central hollow space beneath it. We lifted the glass screen and leaned into the central open area.

It was a massive 3D printer. The Big Daddy of the machine at Keats PR. I'd never seen anything on this scale.

'Absolutely top-of-the-range, cutting edge industrial model. It'll do real-time, high speed, polymer printing in full colour. Must have cost half a million, probably more. And these beasts are much more than printers. They're a mini factory. They manufacture things.' Rochelle seemed impressively clued up.

We stood looking at the machine in awe of its potential. But there were no traces of what the machine had made or what it might be going to make. The central area where the 3D printing took place was spotless with no polymer fragments left behind.

I wondered if Menon was making copies of the Amberger frame. He knew the market for that sort of thing so maybe he was trying to cash in. I wondered if a 3D printer could reproduce a frame that would pass as genuine. It couldn't pass the dendrochronology tests but maybe it would *look* authentic.

There was the sound of movement behind us and a voice said:

'Get down from there, please.'

It was Nassir Hameed. He was standing in the doorway, holding a gun. Next to him was Menon's driver, the taser guy from Keats who had lost the bandage but now displayed a blue-mauve bruise on his neck.

'Mr Hameed,' I said, getting down from the 3D printer's gantry. 'Looks like I didn't kick your gun hand hard enough in that hotel room. Let me introduce Rochelle Smith. Rochelle, this is Mr Nassir Hameed from Qatar's Ministry of Culture and Sport. Supposedly in the UK as part of a trade delegation.'

'Hi there,' said Rochelle. 'Are you the man who killed Jamal Ahmed and dumped him in the river?'

'He probably got his hitman Morina to look after that. A wet job in every sense of the word.'

Rochelle smiled.

'He was on to you, wasn't he?' I said. 'Jamal Ahmed had picked up a lead and was trying to stop you and the others.'

'I don't know what you're talking about,' said Hameed.

'Shame,' I said. 'Well, I've made a long journey to this desolate place so I'd like to see the picture. It is here, isn't it?'

'You'll never see that picture again,' said Hameed. 'It's been destroyed.'

'That's what your boss told me.'

'Boss?' It was an instant reaction from Hameed. It was clear he disapproved of how I described Menon.

'Yes. I didn't believe your *boss*. And I don't believe you.'

He shrugged. 'Then I'll prove it to you.' Hameed waved his gun at us. 'You walk in front. We're going to the next building.'

Chapter 27

We were taken back to the building with the yuccas. But now the room wasn't empty.

Fawaz Menon was there, looking as spruce as when I last saw him. Next to him was the glamorous Yasmine, now in a denim shirt and combat trousers. There were also three youngish Arabic men who I hadn't seen before. They were dressed in casual but expensive clothes and were palpably not special forces or secret service. They had the wide-eyed enthusiasm of recent graduates – or disciples. I put them down as Hameed's personal assistants. Perhaps family.

On a table was a rectangular aluminium flight box with a hinged lid and a padded interior. Like a larger version of the reinforced boxes used by film crews to carry cameras.

'Lower the weapon, Hameed,' Menon said. 'Mr Kite won't be armed and guns just increase the danger for us all.'

Hameed was reluctant to comply. I caught him exchanging quick looks with Yasmine and the taser man.

'Do it, please,' Menon said with a sternness I hadn't heard before. And Hameed returned his gun to a pocket. Menon's aversion to guns was at odds with the fact that his plot had resulted in the death of five men in London already.

'What's in the flashy box?' I said.

'Come and see,' said Menon. 'It's the *remains* of the painting you've been hunting. You can have one last view of it. Then you must report that it's lost forever. I'm afraid you've been on a wild goose chase, as the aphorism has it.'

The word "remains" hit me hard but I still couldn't believe I'd been wasting my time.

234

'A last view?' I said.

'Before it is flown to Qatar.'

'Qatar? Why Qatar?'

'Because Mr Hameed here and his Qatari colleagues are a vital part of my operation. But never mind that. Just admire the skill, the time, the money that's been lavished on creating a new work of art.'

Rochelle and I walked over, nervous and curious, and looked into the flight box. Resting on carefully formed padding was an unframed painting. But it wasn't the Amberger. It was a Leonardo da Vinci. It was the *Salvator Mundi*, or rather an immaculate facsimile of it. I lent closer.

'Good, isn't it?' said Menon.

It was astonishingly good. It was magnificent. Perfect.

'Who did this?' I said. 'Magda?'

'The resourceful Magda, helped by a lot of high tech equipment.'

I carefully picked it up. The surface of the painting looked incredibly authentic.

When I first wondered if Magda had been making forgeries I thought she may have painted a physical copy of the da Vinci on canvas or on paper and it had somehow been fixed on to the surface of the Amberger.

If she had, the paint would inevitably look new and fresh. But the surface I was looking at now was dry and hard. Astonishingly, it looked five hundred years old.

Da Vinci achieved his results with many layers of thin colour and that's exactly what I saw here. There was also the famous *pentimento* in Christ's thumb, which is where the artist had second thoughts about the shape of the digit. He had over-painted his first thoughts, but hadn't completely obscured them, leaving behind the ghost of his original line. The real *Salvator Mundi* picture had been subject to abrasive cleaning several times in its life and also enthusiastic in-painting – the process whereby restorers fill in missing and damaged areas.

All that was reproduced exactly in this copy.

I began to understand how they had achieved this remarkable result. Magda had been brought in not just for her artistic skill but for her expertise in digital art. First of all, she'd been sent to Abu Dhabi to study the original. Then she must have obtained a 3D digital scan of the painting, for even the flattest picture is not as uniformly level as a printed image. This would have needed cooperation from the Louvre authorities which Menon presumably conned them into giving. She would have covertly brought the 3D scan back to the UK and made various test runs. The equipment we saw at Keats was presumably for this preparatory work, for checking settings and colours and working out the best way to get the huge industrial 3D printer to reproduce the surface of the *Salvator Mundi* accurately. Then Magda would have overseen the actual manufacture of the picture by the massive 3D printer at the airport.

The result was remarkable and only complete scientific analysis could reveal the difference from the real thing.

I turned the picture over and looked at the back. There was my first sight of the walnut panel on which the German artist had painted five hundred years ago. But his *Portrait of a Young Merchant* on the other side was now totally obscured.

I finally understood the full implication of what Hameed meant when he said the Amberger painting had been destroyed.

The polymers from the 3D printer would have been jetted directly on to the five hundred year old surface of the Amberger. Polymers are tougher and more resilient than ancient pigment and could not be removed from the surface of the painting without destroying what lay underneath. The *Portrait of a Young Merchant* was buried under, or fused together with, a thin layer of hardened polymer. The Amberger picture was destroyed in the same way Pompeii had been destroyed when it was covered in larva from Vesuvius.

I had finally found the missing picture but it was no more than a corpse. I had failed to save it, failed MacIver, failed Michael Cowper at the abbey, failed Jamie Rind.

We moved away from the crate as the two of the young men in expensive casuals lowered the lid and secured it.

'How are you getting this out of the country?' I asked Menon.

'A normal commercial flight from Heathrow,' he said. 'This was just a convenient place to pull everything together, away from spies and bugs.'

'What about going through customs?' said Rochelle.

'This container is a Diplomatic Bag. These gentlemen are accredited couriers.'

The inviolable and unsearchable so-called Diplomatic Bag, originally invented for the secure transfer of government documents, can be any kind of container, of any size. Even as he spoke Hameed's acolytes were fixing labels to the crate in Arabic and English which stated it contained official government property of the Kingdom of Qatar and must on no account be opened until it reached the Ministry of Culture and Sports in Doha. Hameed was sending this to himself.

I still didn't understand the whole of Menon's plan. 'Explain why Qatar is involved?' I said.

'There's no time,' said Hameed. He looked tense, unlike Menon who seemed remarkably laid-back.

'How did you fix the theft of the *Salvator Mundi* from the Louvre in Abu Dhabi?'

Menon smiled but said nothing.

'You nobbled some cleaners or backroom staff. Probably immigrant workers. Paid them the equivalent of a year's salary. Though that won't help them if they're caught. What would the penalty be? Life imprisonment? Execution?'

'Working as an immigrant in the Gulf is the same as life imprisonment. There's no escape.'

This came from the heart. Rochelle and I exchanged looks.

But Hameed and the others were becoming restless.

'We need to get going,' said Hameed.

'There's time,' said Menon. 'I think it's important that these two know exactly what I'm doing and why I'm doing it. From the horse's mouth as it were. Before the truth gets corrupted.'

'There's no need,' said Yasmine, who was bristling as well.

'And they don't want your autobiography…' said Hameed who had obviously heard it before.

Menon glared at Hameed. 'I'll tell them what I want. And when I want. And since I'm paying you, you'll stand still and listen or else go outside and wait.'

There was visible dissent from Hameed and Yasmine. They said nothing but slipped out of the door, followed quickly by the taser man

237

and the young guys who I now assumed were related to Hameed in some way.

Rochelle and I both exchanged glances again. A division was developing between the plotters. If we could make it worse we stood a chance of stopping their project. Menon, himself, seemed a more conducive and pliable adversary than the others.

'As I see it,' I said, 'what you've planned is a revenge attack against both Qatar and the United Arab Emirates. Though I'm not sure what they did to you to make you so angry.'

Menon held up the hand with half a finger missing.

'I was lucky this was all I lost,' he said. 'Many of my friends and co-workers were killed. Others lost arms, legs. It was not much better than slave labour. Nobody considered health and safety. Living in huts or shipping containers. No rights of any kind. No trades unions. Allowed to work but not become citizens. Almost prisoners in the country.'

'Where did you work?'

'Dubai, Abu Dhabi, then Qatar. I tried to start some kind of protest movement in Dubai for workers' rights. There was just a single demonstration which was broken up by the police. I escaped from the baton charge but they had me on video. I was a hunted man and I knew I'd never work there again. I managed to escape to Qatar and worked on building the football stadia for the World Cup. Inspectors from Amnesty came to look at conditions and wrote a report. Fat lot of good that did.'

'Why did you go to the Gulf in the first place?'

'I was naïve.'

'Very young?'

'Young, but old enough to know better. I had education. School and college. I was married – so not completely innocent. I had prospects. I was doing well.'

'Doing what?' said Rochelle.

'I was an accountant. They're never out of work are they?' He gave a bitter, cynical grin.

'So, what happened?'

'My office was in Dhaka, in the same block as a garment factory. What I've learned to call a sweat shop. Dresses made to sell in the UK for five pounds, worn a few times then thrown away. You know the sort of thing.'

'The building didn't just contain our office, our home was there too. One day there was a fire. Many of the garment workers died. Our apartment was destroyed and also my office. Everything went. Files, papers, computer. Even money in the safe. My business was destroyed and my wife was injured in the fire. I had heard about the building projects in the Gulf and the need for foreign workers. I was fit and young. So I went. I thought I could earn money quickly, more than I could in Bangladesh. I thought I would work maybe a year, then come home with cash in the bank and set up again. It was not to be. I sent money to my wife but I couldn't earn enough. I couldn't even leave. And I saw many thousands of other workers from my country, from Pakistan, from India, all of us in the same boat.'

'I was there twenty-two years. My wife died and I was lucky to be alive at the end of it. I made a plan to get revenge. I escaped from Qatar and made contacts with the terrorists. I had no sympathy with what they do but being a co-religionist gave me access. They had things to sell and I wanted to trade.'

'Didn't you feel guilty buying and selling stolen things? Selling off Iraq's or Syria's national heritage.'

'Better than having it blown up.'

He paused briefly.

'Don't forget museums around the world are full of the culture of other nations. I see nothing wrong in that as long as it is well cared for. Art is universal and for all mankind. It doesn't have to remain in the country which originated it.'

'So now you've set up this elaborate scam. You've had someone steal – or pretend to steal – the da Vinci from Abu Dhabi. You've made a perfect copy of the painting which someone will discover in Qatar. It looks like you're trying to start a war between the two countries.'

'Not at all. Though you might think both countries have been trying to do just that for some years. A lot of posturing, jealousy and envy. But when it comes to working conditions they're both as bad as each other. I leased Mr Sage's facility and brought in IT experts to prepare PR material, emails, that sort of thing and they will be released when we reach Qatar. It'll be the world's biggest publicity campaign ever. I want to show that both countries are more interested in money and self-aggrandisement than welfare or safety.'

I remembered the company name Clark had discovered. The Gulf Financial Settlement Company Ltd. It had sounded like a bland, even meaningless, name for a shell company. But Menon had a political axe to grind and I now realised the company's name was carefully chosen. His aim was to do what it said on the tin. To get his own back on the Gulf states for their mistreatment of him.

At that moment Yasmine, Hameed and the others returned.

'We must get this crate loaded,' Hameed said. 'What are we doing with these two busy-bodies.'

It was a cold, unpleasant look he gave us. Rochelle took a step towards me then turned a little away so we stood at ten to two, facing Hameed, Yasmine and the others who formed a semi-circle in front of us.

I felt her fingers lightly tap the back of my thigh. I took it as a signal she was poised and ready for anything which might confront us.

'I haven't decided,' Menon said.

'You'd better make your mind up,' said Yasmine. 'Nassir has a good selection of weapons ...' And the two of them exchanged private, conspiratorial smiles... 'Or I have the stuff which makes a bigger bang. The choice is yours.'

'I want no more killing,' said Menon quickly. 'You killed enough people already.'

'I've killed nobody,' said Hameed.

'You hired that maniac Morina. He went berserk.'

'He got the job done, didn't he?' Hameed spoke like he was talking about a bolshie bricklayer or a goofy gardener.

'But... the cost! Police everywhere. Mr Kite on our trail. And then this woman. He was bad choice. Very bad. Then you got him killed.'

'You said you wanted rid of him. I did what you wanted.'

'I meant hand him over to the police or something. Not blow him up. Using my car as well.'

'I'm so sorry. My mistake,' said Hameed in a voice so full of cynicism and fake deference it was like sticking two fingers up.

Menon said no more but sucked in breath and took a few paces around the shed.

'You've announced the da Vinci is stolen but it's actually safe in a vault in Abu Dhabi, 'I said. 'What happens next?'

I looked at Hameed. He was saying nothing.

'There will be squabbling, arguments, accusations, threats,' said Menon. 'Our PR assault will encourage this with false stories. We will lead them roundabout until they are dizzy chasing their own tails. Like Puck in Midsummer Night's Dream...'

I glimpsed Hameed and Yasmine raising their eyebrows at each other. No vote of confidence from them.

'... Thorough bush, thorough briar.' Menon was enjoying himself.

I didn't get the reference but I heard Rochelle go, 'Oh, yes,' in recognition of the quote.

'Up and down, up and down, I will lead them up and down.' Menon chuckled as he quoted more lines of what I took to be Shakespeare. He seemed to enjoy the aptness of his reference. 'We will embarrass both countries, show them up as miserly, xenophobic, autocratic, immoral. We'll show they value absurd icons of art – and indeed football tournaments – far more than social justice, democracy or personal liberty. We'll show their values are topsy-turvy. We'll enumerate the abuses suffered by thousands of workers, forced to toil to glorify the state which subjugates them. We will expose their moral bankruptcy.'

Menon looked around the tiny group in front of him as if it was an arena of a hundred thousand, nodding at the rightness of what he had said. But there was no reaction. Hameed and the others were unmoved. More than unmoved. They looked completely blank. Negative.

The crack between the conspirators was developing into a chasm. I felt confident of wrapping the case quickly.

'How does stealing works of art make your case?' I said, feeling I was somehow siding with Hameed and Yasmine.

'Because these states have signed up to a corrupt western value system. The da Vinci painting sold for nearly half a billion dollars. How ridiculous. No painting is worth that. Especially not such a dubious work as this – yes, I have studied it. I know the doubts about its authorship, its condition. They wanted to buy a prestige item, a stand-out statement piece, but were duped by the art trade. My aim is to expose the corruption in the art business as well.'

'Sounds like a man after your own heart,' said Rochelle in a low whisper, quirking her eyebrows at me.

People have tried to expose the art trade before. It never works. Pictures of course have no intrinsic value. The trade sells abstract qualities like workmanship and beauty, rarity and historicity but the value of art depends wholly on fashion.

'It sounds a tricky call,' I said tentatively. 'A lot of effort to make a moral point.'

Menon's plan seemed bizarre. Crazily philanthropic. It wasn't at all what I'd imagined at the outset.

'Shock tactics in aid of good works,' said Rochelle. 'It's a new approach, I suppose, but pretty hare-brained.'

'No,' said Menon firmly. 'Sensible. Measured. Targeted.' He still looked confident and assured.

I was watching Hameed, Yasmine and the others. They had a problem with Menon's scheme too. I felt sure we could crush his plan before it caused an international incident, before it led to an atrocity.

'What about your colleagues?' I said. 'Do they think the plan is hare-brained? Bonkers? Doomed to fail?'

'Of course not,' said Menon, turning towards Hameed whose face remained blank.

'Let's ask them,' I said.

Hameed spoke quietly in Arabic to Yasmine and the others and whatever he said, they agreed with. Rochelle and I exchanged looks, both taking this as an encouraging move.

'You want to give up on Mr Menon's plan?' I said.

Hameed muttered a few words to Yasmine and at that moment Scott Sage walked in.

He looked around, sensed the atmosphere.

'I feel I've arrived at some kind of crisis,' he said with a wickedly teasing look in his eyes. 'Let me know if I can be of any assistance.' He casually took out his nail clippers and snipped at his nails.

Sage's arrival spurred Hameed into action. He took a few steps towards Menon and tapped him on the chest as if he were a friend. Or an underling.

'There's no easy way to say this, Fawaz. But I'm afraid this is what you would call a mutiny. We're taking over from you.'

Menon couldn't comprehend. He opened his mouth, he closed his mouth, he opened it again. But no sounds emerged.

'Your little plan was a delicate thing, innocent, fragile. Like a tender bloom on a tropical plant,' said Yasmine putting on a cartoony, child-like voice. She was good with words and laughed raucously at her own purple prose. I heard Sage chuckling too. Then Yasmine's laughter stopped abruptly and her voice was cold and metallic. 'But it wasn't tough enough to face bad weather. Or a reality check.'

'So we have a new plan,' said Hameed.

'What do you mean?' said Menon, beginning to lose his cool. 'Everything is set up.'

'Yes, it is,' said Yasmine. 'But not what you commissioned.'

'The theft of the painting and the forgery is great,' said Hameed. 'We use that for our own purposes.'

'Which are?' I said, knowing things were about to get worse, not better.

Hameed turned to me.

'To attack Qatar, of course.' Hameed beamed, delighted at his coup.

I was stunned. It didn't make sense.

'But you are Qataris…'

Hameed laughed. 'Only on the surface.'

Rochelle and I turned to each other.

'Sleepers?' she said, hardly believing it.

I nodded, equally astonished. 'Emirati double agents.'

'Menon says he suffered, well we've suffered from the Qataris long enough and like him we want retribution. We want to show the world that the Emirates are on the side of right and the Qataris are not.'

'This is nonsense,' said Menon.

'Shut up,' said Hameed and hit Menon hard across the face. The elderly man fell to the floor but quickly scrambled on to his feet again.

243

The look on his face suggested he had been struck in a similar way in the past. On the construction sites.

'Mr Sage,' Menon said, 'you can't go along with this. You have no quarrel with the state of Qatar.'

Sage shrugged and smiled. 'No,' he said. 'But I suppose I'm a mercenary. You are wealthy. I *was* wealthy. But the Emirates are astronomically, unimaginably rich. I simply sold my services to the highest bidder. And they offered me nationality. So I should be safe from British justice for the foreseeable future. Excellent deal all round. Job done.'

Menon was approaching Sage, livid, fists clenched.

'I paid for all that equipment. You betrayed me.'

Sage took a few judicious steps backwards. 'I took a better offer, that's all.'

Menon just stood there with his former allies, now enemies, ranged around him. His slim frame visibly seemed to shrink and crumble. The light went from his eyes, the flesh on his face sagged, his shoulders slumped. For years he'd nurtured plans for revenge against those who had abused him. His preparations had been involved, expensive and lengthy. It had been his dream. An unreal dream maybe, but it had driven him on. It had been his life's work and now it was utterly worthless, a handful of dust.

I wondered if he was going to collapse and found myself on the point of feeling sorry for him.

Hameed ignored Menon and issued some instructions in Arabic. Two of his team moved towards the flight box holding the picture while two others moved towards Menon. As the young men got near to Menon he launched himself at one of them and wrenched a pistol out of the man's shoulder holster.

'Leave it,' Menon shouted, aiming the gun at the men lifting the flight box, then he whirled round towards Sage and the others, saying, 'Keep away.'

But he was too slow.

Hameed had already drawn his own weapon and two shots rang out.

Menon slumped to the floor, blood rapidly blossoming through his clothes.

'Shit,' said Rochelle.

Exactly. A shockingly casual assassination of the man who was supposedly employing Hameed.

But there was a very different reaction from Hameed's team. Yasmine smiled and put an arm around Hameed. Two of the wealthy young relatives, if that's what they were, nodded approvingly at the killing while a third bent down to examine Menon, crouching on his haunches rather than kneeling, presumably not wanting to sully his expensive designer chinos. The medical man found no pulse and gave Hameed a horrifyingly glib thumbs up.

I'd reckoned Hameed was a bit of a wuss when I first encountered him at the hotel. It's often wrong to make snap judgements on people.

I looked up and turned to Rochelle. Our eyes met. I guess she saw in my eyes what I saw in hers. Horror, fear, uncertainty. Were we to be next? That seemed likely.

Only minutes earlier I'd felt compassionately towards Menon. How stupid was that? His motives were understandable but he'd got involved in a world he didn't understand. With people who were very different from him.

He had let the dogs out. Wild and vicious dogs. And now they were running free, doing what they wanted. They would be difficult to cage up again.

Rochelle and I moved closer, almost back-to-back, checking for any sign of an attack on us. But all we saw was Sage drawing Hameed aside. Their conversation started in a friendly fashion but quickly their expressions grew tense and their voices rose. Hameed turned away from Sage trying to end the conversation.

'We give it at airport. O.K.?'

Sage wouldn't let him go.

'That's not what we agreed. I really need it now. You promised me nationality. Without the papers and the passport, I can be extradited... anything.'

'Have you completed? Finished everything?'

'You know it's all ready. The bots will disseminate the blogs, tweets, press releases and social media messages. Everything is set up for the arranged time.'

'It is automatic?'

'Yes, I've already said. Completely automatic. Pre-programmed. So where's my passport? I was expecting it earlier. That's the only reason I had to drag down here.'

'We give to you. Do not worry.'

Sage sighed with frustration and walked away from the confrontation.

The rapid development of events was breath-taking. A complete reversal.

When severe danger is imminent my policy is to keep talking. To try to engender some rapport between me and my enemy. So they can empathise with me. The reverse of the Stockholm Syndrome, if you like.

'Let me check I've got *your* plan right,' I said to Hameed in as light and disinterested a tone as I could muster. 'You and Sage's computer kids were behind all the World Cup scare stories. You hacked into the ticketing systems to deny service then issued a ton of fake news stories about lost data. You must also have hacked into the World Health Organisation to create the Ebola scare. As for the very fanciful threat of tsunamis, well… brilliant! But tell me how that one worked.'

'There's a network of automatic buoys which float around the world's oceans monitoring sea and weather conditions,' said Rochelle. 'They must have hacked into them and corrupted the data they sent back.'

Hameed smiled. Which proved Rochelle was right.

I also realised they may even have caused the aircraft fault – for fun, I suppose, just because they could – which diverted Hameed's plane to Stansted. Unknown to them, and a fortuitous bonus, it was that which prevented me recovering the picture from the taxi.

'Why do you want to destroy the World Cup? Qatar's the first Arab country to host the tournament. Why aren't you supporting them?'

'They are not worthy,' said Hameed

'Because they got it by bribery?'

He shrugged. 'They pay money, of course. That is just the way business is done. If you British had spent some money you could have had the World Cup. But you wouldn't pay money. You don't like to do that. You think you have royal right to organise these sports. You send a Prince or a Minister to talk but you do not really try. If you really want, you have to pay. You think the way we behave is wrong. Not sporting. Not cricket, old boy.' He laughed and Yasmine laughed too, giving him a congratulatory pat on the back for his colloquial English usage.

Rochelle intervened. 'O.K. Slag us off if you want. But answer Kite's question. Why are you doing this?'

'They know nothing about football. People don't watch it in their country. The people who run football in Qatar are not intelligent, not praiseworthy. And Qatar wants to be most powerful nation in the Gulf. They know the World Cup will get them TV coverage worth billions in every nation on earth. Many of you Brits can't even pronounce the name of the country. In a short time you will hear the name Qatar on every TV and radio channel in the world. That is why Qatar wanted the World Cup – for kudos, for status.'

'Isn't that the reason the UAE did a deal with the Paris Louvre to build a new gallery in Abu Dhabi?'

'No. Quite different. We are supporting culture and art.'

'Seems to me you're jealous of Qatar. They had the World Cup idea before you did.'

'They had the idea because they want to do us down. They want us to be a laughing stock, to lose face among Arab nations. They are upstarts. Who do they think they are?'

'They have different politics from you, that's all.'

'Terrorist politics. It is a crime to say anything in support of Qatar in my country. A serious crime.'

Yasmine took over the lecture: 'They want to make us look like a second class nation. We will show *them* to be a second class nation. And idiots and clowns and, worst of all, thieves.'

I looked at her. She was dangerous, all right. Fanatical. Not open to reason. Like a fundamentalist.

'So your plan is to smuggle the fake picture into Qatar via the diplomatic bag and leave it where it is sure to be found quickly. Meanwhile you slip back into safety in the UAE. You then release news of an invented plot that links the theft to a Qatari-based terrorist group who planned, let's say, to ransom the picture for hundreds of

247

Stuart Doughty

millions of dollars. Nobody will doubt that the fake picture is genuine. And if they do you can submit the rare walnut panel to testing and show conclusively it's original medieval timber.'

Hameed nodded again. 'You understand us well.'

'And here's the best bit…' said Scott Sage with a glint in his eye. He'd been silent for a while but now eagerly took the chance to stake his ownership of part of the plot. 'The best bit is, to coincide with the discovery of the picture in Qatar, there'll be a PR blitz. A PR assault like the world has never seen.'

'Bigger than the outburst on social media when the theft was announced?'

'Yes. That was big. Next time it'll be colossal. Billions of pre-prepared and targeted internet messages, tweets, posts and emails will flood cyberspace. All of them criticising the people of Qatar as thieves and criminals and attacking their links to terrorist groups. There will be massive criticism of the preparations for the World Cup and news stories will show an active terrorist threat to participants and spectators. Like Munich 1972. We'll hack the private emails of world leaders, sending and answering messages that they won't even see and copying them to the United Nations, the EU, to everybody. World opinion will be so stoked up that FIFA will have no option but to cancel the World Cup. All down to me,' said Sage, smiling. 'Or at least the kids I hired. You've heard of the Bilbao effect – how a new art gallery in Bilbao suddenly put that city on the map and brought in tourists and investment?'

I nodded. 'It was the Guggenheim Gallery.'

'That's what they want with the World Cup. To create a Qatar effect,' said Sage.

'But we'll destroy it,' said Hameed. 'We'll create the opposite… a …a…' He hesitated.

'A Hiroshima effect?' I said.

Hameed laughed. Something I hadn't seen him do before. 'Yes. Exactly. Of course we won't physically destroy anything.'

'What about the consequences?' I said.

'What if your PR blitz provokes a military blitz?' said Rochelle.

'We'll be ready. If they attack, the world will condemn them. We have no military objectives, we only want to expose lies.'

'Qatar will not take military action,' Hameed said. 'They talk big. But do small.

'You're trying to ruin another sovereign nation. To destroy them. Without a shot being fired.'

'Ingenious, no?' said Hameed.

'I can't believe this is official Emirates government policy,' I said. 'Are you just a bored billionaire who's trying to ingratiate himself with the Emir?'

'I work for the Emir. I am loyal to him. I have served him under cover for many years, as has my wife.' He indicated Yasmine. 'But this is my policy. My plan. And I have the loyal support of my family.' He indicated the three young men in Saville Row casuals and I knew my hunch had been right.

So Hameed was a renegade, pursuing his own line in the hope it would lead him right to the top. In the Gulf states the centre of power is a small group of families or even just one family. Not unlike England in the middle ages when the king supposedly had absolute power but other ambitious aristocrats jostled for the top job. Control of the country depended on the king's ability to keep these overmighty subjects in check. When he couldn't do that, things fell apart and you had the Wars of the Roses.

Sage took Hameed by the arm.

'Sorry to be a bore, but my passport..?'

Hameed turned on him.

'Why did you hire the Kosovan? Morina.'

'What?' said Sage.

'Menon was right about that at least. The Kosovan killed people. His job was to steal the painting.'

'He did that, didn't he? Water under the bridge, surely. Now sort out my passport. Sort it. Or else.'

'Or else what?' Hameed looked distressed by Sage's presumption.

'Or else I'll call Scotland Yard and explain what's happening. If you don't cough up the cash I'm happy to go to prison for a spell. I'm broke. I've nothing left. Nothing left to lose.'

'You would do that?'

'Yes.'

Hameed thought for a moment then turned away and spoke to the taser man in Arabic. I didn't understand the words but the structure of what he said was clear. Hameed had issued an order which had surprised the other man. He'd queried the order. Hameed had reaffirmed what he'd said in sterner tones and the other had acquiesced.

Hameed turned back to Sage.

'While you talk to the police what about the emails, the tweets? Will they be sent? Are they automatic.'

'They are automatic. Once you activate the programme key.'

'Then it's not automatic, is it? Who has the key?'

'I do of course. So hand over my passport and confirm the money is in my account in the UAE.'

'Show me this programme key.'

Sage sighed. 'It's on a flashdrive.' He dug in a pocket and held up the USB. 'There.'

'Thank you, Mr Sage.'

Then there was a strange pause. Hameed stood still and said nothing. Sage stood still also, holding the memory stick in the air like an exhibit.

'Well?' he said, with an expression of amusement at the hiatus.

Then I saw a flurry of movement to my left. I turned and saw the taser man had drawn a gun.

Sage saw it too and looked horrified. The gun was aimed at him.

'Wha…?' he started to say.

Then a shot was fired.

Rochelle shrieked.

For a moment Sage stood completely still, holding out the memory stick as before, an expression of shock and despair on his face.

Then there was another shot and Sage gasped and collapsed. I think he was dead before he hit the floor.

The taser man holstered his gun and Hameed gave him a nod of thanks.

I'd missed Hameed give the fatal signal but it was clear the murder had been pre-arranged in the brief Arabic conversation I'd heard. A second cold-blooded elimination of a member of the team. Again I reassessed Hameed. He was behaving now like a psychopath, a megalomaniac. Not so different from the unfeeling Morina.

Hameed moved towards Sage's inert body, picked up the memory stick from the floor and pocketed it. I saw Rochelle grim-faced, her jaw clenched shut. But I could see her hands trembling.

Hameed then spoke to his team in Arabic again. Hearing but not understanding his words, Rochelle closed her eyes and looked down at the floor, expecting another shot.

I scarcely took a breath, not taking my eyes off Hameed. He seemed to be discussing nuts-and-bolts issues with Yasmine and the others. His tone was thankfully calm, mundane, practical.

No shot came.

For the moment at least there was a pause in the killing.

Chapter 28

What happened next was Hameed's team produced heavy-duty plastic cable ties, pulled our arms behind our backs, looped the ties round our wrists and pulled them tight so the sharp edges of the plastic cut into our flesh. I heard Rochelle gasp in pain. 'Bastard,' she muttered.

I looked at her, caught her eye, but she shook her head as if to tell me not to worry. Then they drove us at gunpoint into the derelict building we'd seen earlier – the old fuel store.

They hobbled us with another cable tie around our ankles and dragged us along the floor until we were next to one of the giant metal fuel tanks. Using more plastic ties they pinioned each of us to one of the tank's rusty steel legs which were bolted to the concrete floor.

They left us and went out, only to return in a couple of minutes dragging in the body of Sage which was dumped on the floor a few feet in front of us. Again they left and again they returned, this time dumping Menon's body on the floor in a tumbled heap.

The fuel store was turning into a morgue.

It was obvious that Rochelle and I were soon meant to join Sage and Menon in some kind of funeral rite.

One of the young men went over to a draining valve at the bottom of one of the big tanks and tried to turn the control wheel. Nothing happened. It was completely seized. So he found a huge spanner from somewhere and started to hit the valve. The other said something in Arabic and the first guy stopped hitting the tap and instead threaded the end of the spanner through the spokes of the rotary wheel on top of the valve to give him more purchase. He pulled on his spanner, straining hard against seventy years of rust and the wheel suddenly turned. The other gave an ironic cheer and his comrade excitedly turned the wheel until the valve was fully open.

The tank must have been emptied long ago because no fuel gushed out. The man with the giant spanner looked disappointed and hit the tap again in frustration. Slowly a thin trickle of liquid started to drip from the tap and spatter on the floor.

Hameed came in, looked at the measly dribble of fuel and gave the men – his relatives – a curt order. The men moved across the shed and started to unfasten a cast-iron plate in the floor. As the iron plate was removed, a strong smell wafted up from an underground storage tank. The smell of countless litres of aviation fuel.

The funeral rite looked as if it was to be a cremation. A huge conflagration that would leave no trace of any of us. The fact they hadn't shot us first suggested they wanted us to have a horrendously painful death. A ritual burning. Like the Spanish Inquisition. *Auto-da-fe*. That was the phrase I dredged up from school history classes.

I went cold. I looked down at the scarred concrete floor, away from the bodies, away from the men fussing with the fuel tank plate, away from Rochelle. I'd come to this place, knowing the risks, but I'd asked Rochelle for help and she'd volunteered. I thought of the pictures of her near the embassy. Blithe, happy-go-lucky, carefree. I felt guilty.

Then Yasmine appeared. She was carrying a Harrods bag. In any other situation, given her age and style, you'd imagine she'd just been shopping. But the Harrods bag at Kempton Park had been lethal and this bag had to hold something similar.

It was difficult to re-imagine Yasmine, the extrovert, sexy and welcoming receptionist, as a bomb maker. But she placed the bag on the floor with a professional and concentrated care which was stomach-churning. No matches, no kindling, no fuses. No mistakes, no slip-ups, no escape. They wanted to start the cremation ceremony with a bang.

The trickle of fuel from the tank was forming an expanding pool which was seeping ever closer to the Harrods bag.

I wrenched hard at the plastic ties until they bit deep into my wrists and ankles. The pain was intense but there was no movement in the ties. As I knew there wouldn't be. I'd heard about suicide victims who'd hanged themselves and then had second thoughts at the last minute as the noose tightened. Such bodies were found with deep and bloody gouges around the neck where the victim had hopelessly tried to loosen the ligature.

'Goodbye,' said Hameed. 'Maybe somebody finds you here, maybe not.' He turned to Sage's body, regarding him with contempt. 'Mr Sage was thinking he was more clever than us. He was thinking to work for us was easy way to earn money. I think his name in English means magus or wise man or something. But he's not a magus, not a wise man. He made bad mistakes.'

I felt he could have been talking about me.

Hameed turned and left the building with Yasmine. Then we heard voices outside as the box was loaded into one of the cars and directions were given to the team.

I looked down at the pitted concrete, my mind numb, not able to think, not wanting to think. There were grimy paint splashes on the floor, made seventy or eighty years ago by young airmen detailed to keep the tanks in good order. The shape of one of the splashes reminded me of a map of France. There was a protuberance where Brittany stuck out into the Atlantic, a bay-like shape where Cherbourg is and a straighter line for the Bordeaux area in the south. Would I ever go to France again?

Rochelle interrupted my introspection. She could stay silent no longer and her emotions let rip.

'This is a fine bloody mess we're in. We came here to save a picture. But the bloody picture's a write-off. Not just a suicide mission, but a bloody pointless suicide mission.' She spat out the words, her voice full of anger, bitterness and despair and with what sounded like a sob at the end.

I looked towards her. Her face was turned away. 'Yes, but...' I started.

'But fucking what?'

I didn't know what. I couldn't reply. I had nothing to say. No plan, no sparky one-liners. Even so her outburst galvanised me. I had to stop dwelling on the low chance of being rescued and the prospect of a painful death. I had to stop gazing at the floor and moping. I had to work out how to escape.

The picture might be destroyed but there was now a bigger goal than recovering stolen art. Hameed's gang were intent on causing mayhem in the Gulf and starting... what? A revolution? An invasion? A war? Someone had to stop them. Someone... Us. It seemed almost impossible. But I needed to shake Rochelle up and shake myself up as well.

Once again I strained as hard as I could against the plastic ties, twisting, wriggling about, trying to exert some purchase, looking for a weak point, hoping one of the ties hadn't been fixed properly. My shifting and struggling roused Rochelle.

'No point,' she said. 'You know how they work. The little slider moves only one way. Once they're tight the only way is to cut them off and the plastic's heavy gauge. Breaking strain of hundreds of pounds. It needs a Stanley knife or wire cutters.' Once again her voice was flat, hopeless.

But Hameed's people had made what seemed like an error in the way they'd trussed us to the legs of the tank. Instead of putting our arms around the struts and then binding our wrists close against it, they had bound our wrists first and then looped another longer tie from our wrists around the tank supports. It was a small difference but it allowed us just a bit of movement. I demonstrated this to Rochelle.

'Whoopee,' she said in the same fatalistic tone. 'If you just pass the wire cutters we'll be out of here in a jiffy.'

I looked at her but she wouldn't meet my eyes, lost in her own desolate thoughts. Then out of the blue she said:

'Bass Pale Ale.'

'What?'

'The old bottle over there.' She nodded towards a window sill where there was a cobwebby, ancient beer bottle. Left by one of the aircraftmen on a painting detail. 'Broken glass would do the trick.'

'Rochelle...'

'There are tools in your car, as well...'

'Rochelle!'

She wasn't helping the situation. She was rattling me, now. Stopping me from thinking positively.

Then I realised it was selfish to think like that.

Rochelle was tough and resourceful, but everyone has their limits. And she'd been brought to this place because of a case of mine. I'd suggested the observation on Hameed, not her. And because of over-enthusiasm or her general gung-ho, zesty approach to life she'd got captured.

I wanted to comfort her.

I wanted to hold her hand, I wanted to put my arm around her. If only…

There was another silence between us. Minutes dragged by. I looked at the Harrods bag. As if reading my thoughts, Rochelle said:

'How long's the timer, do you think?'

I couldn't answer. An hour? Six hours? A day? Two days? They wanted us to suffer. So I thought it would be longer than shorter. To frighten us to death. To drive us insane.

'The longer it is, the more time we have to find an escape,' I said. Whistling in the dark.

'That sounds like the infinite number of monkeys,' she said.

'What?'

'You know the theorem. If an infinite number of monkeys typed on an infinite number of typewriters for long enough they could reproduce the works of Shakespeare.'

I looked across to her, her face was still turned away from me so I couldn't gauge her expression. It was a typical caustic Rochelle remark, but it wasn't despair. It was humour. It was looking on the bright side of life.

A chink.

I had to develop it.

I looked at the distance between us where we lay tied up on the floor. It was about two metres. Close enough for some kind of contact. I moved my feet sideways towards her and could just reach her legs. I tapped lightly on her thigh with one of my feet.

'Hey, Rochelle,' I said.

'What?'

'I was just thinking. If I could, I'd put my arm around you.'

'Really? Why?'

'Well, you know… to buck you up.'

There was a pause. She still kept her face turned from me.

256

'You did say "buck" did you? Not something else?'

I grinned privately. A bit of progress.

'Anyway, how do you know I'd want physical contact?' she said.

'I'd chance my arm.'

'Hmm. Macho man.' A beat, then: 'I suppose you'd want to smother hot, wet kisses upon my frail and panting body, tear away my shift, clasp my rosebud bosoms with your manly hands and ply your throbbing member to transport me into the realms of ecstasy.'

I broke out laughing.

'Rochelle, I didn't know you did telephone sex in your spare time.'

She turned round to face me. She was smiling. Then she slid her legs nearer to mine and rested both of them on my shins.

'One can but dream,' she said.

Outside we heard Arabic voices. It seemed they hadn't left yet and there was some kind of alert. I heard Hameed issue some instructions and then there was the sound of people running off. Then there was silence.

Except for the steady drip, drip, drip of the fuel on to the floor.

'Tell me about India. How the two of you met. Tell me the background.'

'Why?'

'We've nothing else to do. You might have an entertaining yarn to spin.'

'We don't need entertainment now.'

'We do. I just proved that.' She paused significantly. 'And this may be the last chance you have to tell anybody.'

'For god's sake… Let's not talk about my past when we should be trying to get out of here.'

'Suit yourself,' she said, raising her eyebrows in a disbelieving way.

In desperation I looked over at the body of Sage – and had an idea.

'He may have something that can help us escape.'

Rochelle stared at the body for a long minute. Then she turned back to me. 'Mobile phone?'

'That's what I was thinking of.'

Rochelle looked back warily at the dead body which had been dumped a metre or so in front of her. The blood on his chest had dried to a burnt sienna. It was too soon for any putrefaction but even above the smell of fuel I got from his corpse the bitter aroma of old sweat.

'How do we reach him?' she said.

'You can reach him with your feet. Move as far away from the fuel tank as you can and stretch your legs out.'

Rochelle looked uncertain, but she did what I said. She slithered across the concrete on her bottom until her hands were as far behind her back as they would go. Then stretched her legs forward. The heels of her shoes were just touching Sage's body.

'I can't reach him.'

'See his trousers. There are belt loops on the waistband. Try to hook a heel into one of the loops.'

'Really?' Her voice faltered.

'Yes, really.' Then I looked at her. 'You're not squeamish?'

'Of course not.'

I wasn't convinced.

'Never seen a dead body?'

'Yeah, course'

I gave her another look.

'Well... no.'

'How did you manage that?'

She said nothing.

Police officers have plenty of chances to encounter corpses. Road traffic accidents, deaths by natural causes, suicides, quite apart from murders.

'Now's your chance to get some experience.'

Rochelle gave me a sour look and stretched her legs further out. The nearest belt loop to her was at the side of Sage's waist. She angled her foot, trying to slot the heel in. It was like some perverted fairground sideshow. Trousers instead of ducks. She tried again and again, wincing and breathing hard with the effort, screwing her face up, plainly not liking what she was doing. Then finally the heel slotted in.

'Good. Now drag him towards us.'

Rochelle pulled. Nothing happened.

'Pull harder.'

'I'm trying.'

I saw her face turn away from me and her leg relax, slumping to the ground. She was breathing hard.

'Feeling all right?'

'Course.'

She obviously wasn't. But we couldn't hang about. Quite apart from the timer on the bomb, rigor mortis would begin to affect Sage's body soon. That would make moving or searching him even harder.

'Think of something nice to take your mind off what you're doing. A holiday, a party, something sexy.'

After a few moments her head turned back and the muscles in her leg stiffened as she resumed the pressure on Sage's body.

'Are you thinking nice thoughts?'

'Yes.'

She pulled hard.

Sage wasn't a lightweight and there was plenty of friction between body and floor. But his body moved a few inches.

'Yes!' I said. 'Keep going.'

'This is like some dreadful gym exercise for stomach toning.'

She pulled hard again, but the shoe slipped off her heel so only her toes were still inside the shoe.

'I'm getting cramp!'

'Rest for a moment. Then try again. You can do it.'

She pulled the shoe out of the belt loop and rested it flat on the ground in front of her. I saw her pressing down and flexing her toes inside the shoe to ease the cramp. After a few seconds she lifted her leg again, inserted the heel into the loop and yanked hard.

The body moved a little more.

The sound of car doors shutting and engines starting up outside surprised me. Were the Arabs only just leaving? What had they been doing?

'Keep pulling. You're doing well.'

'It's a killer on the thigh muscles,' she said, grimacing, as inch by inch Sage's body was moving nearer to us.

'Killer heels?'

'Shut up,' she said.

I didn't know why I was making silly jokes either.

Then the trouser loop snapped. With the tension released, Rochelle's leg swung up and her shoe sailed off her foot. The shoe flew up in the air, hit the wall of the fuel store and dropped to the ground behind her.

She groaned despairingly.

'Don't worry. He's nearer now so go for a loop on the front. On his stomach. Use your other foot,' I said. 'I know it's not pleasant but it'll be an easier angle.'

She applied the heel of her remaining shoe to the other belt loop, quickly got the heel hooked in place and pulled repeatedly, remorselessly and enthusiastically. That Sage had once been a living, breathing person no longer seemed to worry her. Bit by bit, inch by inch the body moved closer. Soon his legs were in range of my feet. I put my feet over his knees and pulled as well. This brought him closer so Rochelle looped her legs over his upper body and pulled in the same way.

In this gruesome and ungainly fashion, the body of the dead PR guru moved nearer. I saw blood smears on the legs of Rochelle's boiler suit and I felt the heel of my shoes digging into the pudgy flesh of Sage's calves. But we couldn't afford to be fastidious. Soon the back of Rochelle's thighs were on Sage's chest and mine were on his knees. We could get the body no closer to us without moving ourselves.

'Done it.' Rochelle breathed out as she lifted her legs off the corpse and swivelled her body away from it, moving her legs on to the floor close to the iron tank and relaxing back flat on to the floor. It was like we'd already found a way out of our imprisonment and had time to celebrate.

But how to search the body when our hands were tied behind us?

I stood up.

'I've got to get him closer,' I said.

I stood up, straining at the plastic ties, and began to back heel Sage towards me like a rugby hooker. Rochelle squirmed out of the way as I brought Sage up to where I stood, hard against the edge of the rusty tank supports.

So my hands could reach the body I turned round, then squatted down, half kneeling half sitting on the still warm corpse. Working by touch alone, I started to search his clothes, one side of the body at a time. I felt the side trouser pocket nearest to me, but only found coins there. Then I moved to a jacket hip pocket. Nothing. I found an inside pocket. There was something there, but it felt soft. I pulled hard, ripping the fabric, and something came out.

'Just a notebook,' Rochelle said.

I threw it on the floor.

My range of movement was severely restricted but I needed to search the other side. I grabbed blindly for his jacket, got a grip on it and wrenched the material towards me, fumbling to find his breast pocket. There was a tearing sound and then I felt a wallet in the blood-soaked breast pocket. That was no use either but I pulled it out and put it on the floor between us and felt my way down the jacket towards the other hip pockets.

My fingers felt something hard there. It was unmistakeably a mobile phone. I grabbed it and pulled it out.

Rochelle cheered.

I angled the phone towards her. 'Can you see the screen?'

'Just about. It's locked, asking for a password.'

'Isn't there an emergency call option?'

'Can't see it.'

'Are you sure?'

Rochelle leaned further towards me, desperately peering at the phone. 'No. It's not there. People remove them sometimes. To stop accidental calls.'

I breathed out hard. 'Yeah. Great idea. Like removing lifeboats from a ship to stop stowaways hiding in them.' I paused, mightily frustrated. 'We'd better try for a password then. What do reckon? His birthday?'

'You know his birthday?'

'No. But you're going to find it. He'll have a driving licence in his wallet. Pull it out.'

Rochelle used her feet to drag the bloody wallet nearer to her, then swivelled round, grabbed it and extracted the driving licence.

'I've got it. But I can't read behind my back.'

'Hold it towards me.'

In this way we found Sage's birthday and then Rochelle guided my fingers on to the right keys to insert a password into the phone. We tried day and month first, then just the year. But both tries simply brought up "Password not recognised: Try Again". Then we tried day of the month and the last two digits of the year. We got: "Password failed. Phone locked."

'Shit,' said Rochelle, lying back flat on the concrete.

I let the phone drop to the ground, and lay back too, frustrated and demoralised after all that effort.

Neither of us spoke for a few moments, then Rochelle said,

'Did you know your father was an informer?'

The word made him sound like he'd been talking to the Nazis or the Stasi.

Hulk-like anger swelled inside me. 'Did India tell you? Did she tell you everything about me? Have you known all along who she is?' I looked at her accusingly, bitterly.

'It was only the other day. After I'd been to your place – the day your boss was there. She told me then.'

I breathed out hard. I try to keep a secret for fifteen years and suddenly it's everywhere. What a waste of time. Waste of energy. If I'd had therapy like people suggested perhaps that's what I'd have been told. Don't try to bottle it up.

Bit bloody late for that kind of advice.

'What you tried to do – the vodka and so on – that's understandable. It was fair to try and get him nicked.'

Bizarrely, dragging Sage's body around had removed barriers, stripped away my armour, changed my naturally defensive nature. Secrecy suddenly seemed of no importance. So I replied calmly, honestly.

'I acted stupidly. Thoughtlessly. Emotionally.'

'But you didn't kill them. Nothing was your fault. There's no blame.'

'But I *wanted* to kill them. I thought I had done and then I was in a worse state than before. Still not knowing what to do. I could've been an architect but I joined the police. And you see where that has led. Both of us are completely screwed, stuck in this God-awful place.'

We both lay silent again.

Then a thought burst through my introspection.

'Did I search the other hip pocket?'

Working behind my back I'd literally lost sight of what I was doing.

'I don't know. Stop whingeing and have a bloody look.'

I re-angled myself to attack the remaining pocket. I worked my fingers under the fabric flap and dug down. My fingers found something cold and metallic. I pulled it out.

'Nail clippers,' said Rochelle.

I'd forgotten Sage's obsessive use of his nail clippers.

'Absolutely ideal.'

But they weren't ideal.

They were those tiny, almost feminine, clippers with a small folding lever which swivels to operate the spring mechanism. I swivelled the lever, folded it back and felt for the plastic tie that bound my wrists. I pressed and pressed the tiny clippers against the thick plastic. I felt the jaws sink into it but they weren't cutting through. I worked the clippers again and again but the clippers were small and weak. I'd seen similar ones as gifts in posh Christmas crackers. They were intended for shaping delicate nails, not chopping through several millimetres of industrial-grade plastic. It was like digging a grave with a teaspoon. I squeezed the clippers with all my strength, pressing until my fingers were numb. I pressed and pressed and pulled sideways at the tie. I repeated the movement so many times I lost count.

Finally, mercifully and thankfully the plastic parted and my arms were free.

I sat on the floor and attacked the plastic ties holding my ankles. Again it took what seemed like an age, but in the end the plastic succumbed to my frantic snipping.

I stood up, moved to Rochelle and started on her cable ties.

'Quickly, Kite,' she said.

I was putting as much pressure as I could on the clippers, forcing the thin steel blades together.

Then the clippers fell apart.

Rochelle gasped in horror as I picked up the component parts from the paint-splashed concrete. It was impossible to repair. They were three useless bits of metal. Frustrated, angry and frightened, Rochelle desperately tried to force her wrists apart, straining hard. I saw the plastic cut into her flesh.

'You'll only hurt yourself,' I said, putting a hand on her trembling wrists.

'What the fuck can I do, then?'

We both looked towards the old beer bottle on the window sill. But I thought broken glass might inflict more damage on Rochelle than on the plastic.

'My tools are outside,' I said. 'I've got wire cutters.'

We realised at once the implication. Her alone with the bomb. Time ticking past. A funeral pyre.

'How long would you...?' Her voice was hoarse. She couldn't finish the sentence.

'Thirty seconds. It'll be quicker than trying with the glass.'

We looked at each other. We looked at the Harrods bag. Then, aware that indecision meant more time was passing, she gave a nod.

'Go on,' she said in a whisper.

I ran. I ran as fast as I could. I ran with the image of Rochelle's desperate face going with me.

The wire cutters were still where I'd left them, in the grass by the perimeter fence. There was no sign of Kadir in the car. But I couldn't worry about him.

I grabbed the cutters and ran back to Rochelle. I snipped twice and she was free.

She stood up, massaging her wrists and legs and turned her back to me. I saw she was trembling and breathing hard.

'You knew I'd come back. Surely?' I said.

I put an experimental arm round her shoulder.

'It could still have gone off. In those few seconds...' Her voice was quiet and shaky. I heard a sniff from her followed by a kind of snuffle. Then she gathered herself together, wiped a hand over her face and turned round back to me, whipping my arm off her shoulder. Her eyes were wet but she was once again ready for business.

'Let's get out. Quick.'

'Across the other side of the airport there's...' I was already moving to the door but she silenced me by catching my arm and putting a finger to her lips.

There was the sound of someone moving around outside.

Quietly we moved to positions either side of the shattered door.

To our surprise it was Kadir who walked in.

'Where have you been?' I said.

'You didn't come back. I was hungry so I go to Merlin Café for a meal. Then when I come out, men from this place see me and start to chase. I run and go into Spitfire Museum. I hid inside a plane. They come in but didn't find me.'

I was impressed. Maybe Kadir wasn't such a softie after all.

'I want to go home now, please.'

On the other hand ...

'Pity you couldn't have come in half an hour sooner,' I said.

'What?'

'Doesn't matter.'

'Is Magda here?'

I'd forgotten about Magda.

'In the other building,' said Rochelle.

'She's all yours,' I said to Kadir. 'We're going.'

'How do I get her?'

'Work it out. There are tools here and more in the car boot.'

'How do I get back to London?'

'Use my car. You've got the keys.'

I began to move quickly out of the shed leaving Kadir looking shell-shocked.

'Where are we going, Kite?' said Rochelle as both of us broke into a run.

'The other side of the airport.'

Chapter 29

As a boy I remember once following a country footpath which led straight across a railway line. There was an exciting sense of danger as I read the sign: *Stop. Look. Listen. Beware of Trains.* It was even more thrilling as I balanced on the actual rails the trains ran on and looked up and down the track, half hoping, half fearing to see a train approaching.

Running across an airport runway – even a closed and deserted one – gave me a similar eerie thrill of being an interloper in alien territory. You feel vulnerable and can't help glancing up to check if anything is roaring out of the sky to land on top of you.

The other side is also a lot further away than it looks.

I set off at my usual fast pace and then realised Rochelle had dropped behind. She was having trouble running in the baggy boiler suit and had stopped to roll up the trouser legs. Her heels didn't help either.

I'd halted in the dead centre of the runway and looked down at the dotted white lines leading far away into the distance. Close up, they looked enormous.

'I'm all right,' she said. 'Don't wait for me.'

'Sure?'

'I'll catch you up.'

I took her at her word and raced on. I was heading for the helicopter hire company I'd seen earlier.

I crossed the runway and the aircraft stands. I passed the deserted terminal building with its boarded windows, I ran over the weed-infested passenger car park and came to the main entrance of the airport. The helicopter company was just outside the main gates. The Bell Jetranger was still on the landing pad.

I threw myself at the door of the little office. It smashed into the thin wall of the prefabricated cabin and a young man wearing a white short-sleeved shirt and tie with his feet on the desk visibly jumped.

'Jesus Christ!' he said, taking his feet of his desk. 'What's the matter?' I saw he'd been immersed in Spider Solitaire.

'I need your helicopter. I don't care what it costs. I want it now. For maybe an hour. Two hours at most.' I threw my platinum card on the desk-top.

'The pilot is… is just…'

'Whatever he's doing, stop him. Get him back. Get him ready. Get those rotors turning.'

'He'll need a… a flight plan…'

'From here we follow the A222 then the M2 towards London, then on to the M20. The M26 and the M25 towards Heathrow. Height – as low as possible.'

'If you're thinking of landing at Heathrow we need…'

'I'm not. I want to land before then. Maybe around Sevenoaks. I'll discuss it with the pilot. Now go get him.'

The young man got up from his desk and hurried into a back office. I heard him call 'George' loudly followed by some muttered conversation.

Rochelle burst into the little office, breathing hard. The legs of her boiler suit were rolled up to her knees and she was barefoot.

'You've ditched your shoes?'

'It's a shame: they were expensive. I left them on the runway. Now I suppose they'll be a hazard to aircraft.' She gave me a rueful smile.

The short-sleeved solitaire player returned.

'When do we take off?' Rochelle said, confusing the young man.

'Is it two passengers?' he said.

'It seats up to five, doesn't it?' I said.

'Yes… it's just…' Short-sleeve had noticed Sage's blood on Rochelle's boiler suit.

'You don't have any trainers I could borrow?' said Rochelle who was roaming round the office.

The young man was even more confused.

'You mean like, shoes?' he said.

'Obviously…. Hey! What's all this stuff?' Rochelle was standing by a row of coat pegs and had picked up a backpack. She opened the straps and delved inside. She pulled out a bikini, a scuba face-mask, then some men's swimming shorts and a pair of goggles.

'We had a party spear-fishing in Cornwall. They left some of their stuff in one of the helicopters,' said short-sleeve.

'Wowser! Result.' Rochelle pulled out a pair of sand-covered and still-damp beach shoes which she immediately tried on for size. Meanwhile I'd seen something just as interesting hanging from the clothes pegs. A spear fishing gun, which had obviously been left by the same party. I went over and picked it up.

'I'll hire this as well.' I said. 'And we'll take the shoes.' Rochelle seemed happy with the fit, had tied the laces and was now studying a rack of promotional T-shirts for sale. They carried the helicopter company's name and logo and various not-quite-clever-enough slogans – "I got high with Broadgate Helicopters". That kind of thing.

'And I'll take one of these,' said Rochelle lifting a T-shirt off the rack and slipping it off its hanger.

She took off her battledress top and started to unbutton the top of the boiler suit.

'Avert your eyes, boys,' she said and turned her back on us. Reflected in a window I saw a delicious-looking bare back as she unbuttoned the boiler suit to her waist and put the T-shirt on. She turned back tucking in the T-shirt and re-buttoning the boiler suit.

'That scratchy fabric was driving me insane. You don't sell knickers I suppose?' she said with a disarming smile to short-sleeve shirt. The man simply shook his head, too shell-shocked for any more conversation.

We got straight into the helicopter and were sitting waiting for the pilot when Rochelle said:

'I suppose you've been in a helicopter lots of times.'

'Never before,' I said. 'You?'

'Only once. My Dad bought me a trip as an eighteenth birthday present.'

'Classy.'

'No. It was dreadful. I was sick.'

'Don't look down. That's my advice.'

The cockpit door was yanked open and the pilot – George presumably – hurried into his seat, still buttoning his jacket and adjusting his tie. He was carrying three headsets and a clipboard. He was older than I'd expected, in his late fifties, but didn't seem troubled at being hauled out of the lavatory or woken from a snooze. I explained as quickly as possible what I wanted to do and he simply nodded and said O.K. I got the feeling he was ex-RAF and was happier to bend rules than someone half his age. While he prepared for take-off I signed the forms and fastened them back on his clipboard.

I reckoned that Hameed and his team had a forty minute start. They wouldn't drive too fast because they didn't want to attract attention. It was almost exactly a hundred miles to Heathrow but how long it would take depended entirely on traffic conditions. The helicopter's maximum speed was 150 mph so we had a chance. Everything depended on the traffic.

We took off and banked sharply round to head westwards, climbing fast. The pilot knew the urgency of our pursuit so there were no concessions for civilian passengers. This was great but I quickly understood why Rochelle had been sick on her first helicopter flight. Nevertheless, compared to theme parks with their corkscrew, free-fall and inverted roller-coasters I'd vote for a helicopter in combat mode every time.

We flew over the shed where Rochelle and I had been tied up and as we did so there was an explosion beneath us. The roof of the shed was lifted up and then disintegrated as a fireball ballooned up into the sky towards us incredibly fast. The pilot saw the flames coming and took emergency avoiding action which had Rochelle gripping my arm for support. Then the blast wave hit the helicopter and we were thrust violently upwards and sideways then fell downwards again. I'd experienced bad turbulence on a flight from Orlando with my parents once but it wasn't half as bad as this. Rochelle gave an involuntary scream. Then she clamped a hand over her mouth, trying to stifle any more signs of girly fear. Or maybe to stop herself being sick. She needn't have felt embarrassed. I could easily have screamed myself.

The helicopter rocked and rolled, dipped and rose for a few seconds longer and then everything was back to normal.

'Someone leave the gas on?' said the pilot who was unfazed. Probably a doddle compared to facing missiles or grenade launchers in Afghanistan.

I was beginning to breathe normally again when I remembered Kadir and Magda. I swivelled round in my seat to see if my car was still where it had been left. But I could see nothing but thick smoke and flames.

Rochelle had the same thought.

'I should have defused it,' she said looking troubled.

I bet she could have done, too.

'There wasn't time,' I said.

We looked at each other, wondering. About Magda. About Kadir. Why hadn't I warned him?

'This World Cup scare thing is a bit of a bummer,' said the pilot. 'I've laid out five grand for flights, tickets and all the rest.'

Then one of my phones rang. It was Kadir. He'd found Magda and she was fine. They had just started the drive back to London when the bomb had gone off. He was calling to see if I was all right.

I could hardly believe it. And I suppose I felt touched.

But it wasn't just that. Magda wanted to talk to me.

'Put her on,' I said.

'Mr Kite, did you see it? The fake Leonardo?'

'Yes. The Amberger is obviously ruined.'

'I had to do what I did. I thought they would kill Kadir otherwise. But your picture's not ruined.'

'What do you mean?'

'Before I did the printing I covered your picture with a thickish coat of white acrylic. It'll protect the painting from the polymer but it's water-based so it can be removed and the fake easily exposed. So I think, I hope, your picture will be all right.'

I thanked her and praised her foresight. The call ended and I felt elated. I turned to share the news with Rochelle but her eyes were shut and her knuckles were white with gripping the edge of her seat.

'Open your eyes. Look at the horizon,' I said. 'Don't look down and keep your head still.' She opened her eyes and gave me a baleful look. 'You'll be fine, honestly.'

'Liar,' she said.

'Well, think nice thoughts again.'

We were quickly over the M2 and with our extreme low altitude the sensation of speed was intensified. The ground was rushing past and the traffic below seemed to be crawling. Then I realised the traffic *was* crawling. Looking ahead I could see the inside lane was closed. There were flashing lights and cones around a broken-down lorry while a heavy recovery truck was fixing a tow. There was no sign of the two distinctive cars with their CD plates. But the congestion here would have delayed them for ten or fifteen minutes at least.

At the Sittingbourne exit we left the M2 and took the A249 which links to the M20 through Detling Hill. This was the most direct route to Heathrow and I had to assume they'd come this way.

We were over the M20 quickly, too quickly. Nearly half way to Heathrow. Had I missed the car or were they still ahead of us? They'd been on the road for about an hour and five minutes. Less the M2 hold-up, call it fifty minutes driving time. Their maximum speed would be seventy or seventy-five but there were roundabouts and fifty limits. I juggled figures around. If they averaged fifty-five they should have covered around forty-five miles. We should be near them.

On the M20 traffic was busy but I could see no jams. We passed over the Maidstone exit and then we joined the M26 which led to the M25. Still no sign of them. Were all my calculations wrong?

My phone rang again. It was Leo Somerscales.

'John?... Kite? Can you hear me? There's a dreadful noise in the background.'

'I'm in a helicopter.'

'Of course you are. You may have got your picture back already but something new has come in via the CIA. Satellite observation picked up what looks like troop movements in the UAE and our people on the ground confirm a mobilisation. Their government's giving some poppycock excuse about popular unrest caused by the theft of that painting. But it looks like preparation for something a lot bigger.'

'Any reaction from Qatar?'

'Not yet but we expect they'll follow suit any time. The US Air Force base in Qatar has raised its alert level to DEFCON Bravo.'

Events were moving quickly. Nassir Hameed obviously planned to reveal the discovery of the "stolen" picture as soon as it was in Qatar, while he and his gang slipped safely into the UAE. I redoubled my efforts on scanning the traffic below. Then at Sevenoaks I spotted them.

I put down the binoculars and pointed them out to Rochelle and the pilot. The two black Mercedes S-Class Pullmans were driving together in lane 2 at about seventy miles an hour.

'What instructions?' said the pilot.

'I want to land somewhere and pick up a hire car. Would Cobham services be practical?'

'It's a possibility.'

'Keep them in sight while I arrange a car.' I phoned MacIver. I got through to her PA who said she would interrupt a meeting and MacIver was quickly on the phone.

'Kite. Got the picture?'

'Almost. It's in a car travelling west on the M26 heading for Heathrow. I'm about five hundred feet above it.'

'You're in a plane?'

'A helicopter. I need a car a.s.a.p. Could you pull strings and get some red carpet treatment? Ideally the car needs to be close to the M25 and near a landing ground for the helicopter. In the next fifteen minutes.'

MacIver didn't demur. She just said, 'Anything else?'

'The car must have a bit of poke. At least as fast as a Mercedes S-class.'

MacIver breathed out hard but said nothing. I could hear her tapping on her keyboard. Then I heard her yell, 'Clark!' at the top of her voice, then to me, 'there's something on the news about troop movements in the Gulf…'

'My FCO contact told me.'

'Just checking you knew. I'll call you back.' And the line went dead.

The pilot said, 'Twenty nine miles to Heathrow, but there's another jam ahead.'

The speed limit signs over the carriageway below us were showing 50 and further ahead they were showing 40. A mile further on, the traffic was stationary. The pilot banked left and turned away from the motorway since hovering over slow moving traffic was both distracting for drivers and could well draw our target's attention to us. The helicopter flew in a slow circle a couple of miles in diameter while I kept the binoculars on the cars. After a few minutes we came back to the motorway and flew across it, starting on the second half of a figure of eight.

But as we flew over I saw flashing indicators on the Mercedes.

'They're turning off at Junction 8.'

The M25 is often congested and drivers feel an urge to take an alternative route. The trouble is there are few alternatives, particularly south of London where the motorway skirts the North Downs and the Surrey Hills. The reason the road is so busy is it's a unique route around London. However congested it is, it's usually quicker to stay on the motorway. Trying to navigate the towns and villages either side of it will almost certainly take longer.

Hameed and his gang had followed instinct rather than experience. They were going to exit at Junction 8. Would they go north or south? North was roughly in the direction of Heathrow but to get to the airport would mean toiling through Croydon or Sutton and then Kingston. Madness. It would take a couple of hours. Going south would take them further from Heathrow but on to a more rural route through Reigate, Dorking and Woking. It would be less congested but long and slow.

Down below the cars were inching towards the exit slip.

Then MacIver called back.

'There's a small lay-by on the A25 just beyond Reigate with a football club nearby. If you can land on the pitch you'll find a car waiting for you in the lay-by.'

'Amazing. Thank you.'

'Thank Clark. It's a buddy of his. He lives nearby. Let's hope there isn't a match on this afternoon.'

The call ended and I saw the pilot had already plotted a course for the football club and was altering direction. I looked back at the Mercedes. They'd chosen the southern route. Depending on how their satnav took them it was possible they might drive right past the lay-by where our car was waiting. We might even get to that point first.

Soon the football club was in view and the pitch was thankfully empty of players.

The helicopter touched down, I grabbed the spear gun and hurriedly thanked the pilot. He seemed to have been enjoying himself and gave me one of those exaggerated, cod US Army salutes like Ronald Reagan and John Wayne used to do.

Rochelle and I ran towards the road searching for our vehicle. All I could see was a Range Rover Discovery with a low-loader hitched behind it. Reversing off the loader was a badly dented saloon, hand painted in nursery school colours with a big racing number on the side panels.

I felt let down but there was a shriek of joy from Rochelle. 'Cool bananas! Is that ours?'

I looked at the mud splashes all over it, the cow-catcher grid over the front end and its metal lattice-work in place of a windscreen.

'Two litre Mondeo saloon stock car. Brilliant.'

The man with the Discovery was coming towards me, mentioning his mate Clark and holding out a set of keys and two crash helmets.

Then there was a rush of air from the road as the two S-class Pullmans whizzed past. I clicked the time-elapsed facility on my wristwatch.

I turned to Rochelle.

'Fit to drive?'

'Fit for anything now my feet are on the ground.'

Chapter 30

I smiled at Rochelle's girlish glee as she jumped into the driving seat, fastened the racing harness like it was an old friend and started the engine, revving it hard. I'd barely clicked my own harness together before the clutch was up, the handbrake was down and my head banged back against the headrest as the finely tuned Mondeo fishtailed out of the lay-by throwing a shower of dust and gravel behind it. After just a few seconds we were doing seventy and had already overtaken three cars.

I caught myself wondering if the modified Mondeo was even street legal. But then I found myself not caring. The green mist had descended. Hameed's gang had to be stopped and the picture recovered.

'How far ahead are they?'

We had to shout to each other. The engine was loud, the wind rushing through the car was even louder and the helmets muffled speech. I looked at my watch. They'd passed us three minutes twenty seconds ago doing around sixty.

'A bit over three miles.'

I glanced at the speedo: we were doing eighty.

Maps were spooling through my head.

'If they want to get back on the M25 they'll go for the next junction which is thirteen, fourteen miles away. This road's single-carriageway to Dorking. But the town's a bottle-neck. We need to avoid it.'

'Will they know that?'

'No. But they'll be driving on satnav. They'll set it for the next junction and do what it says.'

'What will it say?'

'I'll give you directions,' I said.

We needed to stop them before they got back to the motorway. There are things you can do discreetly on the A25 that you can't do on the M25. Especially near one of the busiest airports in the world.

'So we've got fourteen miles max,' said Rochelle. 'I don't want to waste time looking at the odometer. Call it twelve *minutes* and give me a countdown from there.'

I checked my watch. 'We've been going one minute fifteen.'

The road we were on had some fast sections but also some slow ones where it went through stockbroker belt commuter towns and pretty villages. But Rochelle used the road as if she were rallying, sliding the rear end round neatly round sharp corners. We flashed past a sign telling us that Betchworth welcomed careful drivers and a squawking cock pheasant only just managed to take off in time to avoid us. There was a thirty limit and one of those roadside signs which light-up and show your speed with either a happy or a sad face. As we shot past, the irate flashing indicator showed sixty-eight.

'Three minutes elapsed,' I said.

There was a roadworks sign, warning of one-way working. The traffic light was green for us but there was a queue of traffic ahead slowly filtering past the cones. As we approached, the light changed to amber, then red but Rochelle accelerated past it. Then she had to brake quickly as she caught up with the tail of the traffic queue.

She drummed her fingers on the steering wheel.

'Four minutes.'

Past the roadworks, Rochelle pulled out and accelerated hard. She passed four, five, six cars but then had to brake before a blind bend. After the bend the road took us uphill and at the summit there was a sudden distant view of the road ahead.

'There they are,' I said. The two black cars were half a mile ahead but there were trucks and cars between us.

I looked at Rochelle who was wriggling her neck and shoulders as if she was in pain.

'Not feeling sick again?'

'Bloody T-shirt. I left the price tag on. It's more itchy than the frigging boiler suit.'

'Five minutes.'

Traffic ahead was slowing because we were reaching a town but Rochelle accelerated and passed a truck and a car before slamming on the brakes and squeezing in front of a VW Golf which gave her a blast on the horn. I consulted the map in my head.

'We need to take a right soon.'

'Tell me when.'

We crawled forward at twenty miles an hour for some seconds then I saw the turning.

'Right in two hundred metres.'

Rochelle pulled out and drove on the wrong side of the road towards the turning, forcing an oncoming Fiesta to take evasive action. Rochelle swung the car into the narrow lane which barely had room for two cars to pass but Rochelle was already flying along.

A black and white cat walked into our path. Rochelle blasted the horn and the cat jumped away.

'Six minutes elapsed.'

A farm tractor was emerging from a field. Rochelle pressed the horn again and didn't vary her speed. The tractor stopped where it was and the driver gave us a vigorous V-sign.

Another rise in the road gave us a view ahead but this time there was no sight of the two black Pullmans.

'Suppose the satnav took them a different way.' said Rochelle.

'It wouldn't.'

'Suppose they're not heading back to the motorway.'

'They've got to.'

'Suppose they've stopped at a pub for pie and chips.'

I said nothing except, 'Seven minutes.'

The shortcut to avoid the town centre was coming to an end. Roundabout warning signs flashed past but Rochelle didn't brake until it seemed too late. There was a squeal from the tyres and some smoke, but we were fine. The back end drifted a little as she accelerated round the roundabout and then we were on a dual carriageway. A sign said the M25 was five miles away.

Eight minutes elapsed.

We were behind the clock.

Rochelle floored the pedal and we were doing ninety. We rounded a bend and there they were: the two black Mercedes Pullmans, one behind the other in lane 1, keeping to the speed limit.

Rochelle eased off the pedal and cruised into their lane, taking up a position behind the second car.

'We can't exactly be discreet in this,' she said.

'Doesn't matter. It's hiding in plain sight again. They'll see the car but never imagine it's a threat to them. Besides, they'll assume we're dead or dying at the airport.'

'What's the plan?'

'Drive level with the rear car. I'll take out one of its tyres.' I grabbed the spear-fishing gun from behind the seats and rested it on the sill of the open side window.

Rochelle moved the car into the outer lane and brought it alongside the Mercedes. One of Hameed's family group was driving, with another in the front seat. The taser man was in the back.

'As soon as I fire, you'd better…'

'I know. As soon as you fire I'll brake and pull back. That shark killer will shred the tyre at once so they'll skid, swerve or even one-eighty. Give me a countdown.'

The offside rear tyre was barely a couple of metres from the muzzle of the spear gun. I took aim.

'Three, two, one, fire.' I pressed the trigger.

The tyre disintegrated instantly with fragments of rubber exploding in all directions. Rochelle slowed sharply and slotted back into lane 1. The Mercedes swerved to the right, then as the driver over-corrected it spun violently to the left. The car left the road and careered down a gravelly slope, flattening a wooden five-bar gate which carried the sign *Broxworth Watermill Closed Today*.

The car continued onwards out of control. It lurched into a forecourt where the tyres sank into soft, deep gravel which caused the Merc to tip over and slide along on its side panels. In the middle of the gravelled area was a pair of huge, ancient grinding stones standing on their edges, erected as a promotional feature for the watermill. The car was still on its side and sliding fast when it hit the mill-stones. The force of the impact toppled the car on to its roof and finally brought it to rest.

Rochelle followed the Mercedes into the car park and stopped. I grabbed my crowbar and made straight for the Mercedes. Shouts and cries from inside the car meant all three men were not only alive but were aware of our attack and wanted to get even. They were frantically trying to get out of the car but the doors had been jammed shut by the impact.

I slipped the sharp end of my crowbar into the small gap between car boot and bodywork and yanked at it savagely and repeatedly. The bodywork was quality engineering but it finally gave up the struggle, bending and crumpling enough to release the lock. The lid of the boot fell downwards, followed immediately by the so-called diplomatic pouch freight container.

Then a shot was fired from inside the car. It was aimed through the rear seat and the bullet whistled between Rochelle and me.

I picked up the freight container and we ran back to the stock car as another bullet zinged out of the Mercedes interior. I was manoeuvring the container on to the back seat when repeated loud hooting made us look toward the road. The other Mercedes had already made a U-turn and chased back on the other side of the dual carriageway. The violent hooting wasn't coming from the Mercedes but from cars behind it. The Merc driver wasn't bothering to find a roundabout to get back to our side of the road. Instead he'd braked hard right in front of the mill entrance and driven up on to the grassy central reservation. He was now poised to charge straight across the other lane of traffic and hurtle towards us. Given the amount of traffic, it was a desperate, almost suicidal, manoeuvre. Seeing a brief opportunity, the Mercedes accelerated off the central reservation, its spinning wheels spraying dirt and grass. There was the squeal of tyres as other drivers braked to let it across the carriageway in front of them. The Mercedes drove over the broken five-bar gate and straight for us. I saw the angry, determined face of Hameed in the front passenger seat. He was holding a gun out of the window as was Yasmine from the rear. One of them fired at us as the car bounced over the gravel.

We were out of the car just a second before the big Mercedes careered into it, sending the stock car sideways.

I grabbed the picture in its freight case and Rochelle and I ran for it, following a tourist path by the millstream which led to the mill building itself. A shot whistled past us but it was well wide. Up ahead I saw a fine brick building and just had time to think it must be eighteenth century before there was another shot. We ducked behind a pallet of thick oak planks destined for restoration work, but the mill building would offer better protection. We ran on down a path that took us beside the mill-race where the stream was channelled underneath the steadily turning water wheel. We could hear the clanking of machinery and the creak of timbers from inside the mill.

There were two entrances, an upper one labelled Grinding Floor and a basement level door labelled Pit Wheel. We headed for the lower entrance. The door was open and we hustled inside where I was hit by the oddly comforting industrial smell of old timber, wood preservative and warm lubricating oil. I'd expected to find an engineer or curator inside but there was no one. A cast iron cog-wheel, several metres across, was slowly revolving, being driven by the water wheel in the mill race outside. This large cog wheel was turning another toothed wheel and, through a number of geared wheels, operated the grind stones on the upper floor.

I was still clutching the Amberger picture in its container and needed to find a temporary place of safety for it. A rustic ladder led to the upper floor where the millstones themselves were. I swarmed up the steps and found a pile of heavy canvas flour sacks. I put the container on the slatted wooden floor, lifted the sacks and heaved them on top. Not ideal, but there were few other options.

Through a window I saw the young man who'd been driving approaching the mill. He was using the path we'd taken and was plainly out of his comfort zone. His movement s were alternatively nervous and reckless, with no understanding of the use of cover, but he had a pistol in his hand. Like me and Rochelle he paused momentarily to consider the choice of entrances. Then he took the steps for the upper floor. I hissed a warning to Rochelle and looked around for a weapon. Nearby was a set of nineteenth century industrial scales for weighing filled sacks of flour together with a set of pre-metric iron weights neatly arranged from 1lb right up to the curious amount of 56lb. I picked up the 4lb weight. It had a convenient ring on top through which my fingers threaded comfortably and I found a place of concealment near the door.

Hameed's driver came into the mill. The din from the groaning wheels, cogs and shafts masked any noise I made as I crept up behind him undetected. I swung the iron weight round in an arc over my shoulder and struck him hard on his gun hand. He screamed in pain and the gun fell to the floor. Four pounds sounds little enough but it's the momentum that counts. As he clutched his broken hand I grabbed an empty flour sack and launched myself at him, pulling the sack over his head. He struggled hard but I was stronger. He was slim and I got the sack down to his chest which was far enough to disable and disorientate him. I wrestled him to the ground but he kept struggling and rolled right under the lower bar of the gallery rail and over the edge. As he hit the wooden floor a couple of metres below he cried out and his impact produced a cloud of floury dust. Then Rochelle was on to him, pulling tight the cords that ran through eyelets round the top of the sack and tying them off. Then she picked up his gun, pressed it to his head and threatened to shoot him if he struggled.

It was all a bit Tom and Jerry, but effective enough. I grinned down at Rochelle from the gallery. Improvisation gives me a buzz.

There was no time for self-congratulation because the lower door clanged open and Yasmine came in also holding a gun in the classic two-handed grip.

'Put down your weapon,' she said.

'Put yours down,' said Rochelle, 'or I'll kill your colleague.'

Yasmine walked further into the mill. She was standing directly beneath my position on the upper gallery.

'I'll count to five,' Yasmine said. 'Then I'll kill you.'

There was a noise from the door as a man wearing a large brown apron walked in. The guy in charge of the mill.

'What's going on? The mill's closed today. Who are you?' he said.

Yasmine turned to face him with her gun.

'Oh my god,' said the mill man.

I jumped from the gallery, Yasmine collapsed under my weight and hit her head on the floor, stunning her. I grabbed her hands behind her back, got her face down on the floor and knelt on her back. I couldn't tell how long she'd stay unconscious.

'Got any rope?' I said to the mill man.

His mouth opened and closed but no words came out.

'Over there,' said Rochelle, pointing. 'Orange bailer twine. Pass it to him.'

The mill man came to, grabbed the roll of twine and handed it to me along with a razor-sharp knife. I trussed up Yasmine's arms and legs. If the knots are good – and mine are – bailer twine is almost as impenetrable as plastic cable tie.

And then the door opened again. Who else but Nassir Hameed himself? With another gun aimed at Rochelle and me.

'Well done,' he said. 'More successful than my cousins. More useful than Mr Sage. And don't bother with threats to kill Asif or Yasmine there. All I mind about is the painting. Where is it?'

I said nothing. Rochelle said nothing. The mill man stuttered, 'What painting?'

'Shut up,' said Hameed.

'Let us do a deal,' he went on. 'I said I would pay Mr Sage fifteen million pounds for his services. What do you say if I pay you the same amount. Each. That is, when you hand over the painting. Then we catch the same flight from Heathrow. This evening. I arrange documents for you.'

'We saw how you arranged Sage's documents.'

Hameed laughed. 'Yes. But he was ... he was a minus for me. I think the two of you can be plusses for me. You will do the same work you do now – you enjoy, I think – but you will live in beautiful country with beautiful weather. You earn times ten, times twenty what you earn now. And no tax. Almost no tax. Best shopping in the world. Most luxurious lifestyle.' He laughed again.

'All shopping's shit,' said Rochelle. 'Nothing luxurious about the way women are treated in your country and I doubt anyone over there can make a decent pisco sour.'

I looked at the gun Hameed was holding. It was a Taurus mini, the kind of weapon Americans with conceal carry permits stick in their shoulder holsters or purses. An unusual weapon for a terrorist like Hameed. Significantly, the Taurus chamber holds only five bullets. How many had he fired already? He'd shot twice to kill Menon: further shots were fired as we approached the mill, but had he fired or Yasmine? Or the man called Asif? One of them had fired as the Merc drove straight at us. He'd maybe used three of his five shots. Or four.

Maybe.

I don't believe in gambling, but I do believe in probability. The probability was he only had two bullets left. But two bullets were plenty to kill both of us.

'Shall we just wait here till it's time for you to catch your plane?' I said.

Hameed raised his pistol towards my head, aimed just to the left and pulled the trigger. I felt the rush of air as the bullet passed a couple of feet from my head and buried itself in a three hundred year old oak beam.

Maybe just one bullet left.

Could I make him fire again? Could I be sure he hadn't reloaded on the drive from Kent? Yes, I could. Too dangerous in the UK to cart around a box of cartridges.

I decided he had just one shot left.

During the stand-off I'd been looking at a rack of ancient tools ranged along a wall. There were outsize spanners and wrenches for fixing the giant cogs and wheels that connected the water-wheel to the grindstones. There were also some long wooden shafts that looked like medieval pikes without the ironwork. I had no idea what they were – spare parts for the milling machinery perhaps – but they looked useful. I shifted my weight from left to right and shuffled my feet; I gained half a metre in the direction of the wooden poles. I did the weight-shift and shuffle again, then said:

'I'd like to accept your offer.' I shuffled again as I spoke, making like I was nervous, and almost without trying I was within reach of the long poles.

Hameed looked surprised. Rochelle knew better than to say anything. The mill man huffed and puffed.

'Good,' said Hameed. 'Where is the picture?'

'It's just up there,' I said, pointing above Hameed's head.

He just laughed. 'Old trick,' he said. 'You must do better.'

'No. It really is up there. Under some sacks.'

I watched his eyes. He was still doubtful but the temptation was too much. His eyes flicked upwards and as they did so I grabbed one of the long-handled tools and hurled it at him. Javelin-like, it hit his chest. He fired and the bullet went into the roof somewhere.

Five shots?

I picked up the pole again and hit his gun hand just as he pulled the trigger again.

The bullet drilled itself into the floor.

I'd miscounted.

I stabbed him hard in the stomach with the pole and he retreated. He aimed his gun directly at my head and I just stood there.

I had to be right this time.

He pulled the trigger.

The gun just clicked.

I smiled. I had the edge.

I stabbed at him again with the pole and he backed out of the mill on to the narrow path by the mill-race.

'Put your gun down,' I said. 'Surrender. Make it easy for yourself. You'll just be expelled from the country. No trial. No punishment.'

There was a blazing fire in his eyes. He threw the gun to the ground and made a grab for the end of the pole. His grip was ferocious; his mood animalistic. I recognised a version of my own green mist. It was a deadly tug of war. Two wrestlers locked together fighting for possession of a two hundred year old, ten foot wooden pole. The only trick worth playing in that game is the one where you reverse your pressure, suddenly pushing after pulling, or vice versa. But the moment had to be carefully calculated.

The moment came. I relaxed my resistance and he stumbled forwards tripping over the stone edging along the mill-race. He took two clumsy steps and tripped again, falling sideways into the water.

The water wasn't deep, but it was cold and it was fast flowing. I saw him floundering, trying to swim, trying to find some footing, but he couldn't. In no time at all he went under the revolving mill wheel and disappeared.

I ran round to the far side of the mill building, expecting to see him flushed out from the mill race. I stood by, on the edge of the stream, ready to stop him climbing out and making a run for it.

But he didn't come out.

What happened was the mill wheel stopped turning. There were ominous creaks and groans from the timbers as the water pressure tried to push the wheel round but something was holding it back. I went back into the mill building where the engineer was white-faced.

'There's a blockage,' he said. 'Something's stuck under the wheel.'

I looked at Rochelle. We knew what it was.

The mill engineer rushed outside to close a sluice to divert the flow of water from under the wheel, but it was too late for Hameed.

It took police divers two hours to extract his body from where he'd been pinioned in the narrow gap between the wheel paddles and the bottom of the mill race.

Yasmine and the wounded Asif were arrested and driven away as were the others trapped in the car. Rochelle and I gave preliminary statements: I referred the local police to Bostock and MacIver.

When we were free to go it was dark. A surprisingly warm autumn evening. Rochelle and I looked at each other wondering what to do next. The Mondeo stock car had been written off when Hameed's car drove into it so we legged it down the dual carriageway until we came to a pub that the mill engineer had recommended.

It wasn't the best pub in Surrey. Or even the best pub in town. But it was all right.

We had a couple of drinks. We didn't feel elated, just tired. And there was that disconcerting anti-climactic feeling that often hits you after finishing something really important.

I put a hand in a pocket, pulled out the little digital device that I'd secreted there and put it on a beermat on the pub table. Rochelle looked at it curiously.

'A memory stick. Is that Hameed's?'

I nodded.

'Why didn't you give it to the police?'

I wasn't entirely sure. I held it up and turned it round in my hand.

'It seemed too dangerous somehow. I didn't want some rookie constable sticking it in his PC, opening the files and ...'

'Causing Armageddon.'

I nodded. 'I'll get Clark to check it over. Make it safe. Then hand it in. Say I got it off Hameed while we were fighting.'

Rochelle leaned over and took it from my hand.

'How much would have been lost if the plan had worked? Billions?'

'I guess. A lot more than that little painting's worth.'

Rochelle smiled. 'I suppose I might watch some of the footy. Are Manchester United playing?' She was tongue-in-cheek of course and grinned as she handed the flashdrive back.

I returned it to my pocket then realised Rochelle was looking intently at me. That made me uneasy.

'Are you about to say something profound?' I said.

'Not profound. But maybe useful.'

'Go on, then.'

'You can't change the past. Get on with the present. Enjoy it.'

I gave her a look. I'd been telling myself this for the last fifteen years.

'I try to,' I said.

'Not hard enough. There's no moral imperative for you to be a white knight. You don't have to be on a mission.'

'I'm not on a mission. I'm just an ordinary guy who recovers pictures.'

Rochelle shook her head and gave me an intense, almost aggressive, look. 'I wish I could believe that.'

'What brought this on?'

Rochelle sat back in her chair and pretended to be uninvolved. 'Has no one ever said this to you before?'

'I've never told anyone the whole story before.'

'Well… I thought it should be said. And…'

She paused.

'And…?' I said.

Unusually for Rochelle she then started to play with her hair, curling it round her fingers. A displacement activity. She looked kind of twitchy. Then she leaned suddenly forward again.

'If you want me to spell it out, it's because I kind of like you, I suppose.'

I looked at her and saw she was blushing. She gave a private, almost nervous, smile. Very un-Rochelle.

Then it struck me that this brief moment of intimacy was the real Rochelle. Much of what I'd seen before was her avoiding the issue, putting on a front. I'd got Rochelle wrong from the start. I'd been puzzled by her yo-yoing between hostility and warmth towards me but the hostility had been a defence mechanism. Like the crossing and uncrossing of legs. To keep her true feelings under wraps.

She'd caught me off guard so I thought I'd throw her a curved ball too.

'What are your plans for after the wedding?' She looked uncomfortable at being asked. Was I trying to get my own back?

'You mean children? That kind of thing?'

'No, I mean work. Will you still do the PI thing?'

'I was thinking of giving it all up. He's got money.'

'I can't imagine you sitting around doing nothing. It would be a waste.'

'A waste?'

'Of your skills. Of your talents.'

'My impression was you thought I was a complete div.'

'You know that's not true. But we both may have got wrong impressions. Of each other.'

She nodded. 'So let's put the record straight... Earlier, and in the helicopter, you said think of something nice, something sexy. So I did.'

She looked straight at me, our eyes met and she held my gaze. Her face was calm and serious but her eyes were wildly alive, glowing with desire. Even in the grubby, old-fashioned boiler suit and cast-off beach shoes her body exuded beguiling sex appeal.

'Would you like to go somewhere?' I said. 'I mean... find a place.'

She nodded.

'I would. Very much,' she said.

# # # # # # # #

If you've enjoyed this book you might like to leave a review on Amazon or Good Reads – or anywhere else for that matter. Reviews help authors like me – and also help readers like you to find books they like.

You also might like to join my Readers' Club. If you join I'll send you a free John Kite story immediately – a story you can't get on Amazon, or anywhere else! For your FREE STORY just go to: https://stuart-doughty.com/freedownload/

Author's Note

As it says below everything in this book is fiction. Nevertheless Leonardo da Vinci's *Salvator Mundi* does of course exist and it was sold for a record sum at auction a few years ago. At the time of publication, though, its whereabouts are unknown. It isn't on display in the Louvre Gallery in Abu Dhabi and nobody seems willing to admit they own it. A recent survey of the unusual situation can be found in *The Guardian* 13 October 2019.

John Kite himself is also fictional of course but people like him do exist. If you'd like to know more about this intriguing world join my Readers' Club. Please go to: https://stuart-doughty.com

 As well as an exclusive FREE STORY I'll also send you interesting info from time to time, including background to the real world of art crime as well as news of forthcoming John Kite titles.

If you've enjoyed this book I'm sure you'll enjoy the second John Kite novel:

PAINT IT BLACKMAIL

It's available now on Amazon

If you want to know more about me – what I've done, where I live, how much hair I have – you can do so at my website. And you can write to me at stuart@stuart-doughty.com

288

And there's also my Readers' Club of course – Did I mention that?
https://stuart-doughty.com
Go on, you know you want to.

And finally, the poem by Philip Larkin mentioned in the novel is called "This Be The Verse" and can be found in *Collected Poems* by Philip Larkin published by Faber & Faber

Printed in Poland
by Amazon Fulfillment
Poland Sp. z o.o., Wrocław

67661531R00168